Di

Hertfordshire market

her incredibly imaginative and creative daughter and her adventurous, adorable little boy. In Sophie's world, happy *is* for ever after, everything stops for tea, and there's always time for one more page…

Melissa Senate has written many novels for Mills & Boon and other publishers, including her debut, *See Jane Date*, which was made into a TV movie. She also wrote seven books for Mills & Boon under the pen name Meg Maxwell. Her novels have been published in over twenty-five countries. Melissa lives on the coast of Maine with her teenage son; their rescue shepherd mix, Flash; and a lap cat named Cleo. For more information, please visit her website, melissasenate.com

Also by Sophie Pembroke

Carrying Her Millionaire's Baby
Pregnant on the Earl's Doorstep
Snowbound with the Heir
Second Chance for the Single Mum

Also by Melissa Senate

For the Twins' Sake
Wyoming Special Delivery
A Family for a Week
The Baby Switch!
Detective Barelli's Legendary Triplets
Wyoming Christmas Surprise
To Keep Her Baby
A Promise for the Twins
A Wyoming Christmas to Remember
Rust Creek Falls Cinderella

Discover more at millsandboon.co.uk

ITALIAN ESCAPE WITH HER FAKE FIANCÉ

SOPHIE PEMBROKE

THE COWBOY'S COMEBACK

MELISSA SENATE

MILLS & BOON

First Published in Great Britain 2020
by Mills & Boon, an imprint of HarperCollinsPublishers,
1 London Bridge Street, London, SE1 9GF

Italian Escape with Her Fake Fiancé © 2020 Sophie Pembroke
The Cowboy's Comeback © 2020 Harlequin Books S.A.

Special thanks and acknowledgement are given to Melissa Senate for her
contribution to the *Montana Mavericks: What Happened to Beatrix?* series.

ISBN: 978-0-263-27890-3

0820

Printed and bound in Spain
by CPI, Barcelona

ITALIAN ESCAPE
WITH HER
FAKE FIANCÉ

SOPHIE PEMBROKE

For my partners in summer fairytale fiction,
Ally Blake and Cara Colter.

PROLOGUE

TALENT IS A funny old thing.

Some people have a talent for business, others a talent for mimicking accents or a talent for baking. Some have a talent for music—for creating it, playing it, sharing it with the world.

Like Daisy Mulligan.

I'm a music lover myself and, as head of the Ascot family fortune, have been able to indulge that love through events such as the Annual Ascot Music Festival and the new Ascot Music Awards. No one queries an old lady like myself meddling in modern music— they just assume I'm in it for financial reasons. Which is partially true, I suppose.

But money is something I've never been short of, and since I took over the family business I've only made more of it. And that financial security is something that gives me the ability to make the most of *my* talent.

I've never met another person with the same talent as me. I don't even know if one exists. It's certainly not something one talks about at the dinner table. Whenever I raised it with my mother I was told to be quiet, to stop being fanciful.

But at seventy-six, after almost a lifetime of study, I can confirm that my talent is, indeed, very real.

I know what people need.

Not what they *want*—which is a very different thing, and something they're far more likely to tell you up front, in my experience—but what they *need*.

And there's no way for me to shut that knowledge off.

As you can imagine, crowded places and large gatherings can be rather wearing, full of people subconsciously blasting me with their deepest needs. But this planet is full of people, so I've had to learn to cope with it.

And sometimes it gives me an opportunity to *do* something with my talent, too.

My talent and Daisy's talent collided at the Annual Ascot Music Festival in Copenhagen two years ago, when my beloved dog Max escaped. I twisted my ankle, and three lovely young ladies came to my rescue: Jessica, a Canadian, sat with me and fetched tea, while Daisy and Aubrey—British and Australian respectively—chased down Max and brought him home. Then the three girls took me to hospital and generally took care of me, making me laugh and keeping me entertained so that what could have been a terrible day turned into one of the best I'd enjoyed in a long time.

Three strangers, with far more important places to be and things to do, took time out from enjoying the festival to look after Max and me.

And I wanted to return the favour.

I kept track of them via social media, to be certain that my first read of their respective needs stayed constant. Then, when the time was right, I acted.

Jessica was first—a job offer in New York that, un-planned by myself, also led to romance.

Aubrey, poor dove, fell sick after we met, but now she's well again I know just what she needs too. Adventures are on the way for her!

But Daisy…

Daisy took a little more time to be sure. Since we met at the festival in Copenhagen her star has only risen. She's becoming a big name in her own right, touring the world and delighting fans with her music.

But that first feeling I had—the first need I sensed—has stayed constant.

She needs a home—something I suspect she hasn't had for a very long time. One that is entirely her own: her sanctuary, her refuge.

So I've given her the old house in Italy. I suspect it'll need some work, but that's intentional. After all, how much value do we place on things we don't have to work for? Making that house a home will be her responsibility and, knowing Daisy, she'll appreciate it far more believing that she's earned it. In fact, if I gave her, say, a pristine villa in Spain, she'd probably run a mile.

This house will take love and effort and care.

But I know that it will repay her.

A home, after all, is one of the greatest treasures we possess. Well, a home and someone to share it with, perhaps. But love is firmly outside my remit *and* my experience.

I have my doggie companions, and they are home enough for me.

But I confess I'm intrigued to see what Daisy will make of her new home…

CHAPTER ONE

Jay Barwell looked out into the stadium, squinting against the lights to try and make out even the front row of the audience. He was losing them. He could tell that much, even if he couldn't see them.

All those adoring fans who'd trailed around after him whenever he was out in LA or London or Dallas with Milli. Those loyal followers who'd been listening to Dept 135's music practically since he and his brother Harry formed the band. The casual listeners who heard them on the radio and found themselves humming along, who'd come to a gig to see if they were as good live.

He was losing all of them.

The band could feel it too, he knew. Harry's guitar riffs sounded tense, somehow, and Nico's beat on the drums wasn't as crisp as it should be. Even Benji's bass guitar was just off, somehow. And Jay knew it was all his fault. He was off his game, had been ever since Milli walked out on him.

He needed to pull it together. He needed to put on a show—one worthy of the ticket price these people had paid to see them play.

Jay just wished he knew how.

He was too far inside his own head, that was the problem. Too caught up in his own failings to be good at anything. Maybe Harry had been right, maybe going out on such a long tour so soon after the break-up was a bad idea. But Jay had been sure it was what he needed—a distraction from the rest of his life falling apart. From the discovery that all the things he'd thought he had were fake all along.

The song wound to a close, going out with a whimper rather than a bang. There was applause, of course, but it felt more polite than genuine.

Jay turned to the side of the stage and saw Daisy Mulligan, their support act, watching with a frown, her bottom lip caught between her teeth. She was young, new on the circuit, technically still star struck by them all—and yet even she could obviously tell something was off tonight.

If it had been one bad gig, Jay might have written it off—every band had an off night now and then, right? But this whole tour seemed to be one bad gig after another, and he just didn't know how to fix it.

At least the next item on the set list was a duet. He and the guys had met Daisy at a festival in Copenhagen a couple of years before, where she'd ended up onstage with them singing one of their bigger hits, 'With You', adding harmonies and a whole new level of meaning to the simple love song. When she'd agreed to come on tour with them as their support act, Jay had suggested they add the duet into the set list. Which was just as well, since night after night it seemed to be the only song that got a genuine response from the crowd.

Picking up her trademark mandolin, Daisy crossed the stage to join him.

'You okay?' she murmured as they took their positions, her words masked by the cheers from the auditorium. They'd already heard Daisy play once tonight and, unlike Dept 135, Jay had to admit that the young singer-songwriter was having a stellar tour. At least the label would be pleased about that much, he supposed. As long as she could continue to keep her notorious firecracker temper in check.

'Fine.' He shook his head. 'Let's do this.'

The difference was obvious the moment the music started. With Daisy onstage beside him, he could focus on her rather than the crowd. He felt the chords vibrate through him, the high counterpoint Daisy played on her mandolin cutting through their more usual riffs.

She caught his eye as they both took a breath, ready for the first words, and for the first time since they'd last sung together the night before, Jay felt centred. Ready. As if he was where he needed to be.

These days, he seemed to be living for these few minutes when he managed to lose himself in the music again, in a way that had been eluding him ever since Milli left. Since he'd realised that what he'd thought was true love was actually all just another performance.

The crowd could obviously feel it too; a hush fell over them as Jay and Daisy sang, the harmonies rising and soaring above their heads. Jay felt the tension start to leave his shoulders. Hopefully they could finish this gig on a high, if he could keep this energy going into their finale number, next.

Maybe he wasn't completely washed up at thirty.

He'd leaned in closer as they sang, he realised, and so had Daisy. There was so much emotion in the words, in the music, that it felt natural. They were singing a love song, after all.

She smiled up at him, her eyes dancing, and he realised—not exactly for the first time—that she was gorgeous. Big green eyes under dark hair, her petite form meaning she barely came up to his shoulder.

Perhaps it was that revelation, or perhaps just the relief that the crowd were back on side, that this song at least sounded good. Whatever the reason, as the last notes faded away Jay wrapped an arm around Daisy's waist and held her close, while the crowd cheered in a way they hadn't since he'd stepped onto the stage.

He leant closer, meaning to murmur his thanks to her. But then he got caught in those eyes, in the cheers, in the atmosphere. And before he even knew what he was doing, Jay pressed his mouth to Daisy's—the brief kiss sending the audience into ecstatic cheers, and his body into the sort of reaction he hadn't felt in months.

It was only as he pulled away and watched the dazed look fade from Daisy's eyes, instantly replaced with a more familiar flashing anger, that he realised how much trouble he was going to be in when he got offstage.

The sound of the crowd still rang in Daisy's ears as she stepped off the stage two nights later—and into her own personal hell.

'Daisy! That was a great gig. You must be so pleased. Do you think you and Jay will celebrate together later? Will you join him back onstage for an encore? Off the record, can you confirm *anything* about your relationship?'

No. Because there is no relationship.

She could tell the damn reporter that, but Daisy knew from experience she wouldn't believe her. And why would she, after that bloody kiss Jay had planted on her after their duet in Philadelphia, two days ago?

He'd apologised afterwards, of course, muttering something about trying to put on a show for the crowd—and Kevin, their manager, had been thrilled. Photos of the kiss had been all over the Internet in a matter of hours, and sales for the remaining nights of their tour had seen a sudden surge with all the speculation about their supposed relationship.

The truth, it seemed, didn't matter so much in situations like this. Another thing to learn about being an almost celebrity.

Daisy knew it was all just an act. But knowing that didn't stop the buzz of connection that had hummed through her like a melody when Jay had kissed her...

The reporter was still waiting for an answer. Daisy yanked her thoughts back to reality and belatedly found some words for her.

'Yeah, it went well. Great crowd out there tonight.'

That much, at least, was true. Unlike all the rumours about her and Jay.

There were more questions—there were always more questions, and too many reporters asking them. Daisy had never imagined anybody being quite so interested in her life offstage. Hell, she'd never imagined them being that interested in her music *on*stage. But ever since that festival in Copenhagen, life had generally been beyond her wildest expectations and dreams.

Copenhagen had given her more than her career though. It'd given her friends too. Not just Jay, and the rest of his band—Dept 135—but also it was where she had met her two best friends in the world. Two women she'd spent mere hours with in person, on that one day at the festival when they'd helped an old lady, Viv, and her dog, and ended up hanging out the rest of the night.

They might not have seen each other since that day in Denmark, but they'd stayed in touch. In fact, Jessica and Aubrey had been a lifeline for Daisy in the months that followed, as her whole world turned upside down when fame came calling.

They'd had their own issues too. Aubrey had been seriously ill, although finally seemed on the mend, and ready to take on life on her own terms again. Jessica, meanwhile, had just been offered an exciting job opportunity in New York.

While Daisy had everything she'd ever dreamt of. She was performing nightly on a world tour, singing her own songs, playing her own instruments, supporting one of the biggest bands in the world. And if you believed the media, she was also involved in a wild romance with Jay Barwell, voted world's sexiest man three years running.

Of course, that part was total fiction, one that had been doing the rounds even *before* the infamous kiss. Daisy happened to know that Jay was still totally hung up on his ex-girlfriend—American popstress Milli Masters. She suspected that was the real reason he'd kissed her—to show Milli he was over her, even if he wasn't.

Daisy could understand that, and could live with the rumours to a point—after all, she owed Jay a lot.

Just not enough to have to deal with the paparazzi quizzing her about her sex life every night after a gig.

Forcing herself to smile, she pushed through the crowd—stopping to sign a few autographs for fans at the edge of the throng—ignoring more shouted questions about her imaginary love life.

'Daisy! Is it true Jay took you to Paris for your birthday?'

'Do you think he's going to propose soon?'

Oh, how disappointed they'd all be if they knew that Daisy had spent her birthday alone in her hotel room, apart from a video call with Aubrey and Jessica during which they sang 'Happy Birthday' to her. She hadn't even told Jay or the guys that it *was* her birthday. It was a rare night off in the tour schedule, after a day of travelling to the next location, and all she'd wanted to do was sleep. That was all she ever seemed to have the energy to do between gigs, these days. The glamour of the celebrity lifestyle had *definitely* been exaggerated in her case.

As for proposing. Ha! Even if they *were* dating, Daisy knew that wouldn't happen.

She wasn't the settling-down type. Staying in one place too long had never been her scene. In fact, she'd spent the first sixteen years of her life fighting to get *out* of the place she'd been born and brought up. There was too much world to see, too much life to live, to settle down and stay with just one person.

Her home was on the road, her people were the musicians she met there and her true friends scattered across the world—Aubrey in Australia and Jessica in Canada, or New York, now. The only things she held sacred were her guitar, her mandolin, and her own voice.

What else did she need, really? Except perhaps a decent night's sleep somewhere that wasn't a bus, and the space to clear her head for a few minutes without someone asking her something or calling her name.

'Daisy Louise Mulligan?'

Somehow, through the clamour of the crowd, the music still raging through the speakers around the stadium, and the questions she was trying to ignore, Daisy heard her full name—spoken softly, but insistently.

Frowning, she turned to try and figure out who'd spoken it. Her eye fell upon a nondescript man in a grey suit. Not a pushy paparazzi for sure, and definitely not one of her typical fans.

'Yes?'

'If you could come with me, please, I have some important legal information to share with you.'

Daisy shrank back. Oh, she didn't like the sound of that. In her life 'legal information' usually meant a lot of trouble. Except she was pretty sure she hadn't done anything even vaguely illegal since she left home at sixteen.

Maybe she was being sued. That was the sort of thing that happened once you started to get famous, right? Jay had definitely been sued before—although the case was thrown out of court because of course he hadn't done anything wrong. Jay was a sweetheart. That was why the whole world loved him so much.

Of course, the rest of the world didn't have to see him moping around about Milli bloody Masters, or deal with his grumpy moods since they split up six months ago. That probably helped.

But back to the problem at hand.

'Am I being sued?' she asked.

The man in the suit gave her a faint smile and shook his head. 'Quite the opposite, Miss Mulligan. In fact, I have some very good news for you.'

Daisy drew back a little more. Somehow, the idea of *good* news made her even more nervous. She was used to bad news, to disaster, to problems. And she figured she'd already used up all the good luck she was entitled to in her whole life by getting the gig as the opening act for Jay and the band.

Whatever this news was, Daisy was certain there'd be a catch. Good things didn't just *happen* to people. Daisy knew that there was always a price to pay somewhere. If her childhood had taught her anything it was that she had to work for anything good that came her way—she couldn't just rely on hope and the kindness of strangers.

'If you could just come with me?' The man held out his arm for Daisy to take.

Her eyes widened even further, and she took a step back.

He dropped his arm, seeming to get her measure. 'There's a coffee shop, just across the way. Brightly lit, plenty of people. If you will join me there, I'll be able to fill you in on all the details of your inheritance.'

Daisy looked across the road and saw the coffee shop he'd mentioned. It looked safe. And not full of reporters asking her questions.

Then her brain caught up with his other words.

'My inheritance?' She didn't have anybody who owned anything to leave her, as far as she knew. Her own family had barely had enough money to buy food for the many kids crammed into their council house. 'Someone left me something? Who?'

But the man in the suit didn't answer the question she asked. Instead, he answered a different one.

'Yes. You've been left a house—well, a cottage. A villa, perhaps? In Italy. Now, if you'll come with me…'

She followed him in a daze. A cottage? Why would *anybody* leave her a cottage, in Italy of all places? A cottage sounded like…well, like a *home*. And she hadn't had one of those since she'd run away from Liverpool at sixteen with her mother's old mandolin and a change of clothes, and barely looked back.

This had to be a mistake. She'd go with the guy, figure out what confusion had sent him here, to her, and then she'd get back to her regularly scheduled life. Her manic, overloaded, exhausting life, full of fake news about her romantic status.

Great.

Another day, another lousy gig. The duet with Daisy had been the only bright point, yet again—although he'd managed to keep his lips off her for the last couple of nights, so even that hadn't gone down as well as it had in Philadelphia.

Jay handed his precious guitar to the stagehand, waved wearily at the rest the band—ignoring a concerned look from his brother, Harry—and headed for the stage door. He should go back to the dressing room, he knew. Get changed, freshen up, hang with the band, listen to their manager, Kevin, tell them what a great job they did tonight. But to be honest? He couldn't face it.

Daisy had come back out for an encore with them, at the end of their set, which he hoped meant she'd forgiven him for the kiss—but might just mean she was trying to save him from himself. She was good, Jay had to admit. From the first time he'd seen her play in Copenhagen, two years ago now, he'd known her talent was something rare and special. It was a point of professional pride that he had brought her on board, although it helped that her music and style, while complementing theirs, was different enough from Dept 135's offerings that they were never in direct competition.

She got on well enough with the rest of the band too—and Jay knew from previous experience that wasn't always the case with supporting acts. Overall, it had been a good decision to ask her to open for them on this tour. But Jay had a feeling it was starting to get to her.

The touring lifestyle wasn't for everybody. Hell, he wasn't even sure it was for him, and he'd been doing it for the better part of a decade now. But it was what you had to do to make it in the music industry these days. And Daisy was great onstage, always had been. The problems only started offstage.

Jay knew that in his current state of mind, he probably wasn't the best choice to be lecturing anybody about positive attitude, or the benefits of not snapping at the management—especially since it was his lips that had increased the pressure on her from the paparazzi. Still, he couldn't help but feel that, as her mentor of sorts, it was his place to have a word with her before she really hacked someone off. Even Harry, the most even-tempered guy Jay knew, had raised his eyebrows when Daisy had stormed off straight after sound check, leaving her precious mandolin behind for someone else to store safely until the gig that night.

When they'd first met, Daisy had hugged that mandolin like a safety blanket. Jay couldn't help but think that this afternoon's mini strop signalled worse things to come, and it was his job as band frontman, and Daisy's sort-of mentor, to try and nip that in the bud.

Leaving the others to head back to the dressing room for a well-deserved drink and pat on the back from the management, Jay followed Daisy's retreating figure out through the stage door instead. She had a head start on him, but he could just about see her mop of dark hair bobbing through the crowd of journos and fans. She stopped to sign some autographs, which was a good sign. When she stopped making time for the people who listened to her music, then she'd be in real trouble.

'Jay!' Pamela Pearson, one of Jay's least favourite music journalists—if he could call someone who only ever reported on the personal lives of musicians, rather than the music they made, that—elbowed her way to the front of the crowd at the stage door to grab his arm. 'It's so good to see you again! And looking so happy, too. Are we to assume that's since you brought Daisy on tour with you this time...?'

She didn't actually wink, but she might as well have done.

Last year, when they'd toured, Daisy hadn't been enough of a name to join them as an opening act, and they'd already had a commitment with another band for the slot, anyway. But ever since Jay had introduced Daisy to their manager, dragging Kevin to see her play in some dive bar in London, after he recognised her name from that festival in Copenhagen, their musical stars had been somewhat linked.

Phoenix Records, their label, had a great reputation for nurturing new talent, and part of that was pairing new artists with established stars to help them through the growing pains that every musician went through, trying to adapt from playing music for themselves and twenty people in a pub to making music for millions. Jay had been an obvious choice to mentor Daisy, so they'd stayed in touch through the year.

Then, it had been low-key enough that no one outside the band or the label had even noticed. Well, apart from Milli, but Jay wasn't thinking about her. Ever again.

Although, it had been his break-up with Milli that had made him so adamant he wanted to get back out on the road, and quickly. He'd assured Kevin and the label that they'd be able to work on the new album while touring, which everyone had to know was a lie, but they'd let him get away with it anyway. Perhaps they knew as well as he did that staying at home, noticing all the places Milli wasn't, wouldn't help him at all.

Heartbreak was supposed to be good for inspiration, but so far Jay hadn't found any music in his misery. At least, nothing that was repeatable to the world at large.

Bringing Daisy on tour had suddenly brought her to the notice of music journos—and gossip reporters— everywhere. And given that Jay was her main friend, supporter and mentor on this tour, people had begun

jumping to the usual boring and predictable conclu-
sions. Helped out by that accidental kiss in Philadelphia.

They were wrong, of course, but it did serve as a nice
distraction from the endless articles about how he was
moping over Milli, while she was off holidaying with
some billionaire businessman in the Maldives.

Not that he read those articles. Much.

Mostly because Harry confiscated them.

'Pamela, I'm always happy after a great gig like tonight.' He flashed the reporter a blinding smile, just one
more person in the industry he was obligated to charm.
'And having Daisy on tour with us is just an added
bonus. She's fantastic fun, onstage and off.'

Dammit. Jay regretted the words the moment they
were out of his mouth and cursed himself doubly when
he saw the shark-like grin that spread across Pamela's
face. She was going to take that as further confirmation of their relationship and run with it, Jay knew. And
since the Daisy being fun offstage part was currently a
total lie, he knew he'd pay for it once it reached her ears.

'I must say, as a friend, it's just so lovely to see you
happy again, Jay.' Pamela laid a hand on his arm, and
he resisted the urge to shake it off. They weren't friends,
they were barely acquaintances. But that wouldn't stop
Pamela butting into his private life. 'Might we keep hoping for an official announcement soon? Maybe even a
shot of Daisy flashing some extra-special jewellery?'

In for a penny, in for a pound, as his gran always
used to say. If Pamela was going to write about him and
Daisy anyway, it might as well be a story that would
show Milli he really had moved on from her and her
betrayal. One that didn't talk about how tired he looked,

how downhearted, how he'd lost his way and his music was suffering. He was so sick of *those* articles.

'Never give up hope, Pamela. That's what I always say.' And with a wink, Jay headed out into the crowd to find his wayward support act, hoping she wouldn't actually injure him when she discovered he was fuelling the rumours about their romantic lives.

CHAPTER TWO

'WHERE WERE YOU last night?'

Daisy closed the hard guitar case with her instrument inside and fastened the clasps. Her guitar wasn't quite as precious to her as her mandolin, but it was still one of the tools of her trade, and that meant she needed to take good care of it. Something she had to remind herself to do when frustration and anger got the better of her, and all she wanted to do was be alone away from idiots. At least musical instruments didn't ask annoying questions. Unlike Jay.

She turned to him with a sigh. 'I was onstage with you, same as every night. In fact, I was carrying the whole damn gig, just like *every* night of this tour. And then I was sleeping on a tour bus to get here. Also the same as you. Except I wasn't snoring.'

'I don't snore. That's Harry.' Jay hopped up to sit onstage beside where she was packing up her equipment after the sound check, close enough that she had to move around him as she worked. One thing she'd learned about Jay while they'd been touring—he had no sense of personal space. Which meant they all got to share his miserable mood. 'And I meant between those two things. Where did you go after the gig? You left me to deal with Pamela the shark all on my own.' He nudged her leg as she passed, obviously hoping to raise a smile with his use of the nickname. He was making an effort, more than he did most days. She supposed she should be pleased by that.

In fact, though, he just reminded her exactly why she was annoyed with him.

'I thought you and Pammy were big mates,' Daisy said. 'At least that's what she's claiming on her blog this morning, as she spills all the details of your private friendly chat about your relationship with me. I understand I should be anticipating some diamonds soon.'

As if. Daisy had always known she wasn't the marrying kind—not even the settling-down sort. Even if Jay was interested in her—which, since she knew he was totally hung up on his ex, Milli, he categorically wasn't, that surprisingly intense kiss notwithstanding— all these stories presupposed that she'd just fall at his feet. Because to the world at large, Jay Barwell was the dream, the fantasy, and no one in their right mind would turn down the opportunity to bed him, let alone marry him.

Well, apart from Milli Masters, who was her own fantasy fodder to millions—even more so than Jay.

And Daisy. Who had absolutely no interest in marrying anyone, especially not a guy who snored on tour buses and tried to 'big brother' her. He called it 'mentoring' but Daisy knew what it *really* was. It was Jay thinking he knew better than her about everything, and that had never gone down well with her.

Especially since *his* attempts at managing the press

now had her practically engaged to him. So much for knowing best. *She'd* never got them accidentally engaged before. Although that might be because she avoided media—social and real world—as much as possible. Something else Jay thought she was wrong about.

Jay laughed. 'You know Pamela. Never one to bother with the truth, when the lie is so much more interesting.'

'Interesting,' Daisy muttered. 'That's one word for it.'

Daisy didn't understand that—or how he could be so blasé about it all. She could sort of get going along with the rumours and the gossip—even her limited PR knowledge told her that people talking about them, whatever the reason, had to be good publicity for the music. Which was, in case the whole crazy world had forgotten, what they were actually there for.

But when it came to outright lies about them, to pretending they were madly in love and getting married... well, that was where she started to get twitchy about the whole thing. Not least because it was completely unbelievable.

She tried to imagine her family, such as it was, back in Liverpool reading these headlines: *Rising star Daisy Mulligan set to tie the knot with superstar Jay Barwell!*

Yeah—no. She could see her gran laughing now, so hard she'd give herself another coughing fit. And her dad would just roll his eyes and toss the paper out. Her little brothers probably wouldn't even remember her well enough to comment, and her stepmum would use the paper to pick up the mess the dogs left in the back garden.

Her life didn't come with fairy-tale weddings and

happy ever afters, even fake ones. Of course, it hadn't come with Italian villas until last night, either.

'You didn't answer my question.' Jay leant closer, right up into her space, and Daisy forced herself to stay still to avoid giving him the satisfaction of backing away. She tried to ignore the way her body hummed with the memory of that fake kiss, too. That wasn't going to be any help at all in this situation. 'Where did you go after the gig last night? I came looking for you.'

She didn't ask why he'd been looking in the first place, because she could guess—and it had nothing to do with getting on one knee with a diamond ring, or even kissing her for real this time. He'd probably wanted to talk to her about her attitude. Again.

As if her basic personality was something she could just change to suit him. Uh…no, thanks.

'Some guy came looking for me. A lawyer, I guess. Wanted to talk to me about an inheritance.'

Jay's sandy eyebrows went up at that. 'Someone died?'

Daisy frowned. The solicitor hadn't explained that part. Usually when you inherited something, someone had to die first, right? But in this case it seemed more like a mystery gift. And it wasn't as if she had any rich relatives to die and leave her stuff, anyway. When her gran went, she'd be lucky to inherit her old Zippo lighter, at a push.

'I'm not sure. It was kind of confusing. But basically, someone seems to have left me some cottage in Italy, for some reason. It's probably some sort of scam, I don't know.'

None of it made any sense at all, and from the baffled look on Jay's face, he knew it. And she'd never even told him about her family, or how she'd left them behind at sixteen and never looked back. Maybe he'd guessed some of it, but she'd never *told* him.

She never told anybody. The past was just that—past. Daisy had no intention of living in it.

But if Jay had questions, he didn't have the chance to ask them, because at that moment Kevin, their shared manager, came bustling into the auditorium, his eyes fixed as ever on the tablet in his hands.

'Guys! Have you seen this? This is immense. The organic reach of this story has been incredible. Ever since that kiss! We *have* to capitalise on this, stat.'

Daisy and Jay exchanged wary glances. Kevin wasn't naturally an over-excitable sort.

'Seen what, exactly?' Jay asked. Daisy was happy to leave whatever this was to him to resolve. After all, he was the senior artist on the roster, the headlining act. She was just support.

Plus he was much less likely to snap sarcastically at Kevin than she was. Daisy knew her limits and, after three months of constant touring, she was pretty near them. She needed her own space—something that was non-existent on tour. Plus the mental strain of keeping everything together when all the reviews talked about how Dept 135 weren't living up to their reputation, how her duet with Jay was the best bit about the show... She was glad people liked what she was doing, of course, but it didn't make for a great feeling on the bus, and she knew it was getting to Jay. She needed some time away from them all.

Thank God tomorrow night was their last show before

a three-week break. Three weeks on her own, without having to make small talk or be polite to people or pretend she cared about marketing strategies and branding... that would be perfect. She could recharge—alone, probably in a hotel room somewhere with great bars nearby, and an anonymous city vibe—and come back to the tour ready to be polite to people again.

Well, as polite as she ever got, anyway.

Kevin turned the tablet towards them, showcasing a shot of the two of them onstage in Philadelphia, the moment that they kissed. The headline above it read: *Wedding Bells for Jay?* Daisy pulled a face and started to turn away—until Kevin flipped to the next photo, one that must have been taken just moments later, after the kiss but before she walked offstage.

She couldn't help herself. Daisy leaned closer and studied the picture.

No wonder people were believing these crazy rumours. They looked like they were in love. No doubt about it, the connection between them onstage was clear for anyone who even glimpsed the photo.

She stared at the screen, fascinated. She'd known, ever since that festival in Copenhagen where they'd first played together, that they had a musical synchronicity. Without ever rehearsing or even playing together before, they'd been able to just sink into each other's style and *play*. When Jay played guitar she could just *feel* where he was going from chord to chord and, with her mandolin in her hand, she could dance around the tune he summoned and add sparkle and chimes and an extra layer of magic.

Of course, they were still much better when they actually practised, but that didn't change what lay under the music, or what she saw in the photo Kevin was proudly displaying.

When she and Jay made music together, she knew him, understood him, in a way she didn't understand *anyone* outside music. Which probably had more to do with her lack of social skills than anything else, but still. When they played, they connected.

And that showed, even in a photo, even without the kiss, even without the music there to explain it.

But without the music that connection didn't make any sense. Unless the two people in that photo were in love.

'That's so misleading,' she said sharply, forgetting her resolve to let Jay deal with this. 'They're reading too much into a fake kiss that only happened because Jay knew the band were tanking that night.'

Jay winced at that, but didn't argue back, which Daisy figured made her case for her.

'Is it?' Kevin raised his eyebrows. 'I mean, it happened—happens every night you play together onstage, whether you kiss or not. And if your fans read a little more into it than is technically true…that's not our fault. It's our opportunity.'

Rubbing his hand across his forehead, Jay sank back down to sit on the edge of the stage. 'This is because I spoke to Pamela last night, isn't it?'

Kevin scrolled up the screen on his tablet to show another headline on the gossip site: *Jay says he's ready to love again!*

Daisy snorted as Jay said, 'I didn't say that!'

'Doesn't matter what you said.' Kevin put the tablet

down, for possibly the first time since Daisy had met him. She suspected he even held onto it in his sleep. 'What matters is what the world believes. And they believe—no, they *know*—that the two of you are in love. And that gives us an opportunity.'

'To do what, exactly?' Daisy asked, instantly suspicious. She had a feeling that whatever it was it would have nothing to do with music—which was all she was interested in. And she was starting to suspect that this had nothing to do with what *she* wanted at all.

'To raise your stars further! To give your audience what they really want!' Kevin's voice vibrated with excitement. 'And to make a lot of money, I hope,' he added, more prosaically.

It always came down to money, Daisy knew. And having lived so long without any, she wasn't about to say it didn't matter. Money—scraped together from gigs in filthy pubs, busking on the street, and even selling her first guitar—was what had allowed her to go to Copenhagen, to the festival, with her mandolin in hand, and play that first gig that really mattered. The one where Jay had seen her, and asked her to come to *their* gig later, a secret afterglow sort of thing for their fans, and pulled her up onstage with him.

She wouldn't argue against money as a motive. But that didn't mean she was just giving in, either.

'*Both* our stars?' she asked sceptically. 'Or is this just an attempt to distract from the fact that ticket sales were trailing off with every tour review, up until the moment Jay kissed me onstage, so now you want us to fleece our fans by lying to them?'

'Of course not!' Kevin sounded far more offended

than Daisy thought was reasonable, since that had totally been his actual suggestion. 'I want to use this interest to bring your music to *new* fans, that's all!'

From the tilt of Jay's eyebrows, Daisy was betting he didn't believe him either. But he also seemed willing to give Kevin's plan a shot. 'How, exactly?'

'Well, now.' Kevin took a seat in the front row of the auditorium and motioned for the two of them to do the same, except then they'd be sitting in a boring row unable to really look at each other, so Daisy ignored him and settled onto the floor, her back against the stage instead. Jay, of course, did as he was told and sat beside Kevin.

'We've got a break in the tour schedule coming up, as I'm sure you both know.'

Did she ever. Daisy had been *living* for this break for the last seven days, ever since the incident with the bus, the muddy back-country road, and the cow, that had led to performing on practically no sleep.

It wasn't that Daisy didn't like touring—well, actually, there was an argument to be made for that, too. But she *loved* performing. Sharing her music with people who actually wanted to listen. Making music with like-minded friends. That was what she lived for.

Sharing a tour bus with five blokes, at least one of whom snored, was not. Neither was dealing with the press, doing interviews, smiling all the time, and living in each other's pockets.

The moving around she was okay with—she'd never been particularly attached to any place anyhow. But she'd like at least a little time to see the places they stopped, beyond the venues and dressing rooms.

And she would *kill* for just twenty-four hours alone, without anyone trying to talk to her.

The break in the schedule was all that stood between her and some sort of furious meltdown that she'd probably end up taking out on poor, placid, miserable Jay. Of course, after the engagement thing with Pamela, he might deserve it.

'Yep,' Jay said to Kevin, his tone wary. 'Three weeks for me to focus on writing the new album, right?'

'I thought we could use this break to capitalise on this fabulous publicity,' Kevin went on, oblivious to Jay's frown and Daisy's suddenly murderous thoughts. 'Of course you'll want to work on the album, but how about working with Daisy, writing a few more duets, since they're what seem to be going down so well right now?'

'More duets,' Jay repeated flatly.

Daisy got the impression he could read between the lines as well as she could. What Kevin meant was, *You can't even perform right now, Jay, let alone write. No one is talking about the music anyway. Let me give you Daisy to distract them all.*

Except she wasn't something that could just be *given* like that. Not like a new watch, or a million dollars, or even an Italian villa...

Kevin continued, regardless. 'And while you're at it, we could set up some public engagements for the two of you as a couple, a few high-profile appearances, maybe even a trip to a jeweller's...'

He left it hanging, as if it were just a suggestion, but Daisy knew from experience that it was nothing of the sort. The label got what the label wanted, and Jay was a far bigger star than she ever hoped to be. If Kevin thought he could use her to save Dept 135 from Jay's blue period, he would, in a heartbeat.

Well, tough. She signed up to play music and sing her songs. Not to get fake engaged to some superstar. She'd probably get death threats from his teenage fans, for a start.

'Sorry, no can do,' she said as breezily as possible to hide her fury. 'I've…just found out I've been left some property in Italy, and need to spend the next three weeks there sorting that out.'

There. Problem solved.

'Italy?' Kevin's brow wrinkled as he obviously tried to make sense of Daisy's statement. Which, Jay knew, would be difficult, since it made basically no sense at all.

Or at least, not a lot more than Kevin's current plan to marry the pair of them off for the publicity.

Except, in the context of the reviews, the ticket sales and the terrible tour, that made *perfect* sense.

Dept 135 fan? Don't look over there at those nasty reviews—look at this photo of Jay kissing a pretty girl!

But just because it made sense didn't mean he was comfortable with it. And he knew for a fact that Daisy wouldn't be.

'Yeah,' Daisy responded nonchalantly, despite the fact that Jay was almost certain she was about to launch into some audacious lying. 'My great-aunt. Lovely woman. I'll miss her so much. But she left me her cottage in Italy to remember her by. And so…' she sniffed, mostly for effect, Jay suspected '…I was planning on spending the break there, sorting out the details.'

Daisy was a terrible liar, but somehow Kevin seemed to be buying it. Probably he was mostly afraid of backlash for not being suitably sympathetic in Daisy's time of great—and probably fictional—loss.

'I'm so sorry, Daisy,' he said, with too much conviction for it to be authentic. 'Of course you must go to Italy. We'll work something out.' The phone in his hand started ringing, and he held it up. 'Sorry, must take this. I'll be right back.'

Jay waited until he was out of earshot and then, knowing that Kevin had never been less than ten minutes on a phone call in his life, turned to Daisy.

'What the hell? I thought you just said it was probably a scam. And now there's a Great-Aunt Felicia or whatever?'

'Felicia! That's a great name for her. Thanks, Jay.' Daisy beamed at him, obviously not mourning the loss of her imaginary aunt one bit. 'It's the details that really sell a lie, right?'

It's not having the worst poker face in history that really helps, he thought, but didn't say.

He quite liked that Daisy was rubbish at lying. He'd been lied to enough in his life already. At least he could be reasonably sure that Daisy would never get away with lying to him.

'But why are we lying to Kevin?' he asked, uncomfortably aware that he was complicit here too. He knew there was no Felicia, but he hadn't called Daisy out in front of Kevin. And he knew he probably wouldn't when the manager returned, either, even though he should.

Daisy gave him a blank look, as if it should be to-tally obvious. 'Um…because I actually *want* a break from this tour?'

Jay shrugged. 'We'll get one either way. I mean, there are no gigs planned for the next three weeks. Did you have plans that are more important than hanging around parties and writing music with me?'

It occurred to him, probably a little late, that she might. That there might be some guy, or some girl, wait-ing for her to finish touring and come home to them. Daisy didn't talk about her private life much. At this point, he knew more about her fictional great-aunt than any of her actual family.

She spoke of her friends, Aubrey and Jessica, some-times, but Jay got the impression that they were scat-tered around the globe and dealing with their own stuff. But maybe Daisy had planned to go visit one of them?

He could sympathise for wanting to get away and back to the people she cared about; normally he'd feel the same way. When there was a break in the tour sched-ule, he and Harry tended to head home to Cheshire to see their mum. But right now, he couldn't take three weeks of his mother lamenting the loss of the love of his life, as if Milli had died rather than just walked out on him.

In his family, true love was for life, just as it had been for his parents. His mum and dad had fallen hard for each other the first day they met, married two months later, and stayed happy and in love until the day his dad died of a heart attack, when Jay was seventeen. His mum had never even contemplated the idea of marrying again. 'Your dad was it for me,' was all she'd say when he or Harry suggested dating. 'I had love. I don't need another poor imitation of it at my time of life.'

That was why he'd always been so cagey about introducing girlfriends to his family too soon. But when he was on the cover of every glossy magazine with Milli, keeping things under wraps had been a little tricky.

But this wasn't about Milli. It was about Daisy, and the album he needed to write.

Because Kevin was right: he needed her help if he was going to shake this funk and write something worth listening to. Which meant he needed to persuade her to forget Aunt Felicia, or whatever she really had planned.

Daisy pulled a face. 'Yes, I had plans. Me, a hotel room, and no people asking me questions or needing me to smile for the next three weeks. Seriously, Jay, if I have to stay on show I'm going to blow a fuse at just the wrong moment. Probably with the wrong person. I'll ruin everything, I know I will.'

Jay hid a smile. For all that Daisy performed onstage as if every moment she lived was for her fans, and for all the engaging and extroverted interviews she gave, he'd long suspected it was all an act. At her heart, Daisy was *not* a people person. Hence the snappy and sulky behaviour over the last week or two. She needed some alone time.

He recognised it easily enough; his brother Harry was the same. Jay tended to be more energised by spending time with people, although he'd withdrawn a lot since the break-up with Milli. Harry, however, could only ever enjoy the company of others for so long before he'd need some serious solitude to find his equilibrium again.

Daisy was like Harry. And even if she wasn't planning on spending three weeks in a scam cottage in Italy, she *did* need time away from the tour. So as a responsible mentor figure he'd back her up on that.

'Okay, fine. We'll go with the cottage story. Rest in peace Great-Aunt Felicia, and all that. But Kevin's going to want to know what we're going to do about the album.' And so was he.

For all his claims of being able to write on tour, Jay knew he wasn't in the right place mentally to do it *and* keep gigging. Plus it was hard to write love songs when he was still mentally reliving what had gone wrong with the only woman he'd ever actually loved.

Even if the love story had been more one-sided than he'd thought.

Daisy's shoulders slumped. 'Yeah. Well, maybe I can just take a week and then we'll get onto it?'

She sounded about as enthusiastic at the prospect of them writing love songs together as he was. But he had obligations, contracts. Fans. Somehow, he had to find a way to get past this writing slump—and Daisy was the best idea he had.

Before he could answer, Kevin returned from his phone call, beaming.

'All sorted, kids! Jay, you're going to go to Italy with Daisy. Kills two birds with one cottage and all that.' Jay shot Daisy an incredulous look, seeing it mirrored on her face. 'You can work on the album together, the media can write about your romantic break away, and Daisy can sort out her inheritance issues at the same time!'

He looked so pleased with himself to have come up

with the solution, Jay didn't have the heart to tell him there might not even *be* a cottage. And that even if there was, Daisy wasn't going to go for pretending to be his girlfriend. One way or another, they were going to have to come up with a solution to this.

But apparently not right now.

Daisy grabbed her stuff, slung her mandolin over her back, and flashed them both a patently false smile. 'Well, in that case, I'll leave you two to decide the rest of my life for me while I go and get some sleep.'

And then she was gone.

Kevin frowned. 'She must really be grieving her aunt,' he said. 'She's normally so happy.'

Jay considered enlightening him as to Daisy's *actual* nature, but decided it probably wasn't worth the time it would take.

'Yeah, that must be it,' he said instead. 'I'll talk to her later, figure something out.'

After she'd calmed down. And in the meantime, he was going to talk to the only stable and sensible person he knew on this tour.

His brother, Harry.

CHAPTER THREE

DAISY SLAMMED ONTO the tour bus, glad that for once it was empty apart from the driver, who was on his phone up front in the cab. She needed to be away from people—especially Kevin.

One thing was abundantly clear to her—she didn't hold enough bargaining chips here to get what she wanted. But wasn't that always the case? It just meant she had to pick her battles. Figure out what she needed most and fight for that—even if it meant giving in on the parts that mattered less to her.

And what she needed most was to get away from this tour.

Flopping onto her bunk, she pulled out her phone. One of the reasons her friendship with Aubrey and Jessica worked so well was that neither of them expected all that much from her. They didn't expect her to be free for a night out when she just needed to be alone. They didn't complain when it took her a few hours—or days—to respond to messages, because she just wasn't in a people place right then.

Daisy liked people—honestly, she did. She just liked them on her own terms.

She thought that Jessica and Aubrey got it. Jessica had a natural gift for connection with others, but she was also generally happiest safely between the covers of a book—well, until she decided to accept the chance to go to New York and interview for a new job, anyway. And while Aubrey was far more extroverted than either of them, after a serious health scare, she hated being fussed over by her loving—but overbearing—brothers, so she got it when Daisy said she was just peopled out.

Now, lying flat on her back on the surprisingly comfortable bunk, she checked her messages, knowing there would probably be something from one or both of them to their message group. She'd texted the group last night to tell them about the solicitor and the cottage, and she was interested to hear what they had to say on the matter.

A cottage? In Italy? Awesome!

Just reading Aubrey's reply made Daisy smile. She could almost hear her friend saying it in her broad Aussie accent.

Italy is totally on my bucket list. But who could have left it to you?

There was nothing from Jessica, which was a surprise. Normally, Daisy would expect her to weigh in with a note about caution, being careful and taking her time. Jessica was always suspicious of change, which was why persuading her to go to New York and find out more about the job had been such a challenge. But she needed it, Daisy knew—and knew that Aubrey agreed too. Jessica had suffered a heart-breaking tragedy years ago that had shrunk her world right down to her small-town life and the books she read. But Jessica was such a friendly, loving soul, she deserved more than to just play it safe her whole life.

Daisy liked to think that she and Aubrey had helped show her that in getting her to accept the New York offer.

That music festival in Copenhagen had given Daisy more than her shot at a serious music career. It had given her friends—a family, almost. She relied on Aubrey and Jessica in a way she'd never been able to rely on her blood relations. They listened to her, gave her advice, helped her stay on the right path. And she knew they only ever had her best interests at heart, which was a lot more than she could say for her actual family.

The day they'd met, at the Annual Ascot Music Festival, had been the day before she'd met Jay and the band. That one festival had given her a future she'd never imagined until then—a successful music career *and* two best friends she could rely on.

They'd come together to save a dog called Max, but once they'd deposited the dog's owner, Viv, and Max at the hospital, the girls hadn't gone their separate ways. They'd stayed up chatting that night, learning about each other's lives. Aubrey and Jessica had come to her gig the next day, had been there when she stepped off-stage to cheer her and celebrate with her.

And they'd been there with her, virtually at least, every step of the way since.

Jessica was still silent, but Aubrey was typing again,

Daisy could see from the screen. She waited to hear what her friend had to say before responding.

And, speaking of awesome opportunities, guess what? Someone has GIVEN me the money to take the round the world trip I always planned! Just given it to me! Like a lottery win!

Daisy's whole body went cold. Of course she could understand why Aubrey was excited, but this seemed like just one too many coincidences to her.

She wrote back.

Wait. They just gave you the money? How did you find out about it?

This solicitor guy came to my house and told me. There's paperwork, bank transfer details, everything. It's REAL, Daisy!

And that doesn't seem a little...weird to you?

No weirder than someone leaving you a cottage. Or Jessica getting the chance at her dream job in New York, totally out of the blue.

Daisy waited a moment.

Hang on...do you think they're connected?

Daisy had known Aubrey would catch on quickly. She typed on...

I can't see how they could not be. I mean, it's just too much of a coincidence, right? You get the one thing you wanted most, ever since you fell sick—the chance to finish your grand tour trip. And Jessica gets exactly what she needs—the opportunity to step outside her safe little world and try out her dream job.

And you get a cottage in Italy.

Daisy had to admit that part didn't make much sense.

I guess I already have my dream—I'm an actual musician.

With a number one hit! Have I mentioned lately how much I love that song?

Yes.

Daisy knew she was blushing, could feel the heat in her cheeks even though there was no one there to see it. She still couldn't believe that she, Daisy Mulligan from Liverpool, had an actual hit single. What would all those teachers who'd dismissed her dreams as impossible say about her now? Not that she planned on going back to find out.

She typed again, bringing the conversation back to what really mattered.

The point is, all three of us have received mysterious but incredibly generous gifts or offers in the last month. Remember, Jessica's job interview wasn't just for her dream job, it involved days in New York too. What company interviews like that?

Not that Daisy had any idea of what job interviews in New York looked like. Hers had tended to be more of the *Can you pull a pint? Great, you're hired!* variety, back when she'd been serving behind bars rather than playing in front of them. Most of them had barely even checked she was eighteen, which had honestly been just as well when she'd been starting out.

Aubrey had replied.

They've got to be connected. But the only thing the three of us have in common is...

Viv.

Daisy finished the thought for her.

Could the older lady they'd helped in Copenhagen two years ago really be behind their gifts? And, if so, why on earth would she do it? Finding a missing dog didn't earn this kind of a reward.

Daisy could almost understand Jessica and Aubrey's gifts—everyone loved Jessica, and it was so obvious she needed to step outside her safe bubble and find actual happiness, not just contentment. And Aubrey... she'd had such a rough time of it with her illness that of course she deserved to finish her bucket-list trip now she was well again.

But why on earth would Viv give Daisy a cottage? She already had everything she needed.

Aubrey had sent another message.

Let me do some research. See what I can figure out. In the meantime…you'd better go see about this Italian cottage of yours!

Daisy typed back.

Looks like I might not have much choice. Kevin wants me and Jay to head there during the break in the tour schedule. We get to write new songs for the album while also pretending we're on a romantic getaway, since he's practically got us engaged in the press now.

I saw that! Well, it might be a good opportunity, Daise.

How?

There was a long pause before Aubrey's reply came through, as if she was thinking exactly how to phrase it.

You've been…kind of tense about the tour lately, right? I mean, some days your messages sound like you're not enjoying playing at all, and that's not you.

Daisy frowned at the screen, but the sad thing was Aubrey was right.

Maybe this cottage is your chance to get away from it all for a bit and figure out where you want to go next. I mean, maybe that's why Viv sent it to you now. You've already achieved your dreams, so maybe it's time to dream some new ones.

And Jay going with me? How is that helpful?

Gives you something pretty to look at while you're dreaming!

Even in her rotten mood, Daisy couldn't help but laugh at that. Trust Aubrey to find a silver lining to everything.

Harry was exactly where Jay had expected to find him—in the dressing room, lovingly polishing his favourite guitar. Harry had rituals and routines he employed to get him through every performance, and it was rare that he let anything or anybody distract him from them.

Jay just hoped he'd be willing to be distracted today.

'So, I understand congratulations are in order,' Harry said without looking up as Jay entered the room. 'Shall I email Mum and ask her to courier Gran's ring over?'

'Kevin wants us to go ring shopping and get photographed doing it, actually,' Jay replied, morosely.

Harry's head jerked up. 'Wait. You're letting *Kevin* plan the proposal? No way. You need someone with a smidge of romance in their soul. Kevin's heart was replaced with sales figures years ago.'

'Since this pretend relationship is all about sales figures, that sounds about right.' Sighing, Jay sank down into the chair opposite his brother, and watched as he ran the cloth over the instrument.

Harry clicked his tongue. 'Shame, really. If you'd just get engaged, Mum would stop worrying that you've lost your one true love and throw herself into the wedding planning. She might even get off my back about finding a nice young man to settle down with.'

'If she had Daisy as her daughter-in-law she'd have much bigger problems than your love life, you mean,' Jay shot back.

He couldn't ever quite shake the vague guilt he felt about dragging Harry into all of this. Yes, his brother loved making music as much as he did, but Harry would have been as happy as a session musician, or even music teacher, as he was as a member of one of the biggest bands to come out of the UK in years. And while he was sure his brother enjoyed the lifestyle and the money, he knew it came at a cost for Harry.

Love.

Starting the band had been Jay's idea. Getting out and gigging, finding an agent, signing with the label... it had all been Jay. He'd dragged Harry along with him every step of the way, and he suspected that one of the main reasons Harry had gone along with it was because he knew that music was Jay's coping strategy. Throwing himself into forming the band had been how he'd coped with their father's sudden, unexpected death. Just as forcing them all out on tour had been helping him cope with Milli leaving. Until now.

'What love life?' Harry scoffed. 'Your imaginary romance is more alive than my love life.'

'You could always try going out on a date,' Jay pointed out. 'Then maybe Mum would get off your back. You know she just worries about you being alone.' She'd had true love, and she was determined that her boys should find the same. It was kind of exhausting, Jay had to admit.

'What, you want me to sign up to some dating app and find a new guy to ask out in every city we play in?' Harry shook his head. 'Whatever would Kevin say?'

'Kevin would be fine with it, as long as you were—'

'Discreet?' Harry interrupted.

'I was going to say happy,' Jay replied.

His brother didn't look convinced. And Jay knew he wasn't entirely wrong. The band had an image, and a lot of fans—most of them female. Harry coming out as gay would probably win him some new ones, but Jay knew they'd take a hit from the girls who fancied him most. Not that he cared about that, not if it meant Harry was able to relax and be himself.

But Harry's answer was the same as always.

'I'll tell you again. I don't want the press picking over my personal life until there's something worth picking at. I don't want them watching me every time I talk to a guy, wondering if he's the one for me. When there's something—or someone, I guess—to tell, I'll tell the world, I promise. Right now, I'm happier being a man of mystery. Unlike yourself.'

Groaning, Jay ran a hand over his forehead. 'You haven't even heard the worst of it yet.'

'Worse than having Daisy Mulligan as a sister-in-law?' Harry looked thoughtful. 'Although, actually, that wouldn't be all that bad. She and I could hide out together at big family events and avoid people. She'd probably remember to bring the good alcohol with her, too.'

'You realise I'm not *actually* proposing to her, right?' Jay asked. 'Whatever the papers—and Kevin—think.'

'What does *she* think?' Harry raised his eyebrows at him and put the guitar on its stand to give Jay his full attention. 'I mean, all this talk about diamonds and a girl could get ideas...'

Jay barked a laugh. 'Not Daisy. All she wants is to get away from all of us and not have to deal with people for a while.'

'I know how she feels.' Harry stretched his arms over his head. 'I'm going to go see Mum, then spend two weeks at the cabin, I think. Out by the lake, just the fish for company...'

'Well, don't forget to come back for that awards ceremony in Rome, right?' Harry's cabin was the one thing he'd bought with the proceeds of their first platinum album. 'Kevin won't be happy if you miss that.'

'Ah, no one will notice if I'm there or not,' Harry teased. 'Not with you there with Daisy on your arm, sporting some giant rock on her left hand.'

'I was hoping that if you went I wouldn't have to. But I suppose at least we'll be in the right country,' Jay mused.

Harry frowned. 'You're going to Italy?'

'That's what I came here to tell you.' Jay explained about the curious cottage Daisy might have been left, and how they were supposed to spend the next few weeks there writing love songs.

'Sounds cosy,' Harry commented.

'Sounds more like she might murder me in my sleep if I get on her nerves. She really is on edge right now.' He shook his head. 'I know I'm meant to be her mentor and what have you, but I don't know *what* to do with her when she gets like this.'

'Then maybe this is exactly what you both need.' Harry tilted his head as he looked at his brother, and

Jay had the uncomfortable sensation of being studied, observed, like a scientific specimen. Like Harry was trying to make sense of him.

'What do you mean?'

'Well, like you say, Daisy's at the end of her temper and needs some time away before she's allowed out in public again, right? And you...well. Maybe you could do with some downtime too. All this gossip about your fake relationship with Daisy is one thing, but it doesn't change the fact that you're not actually over your *last* relationship yet, does it?'

Jay thought about lying, about telling Harry that he was completely over Milli, that he barely even thought about her these days. But Harry knew him too well for him to believe that.

Although even his brother didn't know the real reason the break-up was hanging over his head. It wasn't as their mum thought, that Milli was his one true love and he'd never fall for another woman. It might have been, if Jay hadn't realised the truth—as much as he had believed himself in love with Milli, the woman he'd thought he loved didn't really exist.

Because for Milli, their relationship was as much a publicity stunt as his fake relationship with Daisy.

If their love affair had never been real for Milli, how could he really have been in love with her in the first place? *That* was the question that was messing with his head. What made love real?

But he didn't want to get into that with Harry now.

'I guess some time out of the public eye wouldn't be the worst thing in the world,' he admitted instead. Maybe away from all the chaos of the tour and the cameras, he could get his head around what had happened with Milli, and how he was going to move on.

'You going somewhere, Jay?' Nico, their drummer, swung through the doorway and dropped into a spare chair, followed by their bassist, Benji.

'He's whisking Daisy away to Italy for a romantic break,' Harry said, wiggling his eyebrows.

Nico rolled his eyes. 'Yeah, well, try and write some decent new songs while you're there, yeah? I'm getting bored of hearing the two of you singing the same damn duet every night.'

'I'll see what we can do,' Jay promised dryly. 'You guys don't mind me skipping out during the break in the tour schedule?' They didn't always spend the time together, and Harry would be in Cheshire then at the cabin in Scotland anyway, but as their frontman, their leader even, Jay felt an obligation to check.

Nico shook his head. 'You keeping out of the lime-light for a few weeks gives the rest of us a chance to shine for once. That's fine by me.'

'Plus Daisy might help lighten you up a little bit,' Benji put in. 'No offence or anything, but you've been a miserable bugger so far this tour.'

Jay looked to Harry for confirmation; his brother winced and nodded. 'I wasn't going to put it quite that bluntly but…yeah.'

'Daisy's fun,' Benji said, with a shrug.

'Daisy's gorgeous,' Nico added. 'You'll just have to make sure you don't end up back here engaged for real.'

The memory of that one, impulsive kiss they'd shared onstage flared up in his head, his blood warming instantly. Jay forced himself to think of the diamond ring still sitting in the bottom of his suitcase instead. The one he'd bought for Milli, before she called everything off.

He'd been burnt that way before, no way he'd be stupid enough to fall for it again. Not when, this time, he knew right from the start that nothing about his connection with Daisy was real, however fantastic that brief kiss had felt.

'I don't think we need to worry about that,' he said dryly. 'Now, I need to go find Kevin before the show. And Daisy.'

Apparently, they had travel plans to make.

CHAPTER FOUR

'IS THIS EVEN a real airport?' Daisy asked as she wobbled off the tiny plane that had flown them from Rome to... wherever the hell they were now. The back of beyond, as far as she could tell.

So much for her plans to spend the tour break in a plush hotel with room service on tap. All she could see here was hills, scrub land, and a tiny control building next to the airstrip their minute plane had landed on.

'It's more of a private airfield, I think,' Jay replied, squinting in the sunshine. 'But Kevin said there should be a car waiting for us...'

How Kevin had got so involved in her escape from the public eye, Daisy still wasn't entirely sure. But ever since Jay had come and found her on the bus and declared that he thought they should go to Italy together, things seemed to have been spiralling out of her control.

She'd started off well, putting her foot down on the things that mattered. Yes, Jay could come to Italy with her but only on the proviso that they were going together to write music, nothing else. Jay had agreed easily to that condition, as had Kevin—the latter with a rather suspicious wink that made Daisy doubt he was *actually* going along with her wishes.

But she was escaping, and writing music wasn't exactly a hardship.

Of course, at that point, Kevin had taken over everything.

The solicitor, Mr Mayhew, had been delighted to be dealing with Kevin, someone who seemed to have considerably more understanding of property and law than Daisy. And at least Kevin's involvement had reassured her that it definitely wasn't a scam—although it had also involved some very confusing conversations about Great-Aunt Felicia.

The more she learned about her strange inheritance, though, the more Daisy became convinced that Viv, the lady they'd helped in Copenhagen two years ago, had to be behind it. Apart from anything else, there was literally no one else in the world—apart from Jessica and Aubrey—who would give her anything.

Which was kind of sad, when she thought about it.

But if Viv was responsible, then it linked in with Jessica and Aubrey's recent good fortunes too. Jessica was still radio silent, but Aubrey had been doing some digging, and had sent her a photo of Vivian Ascot, the billionaire owner of Ascot Industries—who coincidentally sponsored the music festival they'd all attended in Copenhagen. The photo was an old one, the woman's face shaded by a large sun hat, but if she squinted, Daisy could definitely see their Viv in the image.

But while she'd been preoccupied with the mystery of why Viv would give her a house, Kevin seemed to have organised everything else. Including the flight from the States, where they were touring, to Italy—and the transfer on the terrifyingly small plane to this airstrip in the middle of nowhere.

And the driver, holding a handwritten sign with their names on that, on closer inspection, appeared to be written on the back of a birthday card. He leaned against a dusty car, his eyes half closed in the sunshine.

Not quite the limos Jay was used to these days, she was sure, but still more than she expected when she travelled, even now.

The driver's English was limited but, by joint pointing at maps on their phones, Daisy managed to confirm where they were going, while Jay loaded their cases into the boot of the car. She slid into the back seat beside him, and held onto the door as the car jerked forward towards what could only charitably be called a road.

'So, have you seen photos of this place?' Jay asked as they bumped along.

Daisy nodded. 'One or two.' She pulled out her phone again to show him the pictures Mr Mayhew had sent her. They showed a single-storey, stone-built cottage with a bright blue door, set against a backdrop of rolling Italian countryside—green and lush in parts, yellow in others, with tall, thin trees jutting up into the sky all around.

'It looks beautiful,' Jay said, swiping through the images. 'Perfect place to get away from everyone for a few weeks.'

'Everyone except you.' Daisy pocketed the phone again. 'Mr Mayhew said that there's a village at the bottom of the hill, so hopefully we can get supplies and such there. There might even be a bar or two.'

'Sounds fun.' The words were right, but Daisy couldn't help but notice that Jay didn't sound exactly excited at the prospect.

'I'm sorry you got forced to come here with me.' Not that spending three weeks in the middle of nowhere with Jay was her first choice for the tour break, either. But it had to beat playing up to the press and pretending to be engaged to him in public.

Jay shook his head and gave her a half-smile. 'Honestly, you're doing me a favour. I mean, even Harry suggested it would be good for me.'

'Because we'd work on some new songs together?' Something she knew Jay had been avoiding ever since the tour started. She hadn't brought it up because, quite frankly, performing every night, zigzagging across the USA in the tour bus, and giving regular interviews at each stop had drained any creativity right out of her, and she imagined it was the same for Jay. But she knew as well as he did that the label had expectations.

'Partly. Mostly I think he hoped it might shake me out of the funk I've been in since—' He broke off suddenly, but Daisy didn't need him to finish the sentence, anyway.

Since Milli, that was what he was going to say. Since the woman he loved walked out on him and their future in the most public, humiliating way she could manage. Really, who dumped someone in a social-media video, anyway?

'Well, if nothing else, you won't have to deal with Pamela Pearson hounding you about whether you've bought me an engagement ring yet,' she said cheerfully. She'd seen the depressive moods Jay could sink into when too many reminders of Milli got the better of him—like the time her new video had been playing on the huge TV screen in the tour bus's living area when they got back after a gig. Or when one interviewer had only asked questions about the demise of their relationship for a full five minutes.

Yeah, the less said about Milli Masters, the better, in Daisy's opinion.

'Harry offered to call Mum and ask her to send Grandma's ring over for you,' Jay replied, obviously relieved at the change of subject. 'I mean, it's a tiny speck of a diamond hidden in a gold band, but if you want it…'

Daisy pulled a face. 'I'll pass, thanks. I'm kind of hoping they'll have all forgotten about it by the time we get back.'

'Does it bother you?' Jay asked, curiosity colouring his tone. 'All this fake relationship stuff, I mean?'

Daisy shrugged. 'A bit. I mean, you and I know it isn't real. But I don't like living a lie.'

'Yeah, I know what you mean.' Jay sounded a little uncomfortable with it all too, Daisy realised. Why? Surely this was just part of the fame game, right? Especially for him, being such a huge star. People had speculated that his relationship with Milli was just for the cameras too, but given his reaction to the ending of it, she guessed not.

'Does it bother *you*?' she asked. 'I mean, it's basically just Kevin spreading gossip, right?' Except Jay had been the one to start the engagement rumour in the first place. And the one to start everything by kissing her during that duet.

And now they were writing more. God, people really were going to start talking. Was that what Jay wanted?

'It doesn't bother me, exactly,' Jay said slowly. 'Not when I know that it's part of the game. More it's just weird, you know? My mum finds it baffling. Like, why would anyone pretend to be in love when they could just find someone to fall in love with for real?'

'Your mum makes a good point,' Daisy admitted. Not that she was looking for love. From what she'd seen, love mostly led to heartbreak. Music was a much safer option.

'But I guess…everything we do is a performance, right?' Jay went on. 'The songs we write—they might have some of us in them, but they're still not a word-for-word rendition of our thoughts.'

'And when we're up onstage… I'm not Daisy Mulligan from Liverpool, exactly. I'm Daisy Mulligan, rock star. And that's something different.' Sometimes, that person felt a world away from the real her. Daisy suspected that might be why she enjoyed playing her so much.

Up onstage, she wasn't the Daisy who everyone agreed would never amount to anything. The useless daughter who wasn't enough to stop her mum from leaving, or the student voted most likely to drop out. Up onstage, she could prove them all wrong—but it never really felt like her.

'I guess it's the same when we give interviews.' Jay sounded thoughtful. 'We present ourselves a certain way.'

'Like a job interview,' Daisy put in. 'Not that I really know much about those.'

'Yeah. So do you reckon pretending to be in love is just like pretending you speak fluent Spanish on your CV?'

Daisy laughed. 'My teachers were impressed I ever managed to learn to speak English properly, never mind a foreign language. But yeah, I guess it's the same principle. You just have to hope you never get caught out—like someone asking you to translate at an important meeting or something.'

'Or in our case, asking us to kiss in front of the cameras.'

Daisy shot him a look. 'That didn't exactly seem to be a problem for you last time.' She'd meant it as an accusation, but it came out a little breathier than she'd intended.

And Jay didn't look exactly apologetic, either. One eyebrow raised suggestively over his green eyes, while amusement played around his lips. And for a moment—just a second, really—she found herself wondering what it would be like to kiss them. To kiss Jay Barwell, world's sexiest man. Not a fake kiss for the crowds and the cameras. A *real* kiss.

Then the car bashed into another bump in the criminally uneven road, just when she'd finally let go of the seat cushion, and lurched sideways, sending her tumbling towards Jay's lap.

Strong arms caught her—stronger than he could have got from just playing guitar, but she supposed that was why Jay had requested that the back of the tour bus be set up as a workout zone, rather than the luxurious master bedroom he could have commanded.

A strange, long-forgotten flutter started deep in her

belly. Suddenly, every single time she'd touched Jay was racing through her mind like a film reel. They'd shaken hands when they met, she remembered. Hugged outside that club in London when Kevin offered to sign her. He'd slung an arm around her shoulder like one of the guys often enough as they took a bow onstage. Then there was that kiss…that she really wasn't thinking about. And just that afternoon he'd put his hand to the small of her back as he guided her up the rickety steps to the tiny plane from Rome, his palm radiating heat. But none of it had felt like this. Not…close. Close enough that she could breathe in his aftershave, feel the heat of his body against hers.

She wanted to reach out and squeeze those muscles—but she didn't. If Kevin was determined to play up some fake affair between them in the press the last thing she wanted to do was complicate that with actual lust or—God forbid—feelings. Any fake relationship was definitely just a marketing strategy.

So as the car righted itself, Daisy pulled away and muttered, 'Sorry,' before tucking herself back into the far corner of the car, glancing out of the window for a distraction. They bumped over a few more potholes in the road—Daisy held tightly to the seat this time to avoid a repeat performance—while they climbed the hill. As they crested it, a small, tumbledown villa came into view. One with the same stone walls and tiled roof as the photos she'd been sent, although this one was in far worse condition. And as the path curved around, she realised it sat right at the top of a cliff, practically on the edge, looking out over the ocean. It must be a typical construction style for houses in the area, she reasoned.

Until she realised that the road they were on stopped at the edge of the cliff. At the faded and peeling blue front door of the falling-down villa. And her heart sank all the way down into the waves below.

Jay was still considering the strange jolt of attraction that had sparked through him as Daisy crashed into his arms, when the car started to slow. Mostly because it was so unexpected. He'd barely felt a connection to anyone, in any way, since Milli—and certainly not that sharp flare of something akin to lust that had taken over his body as she'd pressed against him. Even the night he'd kissed her onstage, he'd been feeling more relief that the crowd were enjoying the show again than lust for the woman attached to the lips he was kissing.

Daisy's gorgeous, he heard Nico's voice repeating in his head. And yes, of course, she was. He wasn't blind, and he sang love songs to her every night onstage. Of course he'd noticed that she was beautiful. Perhaps not in the conventional way that Milli was, with her honey-blonde hair and perfect curves, but in a different, vibrant way that was all Daisy.

He just hadn't thought that beauty was anything he needed to worry about.

Except now he realised he was alone with it for the next three weeks. And it appeared that certain parts of his anatomy were suddenly very aware of what that might possibly mean if, and it was a long shot, Daisy had felt that same spark.

A *very* long shot, he told himself, given that she was currently staring out of the window at the villa outside and paying him no attention at all.

Wait. Villa. Did that mean they were there? He craned his neck to see past her. No, this couldn't be it. The villa in the photos Daisy had shown him had been bright, well-kept and welcoming. This place looked as though the walls might just cave in if he glanced at them wrong.

Except the car had stopped. And the driver was getting out…

'This is it?' he asked, trying not to sound incredulous, and knowing that he'd failed.

'Apparently so.' Jay couldn't quite read the look on Daisy's face as she turned to him. It wasn't quite disappointed. More…resigned? As if she should have known this would happen. 'Sorry.' The apology was short and quiet, as if she wasn't used to giving them.

Actually, from what he knew of Daisy, she wasn't.

The driver had already unloaded their bags from the back of the car, and was hanging around smiling broadly. Jay resisted the urge to ask if he was sure this was the place, and handed over a tip instead, unsurprised when the man jumped back behind the steering wheel and scarpered.

'I guess we'd better see what we're dealing with, then,' Daisy said, glaring at the peeling paint on the door as if it had done her personal harm.

Jay followed gingerly behind her.

When he'd heard 'villa in Italy' he'd imagined spending this break in the schedule relaxing by the pool, sipping cocktails, strumming his guitar under a cypress tree, partaking of the local specialities at a trattoria in the village…and maybe writing a song or two with Daisy.

Instead, it looked as if he'd be searching for a hardware shop to buy a hard hat, and trying to avoid being brained by falling masonry.

'We could just call Kevin and head back to the States,' he suggested as he lingered in the doorway. At least the door frame seemed sturdy. It might be the safest place in the building.

'And spend three weeks smiling for the camera and pretending to be wildly in love? No, thanks.' Daisy shook her head a little too violently, sending a cloud of dust flying up from a nearby table. 'Kevin would have us married by Elvis in Vegas before the tour started up again.'

'True.' Jay took in the very dusty dust sheets covering the furniture and tried to decide which was the worst fate—Elvis, or death by dust inhalation. Thank God Harry hadn't come. It would have played merry hell with his asthma.

Squinting up at the ceiling, he decided it wasn't going to fall down *imminently*, so stepped inside.

The villa's front door opened onto one main room, filled with sheet-covered chairs, tables and—from the shape under the fabric—bookcases. No TV as far as he could see. One door led through to another room at the back that, from the glimpse he could get through the open doorway, was the kitchen. Another opening led to a hallway with several doors off it.

'Shall we explore?' he asked, raising an eyebrow at Daisy. She looked so grumpy about the whole thing, Jay decided he'd have to tease her out of it. Make it all a game, an adventure—the way he used to have to do for Harry when they were kids, and his little brother got into a sulk over something.

'If you're sure you want to risk it,' Daisy replied, looking doubtfully towards a broken window in the open-plan living area.

'Well, then, if madam will follow me?' He held out his arm, elbow crooked. Daisy rolled her eyes, but took it. 'Through the authentically rustic front door we find the spacious living area. With—' he whipped off a few dust sheets and tried not to succumb to the threatened coughing fit '—ample seating for the occupants and their friends. There are myriad entertainment options built in,' he added as another dust sheet fell to reveal shelves of tatty paperbacks—all in Italian—two jigsaw puzzles and a Scrabble set in a beat up box. 'And incredible views through the very clear windows.' Clear in that half the glass was missing. The view part was true, though. From where the villa sat, they could look out of windows one side that showed them the rolling ocean, down below the cliff, and out over the hills and cypress trees on the other.

Actually, if the place weren't in such disrepair, it would be a fantastic little bolt-hole.

Daisy was smiling now, even if she looked as if she was trying not to, so Jay swept her towards the kitchen to continue his tour.

'In here we find a state-of-the-art kitchen, ideal for making, uh…' He looked around him for inspiration but, quite honestly, he wasn't even sure he'd know how to turn the stove on. At home he was an okay cook—he could keep himself fed, at least. But the range cooker here was a mystery to him. Then he spotted the answer.

'Cocktails!' he finished, whipping out a dusty bottle of limoncello from the back of the open shelving.

'Well, thank God for that.' Daisy grabbed the bottle from him and set about opening it. 'Finally something is going right.' She took a swig, pulled a face, and passed it to him.

He copied the motion. 'Sickly sweet.' He pressed his lips together. 'And sticky.'

'Sounds like Milli Masters' last tour,' Daisy joked, then shot him an uncertain look, as if she wasn't sure if he was ready to joke about her yet.

He hadn't been, Jay knew. But here, now, with Italian liquor, a wreck of a holiday villa, and Daisy, he thought he might be. Just.

He grinned, to show her it was okay, and actually watched the tension leave her body. She was so slight, every movement showed in her stance—the stress and frustration in her jaw, the disappointment in her shoulders, the determination in her legs, planted firmly on the floor. She was fascinating to read, Jay realised. A whole story wrapped up in a woman.

He wondered if he'd get to read it, this next few weeks.

Stealing the bottle back, Daisy took another swig of limoncello. 'Come on,' she said. 'Bedrooms next.'

And for a flash of a second as she said the word 'bedrooms', Jay remembered her body against his in the car, and couldn't help but think what a shame it was they needed two.

Yep. Definitely getting over the whole Milli fiasco at last, it seemed. Harry would be so proud.

Jay grabbed the limoncello, took one last gulp, swore, and followed her towards the other side of the villa.

* * *

Daisy woke up the next morning to a drip from the ceiling that landed right on her forehead, and the feeling that she should have known better. Yes, Jessica might get offered her dream job in New York, and Aubrey might get a life-changing amount of money to complete the bucket-list trip she'd had to cancel when she got sick—but that didn't mean that she, Daisy Mulligan, screw-up extraordinaire, would actually get something good too.

Things like just being given a holiday villa in Italy didn't happen to people like her. In fact, she'd obviously used up her entire family's share of good luck by getting signed to the label in the first place. Asking for anything more was just being greedy.

And from that point of view, it was almost a relief that the cottage was a disaster zone. Because if it hadn't been, she'd have spent the next three weeks waiting for the other shoe to drop. As it was, she could just accept that this was another episode in the entertaining but disastrous life of Daisy Mulligan, and spend three weeks swigging limoncello from the bottle and pretending it wasn't happening.

Or she *could*. If she hadn't brought Jay along for the ride.

Now, she had to make this work. Otherwise, Jay would drag her back Stateside to parade her around as his girlfriend, and she knew how that would end. She'd screw it up. She'd lose her temper, say the wrong thing to the wrong person, get filmed doing something stupid. When it was just her, no one much cared what idiocy she got up to, or how much trouble her sharp mouth got her into. But if she were Jay Barwell's fiancée…a whole different level of scrutiny and interest and expectation followed.

Which meant she had to find a way to make this cottage habitable for the next three weeks.

They'd found the bedrooms easily enough the night before—they just followed the scent of mildew. There were four of them, tucked away at the back of the cottage. Two with double beds, one with a twin, and one with a very saggy set of bunk beds. Jay had chivalrously insisted on her taking the one with the biggest bed—and actual windows. He'd taken the other double, using one of the dust sheets to cover over a missing pane.

Her head spinning from the limoncello and the journey, Daisy had collapsed into bed, grateful that at least the bed linens had been packed away in plastic covers that didn't seem to have been eaten by mice or anything. But she hadn't slept, not for hours, her brain spinning as she tried to understand why Viv—if it was Viv—would have left her this wreck of a place.

This morning, however, she knew there was somewhere more important to focus her attention. She had the villa, so now she had to make it liveable. Which meant she needed help, because the last time she'd held a hammer she'd almost lost a finger. And that would be very bad for her future as a guitarist.

She couldn't imagine that Jay was any handier with power tools, so that meant finding someone who was. She just hoped that the people in the village at the bottom of the hill spoke English, because her Italian was non-existent.

The plumbing had proved as erratic as the rest of

the place the night before, so Daisy skipped a shower in favour of a quick wash, dressed in jeans and a flowy tunic top that she thought would suit the weather, and headed out. Creeping past Jay's room, she heard his familiar snores, and figured she had some time to figure this all out before he inevitably woke up and demanded to be returned to civilisation.

At the worst, Daisy reasoned as she headed down the steep hill towards the village, nestled in the valley, there might be a hotel or something they could check into for a couple of weeks. Or Jay could, anyway. All the way out here it was unlikely that Kevin was going to stop by and check they really were fake loved up in Italy, wasn't it?

But the closer she got to the village, the more her hotel dreams started to fade. It was definitely more of a hamlet than a village, she decided—just a cluster of houses scattered in between the trees and scrub. Did it even have any shops? There was no food at the villa, just that rogue bottle of lemon liquor. If there wasn't a shop nearby they were really going to have to find some way to hire a car or something. Or decamp to the nearest city and admit defeat.

No. Daisy couldn't quite explain the defiance that rose up in her at the idea, but she knew it was about more than not wanting to have to pretend to be Jay's girlfriend in public for the next three weeks.

Maybe it was just her natural stubbornness rising to the fore. She'd been given a house and she was damn well going to live in it. Or perhaps it was the feeling that this was some kind of test—one she was expected to fail. And while she'd never been a grade A student, if someone—even herself—told Daisy she couldn't do something, she would bloody well do it. She'd seen the disbelief in the taxi driver's eyes when they actually got out of the car and went into the villa. And she knew that Jay was just waiting for her to come to her senses and retreat to a hotel or something.

Well, he'd be waiting a long time for *that*. Her grandmother always said she didn't have any sense, anyway.

But she did have an appetite. Her stomach gave a loud growl as she reached the edge of the hamlet, and she hoped against hope there'd be a café or something.

It was still quite early, but the place was starting to come to life. People chatted on the street, kids raced past. And actually, now she was down there in the midst of it, it seemed bigger than it had from the top of the hill. More vibrant.

Spotting a few café tables set out on the pavement, Daisy made a beeline for them, grateful for Jay remembering that they needed to change dollars for euros at the airport. She had a feeling that this place wouldn't take cards.

The café, if she could call it that, seemed to be someone's front room. It was set into a traditionally built house in a row of identical ones, the only difference being that this house had the front windows thrown open and a temporary counter balanced on the sill. Presumably it was anchored somehow, although Daisy couldn't see how, as it was laden with pastries and cakes. Behind the counter stood a beautiful, curvy brunette woman in a red dress, laughing as she prepared espressos and handed over plates loaded with bread and jam, or filled pastries or biscuits.

There were a couple of empty tables in amongst the occupied ones, but most people seemed happiest standing up at the counter chatting, espressos in hand. Looking at the beautiful, laughing woman, Daisy supposed she didn't blame them. She seemed warm and welcoming in a way that, so far, Italy really hadn't been. All the things that no one would ever call Daisy. Also, she was hot as hell—even Daisy could appreciate that.

She just hoped she spoke English.

CHAPTER FIVE

JAY AWOKE ALONE, which was not unusual, and to silence, which was. After months on tour he was used to the everyday sounds of the tour bus, or the rare hotel they got to spend the night in. To Harry banging on his bunk to wake him up, or room service arriving with breakfast. Or even his own fast breathing after another alcohol-induced nightmare. Never silence, though.

Then he opened his eyes fully, took in the disaster of a bedroom he was sleeping in, and remembered everything. Especially the limoncello, as his head began to pound.

Daisy was nowhere to be found, so he washed up as best as he could with the creaking plumbing, pulled on some clean clothes, and headed out in search of her—and breakfast.

Outside, the day was already warm and sultry, the sort of heat that made his muscles lazy and his brain switch off. He ambled down the hill towards the village, his hands in his pockets, the start of something that might be a melody humming in his head, just out of reach. He knew better than to try and catch it, though. Any time he tried to force the music, or lyrics, it always fell apart on paper. If he just waited, let his subconscious develop it without any interference from him, eventually it would be ready for him to take and make into something real.

Something he could sing, and play. Maybe even with Daisy.

The village itself seemed bustling with activity, and Jay followed his nose towards a café serving espresso—clearly what he needed to kick-start his day. Conveniently, it also led him to Daisy, who appeared to be having a very convoluted conversation in sign language and one-syllable words with the confused-looking woman behind the counter.

Jay had assumed that the ability to order coffee in any language was a prerequisite for a touring musician, but apparently not.

'Need some help? What do you want?' he asked, sliding in beside Daisy at the counter and flashing the Italian woman serving a smile. 'Cappuccino? Espresso?'

Daisy just glared at him, so he decided to just make the call. He was pretty sure he'd seen her drinking black coffee on tour, so he went with that.

'*Un Americano e un cappuccino, per favore,*' he said, and the café owner smiled and nodded with obvious relief, and headed off to make their coffees.

Jay turned to Daisy, who raised her coffee cup and drank from it ostentatiously.

'You…already had coffee. So what was the problem?'

'I was *trying* to ask her if she knew any tradespeople who might be able to help me fix up the villa.' Her eyebrows lowered over her coffee cup as she glared at him again. 'Until you bumbled in here trying to save me or whatever.'

'Help,' Jay countered. 'I was trying to help. Which I see you do not actually need in respect of coffee. But I'll see what I can do with the other stuff, too.'

'You speak Italian?' Daisy asked disbelievingly. 'Like, not just ordering-coffee Italian?'

'Your faith in me is astounding,' he muttered as he tried to call up his very rusty language skills. 'I actually lived in Italy for a few months on my gap year, working in a pizzeria. Had to pick up at least *some* of the language.' But that had been a good few years ago now, and even then it had been more to do with getting paid on time and spending his money on beers, not home repairs.

Daisy was staring at him as if he'd come down from another planet, although he had no idea why.

The barista returned with their coffees, and Jay took his cappuccino gratefully. Then, in halting Italian, he asked her about local builders or tradespeople, hoping he hadn't mangled the words too badly.

She looked puzzled for a moment, then her face cleared. She pointed up to the hill where Daisy's villa sat, and spoke in a torrent of fast-flowing Italian. Jay clung onto any words he recognised, nodding along as he tried to make sense of it all. He'd told Daisy he could speak Italian, and he was damned if he was going to be proven wrong now.

Then the woman beckoned to a couple of men sipping espressos at a table nearby, and they stood and moved closer, joining in the rapid-fire conversation. Beside him, Daisy's eyes were wider than he'd ever seen them, and he could tell she liked not knowing what was going on as little as she'd enjoyed him playing male saviour for her over the coffee.

Finally, one of the burly guys that had joined them turned to Jay. 'You are English?' he asked, thankfully *in* English. 'You own the villa on the hill?'

'She does,' Jay answered, pointing to Daisy. 'Do you think you could help us fix it up?'

The men looked doubtfully at each other, then shrugged. 'Maybe. We will see.'

Then they put down their empty coffee cups and walked away.

Jay scraped together enough of his Italian to ask the barista, 'Where are they going?'

She shrugged, too, as she cleared the empty cups. 'To work,' she replied, in Italian. 'They will come to the villa when they are done.'

'Right. Okay, then.' He relayed the information to Daisy, who looked as doubtful about this method of hiring contractors as he was. Still, it didn't look as if they had a lot of choice but to wait.

'In that case, I guess we might as well look at finding some food?' she suggested as they finished their coffees and waved goodbye to the barista. 'Also, you know, thanks for sorting that.'

Jay barked a laugh. 'I'm not sure I'd call it exactly sorted. Besides, I'm staying in that villa too, remember? I want to get it fixed up as badly as you do.'

Daisy gave him a sideways look as they strolled along the streets of the village. 'I kind of expected you to demand we move to a hotel.'

He almost missed a step as he realised that had never

crossed his mind since he'd woken up that morning. Why not? It was the obvious solution to the problem of the crumbling villa.

Except…he knew hotels. He'd spent half his life in them, it felt like. And this…hanging out with Daisy, ordering coffees and sipping them in the square, knowing that no one knew or cared who they were, or if they were really together or just faking…he liked that.

He wasn't ready to give that up just yet.

'This is more of an adventure,' he said eventually. 'Come on. Let's find a shop and stock up. I'm starving, and I don't want to have to walk up and down that hill every time I fancy a coffee.'

After a little more wandering between the houses, they found a row of old-fashioned shops selling variously fruit and veg, deli meats and sausages, and freshly baked bread that smelled divine. Along with a more familiar convenience store to provide butter, milk and eggs—plus a couple of bottles of wine—they were able to stock up on pretty much all the essentials of life, and stuff them into the backpack Daisy had brought along, plus a couple of extra shopping bags.

The walk back *up* the hill was rather less relaxing than the walk down it had been, and conversation was little between them as they fought the incline. How was it he could jump around onstage singing until his lungs screamed, six nights a week for months on end, without feeling this out of shape?

At the top of the hill, they paused to catch their breath for a minute, before continuing towards the villa.

'We should make a list,' Daisy said suddenly as they approached the front door. 'Of everything that needs doing to the villa, in case those builders really do come up here.'

'Good idea.' Jay pushed open the peeling front door and stared at the sight before him. A goat—brown and white and with tiny little horns—stood in the middle of the living area, staring back at him. He swung the door open a little wider so Daisy could see. 'We can start with whichever broken door or window let the damn goat in.'

The list—written after they'd chased the goat outside by first roaring at it, then laughing hysterically, which it seemed to find much scarier—was seven pages long. Seven pages of things that were wrong with this inheritance of hers.

Why had Viv given the others perfect, no-strings gifts—and lumbered her with a money pit? Daisy couldn't figure it out. But at the same time, it seemed perfectly in keeping with what she expected from her life.

Things didn't come for free. Fairy godmothers didn't just shower people with gifts—at least, not people like Daisy. She had to fight and scratch for everything she wanted in this life, and even then she had to cling onto it with a death grip, or else it would just melt away.

That was how life worked. She'd seen it clearly enough before she was even sixteen, and had it repeated plenty of times since. Her teachers might disagree, but even Daisy eventually learned her lessons when they were *that* obvious.

Besides, her mother had been her biggest teacher— maybe not in reading or writing, but in how the world worked. She'd taught her that at the age of six, when she'd crept into her room in tears and told Daisy that she couldn't do it any more. She couldn't give up her own life, her own dreams, for a man who didn't appreciate her, who kept her down and forced her into a life she hated. One where all that mattered was whether she had dinner on the table and kept quiet during the football. She loved Daisy, she promised as she laid her old mandolin beside her on the bed, hitching her own guitar onto her back. But she had to chase her own dreams too.

Daisy had learned an important lesson when she'd woken up to find her mother gone: she wasn't enough to make anyone stay. And dreams mattered more than love.

She'd learned it again at fifteen when her stepmother had kicked her out for the first time, after another argument over what mattered more—babysitting her little brothers so her dad and stepmum could go to the pub and spend the grocery money again, or practising with her band so they could play some paid gigs.

She'd come back and done as she was told that time. But she'd started planning, too.

Daisy knew what she needed to know to survive. First, that she had to get out and chase her own future, because she could be damn sure that no one else would do it for her. Secondly, that she didn't want to rely on anybody else to get it. She'd seen too many older girls from the neighbourhood settle for guys who weren't right for them, just because they had a flat, or a job. She'd watched her dad and stepmum relying on handouts from the government just to live, after Dad lost another job. She'd seen her best friend and band mate give up what she wanted—what they both wanted—because she fell in love, and her new boyfriend didn't like her playing in a band, let alone chasing big-time success.

Daisy wouldn't be like them. Not any more. She had made it, at last, and that meant she didn't need to rely on anyone else. She wasn't going to give up *anything*. Love, family…all that stuff came with a cost. And, as she'd learned since she left home and started to make it on her own, so did everything else. It was better to know what the cost was upfront.

Which was why she was almost glad that the villa was a wreck. At least that made *sense*. Viv had obviously needed to get rid of it for tax reasons, or couldn't be bothered doing it up herself, so had passed it off under the appearance of a gift. That, she could understand. It was like those smarmy guys from the record company who talked up all the ways they wanted to help her build her career—mentorships, support, opportunities. Daisy knew what they really meant.

We want to make money from you. Here's what we'll give you so you don't notice we're taking advantage.

She always knew when people were taking advantage, because people were always taking advantage. She just made sure that what she got in return was worth enough to her.

In this case, the villa was an escape, and that was worth a lot. When it came to her career, music had always given her the same thing—the chance to escape home, to escape poverty, to escape fading away to nothing. The rest of it was beside the point.

Except, somehow, it had also given her Jay, sitting

beside her at the rustic wooden kitchen table, chewing the end of his pencil as he added to the list.

'Is "fix the heating" on there?' Daisy asked, shivering. 'Or is that more of a "fix the broken windows" issue?' The day had almost gone, and all they'd really done was potter around the village, buy food, scare a goat and cook a late lunch/early dinner that they'd eaten with one of the bottles of wine they'd bought. It had been nice—a break from the list, at least. But now the sun was sinking outside, although given the time of year she imagined it would take a few more hours to actually dip under the horizon.

Jay looked up, his eyes shining in the fading sunlight. 'Cold? That, at least, I can do something about.'

Dropping his pencil onto the table, he crossed the room to the fireplace, and poked around for a minute or two. Daisy looked on, apprehensively.

'Are you sure we should mess around with that? There might be squirrels nesting in the chimney or something. Maybe another goat.'

Jay turned to her with an amused look. 'You're really not all that comfortable with wildlife, are you?'

'Are you?'

He shrugged. 'I grew up next door to a farm.'

That must have been nice, Daisy supposed, although she couldn't actually imagine it. 'I grew up in the city. I know rats and pigeons and that's about it. Maybe an urban fox or something.'

'And you're right, the chimney probably needs cleaning.' He gave her an assessing look. 'But if you were up for it, we could build a campfire outside? I saw a fire pit out the back earlier.'

'Can't be any colder out there than in here,' Daisy decided. 'Come on.'

Outside, Daisy settled onto a wooden seat, while Jay set about fetching firewood from the store. She watched, enthralled, as he laid the fire, then lit it, coaxing the flames to life. She tried to remember if she'd ever sat by a real fire, out in the countryside—rather than an accidental fire with sirens and engines, like the one at her school that time. She didn't think so.

She knew, in many ways, she was a lot younger than Jay. In years, maybe only six or so. But there were so many experiences out in the world that he'd had and she'd never even dreamt of. Like university—or a gap year in Italy.

Of course, she'd had a lot of experiences she guessed he hadn't either. Like sleeping on London's streets, or running away from home. She wasn't naive, never that. But despite growing up probably only fifty miles apart, their lives had been so totally different—until that festival in Copenhagen threw them together.

She wondered what the label had given him to keep him in the job of her mentor. She couldn't imagine he was doing it for fun. It was clear now what Kevin and the label got out of it—her under control, some great publicity via their new fake relationship, and maybe even some songs, if they ever got around to writing any.

She just couldn't figure out what Jay got.

Once the fire was roaring away, Jay stood up and headed back for the house.

'Where are you going?' Daisy asked, panicked. She *definitely* didn't want to be left alone in charge of wild flames.

He shot her an amused look. 'I'll be right back. Try not to set the whole hilltop ablaze while I'm gone.'

Yeah, that made her feel loads better.

True to his word, he was back moments later, his guitar slung on his back in its case, her mandolin under his arm, and gripping one of his jumpers. He tossed the jumper into her lap. 'Put that on until you warm up.'

She should argue, Daisy was sure. But she *was* cold, and her packing had been more for sultry summer Italy, plus her ubiquitous leather jacket, neither of which were serving her particularly well right now.

She tugged the jumper over her head, breathing in the familiar scent of Jay. Wait. When had that become familiar? On the tour, or when she'd crashed into him in the car…? She wasn't sure. She just knew that for the rest of her life, she'd be able to pick his clothing out of a pile by scent alone.

She was clearly a woman of many talents, most of them less than profitable. It was just as well she could sing, play, and pull a mean pint, or she'd be worthless to the world.

'Are we writing?' she asked, taking the mandolin from him. The instrument felt so familiar in her hands, her fingers smoothing over the wood and finding the strings instinctively, plucking and tuning it without thought.

Jay shook his head. 'Let's save that for the morning. I just thought it might be fun to play together.'

Daisy looked down at her hands, plucking the strings lightly as she refined the tuning. It had been so long since making music had just been about having *fun*, if it ever had been. For her, music had been her way out—

something she had that others didn't, something that she could use to escape her home, her family, and find something *more*, as her mum had tried to do.

Tried, and failed. But she didn't like to dwell on that part.

Nobody really knew what had happened to her mother. But Daisy knew what *hadn't* happened. She hadn't found the success she craved, or else everyone would know her name, her music.

Like they were starting to know Daisy's.

Without her really thinking about it, her fingers began picking out a melody—an old song, a familiar one. One that seemed to have followed her around her whole life. Had her mother sung it, before she left? Maybe. Daisy couldn't remember.

But Jay knew it, too. Because he started playing along—all the right chords, moving with her tune, adding depth and dance to the music.

There were words, too. About luck and stars and moonlight and possibility. As the sun sank behind the hill, Daisy's hands flew over the strings instinctively as she opened her mouth and began to sing, Jay's lower voice joining her on the harmonies.

And for the first time in months, she felt as if she might be exactly where she was supposed to be. Even if she wasn't chasing anything, for once.

Someone was hammering something.

Jay had kind of assumed the banging was just inside his head, after last night's wine and the smoke from the fire—plus the last three hours of trying to drag a tune he couldn't quite hear out of his head. Why was it so easy to make music when it didn't matter, when they could sing and play anything they dreamt of or remembered—but so damn hard to do it when it was important? When they needed to write the songs they'd promised Kevin they'd work on during the break?

'What the hell is that noise?' Daisy scrunched her nose up and dropped her pen on the floor.

Right. The hammering.

'I'll go and find out.' Jay put down the guitar he'd barely played all morning anyway and headed outside.

The source of the banging quickly became apparent: the builders they'd met the day before in the village square had taken out one of the broken window frames.

'We finished our job,' the one with the better English said. 'So now we are here. We fix this.' He gestured to the window. Or possibly the whole house. And the goat that was still loitering on the edge of the cliff.

'Great. Thanks. Um…*grazie.*' See? He hadn't forgotten *all* his Italian.

The builder nodded. 'This place has been empty too long. It is good to see it being cared for again. We're glad to help.'

'We're very, very glad you're helping too.'

Leaving them to their work and heading back inside, he filled Daisy in on the latest developments.

'So they're…fixing my house? I mean, I haven't paid them a deposit or anything. They haven't even given me a quote. They're just…fixing it?' There was a small line between her eyebrows that made her look like a confused child.

'Apparently so. I mean, I expect they'll want paying at some point, but…' He shrugged. They both knew that money wasn't exactly an issue for him—and she couldn't exactly be broke either. He knew what she was getting paid for this tour, and that was before he factored in the income from a number-one record. She could afford it, and if she couldn't, he would.

But Daisy didn't seem quite so relaxed.

'I need to give them money.' She jumped up from where she was sitting, cross-legged on the floor, and headed for the door. Jay watched her go, all fire and fury, and wondered which of her many triggers he had hit this time.

He wasn't under any illusions that Daisy had enjoyed the same happy childhood and opportunities that he had in his life. He didn't know her story—had never felt close enough to her to ask before—but that much was obvious from the barriers she threw up whenever anyone *did* ask about her past. Or her present for that matter. Anything personal, and Daisy wrapped that leather jacket of hers around her like armour.

Her usual weapons of deflection were sarcasm, her incredibly sharp tongue, and a blank, incredulous look that left the object of her attention feeling like the stupidest person on the planet.

He'd been the subject of that look too often already for him to push for more answers.

Except…

He'd sat with her last night and sung to the stars and felt more himself than he had since long before Milli. He'd come here with her to this place. And if they had three weeks together, just them, he couldn't see that distance lasting. She'd managed to maintain it on the tour, even living on a bus together. But this was different, somehow. There was no Harry to run interference, no busy schedule to keep them too rushed to think, no fans to sign autographs for every night, no interviews to give, and no Kevin with that damn tablet scheduling their every second.

It was just the two of them.

And two Italian builders.

And a goat.

Belatedly, Jay followed Daisy outside and found her trying to hand euros to the bemused builders.

'We fix this. *Then* you pay us,' one of them was saying.

'Are you sure?' Daisy sounded so confused, so uncertain, that Jay had to step in.

'Just say *grazie*, and we can get back to work,' he said, taking her arm and tugging her back towards the front door.

'*Grazie!*' Daisy called back over her shoulder.

'Paying people after the job is done isn't exactly unusual, you know,' he pointed out as they headed back inside. 'What's the issue?'

Daisy gave an uncomfortable shrug. 'I don't know. Just…they don't know us at all. They don't have to be here—it's Sunday, for crying out loud. They could be home, with their families.'

'Maybe they need the work,' Jay suggested. 'Or maybe they saw how desperately we needed the help. One of them said to me that this place had been empty a long time. I think they're happy that someone *wanted* to fix it.'

Daisy looked thoughtful. 'When you mentioned it yesterday, and the woman at the café pointed to the hill…they all seemed kind of excited then, too.'

'I guess this place has been abandoned and crumbling a while, but they still consider it part of their village.'

'Or they know who owns it,' Daisy said suddenly. '*That* would make sense.'

'*You* own it,' Jay pointed out.

'Well, yeah, *now* I do. But they don't know that. I bet they know who owned it before me, though.'

'And do *you* know?' It had been a mystery, hadn't it? Some weird legacy from a relative she hadn't even known she possessed. At least, that was what Jay had believed. Watching Daisy squirm now though, he thought otherwise. 'I take it that it wasn't Great-Aunt Felicia?'

She rolled her eyes. 'There is no Great-Aunt Felicia. You know that.'

'So who gave you the cottage?'

'I think… I think it might have been Viv Ascot.'

Jay's eyebrows jumped so high he felt them hit his hairline. Of all the answers he'd expected—if he'd expected any at all—that was probably bottom of the list.

'Multimillionaire heiress and businesswoman Viv Ascot?' he asked, just to be sure.

Daisy nodded. 'I met her at the same festival I met you. My friends Jessica and Aubrey and I—well, they weren't my friends then, because we'd only just met, but they are now—we helped find her dog when she lost it and took her to hospital because she'd hurt her ankle chasing him. We exchanged social-media details, but didn't really hear much from her again. But now Aubrey and Jessica have both received dream gifts this summer too, and I…'

'Got the crumbling villa in Italy,' Jay finished for

her, still trying to process the story she was telling him. 'But why do you think it's Viv Ascot?'

'Because she is literally the only thing the three of us have in common, apart from being female. Different nationalities, different careers, *very* different personalities. The only thing that links us is that we all helped Viv.'

'Huh.' He supposed that made a sort of sense. 'What did the others get?'

'Jessica got the chance at a dream job in New York, which is brilliant, because she'd really shrunk her world to just her hometown since we met in Copenhagen.' That little frown was back, just a small line between her eyebrows. God help him, but it was adorable. 'Although we haven't actually heard from her since she got there. Hopefully that means she's having too much fun, not…' She shook her head. 'Anyway. Aubrey messaged me just before we left for Italy. She's been gifted the money to complete her dream trip of a lifetime, touring Europe. She had started when we met, but then she got sick and had to go home and it was kind of terrifying for a while. But now she's better she can have all the adventures she always dreamed of.'

'Sounds to me like they both got exactly what they needed.'

'Yep. That's what I figured.' Jay was pretty sure he knew exactly what was causing the disappointment in her voice.

'And you can't figure out why Viv Ascot would think you needed this place?' he asked.

'Can you?' She looked up at him, eyebrows raised. He wasn't entirely sure if it was a rhetorical question, but he didn't get the chance to answer it anyway.

Without warning, a huge crash sounded from the side of the house, followed by some fast-flowing Italian that Jay was pretty sure consisted entirely of words he wouldn't repeat to his mother. There was a panicked bleat, and then the goat jumped in through the open window, almost landing on Daisy's guitar before she yanked it out of the way.

'Maybe she thought you needed a quiet, secluded place to write some duets with a friend?' he suggested weakly.

Daisy just raised her eyebrows a little higher.

He sighed. 'Yeah. Come on, this isn't working. I've got a better idea.'

CHAPTER SIX

'WHERE ARE WE GOING?' Daisy's guitar bumped against her back in its soft case as she followed Jay along the cliff top.

While she was glad to be away from marauding goats and the builders possibly destroying her house, she couldn't quite understand how this hike through the Italian countryside was going to help them with the writing-songs issue.

'We're not going anywhere,' Jay said, without looking back.

Daisy looked down at her feet, still moving across the yellowing grass. 'I'm pretty sure we are.'

Glancing over his shoulder, Jay rolled his eyes at her. 'I mean, we're not going anywhere in particular. I always find my best song ideas come to me when I'm walking. Don't you?'

'No.' Her best ideas came in that place between sleeping and waking, when her creativity was awake but the rest of her brain—the part that told her she couldn't do this, that no one would want to hear it—hadn't stirred yet.

'Huh.' Jay stopped walking and turned towards her.

'I guess…we never talked about how we were going to do this—write together, I mean.'

The duet they'd performed every night of the tour so far was one Jay had written before they'd even met—the song that she'd joined them onstage for in Copenhagen. It hadn't been intended as a duet, as such, but it had been an easy enough job to add in some harmonies, switch around who sang which lines and so on. Kevin had suggested they refine it for the tour, and they'd done it in an afternoon.

Coming up with a whole song—or two or three or four—from scratch, together, was an entirely different proposition.

'I've never written a song with another person before,' she admitted. Mostly she liked to have total control over her music. The idea of letting Jay in was kind of scary in the first place. But that was part of the cost of her success, she knew that. 'How do you do it?'

Looking thoughtful, Jay sat down a metre or so away from the edge of the cliff, stretching his legs out on the parched grass. The sun was warm and sultry overhead, and away from the building work and the goat the cliff top was amazingly peaceful. Daisy followed suit and sat too, wondering how long it had been since she'd heard such quiet.

As a musician her life was always full of noise—with melody and harmony, with percussion and the twang of strings, with cheering crowds and sound engineers and managers and the band, with the purr of the tour bus. Out here, there was none of that.

Even the music in her head was quiet. Which would

be a nice change, perhaps, if she didn't need to hear it to write songs.

'Do you have to sit so close to the edge?' Jay asked, his voice a little strained.

Daisy looked down at her hand, next to the cliff drop. She'd sat facing him, but closer to the cliff, her guitar on the ground beside her, and from the look on his face he wasn't entirely comfortable with it.

She couldn't help herself. With a wicked grin she twisted so her feet dangled off the edge of the cliff and she was looking out over the water. There was a thin strip of sand below them, with a few walkers and sunbathers enjoying the beach. If she leaned forward, Daisy could watch them all going about their summer day…

Arms wrapped tight around her waist and tugged her back, her bottom scraping against the grass as she pulled up her feet to stop them catching on the rock of the cliff. Still grinning, she took a moment to realise that her little joke now meant that she was held tight against Jay's broad chest, the scent of him filling her lungs again, and the heat of his body was definitely not unnoticed by her own.

Maybe she hadn't thought this through. Like most things in her life.

'Are you trying to give me a heart attack?' he almost growled in her ear as he moved them away from the edge, and the sound ricocheted through her, leaving tingly wanting feelings wherever it hit.

Yeah. Definitely hadn't thought this through.

She was so tight against him that, as they tumbled onto

their backs together, she could feel his heart beating—too fast. He really had been scared, and for *her*. Huh.

She wanted to make a joke, a 'didn't know you cared,' or a sarcastic comment or *something* that sounded like her, in this place and time where she felt less like Daisy Mulligan than ever.

But what actually came out of her mouth was a question, soft and without mocking. Totally unlike her at all.

'You don't like heights, huh?'

Jay shuddered. 'Hate them. I fell out of a tree when I was about six, and I've avoided them ever since. Better than Harry, at least—he jumped off the roof of the barn next door when he was ten. Lucky for him, he landed on a hay bale. I landed on the tree roots and broke my collarbone.'

She winced. 'Ow. Sorry. I didn't mean to scare you.'

It seemed to dawn on him then just how close they were—his arms still wrapped around her waist, his breath against her cheek, their legs tangled together—because his muscles suddenly tensed against her. Daisy, for her part, hadn't been able to ignore their closeness even for a moment.

Or the effect it had on her.

Perhaps pretending to be in love with Jay Barwell wouldn't be so bad, if she got to feel his body against hers like this when they posed together for photos. Maybe they'd even kiss again…

No. That way lay confusion and feelings and issues, and she wasn't even thinking about it. Not when she was lying in his arms, anyway.

Jay's arms fell away when she wriggled out of them,

sitting up cross-legged beside him. 'Okay, so now we've established that neither of us are going to fall off the cliff, how about we talk about how we're going to write these songs together?'

Nodding, he sat up too, legs outstretched and leaning back on his hands. 'Yeah. Okay. Um, where do you want to start?'

She threw up her hands. 'I don't know! I've never written with another person before. All my songs… they're just me. And I'm not sure they're exactly what Kevin and the label wants for my next album anyway.'

He gave her a curious look. 'What makes you say that? They wouldn't have asked you to do this with me if they didn't want your sort of music.'

Was he really that naive? 'They asked me to do this with you because they can use it to promote our entirely fictional relationship and therefore the floundering tour.'

Jay leaned closer, a teasing heat in his gaze. 'Ah, but there's only a fake relationship in the first place because people watching us perform together sensed the chemistry between us.'

'Because you kissed me, you mean.' Heat surged through her again at his words, and she forced it back down. 'But that was fake too. Just a performance.'

'Was it?' He held her gaze for a moment too long, her mouth drying out as the look lingered.

She could look away. She *should* look away. He couldn't force her to keep looking into his eyes.

So why did it feel as if he were?

With more effort than it really should have taken, Daisy tore her gaze away. 'You're flirting with me.'

And even though she was trying not to look at him, she must have been watching anyway because she saw the amused smile that curved his lips, and the laughter in his eyes.

Damn her traitorous gaze.

'Isn't that what a fake fiancé is supposed to do?' he asked, too casually. Was he as affected by this conversation as she was? Or was this just his rock-star cool at play?

'You haven't actually fake-proposed to me yet, you realise. I'm still technically just your fake girlfriend.' And, right in that moment, something more. Something she couldn't put her finger on, and it bothered her.

'Do you want me to?'

'No.'

She didn't want him to pretend to propose to her. She wanted him to kiss her, for real this time.

She'd always preferred to focus on reality rather than make-believe, even as a child. Except…kissing Jay would be just another sort of make-believe, wouldn't it? Pretending that she could be the sort of woman he'd actually have a relationship with—or even just that she was the sort of woman who could manage a functional relationship. Which, she knew from past experience, she was not.

Men always wanted something from her. Sex, of course, but not just that. Money, even when she didn't have any, and even more so now that she did. An in at a club she'd played, or an introduction to her manager, her label. A leg-up in a brutal industry. Or just to share her fame.

Jay already had all those things, but there were others he could want from her. And nobody gave anything for nothing, not even love.

Why was she thinking about love? She needed to be thinking about music.

'I don't want you to fake propose,' she said, firmer this time. 'I want you to help me write a song. So pick up that damn guitar.'

'Yes, ma'am.' Still smiling, Jay reached for the instrument, and Daisy willed her heartbeat back to normal tempo.

Focus on the music. That was all they were there for.

It took them three days to come up with anything approaching a song idea they could work with. In that time, the builders had fixed the windows, and the front door, made a start on some dodgy-looking roof tiles—and Daisy had named the goat.

'She looks like a Genevieve, don't you think?' she said as she shared her breakfast with the creature on their fifth morning at the villa.

'She looks like a nuisance,' Jay countered. But he had to admit, it amused him to see Daisy—who generally disliked and mistrusted most humans—making friends with a goat.

'Are you ready to get to work?' he asked, watching Genevieve lick pastry crumbs from Daisy's fingers. 'I think we've nearly nailed that first song.'

Daisy pulled a face, but nodded.

Was the face about working or about the song? Either way, Jay shared her sentiments. It wasn't that the song they'd written was no good. It just wasn't…them. Actually, it was more like *fake* them. The song embodiment of the fictional relationship Kevin seemed to have developed for the press.

'It's working like magic!' Kevin had enthused when he'd called the night before. Jay had taken the call in his room, somehow reluctant for Daisy to hear him discussing the fake romance with their manager. 'The photographer I sent to the airport caught a fantastic shot of you with your hand on Daisy's back—you know, loving and protective—and now that photo is *everywhere*. If anyone had any doubts about the two of you before, they certainly don't now. All the gossip sites are talking about your romantic, secluded getaway in Italy!'

'You haven't told any of them where we are, have you?' Jay had asked, sharply.

'Pff! Of course not,' Kevin had replied, and Jay had actually felt a sense of relief—until he'd explained why. 'I don't think Daisy could keep up the facade of *actually* being in love with you in front of the cameras, do you? This way we get all the talk and drama without worrying about Daisy letting on that it isn't real.'

Of course, Kevin didn't have the same concerns about Jay giving the game away. As far as Kevin was concerned, Jay had faked a relationship before, with Milli. Because apparently Jay was the only person involved who *hadn't* realised that relationship wasn't real, until the end.

Which brought him to his current problem. Jay didn't want to write songs about another fake relationship. He wanted to set to music the way Daisy had felt in his arms on that cliff top—as if she might roll over the edge and disappear at any moment if he didn't hold on in just the right way. He wanted to sing about the heat that pulsed through him when she met his gaze, the way his whole body spoke to hers—even if hers wasn't listening.

He wanted to write about what was real. And more than anything else in his world, Jay knew that Daisy was real.

Real and infuriating. Real and insecure. Real and defensive. Real and sarcastic and mean and mocking.

But real.

The only problem was, writing about those things would let on that he'd been *thinking* those things, and he definitely wasn't supposed to be doing that. Their friendship and professional relationship were completely separate from the fake relationship they were supposed to be in, and there was no space between those two worlds for anything else.

Like the desperate need he had to kiss her whenever he let himself look at her lips.

Not thinking about that. Not even to blame himself. After all, if he hadn't kissed her that night onstage, he wouldn't know how surprisingly soft those lips were under his…

Dammit, he was thinking about it again.

They'd taken to working in the main living space, because the sun streamed through the windows almost all day, and they were close to the kettle for coffee in the morning, tea in the afternoon, and near the fridge for alcohol as soon as they decided they weren't getting any more value out of being sober.

This morning, Daisy curled her feet under her on the best chair in the room and pulled her guitar into her lap. On tour, he was used to seeing her mostly in her stage outfits—skinny jeans, logoed vest tops and her favourite leather jacket. Here in Italy she seemed to have lightened up with the weather, favouring flowing skirts with the vest tops instead, or flowy tops with the jeans. The sight of her bare toes—nails painted with unexpected turquoise polish—poking out from under her skirts had been known to distract him for up to half an hour.

God, he was a pathetic individual.

He'd tried telling himself that it was just the proximity, or the music, or the fact that the whole world thought that they were dating. But deep down he knew it wasn't any of those things.

He just wanted Daisy Mulligan. Badly.

'Do you want to go over what we wrote yesterday?' she asked, pulling out a sheaf of notes from the folder on the table.

He should say yes. That was the safe thing for them to do. To go back to fake passion in fake songs about a fake love affair. Just like the songs he'd written for other people to sing, while he was waiting for the band to get their own shot at fame. People like Milli, singing about forever love and then turning around and leaving their supposed beloved behind. At least he knew how that world worked.

'Let's try something new,' he said, before his brain could talk him out of it.

Daisy looked up, eyebrows raised in surprise, but he could see the excitement in her eyes. She was as bored with that song they'd been labouring over as he was. 'You've got something in mind?'

He hadn't, not really. Nothing beyond a feeling and

a few snippets of lines that haunted his sleep at night, and the patches of melody he'd half written in his head walking into the village that first day. But he picked up his guitar anyway. He might be a company man these days, but he still knew how to improvise.

'Maybe something we can work up,' he said. 'I don't know. See what you think. You might hate it.'

But, God, he hoped she didn't.

Gingerly, he strummed a couple of chords before finding his rhythm. Music had always felt like a river to him, flowing through his body as naturally as blood in his veins. He could feel it inside him, working its way to his fingertips and vocal cords, seeking a way out into the world.

His whole life, he'd just had to give himself over to the music and it had come. He hoped that wouldn't fail him now.

As his hands found the melody he'd been searching for, the one that had been writing itself in his subconscious all week, he knew instinctively that this was the song they'd been searching for. And when Daisy picked up her guitar and started playing a counterpoint, a small smile under her closed eyes, brow furrowed with concentration, he knew she felt it too.

But the words. The words just weren't there for him. Harry was more of a lyricist than he was, and for a moment Jay wished his brother were there with him. Then he looked at Daisy again, lost in the music, and changed his mind.

He didn't want to share this moment with anyone else.

As the melody began to repeat, Daisy's warm, husky

voice suddenly joined the song—sometimes just vo-calising with sounds, sometimes singing actual words, even some complete lines. Jay shifted closer to hear them, to understand them, although they were noth-ing like complete lyrics. Still, what he could hear only warmed his blood, and his hopes.

'And when you're close, oh, how I feel you. Down deep inside my soul,' she sang.

And Jay couldn't help but wonder if she could sing that with such feeling if she didn't mean it. If it wasn't real.

Unless she's singing about somebody else, you idiot.

He tried to force reason back into his brain and pull away. But then Daisy opened her eyes and her gaze hit his and he just *knew*. She felt it too. Whatever this ri-diculously strong pull he felt towards her, whatever it was that just made him want to drag her into his arms and keep her there, safe from the rest of the world, *she felt it too*.

And that changed everything.

His fingers stalled on the strings and Daisy's song faded away until they were sitting in silence, just star-ing at each other.

Daisy collected herself first, clearing her throat and looking away. 'Uh, I think that could work. Um—'

No. He wasn't going back to that again now. He couldn't, not now he knew.

So instead, he reached out and grabbed her hand, tugging her towards him so she had to look up at him again. And then he leaned in, just those few precious inches, waiting to see if she'd follow his lead in this, as she had with the music.

A pink tongue darted out and swept across her lower lip. She blinked, slow, and he could see the heat in her eyes. Then she moved, just a fraction, closer, closer—

'Mah!' Genevieve bleated loudly in his ear and Jay jerked back, out of the range of goat spit, trying not to swear. And failing.

'Genevieve!' Daisy scolded, but, given how fast she moved away from him, he wondered if he heard a little relief in her voice.

She'd wanted that kiss as much as he had, he'd seen that in her widened pupils, in the pulse thrumming fast at her throat. But she didn't *want* to want it. Why?

That was what he needed to figure out now.

Just one more mystery of Daisy Mulligan.

'Yes, I know, Genevieve. I'm hiding. You don't need to give me that look.'

The goat stared balefully at her regardless, as if she were as disappointed at Daisy's life choices as her family always had been. As if Genevieve hadn't actually been the one to bring her to her senses two days ago anyway.

If it weren't for the damn goat she'd have kissed Jay Barwell. Again. And then, knowing her, she'd have started getting ideas.

She couldn't afford to get ideas about the world's sexiest man.

It was one thing when she was fourteen, believing that her eighteen-year-old boyfriend really meant it when he said he only loved her, when actually he had two other girls on the go at the same time. It was one thing taking up with a twenty-something guy when she was sixteen because he had a room over the pub where she could crash for a while, in return for her affection. And it was one thing falling for a musician who claimed to love her—but loved her talent, and the prospect of sharing in her fame, a hell of a lot more.

People always wanted something in return, that was the rule, and she had to remember it. At least Jay had been upfront about what he wanted—a fake relationship and some songs to boost their flagging tour sales and popularity, plus probably show Milli Masters that he wasn't still wallowing over her leaving him, even if he was.

She couldn't let herself believe, not for a second, that this was about anything else. That it might just be about how badly she'd wanted to kiss him, before Genevieve had intervened.

So she was avoiding him. Because it was easier than dealing with the butterflies in her stomach—and the other feelings somewhat lower—every time she met his gaze.

Of course, that made progress on the new songs rather slower. Which she felt bad about; she did. Except…she couldn't move past those long minutes when they'd played together, when the words that needed to go with the beautiful melody he'd written had just come to her, complete in parts and a work in progress in others. Those minutes when she'd known exactly what the song was about, because she could see it in his gaze.

It was about wanting. It was about that pull to a person you knew couldn't be right for you, but that you couldn't stop wanting all the same. It was about a voice down deep inside saying that this was the one.

Even when he couldn't be.

And she'd known he was thinking the same as her. They were on the same wavelength as surely as they always were onstage, when they sang to each other in front of hundreds or thousands of people.

Which was why she had to stay away.

'Are you done avoiding me yet?' Jay's voice rang out around the outside walls of the cottage, perfectly audible over the hammering on the roof as Matteo and Lorenzo fixed the roof tiles.

Daisy winced. 'No, not really.'

He came into view around the corner of the villa, skirting Genevieve cautiously, and approached Daisy. 'Tough. I just had a call from Kevin and you're going to have to start talking to me pretty soon.'

'Why?' He didn't ask why she was avoiding him, she realised. Because he already knew. Because he felt the same.

'There's some awards show in Rome I'd hoped we were skipping, but apparently Kevin wants us there. Together.'

'Damn.'

He laughed. 'Is being seen on my arm such a terrible chore?'

'It's more the "dressing up and wearing heels and make-up" part I wasn't looking forward to,' she confessed. 'Plus you know Kevin will probably have an engagement ring waiting ready for me to wear. He probably measured my finger in my sleep on the tour bus.'

Jay shuddered. 'That's worryingly plausible. Actually, Harry offered to bring my gran's engagement ring to the awards if you wanted it. Apparently he really did ask Mum for it while he was at home.'

Daisy recoiled in horror. 'Why would he do that?'

'I think he meant it as a joke.' But even he didn't sound entirely sure.

This was ridiculous. They couldn't carry on like this. They needed to come to some sort of rebalancing here. One that could let them move past this awkwardness and tension and get back to work. And in her experience, only one thing had worked consistently for ruining potential relationships and encouraging men to move on and ignore her.

Getting drunk and sleeping with them.

Jay was an actual rock star. It stood to reason that it would work for him too, right?

Chewing her lip, she tried to figure out how best to suggest it—and if she even wanted to. She *liked* Jay. She wasn't under any illusion that he might be her one and only or anything—they were too different for that, and she didn't believe in all that 'soul mates' stuff anyway. And that was before she got to the part where he was still in love with his all-American, beautiful, successful ex-girlfriend.

But she didn't want to trash the friendship they'd built up, either. They still had to work together, once this was over.

Still, this was the only plan she had—other than hiding out with a goat, which wasn't actually working that well for her.

'Okay. If we need to go back to civilisation and start faking a relationship again, I think we need to do a couple of things first,' she said.

'Like talk about how we almost kissed?' Jay suggested, suddenly closer than she'd thought. Close enough that she could just—

She stepped back. 'Talking is overrated,' she told him, meeting his gaze head-on. 'We need to go and get drunk.'

CHAPTER SEVEN

Jay had no idea exactly what Daisy's plan was here, but so far he was having fun.

The last couple of days had been unbearably awkward. Ever since that almost kiss, Daisy had been keeping her distance, refusing to meet his gaze, acting skittish and un-Daisy-like. He didn't like it. He far preferred her snarky and mocking to this quiet and evasive Daisy.

Fortunately, with her latest suggestion, she seemed to have got back to her old self again.

The village at the bottom of the hill was small, but it did at least boast a bar—one which, so far, they'd discovered had plenty of different sorts of alcohol for them to try. It was a little hole-in-the-wall place, with a barely legible wooden sign over the door. Jay wasn't sure he'd have even noticed it when they walked past, but it seemed Daisy had a nose for places like this.

'It's the many, many years I spent working in them,' she'd explained, when he'd questioned it.

Taking the beer she'd offered him, he'd done some swift mental arithmetic. 'Years? Did you start bartending in secondary school?'

Daisy just shrugged. 'Places like this aren't so fussy about things like age.'

He wondered now how old she'd been. Seventeen? Sixteen? She couldn't be more than twenty-four now, and he knew she'd been playing around pubs and bars for a few years before he met her in Copenhagen, two years ago.

She'd never talked about her family, he realised. Not once. But now, he wondered where her parents had been when she'd been pulling pints and busking in the streets. Who had looked after her?

He almost didn't want to know the answer.

Now, he leaned across the rustic wood table, beer bottle in his hand, and asked her, 'Remind me why us getting drunk tonight is going to solve all our problems?' It hadn't made much sense when he was sober, but he suspected that a couple of beers in it might start to be understandable.

'We're too tense around each other.' Daisy talked with her hands a lot, he realised, watching as she waved her beer bottle around. 'We need to loosen up.'

'We're tense because we're trying not to give in and kiss each other.' *Oops.* Apparently the alcohol had loosened his mouth up plenty already.

Daisy's eyes widened a fraction, before she spoke. 'Well, maybe the drinks can help with that too.'

'I don't think every bottle behind that bar would make me want you less.' Hell, he just had no filter at all tonight, did he? 'So you're going to have to explain to me why I shouldn't.'

Her gaze locked on his. 'What makes you think I'm trying to convince you not to?'

Raising one eyebrow, she got to her feet—not breaking eye contact—and gave him the sort of smile he'd only dreamed of. The sort that sent fire coursing through his veins.

Then she turned and stalked to the bar, leaving him watching her hips sway as she procured them more drinks.

'Why am I not surprised that ordering alcohol is one thing you can do in Italian?' he asked, when she returned with shot glasses for them both.

She laughed, warm and low. 'You know me. Always focussing on what's important.'

He should change the subject from their previous conversation, he knew that. He should get them back to friendly fake boyfriend and girlfriend, to collaborators and colleagues. Mentor and mentee. But the air between them sizzled with potential, with the sort of tension that could just snap at any moment.

He might snap if he didn't do something about it. Either they had to decide to ignore it and hope it went away. Or…

Well. It was the 'or' that had been keeping him awake at night.

'And tonight it was important that you brought me here.' As she sat, he reached across and took her hand, visibly startling her. 'Why, Daisy?'

'Because…' She licked her lower lip again. He wondered if she knew what that did to him, if that was why she did it. Milli would have, he knew. The moment she spotted a weakness in him she homed in on it, exploiting it for all it was worth. But with Daisy…he doubted she even realised she'd done it. 'We need to get past this…thing between us, right? Ever since we wrote that song together—'

'You mean the day we almost kissed,' Jay said, for clarity, and enjoyed watching the slightest hint of pink flush Daisy's cheeks. He'd never imagined that she could blush. He wondered what other parts of her might turn pink with the right attention.

'Yeah.' Her voice was husky on the word, like when she sang deep and full of meaning, and it hit him places even Milli had never quite reached. God, he needed to keep drinking until he stopped thinking about her this way. She'd made it obvious that whatever the attraction between them she didn't intend to do anything about it, which meant he needed to move past it, as she'd suggested.

Except then she said, 'I think we need to have sex.'

It took a lot of effort, but Jay just about managed to not drop his drink, swear loudly, or drag her over the table into his arms in the next instant. Just.

'Is that the alcohol talking?' he asked cautiously. 'Because honestly? I don't see how actually getting to see you naked is going to make me want you any less afterwards.'

'You'd be surprised,' she said, with a wry smile. 'Normally I find that most guys lose interest after they've got what they want from me.'

'I'm not most guys.' He hoped that was true. He definitely knew she was wrong about him losing interest.

She shook her head as if she were shaking away his objections. 'Look, the point is, we need to be able to work together. And we need to be able to pretend that we're a couple. We can't do that if we're flinching every time we touch.'

'Or hiding from each other.'

'Exactly. So we need to get comfortable with each other again. We didn't have this problem on the tour, right? Not even after you, well, kissed me onstage that night.' She rushed the words, as if it would stop him remembering how her lips felt under his. It didn't. 'We just moved past it, right? Probably because we were so busy, and there were so many people around, and you were—'

She broke off, but he knew what she hadn't said. 'I was still wallowing after Milli.'

'Yeah.' Her mouth twisted up into an awkward smile. 'I mean, at least this is a good distraction from that, right?'

'Definitely.' He'd barely thought about Milli since he'd arrived in Italy, while she'd consumed his every waking thought when they were on tour. Until he'd kissed Daisy, anyway. She might have thought they'd moved past it, but for Jay it had felt more like trying to ignore all the strange new feelings it had kicked up in him.

And now, here… It was as if he and Daisy had shifted universes to one where only they existed. Well, them, Genevieve and the builders.

'Plus, people act differently when they've slept together. You can see it just by looking at them.'

He raised an eyebrow. 'So your pitch here is that we should sleep together because then I won't want to do it any more, but Kevin will be happy because more people will believe that we're a real couple?' Because that definitely had to be the shots talking, right?

Daisy leaned forward over the table, low enough

that he could see right down her top to the curve of her breasts. 'My pitch is that we should sleep with each other before I actually lose my mind with lust.'

Any blood in his body that was still doing its actual job, rather than just getting overheated, gave up and flooded south.

Jay swallowed down the last of his drink, got to his feet, then held out his hand to Daisy. He didn't care what her logic was, she obviously needed this as much as he did.

And he wasn't letting any damn goat stop him this time.

'Let's get out of here,' he said, and she nodded.

They were halfway out of the door before he remembered about the stupid hill back to the villa. Even then, he didn't let it slow them down for too long.

Daisy laughed, the sound music on the breeze as he dragged her up the winding path. 'Somebody's eager.'

'You have no idea,' he growled. 'I have been *dreaming* of this moment ever since you tumbled into my arms on the car ride up here.'

'Me too,' she whispered, so softly he only just caught it. The admission just made him more desperate, and he picked up speed again. Hell, he'd pick her up and carry her if he had to.

'No, before then,' he corrected himself. If they were being open and honest, he might as well go all the way. He could always blame the alcohol later. 'Since I kissed you onstage, and pretended it was just for show.'

Her only response to that was a small, desperate gasp. Jay smiled and redoubled his efforts to get them home quickly.

Finally, finally, they reached the top of the hill, and then the front door. It was late enough that the builders had finished work and gone home hours ago, and even Genevieve seemed to have found somewhere else to be.

Jay pulled Daisy close, spinning her so her back was against the front door. He'd intended to give her an opportunity to back out, to change her mind. But as he saw her there, flushed in the fading sunlight, her short black hair just falling against her cheekbone, her skin glowing, he realised something.

'I haven't even kissed you properly yet. Not without an audience. I'm half crazed for you, and I haven't even kissed you.' How could it be she had such an effect on him? When just a week or two ago he'd been so sure no woman besides Milli ever could?

Maybe his mother was right about true love only striking once, but it seemed that true lust could come in many shapes and sizes.

Then Daisy tilted her chin up, looked him straight in the eye and said, 'So kiss me,' and he decided that wondering about that sort of thing could definitely wait for another day.

Right now, he had something much more important to do.

The wood of the door was still warm from the sun, a pleasant heat against her back—but nothing compared to the one between her and Jay. He was going to kiss her. And then he was going to make love to her. And that... Daisy couldn't quite decide if it was terrifying or glorious. Maybe both.

Either way, there was no chance in hell she was going to stop it now.

His mouth met hers and she sank into the kiss, clutching at his arms to get closer, closer. This wasn't like any other first—or technically second—kiss in her experience. Those were drunken, fumbling, probing things. This kiss...

This kiss was something else. Jay's lips were confident and sure on hers, no hint of him being affected by the drinks they'd shared at the bar, although she could still taste the shots. His hands stroked up her side, her shoulder, just brushing against the curve of her breast rather than grabbing and groping her. And when she opened her eyes, he was staring right into them, so she could see the restraint in them. The desperate attempt to hold back from what he wanted.

What they *both* wanted.

'Okay?' he murmured against her lips.

Daisy shook her head, then grabbed him as he made to move away. 'More.'

That was all it took.

Jay fumbled with the handle until the door fell away behind them, and then they were inside, tripping over each other as they kissed their way to the bedroom, reluctant to let go for even a moment. Daisy stripped the shirt from his shoulders as he backed her towards the bed, popping the buttons from their holes in one swift movement to get her hands on the smooth skin of his shoulders and the muscles beneath. His chest was smattered with sandy hair, and she scratched her nails through it, working downwards to the buttons of his jeans.

The backs of her knees hit the bed frame—were they in her room or his? She hadn't been paying attention—and she sat abruptly, smiling as she realised she was now at exactly the right level to get those jeans off him. But Jay had other ideas. Raising her arms, he pulled her top up over her head, revealing the satin and lace half bra she'd chosen when planning the evening. With a small groan, he sank to his knees, taking one breast in his hand, the other in his mouth.

Well. Maybe she could live with him keeping the jeans on just a little longer, Daisy decided as he lowered her onto the bed, one knee on the mattress beside her as he covered her body with his and kissed his way down her body.

Just not *too* much longer.

Jay woke up the next morning to the strange sensation that he was being watched.

He tensed under the covers, eyes still tightly closed, until his brain caught up with his intuition.

Last night. The bar. Kissing Daisy against the door. Daisy.

God, *Daisy*.

His mouth curved into a smile at the memory. Sex with Daisy had been every single bit as amazing as his imagination had told him it could be. From the moment they first kissed for real, her spiky, keep-out persona had dropped away, showing him the passionate woman underneath. Oh, she was still smart-mouthed and sarcastic, keeping him laughing even as he kissed every inch of her body. But there was a softer side, too. One that *wanted*. One that let him give.

And now she was watching him sleep. He loved that.

Smiling, he opened his eyes to wish her good morning—and found himself eyeball to eyeball with a goat.

Letting out a decidedly unmanly shriek, he jumped up to standing on the bed, a pillow clutched to his groin, as Genevieve chewed contently on the corner of the sheet.

'What the...?' Daisy swore sleepily, then sat up, brushing her dark hair out of her eyes. 'Jay? Oh. Good morning, Genevieve.'

'The builders fixed all the doors.' Jay sat cautiously back down on the mattress. 'How is she still even getting in?'

Daisy shrugged, the sheet falling away from her deliciously bare shoulders with the movement. 'Maybe she's a magic goat.'

He shot her a look, and she laughed.

'Okay, what will you give me to get rid of her?' she asked, wrapping the top sheet around her, toga style. It was too hot to sleep with any of the blankets—and they'd definitely kept each other warm the night before.

Jay raised an eyebrow. 'What would you like?'

Tilting her head slightly, Daisy pursed her lips, considering. 'Coffee.'

'Just coffee?'

'And pastries?'

'That's seriously all you want?' Perhaps last night hadn't been as good for her as it had for him, if she wasn't already desperate for a repeat performance. If it wasn't for the goat watching them, he'd definitely have been suggesting it by now.

Daisy nodded. 'Breakfast in bed. With you.' Her grin turned wicked, and his heartbeat kicked up a notch. 'After all, a girl needs sustenance to keep her stamina up.'

Jay grabbed his jeans from the floor and pulled them on. 'Deal. I'll make breakfast, you handle the goat, and we'll meet back here.' He leant in to kiss her swiftly on the lips—a kiss that turned rather more lingering as Daisy grabbed the back of his head and held him to her. Not that he was complaining.

'Breakfast,' he repeated, a little dazed, when they finally parted. 'Goat.'

'Then sex,' Daisy said, bouncing out of bed in her sheet toga. 'Definitely more sex.'

It was just as well that Matteo and Lorenzo had fixed the windows and the shutters, Jay mused the following night as he lounged in the shuttered cocoon of Daisy's bedroom. *Their* bedroom now, he supposed. He certainly hadn't been back to his for longer than it took to pick up a fresh box of condoms from his case.

'And what, exactly, made you think to pack those?' Daisy had asked, eyebrows arched where she'd sat in bed, as he'd returned with them.

'Nico put them in my case as a joke.'

Daisy had shaken her head. 'Knowing Nico, that was *not* a joke.'

'You're probably right.' He'd crawled back up the bed, tugging on her ankle to bring her flat on her back under him, knowing that it wouldn't take her long to kiss away his defences and flip them so she was on top. 'And you definitely weren't complaining when you found that strip of them in my jeans pockets after we made it back from the bar.'

'True. But I'm pretty sure Nico didn't put them there that night,' she'd pointed out.

Ah. Caught. 'Maybe I was just very, very hopeful. Or wishing very hard.'

'You're saying I make your wishes come true?'

He'd caught a bare nipple between his lips, and run his tongue around it, loving how she'd shivered under him. 'You make all my fantasies come true,' he'd murmured against her skin.

They'd had better things to do than talk after that.

In fact, after two whole days spent exclusively in bed with each other, they'd managed to not talk about anything of importance at all. Not what they were doing together, not the awards ceremony in Rome they had to leave for tomorrow, not the songs they were supposed to be writing…they'd just been lost in each other's bodies.

Not that he was complaining about that, either. But tomorrow morning there'd be a car, and a plane, then Rome, and other people. And at some point they really needed to talk about how this was going to work. Would they still be doing…this back in the real world?

'You look like you're thinking too hard,' Daisy murmured beside him. 'You should stop that. You might strain something.'

'I'm more worried about you breaking me than a little bit of thinking.'

'Worried you can't take the pace, old man?' Daisy's naked body slid over his in the dark, her mouth moving across his collarbone with light, butterfly kisses in a way she knew drove him crazy. 'Don't worry. You just lie back and let me take care of you.'

Then her kisses started to move lower, and Jay decided that maybe talking wasn't *that* important. They could discuss everything on the plane.

Right now, he just wanted to *feel*.

'Urgh, clothes.' Daisy threw her favourite short black dress back into her suitcase on top of a few other essentials, along with a pair of biker boots, and called it good. Just getting dressed felt like a challenge that morning. Not that she'd admit it to Jay—especially after her old man jokes—but her whole body ached, in a pleasurable way, from the last few days.

Nearly three days in bed with one man. She'd never done that before. Never *wanted* that before. And that was the part that made her nervous.

The idea had been that they'd get it out of their system, break the stupid tension, then carry on with their lives. Instead, she'd fallen into the best sex of her life, lost two full days and three nights in a haze of lust, and now she had to put on actual clothes and get on a plane to Rome.

Not ideal. Especially since they still hadn't talked about any of it, beyond their tipsy reasoning in the bar.

'The car's here. Are you ready?' Jay asked from outside the bedroom door, and she tensed. Which was ridiculous. She'd literally laid herself bare for the man for the last three days. What on earth did she have to be nervous about now?

She took a breath and opened the door.

It was weird to see him in clothes again, she realised.

To see him dressed like Jay Barwell, lead singer of Dept 135, not the guy she'd been living in a crumbling villa with for the last week or so. The man she'd been kissing and touching and making love with for the last seventy-two hours. He'd worn her out so thoroughly she'd even slept through his snoring.

Jay had also confessed, somewhere in the middle of all the sex, that some photo of them at the airport on their way out there had gone viral, and that, according to Kevin, the whole world knew they were off in some Italian love nest. Daisy was almost certain that Kevin had set up the photographer himself. And the worst part was, she couldn't even reasonably object any more, since it was technically accurate.

So now they were going back to the real world, where the public apparently believed they were a couple and their friends knew that they weren't, and she had no idea which one of those things was *actually* true.

Which meant they were going to have to Talk. With a capital T. About emotions and expectations and stuff—and Daisy *hated* those talks.

At least she already knew how this one would go. They'd agree that this was fun, and good, but they had to keep in mind that it was just for show. That he still loved Milli. That she didn't do relationships and love and all that anyway. She had too many dreams to chase.

As long as she still knew what it was that Jay wanted from her, she'd be okay. She just had to keep her eye on that. The transactional details of the affair, so to speak.

And not deck Nico when he figured out what was going on and started teasing her.

God, she really didn't want to go to Rome.

'I'm not sure we should leave Genevieve alone,' she blurted out, earning herself an amused look from Jay.

'Really? The *goat* is the best excuse you can come up with? I was expecting at least something about leaving Matteo and Lorenzo unattended working on the villa, or how you hadn't paid them yet, or something.'

'Yeah, that would have been a better excuse,' Daisy admitted.

'As it happens, I've already spoken with Matteo. He and Lorenzo will keep working while we're away, and they have my number if any problems come up. I also insisted on transferring some money over for them for materials or what have you.'

Daisy froze. 'You shouldn't have done that. *I* should have done that. It's my villa.'

But Jay just shrugged. 'You can pay me back some time. It wasn't much, Daze. Just a couple of thousand.'

Pocket change to him, of course. But even now she knew, logically, she could afford it, Daisy's heart started to race at the idea of owing anyone that money. She fumbled for her phone, trying to open her banking app. 'I'll pay you now.'

'Save it for the plane, or we're going to be late.' He grabbed her suitcase and lifted it without obvious effort, but Daisy thought she saw a slight wince as he twisted, and realised she knew exactly which of last night's amusements had caused that muscle strain. 'Oh, and I asked Lorenzo to look after Genevieve, too,' he added, seemingly as an afterthought.

Daisy beamed. 'Thank you!'

'I knew you'd worry otherwise,' Jay said, with a soft smile. 'Now, come on, or we'll miss our flight.'

Maybe she was overthinking this. Maybe they could just carry on as before, now that all the sex was out of their system. Go back to being friends without ever having to discuss it.

Her hand brushed against his as she tried to reclaim her suitcase, and sparks sizzled up her arm as her body reacted to his touch—instinctive, automatic, and undeniable.

His gaze met hers and she knew he was feeling it too. She swallowed. Hard.

'Car.'

'Right.'

'Now?'

'Yeah.' He stared a moment longer then shook his head. 'Now. Come on.'

The car bumped back down the hill towards reality. Daisy kept to her side of the back seat, staring out of the window, remembering all too well that this was where it had started. It wasn't that kiss onstage in Philadelphia that had kicked things off, not really. She'd been too certain that the kiss was just for show, so she'd been more annoyed than turned on.

But that moment when she'd fallen into his arms in the car up to the villa, when it was just the two of them and an oblivious driver. *That* was the first time she'd truly looked at Jay Barwell and thought, *Yes.*

Before that, she'd known he was gorgeous, but nothing more. After that…she'd had ideas.

And now? Now she knew *exactly* how he felt against her, inside her, and she wasn't likely to forget in a hurry. And given the sparks still between them, if they didn't want to give the driver a free—and probably very distracting—show they needed to keep their distance.

On the other side of the back seat, Jay appeared to be employing the same strategy, staring at his phone screen as if he cared what was on it and wasn't imagining dragging her back to bed again. Good. At least he couldn't distract her then. And he probably wouldn't notice her sneaking looks at him…

'Kevin sent me another email.'

Oh. Maybe he really *was* thinking of other things.

'What does it say?' Maybe the awards ceremony had been cancelled and they could go home.

Wait. *Home?*

Before she had a chance to analyse that thought further, Jay answered.

'Apparently there's a special live link-up planned from LA for the award I'm presenting, and Kevin wanted to give me a heads-up.'

Daisy frowned. 'Why would you care about that?'

'Because Milli is doing it, and they want me to do some scripted banter with her. Apparently we were both booked before we broke up, and now she's decided not to come to Italy but still needs to honour the contract, so…'

'Oh.' All the passion drained away from her as she realised how firmly back in the real world they were already. The world where Jay Barwell loved Milli Masters, and where she was just a fake distraction for the press.

At least she knew where she stood, and without even having to have that messy emotions conversation. That was a good thing.

Besides, it wasn't as if Jay's prowess in the bedroom

had made her fall in love with him or anything. He was a good friend and a great lay and a fun fake almost-fiancé. That was all.

She forced a smile as the cogs in her brain started turning. 'Then that means she'll be watching tonight. We should put on a show for her.'

Jay raised an eyebrow at her. 'A show?'

'Sure. I mean, we're going tonight as a couple, right? A *fake* couple, I mean,' she added hurriedly, in case he got the wrong idea. 'So we act up to it a bit. Should be even easier now—' She broke off.

'Now we've spent significant time together naked?' Jay finished for her.

'Basically, yeah.' If she was going to be his fake girl-friend, she was going to be the best one he ever had.

Jay looked out of the window for a long moment, before turning back to her. 'Okay. Say we were going to do that. What would it entail?'

Daisy grinned. Acting, that was all this was. Per-forming. And she'd been doing that for most of her life. As long as she didn't let messy emotions get involved, this should be easy.

'Well, for starters, I'm going to need a ring.'

CHAPTER EIGHT

Jay THREW HIS stuff onto the king-size bed of the hotel suite, then fell onto the mattress next to it, face first. He was exhausted. Never mind that his poor body had seen more exercise in the last three days than ever before—that, he could have coped with. Celebrated, even.

It was trawling around the jewellery shops of Rome that had finished him off.

He could hear Daisy pottering around the other bedroom of the suite, probably getting ready for the awards show. They should have had hours at the hotel to prepare, but their detour en route from the airport to procure her an engagement ring had taken *much* longer than he'd expected.

'It doesn't have to be a real diamond or anything, but it does have to be big,' Daisy had said as they'd trawled the racks at the first jeweller's their incredibly patient driver had taken them to. 'We need to make sure it shows up on the cameras from the first moment we step out of the car. We want people talking about it before the awards show even starts.'

'And then we just smile coyly and look adoringly at each other, right?' He knew how this was played. He'd just never actually done it before—with Milli, he'd been so besotted he hadn't needed to act at all. But now, with the benefit of hindsight, he could see all her actions and behaviours for the performance they were.

'Could do.' Daisy had looked thoughtfully at the tray of rings in front of her. 'Or we could just play to our strengths. Coy has never particularly been one of mine.'

'Dare I ask what our strengths are?'

The look she'd given him had scorched him to the bone. 'If I need to tell you, then you really haven't been paying attention the last few days.'

Of course, after that he hadn't really been thinking about rings.

He had, thankfully, noticed the photographer trawling around behind them after the first couple of shops. He'd suspected the driver had tipped someone off. Probably Kevin, who'd tipped off the paparazzi. Perfect.

'Think it better had be a real diamond,' he'd murmured to Daisy as they'd leaned over the latest tray of jewels. 'We're being watched.'

She'd casually glanced over to where he'd indicated, then turned back to the shopkeeper. With one hand possessively placed on Jay's back, she'd pointed to the largest—and most expensive—ring in the tray. 'Let's try that one.'

Of course, it couldn't be quite *that* easy. They needed a ring that was the right size for her to wear to the awards ceremony that night, plus Jay suspected that Daisy had been enjoying leading the photographer a merry dance around Rome, so it had taken another three jewellery shops to find the perfect ring.

Well, perfect for the ruse, anyway. To Jay's mind it hung too big and heavy on Daisy's delicate fingers, clashing with her natural style. It was too sharp, too sparkly, too overwhelming to suit Daisy.

But he had to admit, it would definitely show up on the cameras tonight.

Kevin had cannily booked them a suite with two bedrooms, so they could stay together as far as the hotel and press were concerned but sleep separately. Still, after the last few days, Jay had assumed that they'd share a bedroom here as they had at the cottage. But as soon as they'd arrived, Daisy had taken her bags into the second bedroom and hadn't reappeared.

Jay wasn't quite sure what to make of that.

He'd meant to talk to her on the plane, to figure out exactly what this thing was between them, but instead the journey had been taken up with planning ways to level up their fake relationship. It would help, he supposed, if he knew what he wanted from this fling to start with.

Because it was a fling, right? That much he was pretty sure of.

Probably.

Yeah, he really needed to talk to Daisy.

But not before he'd had a proper, long, hot shower. The plumbing at the villa was still a bit hit and miss, and he'd been dreaming of a hotel bathroom for days. Of course, he'd also been imagining all the things he could do to Daisy in a shower like this…

Later. They'd get through tonight, then come back and enjoy all the benefits of this hotel suite. There'd be plenty of time to talk about what it all meant later, on the plane back, or once they were back at the villa, even. Yeah, that made sense. He'd wait until they had time and space alone again. Well, apart from the goat.

The shower went a long way to reviving him, and once he'd dressed in the suit the stylist Kevin had assigned them had sent up for him, he felt more or less ready to take on the real world again. At least fake-engagement-ring shopping with Daisy had taken his mind off the fact he was going to have to smile and play nice with Milli in front of hundreds of thousands of people across the globe tonight.

And even that was easier than seeing her in person, alone. Then, he knew, he wouldn't be able to stop himself asking her why. Why she'd let him believe that what they had could be real, when for her it was never more than a sham.

He wasn't sure he wanted to know the answer to that.

When they'd met, they'd both been rising stars. But it hadn't taken long for Milli's to eclipse his. From that point on he supposed it had been inevitable that she'd move onwards and upwards to something better.

But he wasn't thinking about Milli tonight. Not until he had to.

Opening the bedroom door, he headed into the suite's lounge, and found Daisy already there, dressed in a shimmering blue floor-length gown he'd never seen before. Cut high at the neckline, instead it plunged low at the back, baring her spine almost to the curve of her backside.

'Wow.'

'Yeah. Apparently now I'm your fake fiancée the stylist decided my wardrobe needed an upgrade.'

'It's gorgeous. *You're* gorgeous.' Her dark hair sat in waves against her head, angling down to her cheek-bone on one side. She looked like a vintage film star, glamorous, beautiful, untouchable.

'It's not exactly my usual style,' Daisy admitted wryly. 'But I guess it goes with the ring.'

'It definitely does that.' His gaze darted to her left hand, and the huge rock sitting there, weighing her down. 'Think you'll be able to play guitar wearing that thing?'

Daisy shrugged, and the dress slid and shifted over her curves in a way that made him want to peel it right off her. 'Probably not. Maybe I'll need a stage ring too.'

'You're just in this for the jewellery, aren't you?' he joked as they heard a knock at the door.

'Because I'm such a magpie?' She patted his cheek and crossed the room to answer the door. 'I'll have you know I'm just in this for the hot sex.'

'More information than I needed.' Harry, standing behind the open door, looked between them, his gaze full of questions. Jay suspected he was going to have to answer at least some of them later tonight. More fun to look forward to. 'Glad to see you both made it,' Harry went on. 'If you're ready, the car's waiting downstairs.'

With a beaming, un-Daisy-like smile, his fake fiancée took his arm, ensuring that her left hand was in full view against his suit jacket. 'Then let's go!'

Daisy knew that the photos of her fake engagement ring would be on the Internet before they even reached the awards ceremony. There had definitely been ones of them ring shopping up online by the time they'd got back to the hotel. The media didn't mess around when it came to Jay Barwell's relationship status.

She just wished she understood it as well as the media seemed to think they did.

Harry had been shooting them both concerned glances since they'd left the hotel, while Kevin just looked blissful the whole time. Nico had elbowed Jay as they'd got into the car, making a joke about the condoms he'd slipped in his case. In response, Benji had rolled his eyes and pointed out that it was all just for show.

Daisy hadn't known how to tell them they were both right, so she hadn't said anything at all.

Jay was quiet too, probably thinking about the impending video chat with his ex. But as soon as they climbed out of the car onto the red carpet, he was all matinee-idol smiles for the cameras, holding her close against his side like a pretty accessory.

God, she hated this, she realised as the camera flashes blinded her. She hated being nothing more than an appendage to some man. She hated that people were more interested in her dress and her ring than her music. She hated that she was lying to the world, pretending to be something she'd never be.

The sort of woman Jay Barwell might marry.

How had it come to this? In some ways, events just seemed to have swept her up and dragged her along. But in others, she knew she'd chosen this. For Jay. To make him feel better.

Because however much she didn't want to talk emotions with him, she knew she had them. About him.

And that, she could already tell, was going to cause her nothing but problems.

'You okay?' Jay murmured softly as they waved goodbye to the press and the crowds and swept into the awards venue. 'You're clinging kind of tight there.'

'Not used to these shoes,' Daisy replied. Not a complete lie.

Just not the whole truth, either.

Basically exactly like their relationship.

The awards were being held in a theatre, newly refurbished inside, but classically styled on the outside. Daisy had to admire the Italian sense of style and she was glad that the stylist had provided her own outfit. Her usual favourite black dress and boots really wouldn't have fitted in here. The women were all so groomed and gorgeous, and the men in their suits all looked like James Bond, even if she knew that they were tattooed under their shirts and usually dressed in leather. Everyone seemed to have made a real effort tonight.

But it wasn't until she saw the signage over the stage that she realised *exactly* which awards ceremony Jay had brought her to tonight.

The Ascot Music Awards.

Ascot. Viv Ascot. How had she missed that?

Because Kevin had sent all the details to Jay, since he was the one appearing. She was just there as a hanger-on, of course. And naturally Jay had been far more obsessed with the details about Milli than linking it to her mysterious cottage acquisition.

'You didn't tell me it was the *Ascot* Music Awards,' she muttered as they took their seats. Jay wasn't needed until much later in the ceremony, so had been told he'd be collected later to have his microphone set up and so . on, and that he should just enjoy the show until then.

'The Ascot… Oh! I guess I didn't even register it. You think she might be here?'

Daisy shrugged. 'She was at the Ascot Music Festival in Copenhagen. Why not? And if she is, I want to ask her about the cottage.'

'About whether she knew what a state it was in? Or why she left it to you in the first place?'

'Both,' Daisy said darkly.

It was hard to concentrate on the actual awards being given out when all she wanted to do was scan the room for the woman she'd met and known only as Viv. She almost missed the moment when the staff came to get Jay to prepare to present his award, grabbing his hand at the last minute as he rose from his seat.

'You going to be okay?' she asked.

He didn't answer, exactly. Instead, he bent down and gave her a searing kiss. One that drove Viv Ascot, and the whole of Italy, from her mind for long seconds after he'd left to go backstage.

Nico leaned forward from his seat behind them. 'Okay, you've got to come clean with us. What's going on with you two?'

Harry pulled the drummer back. 'Ignore him. He only wants to know because he's got fifty quid riding on it in a bet with Benji.'

'True,' Benji put in.

'What's between you two is between you two,' Harry finished as the audience applauded the previous award winner.

'I'll let you know when I figure out what that is,' Daisy whispered to herself, her fingers still against her lips.

When he kissed her like that she wondered. She'd not had many long-term relationships in her life, and none lasting longer than a year. But even then, no other relationship had ever felt so passionate, so involved, in so little time.

Except that was just lust, wasn't it? It didn't mean anything more than that they had chemistry. And she'd known that from the first kiss he'd given her, onstage in Philadelphia, and that had *definitely* been just for show. Chemistry didn't mean anything.

Turning her attention back to the stage, Daisy sat bolt upright. There, just to one side, stood Viv Ascot, dressed in a gorgeous burgundy gown and flanked by a stern-looking security guy. She was talking to one of the other presenters, thanking her probably, Daisy assumed. It would be rude to interrupt.

But then it was pretty rude to leave someone a crumbling building without a single word of explanation, and Daisy had never been particularly polite, anyway. She was almost to her feet and edging her way out of the row towards Viv, when suddenly there was huge applause, and she realised that Jay had come onto the stage. How would it look if his doting fiancée abruptly skedaddled just when he was presenting his award?

Torn, she hovered on the edge of her seat, trying to keep one eye on Viv and the other on the stage as the video link crackled to life and the perfect face of Milli Masters appeared on the screen.

'Hi there, Rome!' She waved, smiling wide enough to show off her perfect teeth, and Daisy tried not to hate her. She was the love of Jay's life.

Except she'd broken his heart. Maybe she was allowed to hate her a little bit.

'Great to see you, Milli,' Jay replied, obviously reading his lines from the autocue, since Daisy knew it wasn't actually great at all. 'And thanks for joining us all the way from LA.'

'Wouldn't miss it!' Milli replied, looking much happier about this whole arrangement than Jay was. Possibly because she was thousands of miles away.

Daisy tuned out for a second as she watched Viv embrace the woman she was talking to, then turn to leave. No! If she lost sight of her now she might never find her again in the crowd. Maybe if she just slipped out no one would notice...

Suddenly, a bright light zeroed in on her eyeballs. She blinked, made sure she hadn't been abducted by aliens in the middle of a music awards ceremony, then smiled as she realised it was just the spotlight from the stage. Shining on her. For some reason she'd apparently missed.

'Looks like they noticed the rock on your left hand,' Harry whispered to her, so she must have looked pretty lost, too.

'So I hear congratulations are in order,' Milli was saying, although she didn't sound particularly celebratory. In fact, her smile was growing stiffer as she made her way through her lines, obviously read off a screen beside the camera. 'I'm just thrilled that you've found someone else—to sing duets with, I mean, of course.'

Forced laughter burst from the crowd, awkward in the face of Milli's obviously unhappy delivery, and Daisy tried not to sink back into her chair and disappear. Oh, God, this was awful. Milli's expression was thunderous, metres high on the TV screen for all to see. And Jay's was even worse, somehow—just completely blank. As if he couldn't even react to what was happening.

He pulled an envelope from his pocket. 'And the nominees are…'

Daisy looked to the side. Viv was gone. She'd missed her chance.

This whole evening was a total disaster.

'Should have stayed home with Genevieve,' she muttered to herself as Harry patted her shoulder.

'Well, that was horrible,' Jay said the moment they were through their hotel-room door and alone again. Dropping onto the sofa in the centre of the suite's main room, he waited for Daisy to join him.

She didn't.

He opened his eyes to find her still standing by the door, her high heels dangling from her fingers and the hem of the gorgeous shimmery blue gown pooling around her bare feet. 'You okay?'

'Yeah.' Crossing to the bar area, she ditched her shoes on the floor and pulled out two glasses, then reached into the minibar. 'Drink?'

'Sure.' She poured two tiny bottles of liquor into the two glasses then handed him one. Jay didn't even ask what it was before downing it. 'I was ready for that.'

'It couldn't have been easy. Seeing Milli again.' Daisy perched on the armchair opposite him, even though there was plenty of space on the sofa.

Jay had to admit that didn't bode too well for his hopes of getting her in his bedroom tonight. Or his shower, for that matter.

No, apparently they had to have a discussion about his disaster of a love life instead. The perfect end to a horrible night.

'At least she was on the other side of an ocean,' he said with a shrug. 'Seeing her in person would be worse.'

'Because it hurts?'

'Because it makes me angrier.' Jumping to his feet, he headed to the minibar for a refill. This was clearly at least a two-drink conversation.

Daisy was blinking at him in astonishment when he turned around. 'You? Angry? I don't think I've ever seen that.'

He huffed a slight laugh. 'I don't suppose you have. I…used to have a temper, as a kid—ask Harry. But I worked hard to control it. It takes a lot to make me lose my temper these days.'

He didn't mention that just dating Milli had been a sore test of that resolve. Or the fact that he'd only taken charge of it after breaking his brother's nose during an argument.

'But you were angry tonight?' Daisy pulled her feet up onto the chair, so just her bare toes poked out from under the hem of her dress. In so many ways, she looked just as she did back at the villa, when it was just the two of them and the goat.

Maybe that was why he answered her honestly.

'Yeah. I was bloody angry.'

'Because they scripted those awful lines about you "duetting" with me?'

Jay pulled a face. 'No. I mean, they were dreadful, but that's just bad writing. I guess someone spotted the ring on our way in and they shoehorned them in. There was supposed to be about another screen and a half of that "banter" between us but I just skipped them. I didn't want you to have to sit there through that with the spotlight on you.'

'Thanks.' Her voice was quiet, no mocking, no sarcasm.

He didn't like it.

Putting his glass down on the coffee table, he knelt down on the floor in front of her chair, his hands either side of hers. 'I was angry because it was all so fake. Her and me smiling and joking with each other when I still just want to yell "why?" at her whenever I see her face. She just walked out, then told me she'd gone in a social-media video shared with several million of our biggest fans and the whole world's media. I never got the chance to ask her why, to have that big argument that ends a relationship.'

Because for her, it hadn't been a relationship. It had been a marketing strategy. But he couldn't admit that humiliation to Daisy—that he'd fallen in love, while she'd just been playing a part. Not tonight, anyway, not in this moment. But he realised to his surprise that he *did* want to tell her. To tell her everything, actually.

'The spotlight on me and the ring probably didn't help either, then,' Daisy said softly. 'I'm sorry about that. Maybe playing up to it all wasn't the best idea I've ever had.'

Jay shook his head. 'No, it was. I needed you there with me tonight.'

He looked up into her eyes and found an expression he'd not seen there before. He was used to seeing passion there now, wicked temptation. He'd seen humour and friendship and even blissful moments of creative synchronicity.

But tonight…was that pity? Or just concern?

Jay wasn't sure. But whatever it was, it drew him in.

'I'm glad I could help,' she said, voice quieter still.

He wanted to say more. There were questions he wanted to ask, things he wanted them to discuss, to clear up or decide between them. But right then he wanted something else more.

Rising up on his knees, Jay took her face between his hands and kissed her, gentle and long. And somehow, it felt completely different from every time he'd kissed her over the last few days.

It wasn't that the passion had changed—he could still feel it, simmering beneath the fancy clothes and the exhaustion. But for the first time, that wasn't all their kiss was about. He wasn't touching her to drag her back into bed, to find their mutual pleasure again.

He was kissing her because he was thankful she was in his life. Because she was the one thing that felt real in his crazy fake world right now.

Except, in reality, she was the fakest part of it.

He pulled back, his gaze drawn to the sparkle of her pretend engagement ring in the lamplight.

At least this time he knew that this wasn't real, however it felt in the moment.

At least discovering the truth couldn't tear his heart out again this time.

'Come to bed with me tonight?' he asked, his words barely a whisper, but she heard them.

'Yes,' she answered. And for a moment, Jay could almost believe he'd asked her another question altogether.

CHAPTER NINE

DAISY HAD NEVER been so grateful to see anywhere as her little cottage on the cliff.

'Genevieve!' she called out as she jumped out of the car. The little goat came trotting over from where she was eating a patch of prickly-looking plants.

Behind her, she saw Jay grabbing their bags and thanking the driver, but she just hugged her goat and gave thanks that she was home.

Home. That was what this place was. Which was crazy, since she'd spent less than two full weeks there in her whole life. But it was *hers* in a way that nowhere else in the world ever had been.

Maybe she didn't need to ask Viv why after all. All she'd really needed was to spend some time away from the place back in the real world, and she'd learned to appreciate the value it held. Far greater than a new job or a trip around the world, for her.

This place was her sanctuary. Her escape. And she had a feeling she was going to need it in the weeks and months to come.

She and Jay still hadn't talked about what was happening between them. After his confession about how he felt seeing Milli again, it just hadn't been the time. He'd said he was angry, but Daisy suspected that was just man-talk for upset and heartbroken.

He'd made love to her that night as if it was the last time, and she'd braced herself for him telling her this morning that he wasn't coming back with her. That he was heading to LA to talk to Milli properly at last.

But he hadn't.

Matteo and Lorenzo appeared from around the side of the villa and excitedly pointed out new improvements to them both, some that they'd finished before they'd left for Rome, but some that were utterly unexpected and new. Daisy suspected they must have had some help over the last couple of days to get it all done. Outside, the finished roof, the windows and the painted front door all finally looked like the photo the solicitor had shown her of the cottage in better days. And inside, all the stained and grubby walls had been painted a fresh, bright white. The floors and bathrooms had been cleaned, and even the dated furniture didn't look so awful against a nice backdrop.

'It's amazing. Thank you!' She threw her arms around each of the men in turn. 'How much do I owe you?'

'We've already been paid,' Matteo replied, looking at Jay. 'But if you need anything else doing, just call us.'

'How much do I owe *you*, then?' she asked, turning to Jay as the builders returned to packing up their stuff.

Jay shrugged. 'Call it a housewarming gift.'

'You can't just fix up my house as a gift.' Gifts were flowers from the service station, or knock-off perfume. And yeah, okay, Jay could afford many times the sort of gifts her old boyfriends used to give her. But this was her *house*. It was personal.

'You let me stay here.' Jay stepped closer, his hands at her waist, his forehead close to hers. 'You helped me find my music again. You got me drunk and made me relax. You gave me the most fun and passionate three days of my entire life. And then you put on a stupid ring you hate and pretended to be in love with me so that I wouldn't be humiliated in front of my ex and the whole world in Rome. I think I can pay for some roof tiles.'

'Well, when you put it like that…' She kissed him. 'Thank you.'

'Thank *you*. I honestly don't know how I'd have made it through last night without you.'

He'd already made his thank-yous for that in bed the night before, as far as Daisy was concerned. And now it was over, she didn't want to dwell on it.

Especially because it made her start thinking about how heavy the ring on her left hand felt—more from the lies than the diamond.

They dumped their bags and wandered down the hill into the village for lunch, pulling up chairs at the café Daisy had discovered on their first day and ordering crispy, thin pizzas loaded with fresh vegetables and deli meat.

'You realise at some point we're going to have to fake break up.' Daisy bit into her pizza and moaned at how good it tasted. Swallowing, she carried on. 'I mean, unless you want to actually fake marry me and fake divorce me later.'

Actually, that didn't sound so terrible. They could just keep hanging out, writing songs, having sex and laughing together until one of them met someone they *actually* loved—that would be Jay, she was certain—and decided it was time to move on.

Okay, *then* it would probably suck a lot. Because she'd have grown used to having him around by then. To the life they had together.

'You'd have to give me a damn good divorce settlement, though,' she said, because she couldn't say, 'I'll miss you when this is over.' That wasn't the deal they'd struck.

Jay pulled a face. 'Maybe you'd have to give *me* one. You might be the one who becomes an amazingly huge star and decides I'm not big enough for you any more.'

There was something in his voice. A hint of bitterness, maybe.

'Is that what you think happened with Milli?'

He shrugged and stared down at his pizza. 'How would I know? She never talked to me directly, remember? But from what I learned later…' He paused, as if saying the words was the hardest thing he'd ever do. 'Yes. She left me when I couldn't do anything more to add to her reputation or celebrity. Because while I thought we were in love, for her it was publicity, like it is with you and me. Only difference is, we both know what the score is this time.'

Daisy's heart hurt for him. He'd been in love and Milli had been faking it all along. God, that had to screw a person up, right?

'We definitely do.' Daisy forced herself not to look at his engagement ring on her finger. Not to imagine for even one second that this relationship was something other than it was.

Even though she was afraid she was starting to want it to be, with every moment they spent together.

Which was why she had to focus on how this was all going to end. She didn't want to end up broken as Jay had been by Milli. She didn't even have the excuse of not knowing that it was all for show from the outset.

'You know, my mum would be completely baffled by this conversation,' Jay said, a fond smile on his face.

'You said once that she didn't understand all this fake relationship stuff? I mean, if anyone actually does.'

'Yeah. She and my dad…they were the real thing. So in love they could never even look at another person.' A shadow fell across his face for a second. 'Until he died.'

'I'm sorry,' Daisy blurted automatically.

Jay shook his head. 'It was a long time ago now, when I was a teenager. Afterwards… I threw myself into music as a sort of coping mechanism, you know?'

'I know,' Daisy said, with feeling. 'When I was younger, growing up in Liverpool, music was my only escape. Practising, getting better, it was a distraction from everything that was awful at home or at school. And I knew, even then, that it was going to be my way out—the one thing that would help me escape the place I grew up and the family that didn't want me. The same way my mum did.'

She pulled back as Jay reached out to take her hand. She hadn't meant to say so much—far more than she'd shared with anyone else since she'd left Liverpool.

'Your mum was a musician?' Jay asked softly.

'A wannabe one,' Daisy said with a shrug. 'She left when I was six to chase fame. But since nobody has ever heard of her since, I'm guessing it didn't go so well. She left me her mandolin, though, so I guess I have her to thank for my career.'

Jay's gaze was soft, sympathetic, but he didn't push her any more on the subject. He had to know her well enough to understand that she'd already said far more than she was really comfortable with.

'My dad taught Harry and me to play guitar. That's why we started the band together, after he died. Sort of in his memory.'

'I bet he'd have loved that. I'm sure your mum did too.'

'Yeah.' His smile faltered a little. 'It kept him alive for us all, I guess. Mum…she's always said that there's only one true love for a person—a soul mate. Dad was hers. She was only in her forties when he died, but she's never even gone on a date since.'

Daisy tried to imagine a love that deep and couldn't. She'd never seen it. But Jay obviously had. No wonder discovering that Milli was faking it had hurt him so badly—he'd been expecting the real thing, like his parents had.

She wanted to say something sympathetic. Something to show she understood him, felt for him, wanted to be there for him.

But she was still Daisy Mulligan, however much he was messing with her emotions. So instead she said, 'Huh. Given how much sex *you've* had since the love of your life walked out, I'm guessing this is one of those things that's different for guys?'

That surprised a laugh from him, at least. 'Only with you,' he said.

His words caught her in the chest, and she fought

to keep her light-hearted, careless composure. 'Okay, then, back to the point at hand. How are we going to do it?' she carried on, forcing a smile. 'Break up, I mean. Milli already stole "dumping you on social media," so we need something new, right? Do you want to dump me this time? Or shall I catch you with another woman? Or hire a skywriter?'

Finally, Jay laughed at her last suggestion. 'This is clearly going to take some thought,' he said. 'I think we'll need to order pudding, too. I bet this place does a great tiramisu.'

'Works for me,' Daisy said, with a smile she couldn't quite feel.

If all she could have with Jay was a few months of a fake relationship, at least she could make sure they both had as much fun with it as possible.

Lunch lingered long into the afternoon, with liqueur coffees to follow the pudding, and their break-up suggestions becoming more outrageous by the minute. By the time they staggered back up the hill to the villa, arms around each other and pausing to kiss at regular intervals, they'd reached 'fighting over custody of Genevieve' in their break-up plans and scripted some hilarious pleas to 'think of the goat!' for the other band members to put out on social media.

Jay couldn't imagine ever laughing so much with Milli, even if he *had* known what the deal was between them.

He swung Daisy around by her hand until she toppled into his arms, and held her close. 'We don't have to do any of this yet though, right? The breaking up, I mean?'

She smiled up at him, but there was something brittle behind that smile. Something at odds with her words. 'Of course not. Not while we're still having fun.'

He bent his head so his lips grazed hers. 'I'm still having a lot of fun.'

'So am I,' she murmured back. 'Want to go have more fun back at the cottage?'

'Definitely.' They raced the rest of the way along the cliff hand in hand, and Jay felt his heart and his spirits rising and rising—

Until he saw the car parked outside Daisy's cottage.

Daisy skidded to a halt beside him. 'Is that—?' She broke off, as Kevin stepped out of the car, raising his sunglasses to look at the building.

'Nice place.' Kevin turned to them and lowered his sunglasses again. 'We thought we'd stop by and hear what you guys have been working on.'

Which, of course, was when the car doors opened and the rest of the band tumbled out.

'Do we even have enough bedrooms for them all?' Daisy hissed to Jay after she dragged him into the bathroom, while outside the locked door Kevin, Harry, Nico and Benji made themselves at home in her cottage's living area.

'As long as I share with you we have,' Jay said. 'And I think I saw some more bed linen in one of the cupboards. Food, however...'

She pulled a face. 'We'll have to go shopping again. Did they tell you they were coming?'

'Not a hint.' And he intended to have very strong words with his brother about that shortly.

'They want to hear the songs we've been working on.' Daisy chewed her lip nervously, and Jay fought not to kiss away her concerns. 'Except we've not exactly been working hard the whole time...'

'I think we worked damn hard, thank you.' He pulled her into his arms again and wished, with all his heart, that it were just the two of them again. And Genevieve, of course. 'Just not on the music.'

'Which is the part they've come to hear. Keep up.'

He kissed her, just because he could. 'Stop worrying. We have two songs.'

'One we hate.'

'And one that will knock their socks off. And that will buy us enough leeway with them to get us time to write the rest.'

She still looked uncertain, but she nodded, all the same. 'Fine. But I'm not playing hostess or anything. Nobody in there actually believes I'm your doting fiancée. They're *your* band, you look after them.'

'Noted. But if you go pour them all drinks, I'll make up the beds for everyone.'

'Done.' She pressed a swift kiss to his cheek. 'But I'm hiding the limoncello in our bedroom.'

'Good plan.'

He gave her a moment to escape to the drinks cabinet they'd stocked up over the last couple of weeks, then slipped out to find the bed linen.

But Harry was waiting for him in what used to be his bedroom.

'Kevin wanted to come on his own, but I thought you might need backup,' he said, before Jay could ask. 'Also, I have questions. Well, one question.'

Jay shook out a pillowcase. 'Which is?'

'What the hell are you doing?'

'Making up the beds.'

'That's not what I meant.'

'I know.' Jay sighed. Of all of the band, his family and friends, Harry knew most how badly he'd been broken by Milli, and the method of her departure. But he'd never told Harry the worst of it. That it wasn't the public humiliation—well, it wasn't *just* that. It was that the love he'd imagined, the future he'd believed in… none of it had even been real to begin with.

But Harry…he wasn't just his friend or his band mate. He was his brother. And he worried, Jay knew, the same way he worried about Harry.

'Look, it's okay. With Milli… I thought I was in love. I thought I knew what I was doing. But it turned out that it was all just a publicity stunt to her. That our relationship meant nothing more than the next headline.'

Harry winced. 'I… I wondered. Because of the way she ended it. And that weird thank-you message from her publicist afterwards.'

'Yeah. That was the real giveaway.'

Jay—thanks for the memories—and the headlines! Milli

If he hadn't already suspected the truth, that would have sealed it.

'On the plus side, at least you can tell Mum that Milli definitely *wasn't* your one true love?' Harry suggested.

Jay chuckled. 'Yeah. I can definitely do that. I mean, how could I be in love with someone who didn't even really exist? Milli, she was just a character, a facade. I see that now.' Because Daisy, even when she was faking being in love with him, was anything but. She was *real*. Even if the game they were playing with the media wasn't.

'So you're not mooning over Milli any more,' Harry concluded. 'That's good. I just don't want to see you getting hurt again.'

Jay shook his head. 'It's different with Daisy…it's not like with Milli. This time, we *both* know what we're doing—we're playing a part, acting at being in love for our fans because it sells records. Nobody is going to get hurt this time.' It was probably a bad thing that he didn't even sound convincing to his own ears.

Because he knew, already, that it would be all too easy to get used to having Daisy around. Spending time with her. Listening to her laugh. Making love to her at night and waking up to her in the mornings.

Daisy was prickly and sarcastic and short-tempered and basically the opposite of the easy-going, relaxed life and personality he'd worked hard to develop for himself. And she was definitely the polar opposite of Milli's sugary sweetness.

He liked all that about her. He liked most things about her.

That was the problem.

'We were just talking today about how we're going to stage our break-up,' Jay went on, not entirely sure if he was trying to convince Harry or himself.

'Why?'

'Because it was funny?' It had been, somehow. Hilarious even, at the time. But thinking about it now gave him chills.

'I mean, why are you planning on breaking up? Did you check your social-media notifications today?' Jay shook his head, and Harry pulled out his phone. 'Then you might not have seen this.'

Holding up the screen so Jay could see it clearly, Harry gave him a knowing look. Jay ignored him and focussed on the photo on the phone.

It was him and Daisy in Rome, of course. But not any of the staged photo opportunities they'd manufactured that night at the awards ceremony. It wasn't a shot of them on the red carpet, or his kissing her ostentatiously in front of the cameras. It was the smaller, quieter moment after it was all over, when she'd taken him aside to check he was okay after Milli, and then told him about seeing Viv and not being able to talk to her.

In the shot, their heads were bent close together, and he had one hand at her waist, while she pressed her palm against his cheek. She looked about to reach up and kiss him—and from his memory, she had.

But most of all, they looked like a couple. A real couple.

A couple in love.

He pushed the phone away. 'Apparently we both have a future in the movies if we want it. Now, if you'll excuse me, I have to make up the beds for our impromptu guests.'

He couldn't start believing there was anything more to this relationship than a good publicity opportunity. Jay didn't want to dwell on possibilities that could only break his heart again. Not when he was only just recovering from the last time.

Harry would have to understand that.

Daisy had been looking forward to waking up to the silence of the villa on the cliff top again, after the busyness of Rome. But instead, she woke the next morning to a headache, an empty bed, and someone shouting about a goat.

'Calm down, Nico,' she heard Jay saying, out in the hallway. 'It's only Genevieve.'

She grinned to herself. At least her gatecrashing guests weren't getting everything their own way. Genevieve was clearly staking her claim to the place, too.

Snuggling back down under the duvet, Daisy grabbed her phone from the nightstand. Jay would probably see the goat back outside, then hopefully come back to bed again. Maybe she'd pretend to be asleep, so he could wake her up properly…

But while she waited, she might as well check in on her notifications.

She scrolled straight past too many reposts of yesterday's star photo—the one of her and Jay in Rome looking a little too loved up for her comfort—to see if there was anything new to report. And stopped as soon as she saw Milli Masters' sugary-sweet smile in her feed.

Why was Milli talking about her?

Apprehension pressing on her chest, she clicked the link.

Jay and Daisy love-fest a fake, claims ex.

Milli says, 'Jay and I are soul mates, even if we can't be together right now.'

Oh, hell.

A message notification pinged—Aubrey.

Anything you want to tell us?

The message was linked to the photo of Daisy and Jay.

She sent one back.

It's a long story. Can I fill you in later? I kind of need to talk to Jay right now.

Aubrey sent back a reply immediately.

I bet you do. And don't worry—looks like Jessica has a 'long story' for us too. I just hope my summer adventures are half as exciting as you two have been having!

Daisy pulled a face at the phone screen. She wasn't sure she'd class this as 'exciting'. More probably a terrible mistake.

She clicked back to the story about Milli. It didn't get any better on full reading.

Anger surged up inside her. This woman had led Jay on, dumped him on social media, broken his heart—and now she had the audacity to come trampling over their relationship? Yes, technically she was right—it *was* fake. But what if it weren't? What if Jay really had

found happiness again? Then she'd be purposely trying to ruin it.

Witch.

Had he seen it yet? Was that why he'd already been
out of bed when Nico started yelling about Genevieve?

Suddenly, Daisy's lazy morning in bed wasn't looking so likely.

The bedroom door opened and Jay slipped in.

'You look tired,' she blurted without thinking.

'Just what every guy wants to hear.' He ran a hand
through his hair. 'I couldn't sleep last night. I was thinking about—'

'Milli,' she finished for him.

He gave her a curious look. 'That third song we
couldn't get right, actually. I think I've got an idea that
might fix it.'

He was focussing on the music. That was a good
thing. She should encourage that. 'Want me to grab my
guitar? We might have to work on it in here though, if
we want anything approaching privacy.'

'Good idea. I gave Harry a shopping list and encour-
aged him to take the others down to the village with
him when he went foraging, by the way.'

'An even better idea. Wait here.'

Daisy crept out into the living area, hanging back
until she heard the front door close behind Harry and
the others, grabbed her guitar and ran back to the bedroom. Maybe they didn't *have* to hide in there with the
others gone, but she liked the more intimate vibe it gave
their work. Plus it meant they wouldn't be interrupted
when the others returned.

'Okay.' Settling cross-legged on the bed, she pulled

her guitar into her lap and tightened up the tuning. 'Tell me what you were thinking.'

This part was so easy, she realised as he started talking—a flow of thoughts on the tone of the song, the way the words and harmonies twined around each other. Here, in the music, was where they understood each other best. Music and sex, that was what they had.

And as she listened to him, as he took her guitar from her hands and played her what he meant, then handed it back so she could repeat it back, with her own flair and additions, she wished they could stay in this bubble for ever.

Just the two of them, the music, and the goat. Here in the middle of nowhere, forgetting about the rest of the world.

Time passed differently when they were lost in the music; Daisy had noticed that before. Still, when the knock on the door came, she was startled out of her concentration.

'Must be Harry back with the shopping,' she said, stretching her arms over her head to work out the kinks in her back—and enjoying the way Jay's gaze hovered around her breasts as she did so. 'How long do you think it'll take them to realise that the door's not locked?'

'If the damn goat can get in here unaided, I'm sure my brother can manage it,' Jay answered, still watching her stretch. 'Do you think this one is ready for Kevin yet?'

Daisy waggled her head from side to side. 'Maybe. It's definitely miles better than it was last week. I can't help but think it's still missing something, though. A last stanza, maybe. It feels…unbalanced.'

Jay shrugged. 'It'll come.'

There was more hammering on the door, and Daisy rolled her eyes before sliding off the bed and heading for the door. 'Harry, you're officially dumber than a goat,' she yelled as she made her way through the living room. At least living in the middle of nowhere meant she didn't have to worry about answering the door in the boy shorts she slept in and Jay's T-shirt she'd pulled on after rolling out of bed. The boys had all seen her in worse on the tour bus; privacy wasn't really a thing for them on tour, and they'd just included her as one of the boys from the start.

'You'd better have brought my limoncello,' she griped as she opened the door—

And stopped.

Because Harry wasn't there. Nor was Kevin or Nico or Benji or even Matteo or Lorenzo or Geraldine.

Standing on her doorstep, one perfectly manicured hand raised to knock again, was Milli Masters.

With half the world's media waiting behind her.

CHAPTER TEN

'JAY! IT'S FOR YOU!'

It was the strain in Daisy's voice that made him jump from the bed and race through the cottage. But even then, he didn't expect to see his ex-girlfriend standing in the Italian sunshine on the cliff top outside Daisy's home.

Daisy stood aside the moment he arrived on the scene. 'This is way above my pay grade,' she muttered as she brushed past him, back to her bedroom.

Their bedroom.

He heard her shut the door behind her, and a horrible sense of foreboding flooded through him as he realised it might not be *their* bedroom any more. This whole charade might be about to crash to a close.

And he couldn't do anything about it, because he had to deal with Milli and her media circus.

'What are you doing here?' he asked in a sharp whisper as he angled himself out of the front door and shut it behind him. He wasn't inviting Milli inside. This was Daisy's place—their place, even—and Milli had no right to be there. Kevin and Harry and the others were one thing, as was Genevieve. But Milli was definitely less welcome than even the bloody goat.

Milli's large grey eyes widened innocently. He didn't believe a millimetre of it. Whatever had brought her here, he knew for a fact that she'd have a plan.

'Aren't you pleased to see me? I just flew in from LA. After I saw you onstage in Rome… I just *had* to come, Jay. You can see that, can't you?'

Was she really talking to him, or to the reporters behind her? Because while he'd kept his voice low, Milli was projecting to the seagulls on the roof.

'No, I can't see that. So I'll ask you again. What, *exactly*, are you doing here, in Italy, and my fiancée's house?' It was amazing how easily that flowed from his mouth. Fiancée. Daisy. Strange how right it felt, when he knew full well it was a lie.

Milli didn't look convinced, though. Some of the studied innocence fell away as her expression hardened, and she dropped her voice a little. 'Oh, come on, Jay. Nobody *really* believes you're going to marry that groupie of yours.'

'Daisy is *not* a groupie.' Was he snarling? He might actually be snarling. God, the media must be loving this.

Time to pull it back. What would that media-training woman Kevin sent him to see say? What about the counsellor after he broke Harry's nose as a kid? Probably both the same thing.

Deep breaths. Only you are in control of your body, your emotions. Don't give that power away.

He knew this. He'd worked hard at this.

Stare between her eyebrows so you're not looking her in the eye but it looks *as if you are. Smile, even if you don't want to. Keep your voice even. Don't let her know that she's getting to you.*

That was all media training. How to fake being a celebrity, rather than a human being with feelings. That was what he was now, right? It was what Milli had wanted him to be, what Daisy wanted. What his fans wanted, even.

It went with the job.

He still wasn't inviting Milli inside, though. And actually, he kind of thought she didn't want to go in, anyway. How would the press report on her every anguished facial expression if they couldn't see her?

Right now, she shot him a warning look, then settled her expression back into earnest innocence. Her words, however, muttered too low for anyone else to hear, were anything but.

'Come on, Jay, you know the game. We've had the dramatic break-up, now it's time for the reconciliation. It'll hit all the papers, boost record sales for the quarter, get us plenty of free publicity. We can probably start looking at rings and wedding venues if that's what you really want—I agree, it's definitely an attention winner, and if we go the "conscious-uncoupling" route in a few years we can probably both retain our images through the divorce.'

'You dumped me. On social media.' His insides felt as if they were falling through the porch steps. He'd known—he'd *known* that this was all just part of the show for her. But she'd never admitted it so clearly before. All those months wasted, thinking he actually mattered to her as more than a publicity prop.

Not a mistake he ever intended to make again.

Milli rolled her eyes. 'Because it was *time*. People don't stay interested in happy couples. They want the drama, the *will they-won't they*. So I gave them that. I didn't expect you to run off and start another fake relationship with the first girl who crossed your path—let alone take her rock shopping. Kevin must have been really worried about your tour figures to push you into that.'

Jay ignored the part about Kevin. 'I thought you were gone. For good.' He didn't bother arguing against the 'fake relationship' accusation. She was right. And, even if she wasn't, she'd never believe it anyway.

'That's because you never paid any attention to everything I was doing to build our profile as a celebrity couple!'

'Because I thought we were an *actual* couple! In love!' Shame burned through him as he admitted it. How much he'd fallen for her charms, for what he'd believed they could have together. He'd thought they'd be like his parents, still in love after forty years of marriage.

How wrong could he have been?

The look Milli gave him was almost pitying.

'Come on, Jay. Really? I knew you were naive, but not even you could have believed that.'

He didn't answer. What else was there to say?

Over her shoulder, he spotted a small commotion at the back of the press pack—Harry, Kevin and the others returning from their jaunt into town. Excellent. Just what this situation needed—more people who thought they had a say in his romantic life.

Where was Daisy? He wanted her beside him, to show Milli how little he needed her now. How he'd found something better—more meaningful, more intense. He and Daisy were friends, they laughed together, they made music together.

But she wasn't there, of course. Because everything he had with her was just as fake as what he'd had with Milli. The only difference was that Daisy had been up-front about that from the start.

Milli glanced back over her shoulder too. He wondered if she saw the thunderous expression on Harry's face. Maybe *that* was why she said what she did next.

'Jay, there's only one reason I've come to Italy.'

Her voice carried out over the cliffs. He wondered if Daisy could hear it inside. If she couldn't, he was sure the video would be on social media for her to watch within moments.

'To win you back. We're soul mates, you and I. And I can't lose you to someone unworthy of your love. Come back to me, my love. We're endgame. Meant to be. And I'm not leaving Italy until you admit it. You know how to find me when you're ready.'

Then, with a swift kiss to his lips, she descended the steps like a princess, climbed back into the car that had brought her, and was driven away down the hill, followed by the scrambling media as they tried to keep up and file copy at the same time.

Leaving just his manager, his brother and his band mates staring at him.

And Jay with no idea what to do next.

Daisy heard the front door open again and people talking over each other as they came inside her house. Her home.

She couldn't hear Milli's voice amongst them, thankfully, but from what she'd been able to overhear through her open window, the pop star had left the ball thoroughly in Jay's court.

She wanted him back. Of course she did. Daisy knew the type perfectly—never more interested in a guy than when someone else had him. Jay had been getting more publicity over his fake romance with Daisy than he had for months before his break-up with Milli. Of course Milli wanted in on that.

And Jay, bless him, would fall for it too. Because he loved her, even though he knew she only loved his fame. More evidence, if Daisy needed it, that love was a ridiculous, hurtful thing.

There's always a price. Would Jay pay it?

There was a soft knock on her door. 'Daisy? Kevin wants us all out here, if that's okay.' Harry's voice, not Jay's, apologetic but firm. Daisy knew it didn't matter if it was 'okay' or not, whatever Harry said. This was part of the job.

Her *heart* was part of the job, now.

She dragged herself off the bed and into the living room, where the others were all ranged around the chairs and perched on the coffee table. She leant against the door frame, outside the group—she wasn't a band member, she wasn't management, and she definitely wasn't actually Jay's fiancée. She had no place here, for all that it was her house.

Jay sat in the armchair, hands folded in his lap, his head bent as he stared at the floor. Daisy willed him to look up, to meet her gaze, to show her what he was feeling, but he didn't.

Kevin was holding court, pacing in front of the window. 'This is actually great news! I mean, Daisy, you've been a real sport and all, but now we can call an end to this fake engagement thing and Jay can get back with Milli! She's a bigger star anyway—no offence, Daisy,' he added, with a brief glance in her direction.

'It's the best of both worlds, mate,' Nico agreed. 'We all still get to tour with Daisy, and you get to sleep with Milli Masters. Living the dream, Jay.' He held one hand up for a high five, which Jay ignored, so he turned to Benji to get one instead.

'Sounds more like a nightmare to me,' Harry objected quietly. 'Jay, you can't let her get to you again. Not when you have the chance at something more. *Think* about this, please. Think about Mum—and Dad. I know you. You've always wanted what they had together. The real thing. You'll never be happy in a fake relationship.'

But Jay stayed silent. Daisy tried to read his face, what little of it she could see from the shadows of the angle he sat at, but there was nothing there. He'd closed off again, completely, the way he'd been when Milli first left.

Harry was right, Daisy knew. Jay wouldn't be happy with Milli, not for ever. He wanted what his parents had, and that wasn't on offer there. But she knew from watching her friends settle for less than their dreams, all because of love, that there was no telling a person in love anything logical. They just couldn't hear it. They had to discover it on their own, as her mother had— eventually, and probably too late.

Kevin obviously took Jay's silence as agreement with his plan. Had Jay ever argued back with him? she wondered. Or was he so focussed on staying calm and being Zen that he forgot to even fight for what mattered to him?

He sure as hell wasn't going to fight for her, she could see that.

'Okay, so what we need to do now is figure out the best way to break you two up—what line to take, so Jay can go back to Milli without there being any backlash,' Kevin said.

'Heaven forbid we fight over custody of the goat,' she murmured—and Jay looked up for the first time and met her gaze.

She wished she could read what was going on behind those troubled green eyes of his, but she couldn't. She had no idea what he was thinking at all.

She just knew that suddenly all the things they'd been joking about yesterday—elaborate break-up schemes, who got Genevieve in the separation—none of them seemed the slightest bit funny any more.

'Stop,' Jay said, from nowhere, still staring at her. 'I need to talk to Daisy.'

She blinked, but nodded, and took his hand as he stood and led her, not to the bedroom as she'd expected, but straight out the front door to the cliff edge where they'd sat and talked music. Where she'd told him she didn't want him to propose to her.

How much had changed since then.

'What do I do, Daze?' he asked, raking his fingers through his hair as he looked at her. 'Tell me what I should do.'

Don't go back to her. Marry me instead.

The thought bubbled up in her totally unbidden, and

she only just caught the words before they flew out of her mouth.

That was crazy thinking. She couldn't—wouldn't—marry Jay. They had a fake relationship, that was all. They weren't in love with each other or anything stupid like that.

Except…except her heart hurt to think of him leaving. Every muscle in her body wanted to grab him and make him stay here, at the cottage with her and Genevieve, for ever. She wanted to wake up to him in the mornings, make love to him before she fell asleep. She wanted to laugh at ridiculous jokes with him and write countless songs with him and go out for pizza and coffee and laugh at his attempts at Italian.

She wanted him. For her own.

For ever.

Oh, God, she was in love with Jay Barwell. How *stupid* could she get?

She'd let a fake romance feel real, and now look where she was. About to get her heart broken, just as she'd sworn she never would again.

She knew what love did to people. It made them give up their dreams. Would her mum have been a success if she hadn't married her father? Daisy couldn't know for sure.

But she knew that Jay wanted forever and everything, the way his parents had loved. And she wasn't that, for him. She was a pretend fiancée to boost ticket sales.

Which was why she couldn't let him know how she felt. They had passion and they had friendship, but he'd never even hinted at anything more between them. If she wanted to keep at least the friendship, and the music, and her career, and her heart vaguely intact, then she had to make sure Jay never knew how she felt.

Swallowing hard, Daisy put on her best mask, and prepared to lie.

'Kevin's right,' Daisy said. 'Milli would be better for your career than me. You should get back together with her. I mean, you know we'll come up with a great break-up, right?'

The words hit him harder than he'd expected. There were no surprises in them, nothing he didn't already know. They'd been joking about their break-up plan just yesterday, after all.

But somehow, it hadn't felt really real then.

It did now. And somehow it hurt, far, far more than he'd thought it would.

'You...you want me to get back together with Milli?' He had to be sure.

Daisy gave a nonchalant shrug. 'Sure. I mean, if it keeps the label happy. One fake relationship is much like another, right?'

But they weren't, he realised. Not at all.

He'd assumed the difference between his two relationships was that he'd believed in true love with Milli but known the score with Daisy from the start. He'd thought it was more fun, more real with Daisy because he *knew* it wasn't.

But that wasn't it at all.

His fake relationship with Daisy felt more real than anything before in his life. Because it was *Daisy*.

Because she felt music the way he felt music. Because his skin fizzled when she touched him, and because she came alive under his fingers too. Because when he made her laugh it felt like a victory, and when they laughed together it felt like *life*. Because kissing her was his new favourite hobby. Because when she thought he needed something, she stepped in and went the whole way—diamond, dress, heels and all.

Because she named the goat Genevieve, and worried about who would look after it while she was gone.

Because he didn't know her whole story yet, and he wanted to. He wanted to know her, understand her, more than anyone else on the planet.

Because he wanted to be part of her story for the rest of his life.

Oh, hell.

Because he was in love with her. In a way that he'd never felt before, even with Milli.

He didn't want Milli back. He never had.

He didn't want another fake relationship. He wanted the real thing.

With Daisy.

Except she was standing there telling him to go back to Milli because one fake relationship was just like another.

'Is everything between us fake for you?' Jay asked, his head still spinning from his realisations.

Daisy gave him a sly smile. 'Is that a question about my bedroom satisfaction levels? Don't worry, Jay. I'm not going to go giving interviews casting shade on your manly prowess. You know that side of things wasn't fake at all. But that's just lust. Passion. Friends with benefits, right?'

'Friends with benefits.'

'Sure! Well, not now you're back together with Milli. But we'll still be friends—just like Nico said. It's the best of both worlds, right?'

'And you can give up what we had that easily?' Because he wasn't sure he could.

More than that, he knew for certain now that he didn't want to.

She shrugged again. 'We always knew it wasn't going to last for long, right? Once the new album came out, or the tours were over, we'd be going our separate ways anyway. This just brings it forward a bit.'

'I just…' He couldn't find the words.

'What? You thought I was just going to fall in love with you, like all those screaming fans?' She shot him an amused look, and Jay felt it stab his heart. 'Come on, Jay, you know me better than that.'

'I thought I did.' He'd thought he'd seen a new side to her, the last few weeks. A Daisy no one else got to see, or have, or hold.

But apparently that had all been fake too.

'I might be younger than you, but I think I learned the most important rule a lot sooner than you did,' she said contemplatively. 'Always know what the person you're with wants from you. Because they always want something. Kevin wants you to be a star—and make him a lot of money. Nico wants you to leave him enough of the groupies to keep him happy. Harry, bless him, just wants you to be happy—but he's better than most people.'

'And you? What do you want from me?'

'I wanted to escape the tour and write some songs,

and pretending to date you let me do that,' she said simply. 'And you wanted me to hang on your arm to show Milli you'd moved on, even when you hadn't.'

'That was then,' Jay pressed. 'That was before…everything that's happened between us. I'm asking you, what do you want from me now?'

Daisy shook her head. 'We agreed upfront what we both wanted, Jay. There's no point trying to change it now, just because we had sex and you're feeling sentimental about it.'

How could she feel so little, when he felt so much?

But then, it had been exactly the same with Milli, hadn't it? He'd been struck down by her leaving, and she'd just been playing a game.

He'd fallen for it again, when he'd sworn to himself that he wouldn't. He'd thought he was too wise, too cynical to the way this industry worked to be fooled again. But he was the same idiot who'd thought he was in love with Milli Masters.

Except this time it was Daisy, and he knew that was going to hurt a thousand times more.

'You're right.' The words didn't even feel like his. He couldn't believe he was saying them.

'I am?' Daisy asked, eyebrow raised. 'I mean, I usually am, but about what in particular?'

'One fake relationship is as good as another. And if I have to pick I might as well go with the one that's best for my career, right?' Swallowing, he drank in the sight of her one last time, here, in this place that had meant so much to them.

'Right. Of course.' Daisy shrugged. 'Makes sense.'

'I'll get the guys to get their stuff together, we'll head

to wherever Milli's staying so I can talk with her. Then I guess we'll see you back on tour.'

'Great. I'll see you there.'

He wanted to kiss her. Or shake her. Or fall to his knees and beg her to think about this. To open her heart to the possibility of more.

But he didn't.

He turned around, walked back into the house, and consigned Daisy Mulligan to the graveyard of his heart.

CHAPTER ELEVEN

DAISY COULDN'T BEAR to be there when they left, so she walked down the hill into the village, glad she'd changed out of Jay's shirt and her shorts while Milli had made her impassioned plea for his heart. Not only was it not suitable attire for going out in public, but it smelled of him. Warm and comforting and safe.

She couldn't be smelling his clothes for comfort when she'd just walked out of his life. Or, not, because she had to face him on tour again in a week's time. And before then, she had to get him comprehensively out of her system.

So, first rule: no smelling his clothes. If he even left any behind.

God, she hoped he didn't find that T-shirt of his she'd hidden under her pillow. Not that she was going to smell it, because that was breaking the rules and—

She sobbed, stopped walking, and sat down on the grass at the side of the road.

Okay. So it was possible she'd just made the biggest mistake of her life. But she'd done it to protect herself, the same as always. She was keeping her eye on the prize—chasing her dreams.

Except what was that dream worth without someone to share it with?

Pulling her phone from her pocket, she sent a group message to Aubrey and Jessica.

So, I might have done a stupid thing.

Aubrey responded almost instantly.

You? I don't believe it! Teasing! What's happened? Is it something to do with you getting engaged to Jay Barwell…?

It took surprisingly little time for Daisy to recount everything that had happened over the last couple of weeks to her friend, and by then Jessica had also jumped on the group chat.

Hmm… Are you sure he doesn't feel the same way about you?

Aubrey answered that.

Of course she's not sure! Because she never let on that she loved him! So how could he know?

Jessica came back:

Well, then. Maybe she should tell him.

Daisy shuddered at the thought of putting herself in

that position—of opening her heart to Jay only to let him tear it apart.

If he felt the same he would have said, wouldn't he? I mean, he had the chance, when I told him that we'd agreed to a fake relationship. He could have said if he wanted something more, and he didn't.

Aubrey: But neither did you. And you obviously do.

Jessica: Aubrey's right.

Aubrey: I love it when you say that!

Jessica: He might be scared, like you.

Daisy: He's been voted world's sexiest man. Three times. How scared can he be?

Aubrey: That's not the same as love, and you know it.

Jessica: Plus his ex dumped him on social media before she came grovelling back. Trust might be an issue.

Daisy thought of Jay the night after the awards ceremony in Rome, telling her how he just wanted to demand Milli explain *why* she'd done it. She knew that feeling of not understanding something that had turned her life upside down.

She'd never been able to ask her mother why she'd left, either. Nothing beyond her parting words about chasing her dreams.

She didn't even know if she'd ever found them.

That kind of uncertainty…yeah. That had an effect on a person.

But even if he did have non-fake feelings for me, he loved Milli. Of course he's going back to her if there's a chance of them being happy together.

Even though she was pretty certain it would only end the same way again.

Aubrey replied.

Then why did he ask you what to do?

Daisy bit her lip. As ever, her friend had a point. She'd been so busy protecting her own heart she hadn't even thought about his.

What if he'd wanted her to say, *Don't go back to Milli*?

She frowned. No. She wasn't going to blame herself for this. If he wanted her he could have said as much too.

But if neither of them had the courage to try…

Jessica replied.

I guess the biggest question you have to ask yourself is…if you weren't afraid of anything, what would you want to do right now?

She didn't even have to think before answering.

I'd run back up the hill to the villa, to my home, and ask Jay to stay there with me. For real this time, not fake.

Then that's what you need to do. Run, girl! Or, trust me, you'll always regret it.

Could she?

Daisy shook her head. How could she not?

Jumping to her feet, she ran, only slowing as she crested the top of the hill and saw the driveway, empty except for a forlorn-looking Genevieve.

She didn't need to open the front door to know for sure; she could feel it already.

Jay had gone.

'You're being an idiot about this.' Harry, as ever, was perfectly happy being blunt about his brother's life choices, Jay realised.

'No. I'm focussing on what really matters. The band. The music,' he argued as he dumped his suitcase on yet another hotel bed. Just like all the other ones, except for one important fact. Somewhere in this hotel, according to Kevin's mysterious means of intelligence gathering, was Milli Masters. Probably the penthouse suite, if Jay had to guess.

He hated hotels, he'd decided. Even penthouse suites.

He missed the cottage already. He missed Daisy. He even missed the damn goat.

'I heard the song you and Daisy were working on when you played it for Kevin last night. She's better for the music than Milli could ever be.'

'I'm not disagreeing with you on that.' Jay pulled out a pair of tracksuit bottoms and searched for a T-shirt to wear with them. He was going to order room service, watch bad hotel TV, and slob about. That was his entire plan for the evening.

Milli and everything else could wait one more day. He couldn't take another emotional conversation today.

'Then why the hell are you running back to Milli Masters?' Harry grabbed the clothing from his hands to make Jay turn and look at him.

Jay wondered quite how stupid his brother thought he was. 'I didn't say I was going back to Milli.'

'That's what you told Daisy. And Kevin definitely thinks you are.'

'Firstly, you shouldn't be eavesdropping on my conversations. And secondly... Kevin believes what he wants to believe. But this time he's going to be disappointed. Now, can I have my clothes back, please?'

A calmness had settled over him as he'd walked away from Daisy. A certainty, one that made everything suddenly very simple.

He wasn't in love with Milli. Daisy wasn't in love with him.

And Jay didn't want a fake relationship with either of them.

He wanted the real thing. And if that meant waiting until his star had faded and no one was interested in dating him for his celebrity, that was fine by him.

Harry handed him his trousers. 'So...what are you doing?'

Jay changed out of the jeans he'd travelled in. 'I'm taking a leaf out of your book, Harry. I'm waiting for the real thing to come along. No more fake celebrity romances. The next time I get into a relationship it will be a real one. Now, where the hell are all my T-shirts?'

'You're waiting for a real relationship,' Harry said, disbelief colouring his voice.

'You don't think I can do it?'

'I think you're even more of an idiot than I thought.'

Jay stopped searching for a T-shirt and raised an eyebrow at his brother. 'Excuse me?'

'What do you think you had with Daisy?'

Everything I ever wanted.

Jay clenched his jaw and forced the thought aside. 'Exactly what we agreed we'd have. A fake relationship—fake engagement, even. And a friends-with-benefits arrangement. That's all.'

'Did she tell you that?'

'She didn't need to. It's what we agreed.' Except he couldn't remember actually agreeing to it. It just sort of happened. Like falling for her. He definitely hadn't planned to do that.

'She told you that,' Harry said smugly. 'Okay, Jay, think about what you know about Daisy.'

How she laughs. How she looks when she's sleeping. How she kisses. How she writes songs. How she feels in my arms...

'She's defensive, prickly, sarcastic and mocking is her favourite hobby,' he said instead.

'Exactly.' Harry beamed. 'Now, look at this.'

He pulled out his phone, but Jay pushed it away.

'I don't want to see any more photos of Daisy pretending she's in love with me for an audience.'

'That's not what this is,' Harry said. 'Just watch it. Please?'

Sighing, Jay took the phone and pressed play.

He recognised Daisy's cottage instantly, but not the

angle. In the video, Daisy was sitting cross-legged in the armchair, her guitar in her lap, laughing at something he'd said.

'Play it for me again,' he heard his own voice say, and saw himself appear on the screen, perching on the coffee table opposite her, his own guitar in his hands. 'I want to try something.'

Daisy nodded, then started to play.

It was the second song they'd written together. The one that had led to the almost kiss that had led to everything that came after.

The moment he'd realised that she might want him too.

'Where did you get this?' he asked, hoarsely.

'Daisy sent it to me. She said she always records song-writing sessions on her phone in case she forgets something later. I asked her if she had any footage of the songs you were working on together and she sent me this.'

'And when you're close, oh, how I feel you. Down deep inside my soul,' Daisy sang on the screen.

Jay pressed stop.

He couldn't hear that right now.

He handed Harry the phone back, and his brother took it reluctantly.

'I'm sending you the file,' he said, tapping the screen. 'Watch it to the end, will you? Then tell me if you honestly think you still have to wait for the real thing. Because I'm telling you, if I had someone who looked at me the way Daisy looks at you—or the way you look at her—I'd be shouting it from the rooftop.'

'You're wrong,' Jay said. But somewhere inside, part of him was wondering. Hoping.

'No,' Harry said. 'I'm not. Watch the video. I'm going to go tell Kevin to stop planning your grand reunion with Milli.'

She didn't want to leave.

Daisy looked around her cosy villa, no longer crumbling quite so much, but still in need of some redecoration and sprucing up. Maybe she could just stay here. Cancel the tour—or, better yet, Kevin could probably get Milli Masters to fill in for her. Jay would like that.

Except Milli would expect to headline, of course.

And she didn't want to think about Milli and Jay.

She'd known, when she'd ended things with him, that she'd have to be back on that tour bus with him within the week. But she'd hoped the few days apart would help her get over that crushing sense of loss that had hit her when she'd returned to the villa to discover it was just her and Genevieve now.

They hadn't.

Jessica and Aubrey had been great, messaging every day to check in with her, trying to keep her spirits up. They'd both also tried to talk to her about the conversations she needed to have with Jay when she saw him again, but she'd managed to shut them down. She wasn't ready to think about that just yet.

She knew what she needed to do to get through the first couple of weeks back on tour with the band—the same thing she'd been doing since long before she left home at sixteen. Toughen up and not let anyone see she cared.

If the guys realised how she felt about Jay it would be awkward. If Milli realised, it would be humiliating. And if the world knew…she'd be a laughing stock.

'It's not like I'm the first girl who had a guy not love her back,' she said to Genevieve. 'I'll survive.'

The only thing was, when she'd been with Jay, for the first time in so long it hadn't felt like surviving.

It had felt like really living.

On the counter, her phone flashed with an alert, and she picked it up to find a message from Aubrey.

Did you see this?

Frowning, she clicked the link. Milli Masters' perfect face filled the screen—except she didn't look *quite* so perfect for once. There were artfully placed tears in the corners of her eyes, but Daisy suspected that was a filter, because if anything her expression looked more annoyed than upset.

She turned up the volume to hear the words, and her breath caught in her throat.

'I mean, when it comes down to it, I'm just another heartbroken girl. I thought we were soul mates, but I guess sometimes true love just doesn't work out, right? But I wish Jay every happiness, and I'd hate for any of you to give him a hard time.'

Daisy scoffed at that. Knowing Milli's fans the hate mail was probably already in full swing.

But she'd worry about that later. Right now, she needed to understand what this meant.

'Does it mean he hasn't gone back to her after all?' she asked aloud.

Genevieve remained unhelpfully silent, busy chewing on the fringe of an old sofa cushion.

'Or does it mean...?'

'It means I'm in love with someone else. And I'm hoping she's in love with me too.'

Daisy spun around at the sound of Jay's voice, half expecting it to be her imagination tormenting her. But no, there he was, standing in the open doorway, the Italian sun streaming through his light hair, his hands in his pockets as he squinted at her.

'Are you wearing my T-shirt?'

'Are you really here?' she countered. She wasn't about to confess now that she'd been wearing one of the three T-shirts he'd managed to leave behind every day for the last week.

'Yeah. I figured I left some stuff behind here.'

'Like your T-shirts?'

'And my heart.'

'Oh.' Her own heart was hammering against her chest, a constant reminder that it was still inside her and beating and loving and that maybe she might consider just *listening* to it for once.

And for the first time since she couldn't remember when—Daisy decided to do just that.

This would be so much easier if she didn't look like a startled rabbit. An adorable startled rabbit wearing his T-shirt, but still. Her eyes—wide and confused—were giving nothing away. He'd been so sure—well, Harry had been sure enough for both of them—that if he came back then they could figure it all out. Even Kevin had thought it was a good idea—if only because, if Milli wasn't in Jay's future, he wanted to make sure that they at least had Daisy back on tour, along with the new songs they had written.

But now he was here, looking into those wide eyes, other than the relief of being with her again, Jay wasn't sure of anything at all.

No. That wasn't true. He was sure of one thing: he couldn't risk not trying.

He'd called his mum, in the end. Asked her to tell him all about his dad, about their relationship. How she knew it was the for ever kind of love.

'Honestly, Jay?' his mum had said. *'I'm not sure you can ever know for sure—maybe not until it's gone. But you can hope. You can take a chance and you can work for it, if she's worth it. Because if it is true love, then it'll all work out. If it doesn't it wasn't meant to be. You can't know which it is without trying, and without hope and hard work.'*

So Jay took a step closer, and hoped.

'I came back because I realised I was wrong. One fake relationship wasn't anything like the other. When I was with Milli… I thought our relationship was something that it wasn't. I believed that we could have a future together. That we could love each other. And when I realised that she'd never believed either of those things…it shook my faith in love altogether.'

'I know,' Daisy said quietly, but there was still a hint of her old mocking tones in her voice that made him smile. 'You were grumpy as anything when we started this tour together.'

'But you changed that.'

'That much sex will cheer anyone up,' she joked.

Jay shook his head. 'You just can't stop yourself, can you? I meant the faith-in-love thing, not just the being grumpy.'

'Oh.' That, at least, seemed to render her speechless. Jay decided he'd better get in with what else he needed to say before she found another flip remark to make.

'Because the thing is, Daisy, being in a fake relationship with you felt more real than any real relationship I've ever had. And I think we gave up on it too quick, because we were both scared of getting it wrong. At least, I know I was. You were so adamant that it was all for show that I believed you, even though I knew for me it was something more. And maybe you don't feel the same—maybe it really was just all fake for you. And if that's the case, I'll get over it, eventually, I'm sure. But if you *do*—if you think there might be something real between us underneath all the pretending…well, I'd never forgive myself if I didn't find out.'

He stopped and waited for her response.

It didn't come.

Doubt started to creep into Jay's mind. Maybe her jokes were attempts at deflection—to avoid having this conversation in the first place. To stop him making a fool of himself because, despite everything, Daisy wasn't cruel.

Maybe Harry was wrong.

He felt a rough lapping at his hand and looked down to find Genevieve nibbling on his fingers. At least someone seemed genuinely pleased to see him, if only because she was hoping he'd brought food.

But Daisy was still staring at him.

'I'm sorry,' he said. 'Maybe I—'

'No!' Lurching forward, Daisy grabbed his hand and held it against her T-shirt-clad chest. 'No. I'm sorry. I... I lied when I said it was all fake. I lied because I was scared. Because I'd just figured out that I was in love with you, and you were going back to Milli—'

'I never went back to Milli. Not for one night.'

She shook her head. 'It doesn't matter. The point is, I was terrified of getting my heart broken. Of feeling more for you than I knew what to do with and not wanting anything in return. And if you didn't want me as a fake fiancée, I didn't know what you wanted from me at all, and that scared me. In my world...you always need to know what the deal is. What you're giving and what you're getting. Or what you're giving up.'

'I would never ask you to give up anything,' he swore.

She flashed him a small smile and carried on. 'And with you... I just felt so much, *got* so much. And I didn't know what you wanted in return.'

'You,' he whispered. 'All you ever have to be for me is yourself. Because just being with you gives me everything I need. Music, laughter, passion—and love. Those are all I want in this world. Well, those and truth.'

'I could give you those,' Daisy whispered, and when she looked up at him there was such hope in her eyes that Jay knew that, from now on, everything would be all right. As long as they were together.

Reaching into his pocket, he pulled out a small box. 'Harry gave me this to give to you.' He flipped it open. 'It's our grandma's engagement ring. Seems he knew how I felt about you before even I did, when he asked mum for it.'

'It's beautiful.' Daisy seemed mesmerised by the twisting lines of silver, specked with tiny diamonds and sapphires.

'It's nothing like as valuable as the one I bought you in Rome, but—'

'But it's *real*.'

'I was going to say you can play guitar wearing it.'

She grinned at that. 'That too. But, Jay—'

'The whole world already thinks we're engaged. And I don't want to rush you into anything—we can wait years to get married if that's what you need. But I'd like you to wear this ring. So whenever I'm not there to remind you, you'll know that I love you.'

Wordlessly, she held up her left hand and Jay slipped the huge diamond from her finger and replaced it with his grandmother's ring, love and happiness pulsing through every inch of him. 'Marry me, Daisy? For real?'

'For real,' she agreed, reaching up to kiss him. 'And for always.'

EPILOGUE

WELL, I HAVE to confess that's not exactly how I expected things to go.

I didn't need the report that landed on my desk that morning to follow the effects of *this* gift. Max and I had watched the whole thing play out in real time on social media, with Max begging for snacks at my side and me handing them over because I was so distracted by the twists and turns of the story.

One thing I didn't know, however—and possibly never will—was how much of what I saw was real and how much fabricated for the media. Maybe Daisy will tell me one day if I ask.

She hasn't contacted me yet, but I suspect she will soon. She'll have questions, I'm sure.

I spotted her through the crowds that night in Rome, but resisted the urge to seek her out. When one is giving a person something they *need*, sometimes it's better to stay out of the way until *they* realise that they need it too. At least in my experience.

When I saw Milli Masters, of all people, standing in front of the old cottage where I used to holiday as a child, I was worried that the whole plan might have backfired horribly. The romance part was outside my control, of course—all I did was give Daisy a place to escape, a place to call her own. Who she took there with her was entirely her own choice.

But I hated to think that the place might become associated with such bad memories that she'd shut it up and never go back there. Max and I definitely had a few sleepless nights over that one.

Then, this morning, when I knew that Daisy must already be back on tour with her beau and his band, she posted a photo on social media. Her and Jay and a goat, standing on a cliff, with the cottage in the background. He had one arm around her waist, the other presumably holding the camera, and she was on tiptoe kissing his cheek. The goat was eating his shirt, but he didn't seem to have noticed.

The caption underneath? One word: *Home*.

And that was when I knew that my gift had steered me right once again. I've given Daisy what she needed most in the world: a place of her own, where she can just be herself and know that's more than enough.

I just hope I can have the same success with Aubrey's gift…

* * * * *

THE COWBOY'S COMEBACK

MELISSA SENATE

For my aunt Arlene, with love.

Chapter One

Holt Dalton had turned around for three seconds—his attention snagged by two kittens playing with a piece of hay—when his son called out, "Look at me, Daddy!"

Holt's gaze shot up at the sound of the voice in the cat barn at Happy Hearts, an animal sanctuary where he'd come to adopt a *dog* for Robby. But they'd passed by the cat section of the "Adoptable Animals" barn first, and Robby had begged to go in after seeing kittens climbing up a hay bale.

Like kittens, like boy. Robby, seven-going-on-daredevil, was suddenly at the top of a huge stack of hay bales, swinging back his arms as if prepared to jump—onto a shallow pile of hay a good ten feet below. A few cats on varying levels of the hay bales were watching him, while others were either napping, doing a little grooming, or playing with toys and hay.

How his son had gotten up there so fast was beyond Holt, but that was Robby for you. Look away from the forty-eight-pound whirlwind at your own peril.

"Robby, no!" Holt called up. "The hay won't break your fall. You don't want broken bones keeping you from doing all your favorite activities the last month of summer and playing with your new dog."

"That orange cat jumped down and was totally okay!" Robby said, pointing at the tabby now grooming himself in a patch of sunlight.

"You're not a cat, Robby," Holt reminded him.

And cats supposedly had nine lives. Robby had *one* and was everything to Holt. He'd raised his son single-handedly since his ex-wife had left when Robby was three years old. Their marriage had always been rocky, but Holt had tried—hard—and signing the divorce papers he'd been served had felt like the ultimate failure. His ex had made it clear before they were married that she wasn't sure she wanted kids, but they'd gotten pregnant accidentally. She now lived in Colorado with a guy named Enzo and sent birthday and Christmas cards with age-appropriate small gifts to Robby every year. Holt wished things could be different between his son and his mother, but Sally Anne had never deceived him about what she wanted.

"Cowabunga!" Robby shouted and leaped—without looking.

Luckily, Holt was right there with his arms extended and caught his boy, getting a kid-size foot in the gut for his trouble.

"Thanks for catching me, Daddy," Robby said with a huge smile, wrapping his skinny, freckled arms around Holt's neck for a hug. Not an impish, *ha-ha, you know I never listen* smile of victory. Just pure happy.

His dad caught him—and always would. Robby knew that. Holt's own father, Robby's gramps, would have said: *You shoulda let Robby fall, splat, right on the barn floor and broken a wrist or an ankle. That'll teach him. Being soft or coddled never got anyone anywhere.*

The problem was that his dad was right *and* wrong, just as Holt was both plenty of times. Sometimes you had to let a child learn a lesson. And sometimes *being there* was the right answer. Holt's life was a constant judging of that. Three-quarters of the time he thought he got it right. Like now.

He gave Robby's dark hair a tussle. "Robby, I said not to jump and that means don't jump. If I'd missed—"

"Like you'd ever!" Robby exclaimed, wriggling out of his arms and dashing to the glass door that led to the vestibule of the cat barn and exit.

"Robby, wait," Holt called, but his son was halfway up the path of the vast farm to where a bunch of cows were grazing in a pasture.

Holt was sure a few grays hairs had sprung out in his own dark hair. He headed after his son who was already chatting away with one of the cows, a Belted Galloway. Holt stood a few feet behind, ready to catch Robby if he ran off toward the barns again.

Of course he'd reprimand Robby for disobeying, for not following the rules about running around the animal sanctuary. But part of him always felt he needed to give his son some leeway, when it felt right, to be seven and do what was natural for him. Like running around a wide-open farm. Robby's first grade teacher had said he was a typical child, just rambunctious and that time and a little maturity would help. She'd given Holt some great tips that had worked wonders for her in the classroom—letting Robby take breaks and "shake out his legs," making sure he had a good snack, allowing him to use a squeeze ball that he could keep in his hand while she was instructing and listening wasn't easy. But the director of the camp Robby had attended a few days each week this summer had complained that the seven-year-old required too much of the counselors' attention and could he *please* speak to his son. That had made Holt feel like hell.

Even if he'd been expecting it. Holt had done his research on his son's impulsivity and consulted with Robby's teachers and the guidance counselor and read all sorts of articles. There was such a vast pool of information, with so many recommendations, that Holt would just do his best with what made sense to him. The guidance counselor had recommended getting Robby tested for ADHD, attention deficit hyperactivity disorder, at the start of second grade, to allow him to mature some, and that was what Holt would do.

He was about to call Robby over for a chat about following the rules—*and if you break another we'll leave*—but the boy was deep in conversation with the cow.

"I sure would love to take you home," Robby said to the cow. "I'd name you Daring Drake after my favorite Bronc rider. Or should I name you

Holt? That's my dad and he's my number one hero but it would be weird to name a pet cow after him, right? Anyway, Daring Drake is my number two hero. Want to know who number three is? You!"

As Robby continued to talk to the cow, telling the ole girl about the teacher he got for second grade, which started at the end of the month, Holt relaxed. Talking to animals really seemed to calm his son down. Robby wasn't jumping or running or trying to climb over the fence. He was just talking and fully engaged. Coming here, deciding to bring a pet into their home, had been a good idea. Holt had done his research, knew *he'd* be doing the brunt of the work, but Robby would have a living creature to care for and love, to talk to, to turn to.

"Is your dad your hero too?" Robby asked the cow. "Which one is your dad, anyway?" The boy glanced around the pasture, and Holt had to admit, his heart had moved in his chest. His son might be a handful, but he was incredibly loving. Holt considered himself very lucky.

"Awww," said a woman's voice. "That is sure sweet."

Holt turned around—and the man who thought nothing could ever shock him anymore felt his knees wobble.

Because there was no way Amanda Jenkins

was standing right there in the middle of Happy Hearts Animal Sanctuary in Bronco, Montana. He *had* to be seeing things.

But he blinked and there she definitely was.

Ten years older, yet it seemed as though she hadn't changed a bit. The same long, dark wavy hair halfway down her back. The same beautiful dark eyes and full pink-red lips. She was petite and had been on the shy side, not one to make herself stand out. But man, did she, then and now. The minute he'd laid eyes on her that long-ago summer they'd met while working at a camp for special needs kids, there were no other girls at Camp KidPower. Let alone Montana.

What could she be doing in Bronco, though? Neither of them was from here, though Bronco Heights was home to him now.

"Holt?" she said on a gasp, her expression as shocked as his must have been.

He nodded. "It's good to see you again, Amanda." Major understatement. He couldn't take his eyes off her as memories of their summer together hit him. All they'd shared and talked about. The feel of her lips on his. Her soft hands on his body. It might be August, but a chill, a good one, ran up his spine. Amanda Jenkins. The woman he'd let get away.

She didn't respond to that. "What in the world

are you doing in Bronco?" She glanced at Robby, still talking to the cow, then back at Holt. "And you have a kid. Wow."

He nodded and took off his Stetson, holding it against his stomach and running a quick hand through his hair. "I live here now. In Bronco Heights. My family bought a big ranch last year. Dalton's Grange. I have a cabin on the property for me and Robby."

He could see her taking that in—the *me and Robby*. Not *me and my wife and Robby*.

"You've been living in Bronco Heights for a year?" she asked. "I've been here two years. I can't believe I haven't run into you."

"Well, we never ran with the same crowd," he said. Also an understatement.

She narrowed her brown eyes at him. "The same crowd? We were practically the same *person*, Holt. Remember how we always used to say, 'I'm you and you're me'?" She smiled as if lost in the sweet memory, then frowned, then seemed embarrassed she'd said it. She lifted her chin. "Well, I don't know why I brought that up. Old stuff that doesn't matter anymore."

It did to him and always would. He remembered. The way they'd lie on the grass by the lake after they were free for the day—she'd been a counselor while he was on the kitchen staff—

holding hands, making out, talking about everything and anything. *I'm you and you're me*, she'd say, and he'd repeat it back with absolute wonder in his heart, in his gut, in every cell in his body. Those times when he was with Amanda like that, just the two of them when it felt like there was no one else in the world? Yeah, he was her and she was him. But in reality? They were nothing alike.

He'd never told her the truth—*why* he'd been working at that camp, making industrial-size pots of scrambled eggs and spaghetti and vats of "bug juice" and scouring dishes and counters and mopping the huge kitchen floor. He hadn't told anyone. She'd made some assumptions about him back then that he liked, that he was a college student on summer break, as she'd been, and he hadn't corrected her. For those nine, ten weeks, he'd been the guy she thought he was. But that was summer. Like all good things, it always came to an end.

"Daddy, I definitely want a dog but I also want a cow!" Robby called out as he turned and simultaneously rushed ahead, clearly having no idea his dad was right behind him. He almost barreled into Holt's waist and legs. "Oops!" He squinted up at Holt in the sun. "See him, Daddy?" he said, pointing at the Beltie. "His name will be Daring Drake after the greatest bronc rider in Montana."

"Hi there," Amanda said, extending her hand to Robby. "I'm Amanda Jenkins and you can call me Amanda."

Robby gave her hand a hearty pump. "I'm Robby. My principal at school always shakes my hand. I get called down to her office a lot and when I leave, she always shakes my hand. I like her. Some kids think she's mean but I don't. There was a girl named Amanda in my class last year. She was in the best reading group. I was in the worst."

Amanda seemed about to say something, but Robby beat her to it, his trademark.

"Can we adopt the cow, Daddy? He's the one I want." Robby turned and beamed at his new friend.

Happy Hearts Animal Sanctuary wasn't a working farm; it was a place where animals lived in peace and harmony with nature. The owner, an animal rights devotee named Daphne Taylor, rescued farm animals—and everything in between, from dogs to rabbits to guinea pigs—and gave them a home on the huge property. She adopted out the animals that would do well in forever homes, which was why he and Robby had come. To adopt a *dog*. Not a cat. Not a cow.

"That cow's a beaut—a female, by the way—but the cows at the Dalton Grange aren't pets, they're hardworking members of the ranch." His family ranch, where he, his parents and his four brothers lived and raised cattle. Daphne had full respect for the ranchers in the area, and he was glad to know that someone who had the means—Holt's father referred to her as "that hippie-socialite"—to run a sanctuary for animals had created this special place. Not all the ranchers in town understood Daphne, but Holt admired her.

"Oh yeah," Robby said with a frown. He turned to the cow. "Sorry, buddy. I can't adopt you. But maybe I could come see you sometimes."

"That would be very nice, Robby," Amanda said, her smile so warm that Holt wanted to reach out and squeeze her hand.

"Can you show us the dogs now, Amanda?" Robby asked, his blue eyes excited.

Holt glanced at Amanda. She wore a yellow knee-length dress with a short, fitted white blazer, and there were a few gold bangles on her wrist. Her shoes were flat but shiny and looked expensive. He doubted she worked here. Not in that dressy outfit.

"Well, I'm not involved with the adoptions," Amanda explained, "but I can find Daphne Taylor for you two. She owns Happy Hearts. I do social media for the sanctuary."

"Social what-ee-ah?" Robby asked, tilting his head.

"Social media refers to websites online—on computers—that let people communicate with one another in all kinds of ways. Facebook, Twitter, chat groups, that kind of thing. I promote Happy Hearts online and around the state so that people know about the animals and adoption events and fund-raising opportunities."

Robby nodded. "Isn't it so awesome that I'm getting a dog?" he asked. "My mom has a dog but I've never met him. Well, it's not really her dog. It's Enzo's. That's her boyfriend. They live in Colado."

"Colorado," Holt corrected, the neckline of his Henley shirt tightening on him. The way Robby talked about his mom just then, you'd think it didn't bother the boy at all that he'd barely had contact with her—and hadn't for four years. But it did. Sometimes, that stupid saying Holt couldn't stand—*it is what it is*—brought Holt to his knees, but it mostly just kept him from getting a decent night's sleep. Some things he didn't know how to fix.

Amanda's expression was a mixture of so

many emotions he couldn't pick out the strongest. Robby sure did like to talk.

"Well," Holt said, forcing a smile. "Let's go check out the dogs, Robby." Not that he wanted a fast getaway. Or any getaway from Amanda.

"I'll text Daphne to meet you two there," Amanda said, pulling out her phone and double-thumbing away. Seconds later she nodded. "Yup, Daphne will be over there in a few minutes. I'll show you the way," she added, tucking a swath of her long hair behind one ear. He noticed her delicate gold and ruby earrings, a sweet sixteen gift from her parents, he recalled. "The dogs have their own separated section of the barn with large cozy kennels that lead to outdoor runs for them."

She started walking and Holt had to tell his feet to move—that was how startled he was by her presence in the first place.

They went into the dog area, which managed to be sunny and shady, tranquil and energetic all at once. There were large white boards with dog names and schedules of who was walked when, and pegs that held many leashes and tables beneath with supplies, from dog food to treats. Robby walked up and down the rows of kennels, Holt trailing behind him, too aware of Amanda standing by the door and probably still reeling, as he was, from the craziness of running into each other ten years later.

Unless he was flattering himself. They hadn't exactly parted on good terms, and it was one summer out of her life. Maybe she hadn't given him a thought in all these years.

Robby was greeted by barks and dogs jumping up against the kennel doors. The seven-year-old stopped in front of the kennel of a medium-size black-and-white dog—a border collie mix, if Holt had that right.

Robby grinned at the dog, who sat staring at him, head tilted. He didn't jump or bark. The dog put his paw up on a bar of the door as if to say hi. Some dogs looked like they were smiling, and this was one of those.

"He likes me!" Robby exclaimed. "Hi. I'm Robby! I'm seven. I like running, talking, TV shows, Minecraft, cheeseburgers, ice cream, my grandparents and my uncles, and Daring Drake the bronc rider."

Holt glanced at Amanda, who was smiling. He had to admit, he liked that she seemed charmed by Robby instead of irritated by his happy chatter. He'd dated quite a few women the past couple of years, thinking about trying to settle down, to find his Ms. Right and Robby a wonderful mother. But any woman he'd been attracted to had not been mom material either because she showed no interest in Robby at all or because she couldn't handle his energy.

The dog wedged his snout through the bars as much as he could, his head tilted. One side was white, the other black, one ear white, one ear black, his furry body big sections of either color while his legs were mottled. The dog was particularly cute.

"Bentley is superfriendly," another voice said, and they all turned.

Daphne Taylor, around his age with long, wavy red hair and a warm expression, came toward them with a smile. Over a week ago, Holt had filled out an application to adopt a dog, then a few days later, Daphne had visited Dalton's Grange for a home check, scoping out his house and walking around the property. He, Robby and their cabin had passed with flying colors.

Daphne smiled at Robby and shook both their hands. "Nice to see you two again," she said. "I'll get a leash and let him out."

When Daphne brought the dog over to Robby, he fell to his knees in front of him and Bentley licked his face twice, calmly, not jumping, not barking, not knocking him over, then actually put his head on Robby's shoulder.

Holt almost gasped.

Amanda put her hand over her mouth.

Robby threw his arms around Bentley. "You really like me! I like you too." Bentley licked Robby's cheek again, his tail wagging. While petting him, Robby began telling Bentley his life story. "I was born in Whitehorn. That's a town in Montana. And then we moved to Bronco. You're gonna love Dalton's Grange. That's our ranch…"

Daphne's phone pinged and she excused herself for a moment.

Holt stood and read the information on the sheet attached to the Bentley's kennel. "Bentley, age four. Elderly owner surrender. Gets along with kids, other dogs, cats, animals, friendly and housebroken, nicely trained in the basics. Bonded pair with Oliver."

"Bonded pair?" Holt asked, looking at Amanda.

"Oh that's right," she said, biting her lip and clearly worried she should have said something earlier. "Bentley was surrendered with Oliver—a cat. They were raised together as a pup and kitten and they're very close. Daphne is firm on adopting them out only together."

Robby turned to Holt, his face falling. "Does that mean we can't get Bentley?" he asked, his lower lip trembling. He turned back to the dog and hugged him, the dog seeming to actually like the heavy affection. "Is Oliver your best friend? I don't have a best friend. You're lucky." He stood up and wiped under his eyes. "I think Oliver and Bentley should stay together. They're best friends."

"Well, I guess that means we're bringing them *both* home," Holt said, a sucker for bonded pairs. Plus he'd always liked cats. Sleek and independent creatures.

Robby's eyes widened like plates. He flung himself at Holt and wrapped his arms around his father's neck. "Thank you, Daddy."

"Now, the *three* of you will be best friends," Amanda said with that dazzling smile. "I'll text Daphne to bring Oliver on her way back in so that you can meet him."

Holt glanced at her. There was a time when he'd thought of Amanda as *his* best friend. Just for those two months that they'd been a couple, but she'd had a big influence on him afterward. He'd never stopped wanting to be the guy she'd thought he was. By the time he'd realized that, it was too late. He'd actually driven out to her college about six months after they broke up, but as he'd arrived in the parking lot of her dorm, he'd seen her going in with a guy, his arm around her shoulders Amanda laughing at something the guy had said. Holt had sat there in his car for a good ten minutes, feeling like absolute dog-doo, then had finally gone home and dated as many women as he could until he stopped thinking about Amanda Jenkins so much.

Robby beamed and wriggled down, continuing to tell Bentley all about Dalton's Grange, and that Oliver was going to love it too even though he hadn't even met Oliver, but if Bentley loved Oliver, then Robby would too.

Amanda was chuckling and wiping her eyes. "I'm sorry," she whispered. "But your son is adorable. I always think the animals that find good homes are lucky, but I know that Bentley and Oliver will be *very* loved and very well cared for."

Not that you took good care of me, of us, he imagined her adding. Which was nuts. Her expression hadn't changed. He supposed he just felt guilty at how he'd left things, even if she'd clearly moved on. She'd thought they'd figure it out once camp ended but he'd just walked away, barely saying goodbye.

This whole summer you made me forget that people can shock you, she'd called after him. *Maybe it's good you just reopened my eyes to reality.*

He'd stopped in his tracks and wanted to run back to her and apologize, tell her who he really was, no one that she'd want to be involved with if she knew the real him. A dropout. A troublemaker. He'd been arrested twice for stupid stuff, but he'd been in a jail cell, if only for less than an hour. His reason for working at Camp KidPower? Court-ordered community service. He'd been going nowhere fast at twenty-two, and Amanda had had the world at her feet. She hadn't had the easiest childhood but had been focused and self-motivated. Then again, her parents had been financially comfortable if on the negligent side, leaving her to fend for herself, which she had.

His parents had had nothing until his dad had struck it rich gambling just over a year ago, enabling his parents to start fresh in Bronco—specifically Bronco Heights, the "right" side of town for once. Holt and his four brothers would have stayed where they'd all been scattered across Montana, but their mom had had a heart attack last year, and the scare had made them all want to stay close, look out for her. His dad wasn't always easy to be around, even with money taking a huge stress load off his shoulders, but Holt had to say, he loved Dalton's Grange. And he loved having his family right there for Robby.

Daphne came back in with Oliver in a cat carrier and set it on the floor of the barn. "Oliver is four years old just like Bentley. He likes back scratches, playing with string and little balls, and curling up next to Bentley for his many naps. He's a real sweetie."

Robby knelt and peered in. "He's black-and-white just like Bentley! I love Oliver!" The boy stretched out on his belly, smiling at his new cat through the barred door of the carrier and now telling Oliver his life story.

"Looks like our little family just grew by two," Holt said, nodding at Daphne. "Let's bring our new family members home, Robby. You can show them your room. I'll bet that's where they'll want to sleep."

"Thanks to a generous donation from Bentley and Oliver's previous owner's family, Happy Hearts has everything you may need for them, from a dog bed to food they like, to brand-new bowls and toys," Daphne said. "I'll go grab those bags and the paperwork. We'll meet in the lobby in five minutes."

"I'm headed out," Amanda said to him. "I'll show you the way."

Headed out. No, he thought. Not yet. He could still barely believe he was actually standing a few feet from Amanda Jenkins. He was far from ready to say goodbye.

"Well, goodbye," Amanda said as she stopped near an archway—she certainly *was* ready.

"Thanks for helping me," Robby said, beaming at her.

She grinned at him. "My pleasure. Bentley and Oliver sure are lucky to be going home with such a wonderful boy who loves dogs and cats and cares so much about their friendship."

Robby beamed and looked at his dad to make sure he'd heard such praise. Holt sent her a smile of thanks. Amanda met his gaze and held it for a moment as if she wanted to say something. But she didn't.

Daphne came back in with papers in her hand. "Oh, Amanda—I just thought of something! Remember how we talked about you doing a story for the Happy Hearts website on a new adoption? How about you cover this adoption? Bentley and Oliver joining the Dalton family. It's such a great story—two best friends going home with a little boy to a beautiful ranch."

Holt raised an eyebrow. He noticed Amanda pale.

"Um, sure," Amanda said.

Holt nodded. "Happy to help."

"We're going to be famous!" Robby said to Bentley and Oliver.

Daphne smiled. "Amanda, I'll text you the contact info. And then you two can set a time for the interview. Get lots of great photos," she added.

Amanda managed a smile but looked like she wanted the ground to swallow her. "I sure will."

He was assured of seeing her again. Thank you, Daphne.

Even if Amanda Jenkins looked like she never wanted to lay eyes on him again.

Chapter Two

Amanda got into her car in the gravel parking area at Happy Hearts, expecting to hightail it out of there to put some space between her and Holt, but she needed a minute in her car to decompress. Maybe a few.

Holt Dalton. In the flesh. After all these years.

Her first love, her first *everything*. She'd had crushes and a few boyfriends before Holt, but when she met him at age twenty-one, the summer before her senior year in college, she finally knew what everyone was talking about when they used the words *in love* and *you'll know* and The One.

The tall, sexy, dark-haired, dark-eyed Holt, on whom every female KidPower staffer had had an immediate crush, had surprised her with his attention the first day. *There's just something about you*, he'd say, staring into her eyes, talking away, asking her questions, listening to her. He'd truly *seen* her, seen something exciting and irresistible in the shy, quiet, bookish young woman in the ponytail and glasses. She'd opened up with him, become more herself. She'd thought they'd always be together. But he'd just walked away from her at summer's end as if she'd meant nothing to him.

What did Amanda expect? she'd heard girls around her whisper on that last day, when everyone was hugging goodbye. *Holt the Hottie with Nose in a Book Amanda Who Doesn't Want People Calling Her Mandy? Like* that *would last.*

Well, they were right. And dammit, she didn't like people calling her Mandy because her grandpop had called her that her whole life, just him, and when she'd lost him, she didn't need people she barely knew giving her that special nickname because Amanda was too long or they wanted to tell her who she was. She'd tried explaining that to a blind date a few years ago, and he'd told her to lighten up. Sigh. Amanda was used to not easily connecting with people.

She slid down in her seat and glanced toward

the door of the barn where she could just make out Holt and Daphne sitting at a table, going over paperwork. No surprise that he had grown into a gorgeous man. Getting over him had been rough. She remembered how she'd forced herself to finally go on dates, mostly involving studying at the college library or the lounge of her dorm, and how she'd tried to *lighten up*. She'd had some short-term relationships over the years, no one measuring up to Holt Dalton. Until she'd met Tyler two years ago. She'd thought she'd finally met her guy and had gotten swept up in the whirlwind of them and had even agreed to his crazy, romantic plan of eloping to Las Vegas.

She turned to face away from the building, staring at the peaceful cows that Robby Dalton had been mesmerized by. She willed herself to think about the social media posts she'd schedule for Daphne and Happy Hearts and not let her mind go deeper into her almost-marriage, not right now, not after seeing Holt—talk about a double whammy—but the memories came.

Tyler had booked a honeymoon suite with the glittering lights of the strip outside their window, way up on the forty-second floor. That night, the plan was to go to the elegant wedding chapel in their hotel, her in the beautiful white dress she'd bought—not quite a wedding gown but still bridal—Tyler in his tux. Her handsome fiancé, a businessman she'd met through a work-related fund-raiser, had gone down to the casino to let her get dressed so he wouldn't see his bride until she was all dolled up. She'd texted him to let him know she was ready, but he didn't respond. Not to her texts or her calls. She'd waited and waited, pacing and calling and texting him, wondering what the holdup was, praying he hadn't gotten into an accident—she'd actually been about to call local hospitals—and then came the text.

I'm so sorry. The reality of almost doing this made me realize I can't. Sorry. You deserve better. I paid for the room till the morning, so no worries.

Right. No worries. She'd gotten herself together after ugly-crying for a good hour and checked out that same night, renting a car and driving north as long as she could before the tears made her eyes too blurry. She'd found the closest motel, somewhere in Utah, and checked in. In the morning she'd driven home to Whitehorn, Montana, and made some decisions. There hadn't been much for her in her hometown; her parents had retired to Arizona years before, she was so shy that she had few friends in town, and her job as the social media liaison for a county-wide bank was pretty dull. She'd typed *Best places to live in Montana* into her search engine, and the first town that popped up was Bronco, a bit farther north. It was part Wild West with an old ghost story legend, part glitzy with a vibrant but small downtown, and she liked that it was bigger and more diverse than she was used to. But best of all, a very good friend from college, Brittany Brandt, lived there, and she was looking for a roommate. Amanda had sent up a silent prayer of thanks to the universe for that.

Bronco, here we come, she'd said to her cat, Poindexter, and two weeks later they headed north. She'd instantly loved the swanky BH247 apartment complex with views of the mountains, indoor and outdoor pools, a hot tub and lots of singles. That was the strange thing about Amanda; she liked being around people and hoopla, just not for long. She'd pretty much stayed in her shell, much to her very outgoing roommate's chagrin. What would be the point of dating when it led to having your spirit crushed, your heart irrevocably broken, your trust obliterated? And so Amanda had focused on work, leveraging her social media and marketing work experience into her own small business, and now she had a solid list of clients, from Happy Hearts Animal Sanctuary to Bronco Bank and Trust. Since most of her work was online, intro-

verted, shy Amanda had found her sweet spot—
and on her sofa most of the time.

But then something happened that had changed
everything. Something very unexpected. Soon
after moving to Bronco, Amanda had walked into
Tender Years Daycare for a preliminary meeting with the owners on plans for marketing, and
those little kids singing their ABCs and running
around in the playground had stopped her in her
tracks. She wanted a family. A child. The feeling
had gripped her and hadn't let go. A baby. Problem was, she didn't want to have a child on her
own. Every time she envisioned holding a little
hand, there was a man beside her, holding the
other tiny hand.

A problem, since she wasn't letting a man anywhere near her heart, mind or soul for the fore-
seeable future. She'd thought Holt had broken
her heart ten years ago? Getting left at the altar
in her wedding gown had been a hundred times
more painful because it had taken her so long to
find Tyler, to let herself give into her feelings for
him, to open up. Then whammo, bye.

But if she'd thought ten years and a two-year-
old broken spirit would have protected her from
seeing Holt again, she was dead wrong. She'd
barely gotten through the twenty minutes she'd
spent in the Dalton boys' company.

That Holt was a dad wasn't a surprise. Back at camp, he hadn't been a counselor; he'd worked in the kitchen, but any time he had been around her campers, he'd been so warm and fun and kind to them. He hadn't ignored them or spoken down to them, hadn't been turned off by their special needs—and those issues had varied. He'd treated her campers like the individuals they were.

Maybe she'd tell Daphne she couldn't do the interview and photo session with Holt and his son—and come clean as to why. She and Daphne had become friends. Daphne, daughter of the richest family in town, had nonetheless been through her own share of life and would definitely understand. Amanda pulled out her phone but then put it back. Nope. She was a professional. Daphne was a great client, kept her very busy, and Amanda wasn't going to let her personal life get in the way. She'd just be all business when she went to Dalton's Grange, and that would be that. Holt had been in a town a year and she hadn't run into him, so after their interview and photo session, certainly another year could go by without her seeing him. Or his cute son. Or their precious new family members, Oliver and Bentley.

Feeling more in control of herself, she started her car, just in time to see Robby Dalton, his brown bangs blowing in the late-afternoon breeze, come out of the barn with Bentley on a navy leash, a matching collar around his neck. Amanda could see they'd already gotten Bentley his own name tag in the shape of a silver bone. Holt came out behind his son and called out to Robby to be mindful of the cars, but their truck was parked right by the barn. Amanda ducked down a bit, unable to drive away, unable to stop watching them. Holt was carrying the cat carrier in one hand, and two Happy Hearts reusable tote bags, filled to the brim, were dangling off his other wrist. Robby walked Bentley over to the grassy area in front of the truck as Holt put the carrier and bags on the floor of the back seat so that Oliver wouldn't be jostled, then Robby and Bentley got in.

When they drove away, Amanda realized she wanted to follow them, watch them introduce their new pets to their home. She shook her head at herself and turned on the radio to her favorite country station, as always playing a song about a love gone wrong. That would set her straight.

"Amanda, put on your dancing shoes!" Brittany called out as she came into the kitchen of the condo they shared. As always, Brittany Brandt looked fabulous in a strapless, billowy red jumpsuit and sky-high silver heels. Tall and willowy with light brown skin and long black curly hair, the thirty-three-year-old event planner—for Bronco Heights Elite Parties, no less—had just gotten home from work for a quick refresh of her makeup, change of outfit and a dab of her favorite perfume, which smelled heavenly. Brittany's social calendar was always packed, whereas Amanda's revolved around whatever binge-worthy TV shows she might watch. "DJ's is having a fundraiser and I've put you on the guest list," Brittany said. "Wear something swishy."

Amanda stopped midpour of the hot water from the kettle onto her herbal tea. She ran her free hand down her body, indicating her polka-dot yoga pants, long tank top, and socks with the cartoon owls. She did love DJ's Deluxe—the very popular upscale rib joint where their next-door neighbor, Mel, used to be the manager before taking a big role as CFO of DJ's, Incorporated—but after running into Holt she had zero appetite. "I've got a date with Poindexter tonight. There's a documentary on the history of Montana on that I've been meaning to catch. It even covers Bronco and the 'unexplained phenomenon' and ghost tours." Bronco had quite the history. No wonder it was always on "Best of the West" lists of places to visit and live.

Brittany raised an eyebrow. "Well, I'm not

gonna lie. That sounds good too. I wouldn't mind putting on my jammies and curling up on the sofa with a bowl of popcorn. But work calls! Sure you don't want to go? Lots of hot single men will be there." She grinned and flipped back her gorgeous wild long hair.

"I'm sure. Have fun, Brittany."

"I'll try to be quiet when I come in," her sweet roommate said, gave Poindexter a scratch on the back, then headed out.

Amanda looked at Poindexter. "Brittany and I sure are going to have different nights, Poin."

Her cat started grooming himself. Some conversationalist. Then again, if Amanda had wanted conversation, she'd be at DJ's with Brittany and a couple hundred of Bronco Heights residents. She hadn't shared too much of her romantic past with Brittany—Amanda just hated talking about it—but her roommate knew she'd been through the love wringer. The interesting thing about bubbly, constantly going-out Brittany was that she wasn't looking for a husband because she wasn't sure she wanted to have kids. The eldest of five siblings, her roommate liked single life and wasn't interested in a family of her own. *Yet*, Amanda figured. Men loved Brittany, and one day someone would likely turn her head even if Brittany wasn't too sure it was possible.

So Brittany liked dating but didn't want it to go anywhere because her biological clock was definitely *not* ticking, and Amanda's was ticking out of control but she hated dating because it either led nowhere or straight to heartache. No wonder they got along so well despite being very different. They were simpatico.

Amanda was about to turn on the *History of Montana* when her doorbell rang. She popped up and headed to the door. Her neighbor, Melanie Driscoll, dressed to kill like Brittany, stood there.

"Wow, you look amazing, Mel!" Amanda said, admiring her gorgeous hot pink dress—swishy indeed—and her sophisticated blond chignon. Mel's diamond engagement ring shone on her finger. Her friend had recently gotten engaged to Gabe Abernathy, from a prominent ranching family in Bronco Heights.

"I guess this—" she swept a hand down Amanda's outfit "—means you're not coming?" She grinned, knowing the answer would be no. Amanda stayed home unless she had to be somewhere for business reasons or to support a friend. And with the wealthiest ranchers in Bronco attending the fund-raiser tonight, her friends were all set.

"Poindexter and I are watching a documentary," she said. "It's been a long day. Trust me."

Mel's pretty blue eyes were sympathetic. "I get it. Listen, Amanda, I'm here because I'm ready to take you up on your offer to find out what you can about Josiah and Winona's long-lost baby."

Amanda squeezed Mel's hand. Not long ago, Mel had asked for Amanda's help with a very poignant family mystery, but then had asked her to hold off just in case Mel herself found any new information.

"I haven't been able to learn anything new," Mel said, "and all my searches have gotten me nowhere."

"Can you refresh my memory?" Amanda asked. "I just want to be sure I have it all straight in my head."

Mel nodded. "Beatrix Abernathy is the long-lost daughter of relatives of Gabe's. His great-grandfather, Josiah, kept a diary that was found buried under floorboards in the old Ambling A out in Rust Creek Falls, which his family abandoned before moving to Bronco decades ago. The new owners of that ranch were deeply touched by the seventy-plus-year-old old diary and its beautiful love story. Turns out, when Josiah Abernathy was a teenager, he had a secret love, a girl named Winona Cobbs, who'd always been on the 'delicate' side. Winona got pregnant, and I'm not sure of all the details, but she was institutionalized after she was told her baby died. But that was a lie."

"Oh my heart," Amanda said. "I wish you could say that true love won out, that mother, father and baby were reunited. I totally understand why trying to find Beatrix is so important to you and Gabe."

Mel's eyes clouded, and Amanda could see how affected her neighbor was by the story. "I keep thinking about poor Winona. How when she delivered, she was told her baby was stillborn and that Josiah learned that the baby was alive and well. How he wanted to raise her, but he was forced to place her for adoption. And remember, in a letter to Winona found tucked into the diary, Josiah wrote that he figured out who adopted his daughter and that someday, he'd bring her home. But I've done some digging, and no one has ever heard of a Beatrix Abernathy. So clearly, Josiah wasn't able to reunite with the baby. I want to find her—Beatrix. I *have* to find her."

"And that's where my online skills and I come in," Amanda said. "I can help. I can try, anyway."

Mel nodded. "Thanks, Amanda. This is personal for me on two counts. As you know, I'm going to *be* an Abernathy. And as I said when I first told you about all this, I *know* and adore Winona—she lives near my parents—she's wonderful but definitely is delicate. She used to be the town psychic and was often written off as an oddball." She shook her head. "She's not doing too well these days. And Josiah is in a nursing home with Alzheimer's. Can you imagine how surprised Gabe and I were when, in a moment of absolute lucidity, Josiah remembered his baby and asked me and Gabe to find her? But I can't so I'm seriously hoping that with your online skills, your sleuthing will find her. The baby was likely born in Rust Creek Falls over seventy years ago and then given up for adoption."

"And Josiah didn't say anything in the diary that might help locate her?" Amanda asked.

"No. All I have on that end is the letter that was tucked inside. I can recite that verbatim. It said, 'My dearest Winona, please forgive me. But they say you will never get better. I promise you that your baby daughter is safe. She's alive! I wanted to raise her myself, but my parents forced me to have her placed for adoption. She's with good people—my parents don't know, but I have figured out who they are. Someday, I will find a way to bring her back to you.'"

Amanda felt tears poke the backs of her eyes. "Oh, Mel. We have to find that baby girl!"

Mel nodded. "We have to. I'm not saying a word to Winona about it until her long-lost daughter is found—if she's found. But I just know this is important."

"I'll do everything I can to find a connection," Amanda said, already thinking how she could go about it. Time frames, hospitals, adoption agencies. Even putting out a general feeler could bring forth leads.

Mel bit her lip. "One major reason why I haven't gotten anywhere is because the psychiatric institution where Winona was sent in Kalispell burned down forty years ago. I wish I had more for you to go on."

Amanda frowned. If the records were gone, then so was any information about why Winona had been sent to that place and details about the baby. Finding Beatrix Abernathy would definitely be harder. She grabbed her phone. "I want to input all of this into my notes app again while it's all fresh in my mind, especially the letter you recited. Can you repeat it—slowly?"

Mel did, and again Amanda's heart clenched with Josiah's clear love for Winona and his determination to reunite with her and their baby girl.

"And you know what else is interesting about the story, Amanda? It seems like everyone who's had something to do with the diary has been truly touched by the story. Hey, who knows? Maybe the diary will bring some romance into your life.

If anyone had told me that after all Gabriel Abernathy and I had been through that we would actually end up engaged..."

Holt Dalton flashed into Amanda's mind. There was no way their brief reunion, even with a future meeting for the interview and photos for the Happy Hearts website, would go anywhere. Because Amanda wouldn't let it. Love—the love she'd felt for Holt, the love she'd felt for Tyler—meant eventually hurting in a way she couldn't bear to go through again. Twice burned, quadruply shy. If *that* wasn't a saying, it should be.

Amanda smiled. "Well, I don't know about that, Mel, but I've got a whole night to see what I can do with my social media skills. I'll be discreet and put out some feelers. I'll keep it to surnames only for a start and see what it leads to."

"Perfect. Thanks, Amanda." Her phone pinged. "Gah. Being CFO of a company means always being on duty. Couple fires to put out, and I'm supposed to be heading out to the party at DJ's. Brittany already leave?"

Amanda nodded. "Yup, you know she likes to be the first on scene of every event she runs."

"Thank God for Brittany. Thanks again, Amanda. See you, Poindexter," she added to the cat, who stood beside Amanda staring up at Mel.

Amanda smiled and shut the door. The documentary on Montana could wait. She had a very interesting mystery to help solve. That would keep her mind off Holt Dalton for sure. For a little while anyway.

Her phone pinged with a text, and she was sure it would be Mel with something she wanted to add about the Winona and Josiah mystery. But it was Holt Dalton.

Got your number from Happy Hearts. I could really use your help. Oliver ran under Robby's bed when we got home and now Bentley's under there too and Robby's worried they both hate him and his room. Robby keeps asking if that "nice Amanda" can come talk to them. Can she? P.S. Sorry if this is way out of bounds. I'll understand.

She swallowed. Oh boy.

Dalton's Grange, right? she texted back. She quickly called it up on her maps app. All the time, the past year, he was right there. I can be over in fifteen minutes.

You're a lifesaver. Log cabin with the bright blue door a half mile back from the main house, nestled in the woods. Tire swing hanging from the big oak out front. Can't miss it.

See you soon, she texted back.

Appreciate it. He added an emoji of a smiley face in a cowboy hat.

She stared at the cowboy smiley face. *Careful, girl*, she told herself. *This is not a guy to be trusted. Don't let a cute kid and two animals you've loved since they came into Happy Hearts get you overinvolved with Holt Dalton.*

Cowboy heartbreaker extraordinaire.

Chapter Three

When the doorbell rang, Oliver was still under the bed—way under—and so was Bentley. Robby was in tears, lying on the floor, head smushed in the crook of his elbow as he'd long given up trying to coax them out.

"Hey, Robby," Holt said. "I'll bet that's Amanda. Want to come to the door with me?"

Robby lifted his head. "I'll wait here. I don't want Bentley and Oliver to think I went away."

Holt nodded and went to the door, barely able to believe that when he opened it, Amanda Jenkins would be standing there. The woman he'd never forgotten.

He'd thought a ringing doorbell would have brought at least Bentley barking and running, but nope, he'd tried that ten minutes ago, and Bentley had stayed put, silent as could be next to his buddy.

Holt opened the door—and whoa. Despite being ten years older, Amanda, in a casual summer outfit of white jeans and a black tank top with a ruffle down the center, looked so much like the girl he'd loved. She wore flat silver sandals, and her toenails were painted a sparkly pink. Her long, lush hair was in a low ponytail, her neck and shoulders exposed. She was so pretty—and sexy.

"Thanks for coming out," Holt said.

"I have to admit, I stood on your porch for a good five minutes staring at the cabin and then up at the main house and the property," she said. "*Wow* does not do Dalton's Grange justice."

The property was definitely spectacular. When his dad said he'd found their ranch, a place for all of them to build the cattle empire they'd always talked about, Holt hadn't expected this. Nestled into the mountains, the main house, which looked like a log mansion, caught his breath every time he passed it. His own house, a miniature version of the main house but still large and comfortable for him and his son—and now a dog and cat—had instantly felt like home. Holt had always been a cowboy through and through, and the log cabin, upscale though it was with its floor-to-ceiling stone fireplace and expert craftsmanship, spoke to him.

"It's so peaceful," he said. "When my head is about to explode, I just have to look up and take in all this wilderness, the mountains, the trees, the cattle, and I can breathe again."

"Is your head often about to explode?"

He nodded.

She stared at him for a moment. "Then I'm glad all you have to do is look around you. Other than try to find peace in a lot more destructive or expensive ways."

"Daddy, is that Amanda?" Robby called out. "Can she come to talk to Bentley and Oliver?"

"Aww," she said. "They're still under the bed, huh?"

"Yup." He gestured for her to come in, and she followed him into the hall, looking all around. "Wow again. This place is incredible. I love everything. It's so wide open yet cozy at the same time."

He watched her take in the vaulted wood ceilings and arched doorways, the warm, colorful rugs and the big leather sofas in the living room, the grand, curved stairway with its tribal treads and photo gallery covering the wall all the way up. "Robby's room is upstairs."

"Four brothers," she said, eyeing the photos of him, Morgan, Boone, Dale and Shep over the years. "I guess the family must have expanded a lot in the past ten years. How many cousins does Robby have?"

"None. My brothers are all single and seem to like it that way. And my ex was an only so no cousins for Robby on that side, either."

"Well, in time I guess the Dalton brothers will settle down. You're so lucky to have a big family. I'm an only myself, as you know, and my parents were onlies, and both sets of grandparents are gone. My parents are all I have, but they retired to Arizona so I don't see them as often I'd like."

"Thanksgiving must be quiet," he said.

She nodded. "Last year my folks went on a cruise with their bridge group, so I was on my own. Luckily, my roommate Brittany invited me over to her family celebration. She's also one of five. I don't think I've ever seen a turkey that big before."

Huh. He was glad she had a kind roommate who looked out for her, but to be alone on Thanksgiving had to hurt. Christmas probably wasn't a blast either.

"Daddy?" Robby called, his voice choked.

"I'm here with Amanda," he called out as he arrived in the doorway of Robby's room. His son had a great bedroom with all his favorite things—lots of hunter green, his favorite color, a shelf devoted to his favorite book series about an amateur detective raccoon in a Hawaiian shirt who solved light, funny mysteries at school, and now Bentley and Oliver's shared bed, which Happy Hearts had wanted Robby to have, and all their toys.

"Hi, Robby," Amanda said, stepping in. "When I brought my cat Poindexter home for the first time after adopting him, he wouldn't come out from under my bed for over four hours."

Robby's eyes widened. "Really? But you're nice."

She sat down beside him. "So are you. It's not that Oliver and Bentley don't like you and aren't happy to be here. They do and are. But animals, particularly cats, get very nervous when they move into a new home. Nothing smells familiar. So they tend to hide under a bed or table until they feel more at home. Then they come out and do a little exploring. Bentley is braver but he's keeping his buddy company so Oliver feels safer."

Robby's face brightened. "That's what Daddy said."

Amanda smiled. "Your daddy is definitely right. So, Robby, why don't you hang out on the rug and just play with a toy or read or whatever you usually do in your room, and I'll bet Oliver comes out to explore. Bentley will be right behind him."

Robby started reaching for his stuffed animals. "I can set up a party of my stuffed animals and toys so that when Bentley and Oliver come out, they can meet everyone."

"That sounds good, Robby," Holt said. He turned to Amanda. "I was about to make some coffee. Sound good?"

"Sure," she said.

"We'll be in the kitchen, Robby. Call down if they come out."

"'Kay, Daddy," Robby said, the anticipation of that in his voice a relief compared to the teary sadness of earlier.

Holt ran a hand over Robby's hair, and Amanda smiled at the boy, then they went downstairs into the kitchen.

"Even the kitchen is gorgeous," she said, looking all around the room. "How does it manage to look antique and state-of-the-art at the same time?"

"Right? Even I don't mind cooking since I moved in."

"*Can* you cook?"

"Hell yeah, I can. For a while there after our

summer at camp, I didn't know what to do with myself. I was always a cowboy, working as a hand, but the places that took a chance on me didn't pay much, so I supplemented my income as a short order cook, thanks to my brief experience in the kitchen at Camp KidPower. Turned out I could make a cheap cut of anything tender and delicious."

"What do you mean you didn't know what to do with yourself?" she asked, clearly confused. "You were in college, majoring in agricultural development, right? You were planning to run a ranching empire."

He moved over to the coffee maker. "I dropped out of school after two years, Amanda. And the summer job at KidPower was court-ordered stupid trouble with the law, petty stuff, disorderly conduct, drinking in public, drag racing, that kind of thing. My life had been going nowhere fast at twenty-two. Till that summer I met you turned me around."

She stared at him, disbelief and resignation in her pretty brown eyes. "Why didn't you tell me?"

He hesitated at first. Then just blurted it out. Finally. "You seemed to like me as I was and I didn't want to spoil it by letting you know I was a hooligan, as my dad used to call me."

She seemed to think about that for a moment.

"You liked me as I was, so I get it. A lot of guys found me boring and thought I was stuck up."

"Shy for sure. Only until someone gets to know you. Then you never stop talking." He grinned, and so did she, and just like that, the ice was broken. Whatever residual anger she'd been holding on to the past ten years seemed to have dissipated. Or maybe that was just wishful thinking on his part.

The relief that hit him was a surprise.

"Well, I wish you'd told me, Holt. I wouldn't have liked you any less."

He wasn't so sure of that.

"Speaking of your father," she added, "I'm surprised you live on the same property with your folks. I remember you saying you and your dad didn't see eye to eye."

Whenever he had opened up to Amanda, he'd been honest. He'd omitted quite a lot, yes, but it had helped back then to talk about his fraught relationship with his dad.

The coffee finally brewed, giving him something to do, somewhere else to look. He poured two mugs, and brought over cream and sugar and sat down across from her.

"No one was more surprised than me," he said. "I still don't get along great with my dad, but I'm working on it. It's my summer plan, actually—to make peace with him. I have barely a month left."

She added cream and a sugar cube to her yellow mug. "Do you argue a lot?"

"I want my father to be someone he's not," he said, taking a long sip of his coffee.

"Sounds like something someone else told you."

He smiled. "All the time. My mother. And all four of my brothers."

"What do you want him to be?" she asked.

"More patient with his grandson." Holt got up and walked over to the counter, where a half-eaten pie sat. "Slice of pecan pie? I made it."

"I never turn down pie," she said. "Especially homemade."

He cut them both a slice and sat back down. Why had he brought up the issue with his dad and Robby? Now he had no appetite for the pie, which he'd only thought of in the first place to have something more to do with himself since the subject of his dad's lack of patience for his grandson grated on him.

"So," she said, taking a bite. "How *does* your dad treat Robby?"

He sighed. "He wants him to stop talking quite so much, stop running quite so fast, stop asking quite so many questions. He wants him to stop being such a whirlwind."

"Too much energy for grandpa?"

He shrugged. "Robby's a great kid. Very energetic, yes. Very talkative, yes. Doesn't always listen, yes. Clumsy as heck, yes. He's seven. He's a lot, I know that."

"Does your father yell at Robby?" she asked, sipping her coffee.

"He's more just gruff. My mother more than makes up for it, but it rankles me. I know my son is a handful, but my dad would be annoyed by any kid who wasn't like a church mouse."

Holt often thought that maybe he should pack Robby up and leave. But the whole reason Holt was here was for his mom. Deborah Dalton had given up so much of herself—including a career she cared about—to help her husband with his dream of having his own ranch, a small place they'd bought in Whitehorn after they'd gotten married. Worrying with him over taxes and cattle prices falling. Up before the crack of dawn to make breakfast, to muck out the barns and stalls, to do just as much heavy lifting. Had his dad appreciated it? Did men who appreciated their wives cheat on them?

No.

A familiar hot pit of anger rose in his gut as he

thought about it. He wouldn't even know about this—and hell, he wished he didn't—if he hadn't overheard an argument as a kid. Another as a teenager. Once, a few years ago, he'd seen his dad standing a little too close to an interested-looking woman in a bar, and Holt had left, feeling sick. Before they'd ever moved to Bronco, when his mom was recovering from the heart attack that had scared them all, he'd overheard his dad talking to the hospital chaplain, asking forgiveness for not loving his wife right or good enough, admitting he'd cheated and making a solemn vow to never betray his marriage vows again. His father had been crying, and Holt had retreated, bursting into tears himself.

He could count on his hands the times he'd cried as an adult—when he'd walked away from Amanda ten years ago, not sure why he was so upset over something *he* was actually doing. When the divorce papers arrived. When his son was placed in his arms for the first time less than a minute after he was born. And that day he'd overheard his father with the chaplain.

Amanda took another bite of the pie. "I guess your family chose Bronco for the same reason I did. And most folks. It's pretty great here. The Wild West, the old ghost legends, downtown Bronco Heights. I love it here."

"I do too. So does Robby. When the ranch in Whitehorn failed, my dad was thinking of moving to Rust Creek Falls, where we have a lot of family, but our branch didn't exactly have a good reputation then, so my dad just said Rust Creek Falls was too small town for his taste and that Bronco had everything we could want. He got lucky gambling, which was how he was able to afford this place. And because we know my dad has a penchant for letting good things slip away, we all moved to the ranch at my mother's request to make sure the place runs smoothly and to keep an eye on our mom, who'd had a heart attack not long before."

He'd never forget how he'd ended up here with his dad—how all his brothers had. Their first night in Bronco, sitting around the big dining table in their huge new dining room, his father had said he had his own personal kind of grace to say and went on to announce that he'd been lucky a few times in his life. The first was when Deborah had agreed to marry him despite him having not a nickel to his name. The second was when he won the money to give her the life she deserved. When Neal had brought Dalton's Grange, he'd asked his sons, scattered across Montana working on other ranches, to come work for him, assuring them there were houses on the property for all of them to live separately if they wanted. All five Dalton brothers refused. But then their mother asked them to reconsider. She wanted her family together, a true second chance for them all. How could they possibly refuse after what she'd gone through?

"Is she doing all right?" Amanda asked.

"Good as gold," he said. "But we almost lost her and none of us had ever been so scared."

"So the seven of you got to start fresh in Bronco. Like me."

"Like you?" he asked, raising an eyebrow. He should have figured something had made her leave Whitehorn, besides just her parents retiring and leaving themselves.

She frowned and then dug into her pie, clearly not wanting to talk about it. He got it. There was a lot he didn't want to talk about either.

"There are some other prosperous ranching families who aren't so welcoming," he said. "I guess we're considered 'new money' without a family history or legacy in town. And a little rough around the edges to say the least."

She smiled. "Well, if you're rough around the edges, Holt Dalton, you're a diamond in the rough. I spent a lot of time with you ten years ago, even for just a summer, and there's nothing rough about you."

Without thinking, he reached out for her hand and gave it a gentle squeeze. "That's nice of you to say."

"Daddy! Amanda! Come look!"

Amanda's smile lit up her face. "I have a feeling a certain cat and dog have come out from under the bed."

They both took one last sip of their coffees, then went upstairs, stopping in the doorway to Robby's room, mostly because Holt was so surprised. Robby was sitting cross-legged on the rug in front of the fancy memory-foam pet bed, where Bentley and Oliver were lying down, Oliver curled up along Bentley's belly.

Robby was reading from a chapter book, "'And then…'" He stopped and put his finger on the page. "'And then Rocco…'" He bit his lip, moving his finger to the right. "'Rocco the raccoon said…'" He moved his finger and stared down hard at the page. "'Well, that.'" He stopped and shifted his body a bit. "'Well that sure is…is a mystery!'" He looked up at his pets with a smile. "Bentley and Oliver, I know that word by heart now! Mystery! Isn't that a big word? It means something that no one can figure out." He looked back down at the page. "'But don't worry, I can…'" He stared at the page, his face scrunching in concentration. He turned around and looked at Holt. "Daddy? What is this word again?"

Holt came in the room and glanced at where Robby pointed. "Solve. Do you remember what that means?"

Robby nodded. "That's the figuring out part, right?"

Holt nodded. "You got it, Robby."

The boy continued reading. "'But don't worry,'" he said again, "'I can solve it!'" Robby glanced up from his book at Bentley and Oliver. "Guys, don't worry about the missing chalk in the classroom because Rocco the raccoon is really good at solving mysteries!"

Amanda moved beside Holt. "Oh, my heart," she whispered to him. "He is the sweetest."

Holt smiled at her, holding her gaze a beat longer than he should have, but he could barely drag his eyes off her. "Good job, buddy," he said to his son.

"Do you think Bentley and Oliver like being read to even by me?" Robby asked, his blue eyes worried and his mouth kind of scrunched up.

"I can tell they love it," Amanda said. "Look at how calm they are. They seem very happy you're reading to them."

Robby brightened. "I'm not a good reader, though. I'm in the worst group at school. But maybe I'll get better if I read to Bentley and Oliver."

"That would be great practice," Amanda said with a nod.

The doorbell rang, and Holt excused himself to answer it, his heart in his throat as it often was when Robby opened up about his struggles with reading. A glance out the window showed his dad's pickup in the drive. Great. His father was here with some complaint, probably about how Robby was running too close to the bulls pasture this morning and it wasn't good for them.

But it was Holt's mother on the porch with a red bag in her hand. *Bronco Pets Emporium* was in gold across the bag.

"Special delivery for Robby Dalton," she said with a smile. Tall like all the Daltons but with short blond hair cut to her chin and warm blue eyes like Robby's, Deborah held out the bag.

He gave his mom a kiss on the cheek. "That was nice of you, Mom."

"And your dad too," she added quickly. "He's the one who drove us into town to the pet shop. Even tested out the squeaker in Bentley's new toy."

"Thanks for the warning," Holt said with a smile, hating the loud squeakers. "Dad not here too?" he asked, glancing past her into the truck.

Empty. He'd let his parents know he'd adopted not only the dog he'd promised Robby but a cat, and that they'd both stay in the house, not roam around loose.

"He's rolling out the dough for pizza night, actually," she said. "The man can't cook but he likes to roll out the dough."

Holt had definitely gotten his skills in the kitchen from his mother, who was a great cook. His father managed to scorch pots of spaghetti, always letting the water boil out because he completely forgot he was cooking in the first place. Deborah had pretty much banned him from their state-of-the-art kitchen.

"Come on upstairs," Holt said. "Robby just managed to coax his pets out from under his bed, so your timing is perfect. Oh, and I have a visitor—Amanda Jenkins. We worked at that summer camp together ten years ago. Turns out she does social media for Happy Hearts, and I ran into her there earlier today."

He did catch the look of surprise and curiosity on his mom's face. When was the last time he'd brought a woman into his home? Not this year, certainly.

They'd reached Robby's bedroom, and his mom walked in quietly so as not to scare the pets. She looked at Amanda and smiled, then turned to her grandson. "Robby, I have a happy-new-pets present for you!"

Robby's face lit up. "Thanks, Gram!" He stood slowly as if he knew any sudden movements would send Oliver racing back under the bed. He opened the gifts and again, it might as well have been Christmas morning. "A stuffed rabbit for Bentley and a catnip mouse for Oliver!"

Deborah grinned. "We also got Oliver his own cat condo so he has a place to scratch and climb and get high up the way cats like. That's in the car. Holt, you can bring it up before I go. And we got Bentley his very own indoor doghouse. It's made out of sturdy foam and has a cushy bed."

The trip to the pet store and all the gifts might have been his mom's idea, but his dad certainly hadn't vetoed it. His father was overly generous with his wife, especially, but his sons and Robby too. If he had it, he'd share it. That had always been his dad's way.

"That was above and beyond," Holt said. "Thank you."

"You're the best gram in the whole entire world!" Robby said, propelling himself at his grandmother for a hug.

She laughed and wrapped her arms around him, then looked at Amanda.

"Mom, this is Amanda Jenkins," he said.

"Amanda, my mother, Deborah Dalton. I was just telling my mom that we met in camp all those years ago and ran into each other at Happy Hearts."

"Isn't that something," his mother said. "Such a small world. Amanda, why don't you stay for dinner tonight? It'll be ready in about thirty minutes. I have this fancy brick-oven-style contraption in the kitchen, so how could I not use it on everyone's favorite food?"

Amanda bit her lip and glanced at Holt. Was she looking for help getting out of the invitation? Thing was, if she did want him to give her an easy excuse, he didn't want to.

He wanted her to stay.

"Yay, Amanda is having dinner with us!" Robby said with absolutely no assurance of that and shooting her a big smile. "Gram, Amanda helped us at Happy Hearts. She's so nice."

"She certainly is," Holt said, hoping she'd say yes. "I hope you can stay, Amanda. Unless you have plans." There—he'd provided her the out.

Don't take it, he willed her. *Don't say, "Well, actually, I do have plans, sorry."* She probably would say that—and not even add "another time."

Because from the look on her pretty face, she didn't want there to be another time.

After how he'd treated her ten years ago, who

could blame her? Even if he had explained himself. Maybe the truth was worse than the crime itself, despite what she'd said in the kitchen a little while ago. He hadn't been anyone she'd have wanted to be involved with.

"I'd love to," she said, surprising him and getting a hug from Robby, who'd gotten up again and wrapped his arms around her. Amanda laughed. "Thanks for the invitation," she said to his mother. "Can I help?"

"Oh no, you enjoy your visit with Holt and Robby," Deborah said. "But thank you."

"I'm going to teach Oliver and Bentley tricks," Robby said, getting back down on the floor to tell them about pizza night and how Gram always made his favorite, half pepperoni, half mushroom. Robby loved mushrooms on everything.

Holt could give his mother and son five hugs each. They'd gotten Amanda to stay for dinner. That he didn't want their time to end registered loud and clear. He wanted to get to know this new, older Amanda. But he could see from her expression that she was very wary of him. Maybe that was a good thing. Yeah, it probably was. He had a lot on his plate. His work on the ranch, which kept him busy. Almost a full month of summer left without childcare or camps, thanks to the camp director making him feel Robby wasn't welcome.

And this thing with his dad, which had come to a head last week when Robby was doing his chore of feeding his beloved chickens. His father had told Holt that Robby had let one of them get out and if it happened again, his son would be banned from the coop.

Holt had stood up for Robby—the boy was seven and chickens were sneaky. Seemed like his dad was always complaining about something; it was the Neal Dalton way. Holt had barely spoken to his father the past few weeks, mostly because Holt was keeping his distance. But his mom had specifically asked him to come tonight since all the Dalton brothers were attending.

Now tonight he'd have to deal with his dad *and* having Amanda Jenkins back in his life— and he didn't know what the next steps were in dealing with either.

Chapter Four

Amanda had never been inside a log mansion—and boy, was she glad she'd changed out of her yoga pants, long tank and owl socks when she'd first been asked over to Holt's and into something presentable for an unexpected family dinner. The gorgeous main house at Dalton's Grange went on forever, sprawling against the mountains. The home was a lot like Holt's much smaller version, vaulted wood ceilings, huge windows, arched doorways, a floor-to-ceiling stone fireplace and rustic-luxe furnishings. The dining room alone was almost twice the size of Amanda's big bedroom at BH247. Then again, with eight Daltons living on the property, Amanda supposed they'd need a big dining space for when they all got together.

The polished wood table also went on forever, comfortably seating everyone. Holt and Amanda were across from each other at the center of the table, Robby beside his father and next to his uncle Morgan. The oldest at thirty-four, Morgan was as blond and blue-eyed as Holt was dark-haired and dark-eyed, though the family resemblance was easily seen in the shape of the eyes, the nose, even their expressions. Holt was second oldest at thirty-two. Thirty-year-old Boone was somewhere in between, coloring-wise. Rounding out the Dalton siblings were Shep and Dale, both in their twenties, who lived in the house with Neal and Deborah. Amanda had felt eyes on her constantly when she'd first been introduced to the Dalton men. The siblings all had teasing grins on their faces for Holt, who apparently wasn't one to bring a woman home for dinner. Neal had welcomed her kindly and made some small talk about Whitehorn, which he said he didn't miss one bit.

As Amanda helped herself to a slice of roasted vegetable pizza, which looked delicious, she gazed around the table, the Daltons all chatting away about the ranch and a runaway horse, who'd been caught eventually, and then talk turned to Bentley and Oliver. Before Deborah had left Holt's house earlier, Amanda and Holt had carried up the indoor doghouse and cat condo. Oliver had explored his new catnip-scented playhouse immediately and seemed to love the high perch. Bentley had gone inside his doghouse, which Robby had festooned with toys, but since Oliver had seemed content enough, the dog had jumped up on Robby's bed, turned around three times, and then settled down with a happy sigh. Robby had hugged his grandmother again and again, beside himself with happiness.

Amanda already adored the kid. She'd used the rest of the time before dinner to interview Holt and Robby for the Happy Hearts website and take photos. In addition to photos of little Robby and his new pets, she now had one too many pictures of Holt Dalton on her phone. Available to ogle anytime.

As Robby talked more and more about his new pets, his grandfather, sitting at the head of the table, seemed to be a bit irritated by his grandson. Robby was talking a mile a minute, answering his uncle's questions, and Holt was focused on their conversation.

Amanda hadn't been sure if Holt had been overstating his father's impatience with Robby in his own anger over it. Given Neal's frustrated expression as he glanced at Robby, Holt hadn't been exaggerating. Neal, in his sixties with salt-and-pepper hair, tall and muscular like his sons, was now having a completely separate conversation with his son Dale, who sat to his left.

At the other end of the table, Deborah asked Robby questions about Bentley and Oliver, the boy excitedly answering.

"Gramps, will you come meet Bentley and Oliver too?" Robby asked. "Everyone's coming over after dinner to meet them."

All eyes were on Gramps. Amanda noticed Deborah Dalton's blue gaze was fierce on her husband, daring him to make an excuse.

"Sure I'm coming," Neal said with a smile at Robby—a genuine smile.

Robby beamed and reached for another slice of pepperoni and mushroom.

Amanda glanced at Holt. Whew. There was hope here. Neal could have said no, that he was tired, but he clearly did care deeply about his grandson.

As dinner went on, with so much talking and laughing, folks from each side asking her questions about living in downtown Bronco Heights and if she thought social media was going to be the downfall of global society—that one came from Holt's dad, of course—Amanda felt herself growing more and more wistful. Dinner growing up in the Jenkins family certainly hadn't been like this. With three shy Jenkinses at the table, no one had said much of anything. Every now and then, one of them would bring up something light and then go back to chewing and dabbing his or her mouth. Amanda had always figured it was the reason she'd become such a bookworm: reading allowed her to inhabit other worlds, be a part of the story, the family in the book. She got to be both Fern and Wilbur in *Charlotte's Web* and Anne and Anne's best friend, Diana, in *Anne of Green Gables*, and in all the romances and mysteries she read now, she got to be all different kinds of heroines. Being here at Dalton's Grange reminded her of being in a very good book.

Amanda had gone to quite a few gatherings that Brittany invited her to, forcing herself to be social, but she felt so out of place, wishing that piping up with an interesting thing to say came easily. Tonight, she found herself talking easily with this crew. They were a warm, welcoming bunch, even if Neal Dalton had too much of the "get off my lawn" at the ready.

"So, dessert at my house," Holt said, glancing around the table at his family. "I whipped up three pies this morning. Well, four, but I'm almost through one already."

"Daddy is the best cook," Robby said. "After Gram," he added quickly.

Deborah laughed. "I'd like to think I taught your daddy everything he knows about the kitchen."

"Why didn't it rub off on me?" Morgan asked, stealing a pepperoni off the edge of a pizza and popping it into his mouth.

As the brothers ribbed one another, again Amanda wished she had a family like this. Close, loving, sharing a weekday meal because they happened to live very close by and because they loved one another.

As they all headed out to walk in the gorgeous night air down to Holt's cabin, Amanda whispered, "I'll leave when we get to your house. I don't want to intrude any more than I have already."

Holt stopped in his tracks. "And miss my chocolate cream pie? My lemon chiffon? Are you kidding me?"

That was how Amanda ended up staying for dessert, sitting on the big leather chair by the fireplace and watching as Holt's brothers made a fuss over Bentley. Oliver had come as far as the stairs and refused to go farther, but Amanda was sure he'd warm enough to the house by tomorrow. Holt had set out the pies and plates and forks on the buffet in the living room, and had brought out the coffee maker, which made individual cups. The Daltons were again eating and sipping and talking and laughing, Amanda loving being part of this big rowdy crew.

But then Robby tried to see if Bentley knew how to play fetch, which meant grabbing a remote control and tossing it across the room, which hit a lamp and knocked it over, and Neal Dalton had an absolute fit.

"Robby! What in the world were you thinking!" Neal said. "You don't throw things! Is a remote control a stick? And you don't throw sticks in the house anyway!"

Robby's eyes got wide and he hung his head, dropping down and burying his face in Bentley's black-and-white fur.

"Dad, tone it down!" Holt said to Neal, holding up a hand. "It was an accident."

"Yes, just an accident," Deborah put in. "Let me get a broom and dustpan."

"I've got it, Mom," Holt said. "Enjoy your coffee."

"Who can enjoy their coffee with glass shards all over the place?" Neal said, shaking his head.

"You had five sons, Dad. You're gonna tell me you're not used to broken lamps? Come on. You've got to lighten up."

Neal frowned. "I'm grumpy because I'm tired." He sent Robby something of a smile, then got up and headed to the door. "Come on, Deborah. We both have to get up early."

"It's okay, Mom," Holt whispered.

Deborah kissed Holt on the cheek. "The pie was delicious." She looked at Amanda. "Lovely to meet you, Amanda."

The parents were suddenly gone, and then the brothers all headed to the door within minutes. "Don't mind Grumpy Gramps, Robby," Morgan said to his nephew.

"Seriously, Robby," Boone said, running a hand through his nephew's tousled hair, "Gramps didn't mean to yell. He's just tired from a long day with a sick bull."

"Yeah?" Holt asked. "Bull okay?"

Boone nodded. "He'll be fine. Dad stayed with him most of the day and once the meds kicked in, he was better."

"Hey, Robby," Dale said. "I once threw the TV remote at Shep's head when he was making fun of me for something in middle school, and it knocked over Gramp's favorite coffee mug that was on an end table. He lit into me for a good ten minutes and grounded me for a year but he was mad at something else, not me. Mom said he'd gotten a huge tax bill that day and his patience level was at zero."

"I remember that," Shep said. "And your aim is still terrible by the way."

Robby laughed. "So Gramps isn't really mad at me?"

"Nah," Holt assured his son. "An accident is an accident, right? You didn't mean to knock over the lamp. But you did break it because you were playing fetch in the house. Next time you want to play fetch with Bentley, you have to go outside. Understood?"

"Yes, Daddy," he said, wrapping Holt in a hug.

"And don't use a remote control, Robby," Holt added. "Use Uncle Morgan's shoe instead."

"I'll get you," Morgan said with a grin, fake punching Holt in the gut.

Robby laughed.

Amanda felt tears poke the backs of her eyes. Could this family be any lovelier?

Suddenly, it was just three of them. Bentley and Oliver had *long* come out from under the bed, the whole reason she'd come over in the first place. They'd eaten dinner. They'd had dessert. But Amanda didn't want to leave.

Holt had to somehow prolong Amanda's time in the house, so when Robby asked her to read him a bedtime story, he could not have been more grateful to his son.

"Sure, Robby," Amanda said. She seemed to like that she was a little kid's favorite new person in the world.

Back up in Robby's room, Amanda pulled over the desk chair by his bed while Holt sank down in the easy chair by the window. He'd read his son countless books over the past seven years, starting when he was just two days old and home from the hospital. Sally Anne, Robby's mother, had been rightfully tired, but as time passed, she'd never seemed comfortable feeding him or giving him his bath or taking care of him in the middle of the night. So Holt had done all that. He'd taken to fatherhood so easily because he loved Robby from the moment he knew about him. He and Sally Anne might have always had their problems, but ever since she'd told him she was pregnant, he was madly in love with his child.

Robby was a mini Holt, too, except for the eye color. He'd gotten his mother's baby blues but the rest was all Holt.

"'*Rocco and the Case of the Missing Chocolate Cake*,'" Amanda read, holding up the cover for Robby to see. His bedtime story was always a few chapters from a Rocco the Raccoon mystery.

"Yay, I love that one," Robby said. He'd asked

Amanda to pick out one from his favorites shelf. He yawned and pulled the blanket up to his chin.

Holt had no doubt he'd be asleep by chapter two. "Night, buddy," he said. "Just in case you fall asleep while Amanda's still reading."

"Night, Daddy. Night, Bentley. Night, Oliver."

Oliver was on the top perch of his kitty condo, which seemed his favorite place in the room. Bentley was sprawled across the foot of Robby's bed as if he'd always been part of the family. Holt could barely believe they'd just brought these two home *today.*

Bentley lifted his head, tilting it that adorable way dogs did, then closed his eyes. Amanda started reading.

"Oh wait. Good night, Amanda," Robby said. "Thanks for reading to me."

"Good night, Robby. And it's my pleasure."

Robby's eyes drooped with every word Amanda read. She'd gotten to page three, which was the end of chapter one, when Robby was clearly asleep.

"And my work here is done," she whispered with a smile.

"Hope not," he said. "I thought I could tempt you to stay for a cup of coffee. Dessert got kind of interrupted earlier."

"Sounds good," she said. Warily.

I'm more scared of you than you are of me, he wanted to tell her. *I might have hurt you ten years ago, but I'm not in a place to fall for someone. Or to get kicked to the curb.* But there was no way he was backing away from what he was feeling. Which was simply wanting to be with Amanda.

Downstairs in the kitchen, he brewed more coffee and suggested taking it out to the back deck so that Bentley could go out for a while. Amanda said something about the weather and the moon being gorgeous tonight, but he really had eyes only for her. It was just like the first time he'd seen her and had been so struck by a feeling—not just attraction but a feeling of *rightness*. He didn't know what that had meant at the time or even now, but when he looked at Amanda Jenkins, everything about his world felt right. Over the past few years that he'd been on his own, a single guy, he'd gone on dates his brothers had set up for him or with women who'd asked him out in the bakery aisle of the grocery store or in the pickup line at school, and half the time, he felt like they were on different planets. Lack of connection, of chemistry. With Amanda, it just felt *right*.

He went upstairs and whispered to Bentley to come, which the good boy did immediately, then the two joined Amanda on the deck. Holt set down the mugs of coffee on the table between their chaises, then stretched out, watching the border collie explore the backyard and sniff every blade of grass.

"Sorry you had to be there for that awkwardness with my dad and Robby," Holt said. Granted, Robby had done wrong and been wrong, but for his grandfather to yell like that—Holt didn't like it. Rage might make people, particularly kids, fearful, but it certainly wouldn't turn an impulsive kid into a more thoughtful, careful one.

"Well, I got to see firsthand what you meant," Amanda said, crossing her long legs at the ankles and picking up her coffee. "About your dad's lack of patience. I like how you handled it—explaining why it was wrong, that it was wrong. But it was an accident."

Holt ran a hand over his face. "I'm glad you said that. Half the time I don't know if I'm being too easy on him or if I just get him."

"Thank God you get him, Holt. Why do you think you're his hero?"

A warmth started in his gut and traveled straight up to his chest, left side. Damn. She got *him*. "I almost forgot you heard all that at the Happy Hearts. When he was talking to the cow."

She smiled. "I still can't get over saying 'how sweet' thinking I was talking to a complete stranger and finding the—" She stopped talking, watching Bentley intently as he explored the large yard.

"The guy who acted like a heartless jerk to the woman he loved," he finished for her.

"Well, you definitely didn't love me, Holt. Or you wouldn't have walked away."

He shook his head. "At the time I walked away because I *did* love you. I know that sounds nuts. You were the first person to treat me like I was not only worth something, but special. Almost like a golden boy—me." He shook his head, hardly able to believe anyone thought he was that guy. "Guys who had everything."

"You *were* that guy, Holt. I didn't create you. I met you and got to know you and fell in love with exactly what was in front of me. You."

Huh. He'd never thought of it that way. Certainly not back then. He'd been so sure she'd never accept the "real him," and he didn't have the heart to test out his theory. So he'd said something awful about being a rolling stone and wished her well. He'd never forget the look on her face. The confusion, the betrayal, and what she'd said about forgetting how people could shock you. And his own anguish at the time was something he'd never stopped carrying with him.

"I'm surprised you didn't become a teacher

for kids with special needs," he said, wanting to change the subject.

She sipped her coffee. "That was my plan, but turns out that in college, during my fieldwork of observation and student teaching at an elementary school, I was so shy I couldn't speak up or exert myself and I realized I couldn't stand up in front of twenty-five third graders and lead a classroom. I liked learning about education—theories and new practices—but being a teacher required something that I just didn't have and I knew it."

"That must have been rough to discover about yourself," he said. "Was it?"

"Well, it's important to know who you are and figure out where your strengths can take you. For a shy, bookish girl, I was shocked to find out I was good at marketing and social media outreach—promoting all kinds of businesses. I got to shower all my ideas and pep and passion on my work and in my campaigns—it's less about dealing with people than about the campaigns. My work just has to do my talking for me."

"That's really interesting," he said. "How'd you even find out you were good at marketing?"

"I took a marketing class in college and then did an internship at a really luxe dude ranch that celebs and their kids would vacation at. I found my calling—social media in the wilderness of

Montana. I love my job and being surrounded by ranches here in Bronco. Best of both worlds. But I do volunteer at the elementary school. I didn't entirely walk away from education and helping kids. I help out with reading and math for kindergarten through third grade. I've never been assigned to Robby's classroom, though. Dalton isn't that uncommon a name, but it would have stood out for me."

He sat up and turned to face her. "You tutor kids in reading?"

"Sometimes, yes. Why?"

"Would you consider privately tutoring Robby this summer? His confidence is so low. I'd love for him to walk into second grade the very first day knowing that he'll be moved from the 'worst reading group.'" He shook his head that Robby even knew he was in the lowest group.

"Kids are so aware—self aware and aware of others and where they fit in academically and socially. Even in the very early grades. It's awful."

"Yeah. Unless you really *are* a golden boy," he added with a grin. "Then you're on easy street."

"Eh, no one gets away from bad stuff happening," she said.

"True," he said, holding her gaze.

Bentley walked up to the deck and tilted his head as if deciding who to lie next to. He chose the soft mat in between their chairs and stretched out. Holt gave him a scratch and he got a pat from Amanda.

"I'd be happy to work with Robby," she finally said.

He wondered if she'd taken a few moments to respond because she didn't really want to but felt she couldn't say no. She seemed to like Robby—a lot, actually. But he could tell Amanda was ambivalent about spending time with her new student's dad. The one who broke her heart and walked away.

He wanted to ask about her hesitation in saying yes, but he figured he'd just accept that she *had* said yes and not look the ole gift horse in the mouth. "I'll warn you," he said. "He's not easy. He gets distracted and bored and unless he can read Rocco the Raccoon mysteries, he's not too interested in reading. But I'll pay you well." He named a figure that was at least a third more than he'd been quoted by other tutors that hadn't worked out—at all.

"I won't take a cent from you, Holt. Call it the we-have-a-past one-hundred-percent discount." She smiled. "Besides, I really like Robby and already think of him as my little buddy, not a client. He might be a whirlwind chatterbox to others, but I find his energy and excitement life-affirming."

Again, there was that feeling in his chest—warmth, gratitude. "Wow. How'd I get so lucky to have you walk back into my life?"

Oh, crud. The moment the words were out of his mouth he realized he shouldn't have said them. Or quite that way.

She sat up and faced him. "I'll be upfront, Holt. I'm not looking to reunite here."

He stared at her. "I'm not either." He was but he wasn't. He hoped that was what she meant too.

"Good," she said. "Nothing against you or what happened ten years ago," she added. "But I've been through…stuff since. And I'm done with all that."

"All that? You mean dating?"

She glanced away. "Well, I mean love. I'm done with love."

He raised an eyebrow. "You can't be done with love. You can't possibly control it."

She looked him right in the eyes. "You did, remember? You said just a little while ago that despite loving me, you left me."

Oh hell. He did say that. "But it cost me, Amanda. I didn't even realize what a bad state I was in at the time, leaving you like that. Not having you in my life anymore. I wasn't exactly Guy of the Year. And then I met Sally Anne and I thought, okay, she's rough around the edges like me, my kind of woman. She got pregnant by accident, and I'll tell you, Amanda, my life changed in that moment. Every bad habit I had I kicked to the curb. Driving too fast, drinking too much, running wild like I didn't have a care. I *had* a care—a baby. That was it. I changed like that." He snapped his fingers for emphasis.

"But it didn't work out. You and Sally Anne."

He really didn't like thinking back to his marriage. "I was a lot more into making it work than she was. She wasn't even all that interested in marrying me but her parents, who had a lot of problems with her, told her they'd cut her out of the will if she didn't make them respectable grandparents. They didn't have much, but they had enough to make her say I do."

"Oh God, this sounds awful."

"It gets worse." He took a long sip of his cooling coffee. "We got married when I was twenty-five. She was just twenty-two. She'd always told me she wasn't cut out for motherhood and I guess she tried here and there, but she left when Robby was three. When her parents passed away in a car accident, nothing in her life felt right and she moved out to Colorado where she had some friends. And now she sends cards and small gifts for birthdays and Christmas, but that's it. She doesn't come visit."

"Robby must ask about his mom," she asked softly.

"He does. Less now than the first year she left. But he's often reminded of her absence in other ways. You know how it is at school since you volunteer—moms coming in for special class events and choral concerts and to be the guest reader. It's always just me or his grandmother."

Amanda touched a hand to her chest. "Oh, my heart hurts thinking about that."

"Keeps me up at night, Amanda. But that's our life. And we have a good one. Robby has a de-voted father, grandparents who love him, uncles who dote on him. Morgan taught Robby to ride a two-wheeler. Boone takes him fishing every Sunday. Dale's the one who got Robby interested in the rodeo and takes him to all Daring Drake's events. And Shep takes Robby hiking up in the mountains, tiring him out good."

"That's wonderful. He's truly lucky to have all of that love."

Holt nodded. "Yeah. It's why I know I made the right decision coming back, working for my dad, hard as it is to be around him so often. I try to keep my distance." He was still sitting facing her, their knees almost touching. He wanted to reach out and touch her face, her hair.

"Did I just tell you my life story?" he asked.

She smiled. "I'm glad you did."

He wasn't sure if he moved forward or if she did, but suddenly their lips met in an unexpected kiss.

"Whoa, cowboy," she said. "How'd we get here?"

"I don't regret it," he said, looking right into her beautiful dark eyes.

"I have to," she said, standing up. "I'm not going there, Holt. I can't. If I help Robby this summer, you have to make me a promise that we'll be platonic. Don't flirt, don't sweet talk me, don't come near me with those lips."

He stood too. "Well, it's not going to be easy but given how crazy my life is right now, I shouldn't be trying to start something with anyone." Especially not the one woman who could bring him to his knees. Sometimes he thought the real reason he left Amanda was because he knew she would have left him if she knew the truth about him, and he wouldn't have been able to survive that pain.

"So we have a deal?" she asked.

"A tough deal, but a deal."

"Shake it on. Cowboy's code means you can't break it."

He smiled and shook, mostly just to feel her hand against his, but inside he was sweating. Because he was already dreaming of breaking that code.

Chapter Five

Ten minutes after Amanda had gotten home from the extended trip to Dalton's Grange, she was back in her jammies and sitting at her desk in front of her laptop, determined to focus on the decades-old mystery of what became of Beatrix Abernathy. If she worked on helping Mel track down the long-lost daughter of the two young separated lovers, Amanda wouldn't think about Holt. Or the kiss. Or the agreement she'd made to tutor his son.

Yet all she was thinking about was the unexpected kiss. Their chemistry was on fire, always had been, so the kiss was no surprise. There was just something between them as there had been from the first day she'd seen Holt Dalton ten years ago at Camp KidPower. And the more he opened up to her about what was really going on in his life, the closer she felt to him. Unfortunately.

She should not, could not feel close to him. Not after how badly he'd hurt her. As she'd told him on the deck, she was done with love, done with opening herself up to heart-wrenching pain. She had to keep some distance from Holt, somehow. His promise to keep his lips to himself was a good start.

Beatrix Abernathy, she told herself, staring at the search engine. Amanda went over her notes in her phone app, reading the words in the letter found tucked between the pages of Josiah Abernathy's diary.

My dearest Winona, please forgive me. But they say you will never get better. I promise you that your baby daughter is safe. She's alive! I wanted to raise her myself, but my parents forced me to have her placed for adoption. She's with good people—my parents don't know, but I have figured out who they are. Someday, I will find a way to bring her back to you.

Winona Cobbs was in her nineties now. And according to Mel she was delicate and frail these days. They had to fulfill Josiah's promise as quickly as possible—especially now that Josiah had had that moment of remembrance.

I'll do everything I can to help. Amanda sent the promise silently into the universe.

Hmm, Amanda thought, staring at her computer screen. She'd done some marketing work for a hospital and recalled there was an online group of adoptees looking for information about their birth parents. She could start with a group such as that one. But where to focus the search? Winona and her family had lived in Rust Creek Falls back then, where she'd likely given birth.

Since the Abernathys had moved to Bronco after the baby had been adopted, Mel had said she had a feeling the baby had been adopted to a Bronco family. Perhaps, like Josiah, the Abernathys also knew which family the newborn had been placed with and wanted to keep tabs from a distance or just live in the same area with the little girl who wouldn't be part of their own family. Mel hadn't been sure of any of that.

Amanda figured she'd start with online groups related to Rust Creek Falls, a very small town, and Bronco. With Poindexter on her lap, she did some searches for online groups concerning adoption in Kalispell and bingo—there was a public chat group of people looking for information. Amanda typed her own new post into the site:

I'm looking for information about a baby girl likely born in Rust Creek Falls seventy-plus years ago to teenaged parents and placed for adoption by the birth father's family. The families—the surnames are Cobbs and Abernathy—would have originally been from Rust Creek Falls. I have reason to believe the adoptive family was from Bronco. Please contact me with any leads.

She closed her laptop. Her post was pretty general, but there was a time frame, a place, surnames—and all that was a good start. You never knew what could resonate with someone out there and bring forth a lead.

I hope we find you, Beatrix Abernathy, Amanda thought, giving her cat a few scratches by her tail.

She heard a key in the lock, which meant Brittany was home. Her roommate came in and locked up, then took off her high heels, sighing with relief.

"Ahhh. These pinched me all night. Gorgeous

but painful," she said, wagging her finger at the sexy stilettos.

Amanda sent her a rueful smile. "Just like the guy I spent the past few hours with." She felt her eyes widen as she realized what she'd just blurted out. "Did I just say that?"

Brittany came rushing over to the sofa and plopped down. "What guy? I thought you were spending the evening on the sofa with that documentary." She reached into her purse and pulled out a velvet scrunchie, then pulled her long hair into a low ponytail.

"Well, that was the plan. And then Holt called."

Brittany raised an eyebrow. "Holt? I like that name. Sounds sexy."

"Oh, he is," Amanda said, feeling herself blush. She was very comfortable with Brittany and always felt like she could be herself and say what was on her mind. But she hadn't had a guy to gush about in the two years she'd lived here. Not that Holt was hers. "I've mentioned him, though not by name. He was that summer love ten years ago at a camp where we worked. I thought we'd be together forever, but he dumped me the last day. I ran into him late this afternoon when I was at Happy Hearts to go over some work with Daphne."

"He was at Happy Hearts? Is he a vegan who doesn't wear leather shoes?" she asked.

Amanda laughed. "The opposite. He's a cattle breeder. His family owns one of the biggest and most gorgeous ranches in Bronco Heights—Dalton's Grange."

"He's a Dalton? There are a zillion of them and each one is better looking than the last."

Very true. Holt was the cutest, in Amanda's opinion—then each was cuter than the last. "Five brothers to be exact. And yup, I met them all tonight at dinner at the parents' house. Holt's mother invited me to stay."

"Oooh," Brittany said. "Tell me every detail."

Amanda did. She left nothing out. Starting with Robby Dalton wanting to adopt a cow and ending with the hot kiss from Holt on the back deck. And the promise they'd both made not to repeat it.

"Oh sure," Brittany said, shaking her head with a grin. "Like *that* will happen. That was some intense evening, Amanda. You two will be lip-locked within minutes of seeing each other the next time."

"He's an *amazing* kisser," Amanda said, biting her lip as she recalled every delicious sensation that had consumed her. "But I mean it. No more. First of all, he completely broke my heart and was careless about it too. He just walked away, Brittany." She'd never told her roommate about getting left at the altar two years ago right before moving to Bronco. When she'd arrived in town, she'd wanted this to be about a fresh start, not re-hashing everything that went wrong in her life, so she'd just said she'd had her share of heartache and wasn't looking to get involved with anyone. "I guess I just don't have faith in love anymore."

"Your trust was shot," Brittany said, her dark eyes sympathetic. "I can understand that. But life and love are about risks."

Poindexter moved and Amanda petted his back and cute head, her gaze on the sweet, loving cat who never gave her any trouble. "That's just it. I don't want to take risks. I never want to be that hurt again. There was a next time with someone else too. I did try again and look what happened. Same thing."

Brittany tilted her head, her expression sym-pathetic. "Well, since you'll be tutoring Holt's son, it sounds like you agreed to spend some se-rious time with the Dalton duo. And that means you might not have any say over what your heart says and does."

She'd become an expert at just that these past couple of years. A handsome face and a list of quali-ties she'd like hadn't been able to tempt her into dating anyone. "I pride myself on being levelheaded. Even if I'm attracted to Holt, I won't get involved with him. Tutoring his son will be about Robby. Not about me and Holt. There is no me and Holt."

"I do hear you, Amanda. But I'll say this. I'm glad you're going to tutor his son. Because you're putting yourself in the path. And that's where you should be, sweetie. Not hiding out in your room with Poindexter. Much as I love that cat."

Amanda wanted to tell her roommate—whom she adored—the same thing back. Brittany dated up a storm, but she never let anything escalate because she didn't want more than a good time. But what if her roommate did want more deep down where she wouldn't admit it to herself? Amanda had always figured the right guy would come along and Brittany's own words would be used against her. She'd be in the path and wouldn't be able to get out of the way.

Eh, life and love and relationships were complicated.

Brittany let out a giant yawn. "I'm zonked. And I can't wait to get out of this jumpsuit and into my pj's."

"The party was a huge success, I'm sure."

Brittany grinned and stood up. "It definitely was." She gave Poindexter a pat. "See you in the morning, roomie."

"Night, Brittany. Thanks for the talk."

With Poindexter in her arms, Amanda went into her bedroom. She got under the covers and knew she wouldn't be falling asleep any time soon. She stared up at the ceiling, trying to bore herself to sleep. But all she saw in her mind was Holt Dalton's face. And how sexy he was. She sighed and grabbed her phone, opening up her photos app.

Photos of Holt and Robby and their new dog and cat filled the screen. The craziest thought hit her and she quickly turned off her phone. She'd imagined herself in that last photo, sitting with Holt, her husband, Robby, her son, Bentley and Oliver—and of course Poindexter—her sweet pets.

She was getting all mixed up. She wanted a child—and obviously, Robby, with his put-it-out-there honesty and adorableness, had plucked her heartstrings something fierce. Throw in his gorgeous single father with whom she had a past, and of course her emotions were all over the place.

She took one last look at a photo of Holt before shutting off her phone and staring back up the ceiling. But all she saw was Holt's face. All she felt was Holt kissing her, his hands on her back. He was so familiar and so not at the same time.

How exactly was she going to keep herself from falling for him all over again?

* * *

Thunk.

Thunk-thunk.

Thunkety-thunk.

It was just before midnight. Holt glanced toward his bedroom door, not that it would reveal anything about the strange noises coming from down the hall. Sounded like Robby was bouncing one of Bentley's balls, but his son was fast asleep. He knew that because he'd come upstairs just a few minutes ago, checked on Robby, nodded at Bentley, who was lying at the foot of the bed, then went into his own room and slid under the covers, hoping he'd get some sleep tonight.

But doubting it. He could not stop thinking about Amanda and that kiss. Wanting more. Despite agreeing there would not be a second kiss.

Thunk.

Holt got out of bed and went to investigate.

"Daddy?" came Robby's voice.

"Already on my way," he called out, going into Robby's room.

Bentley was sitting on the floor by the bed now. Oliver was on his perch and jumped onto the foot of the bed, and the dog jumped up onto the bed too. Then the cat jumped down and Bentley did too.

Hence the thunks. Great—pet acrobatics at midnight.

"Bentley and Oliver," Holt said, wagging a finger. "You woke up Robby. Shhhhh from now on."

Bentley tilted his black-and-white head as if apologizing and agreeing. Oliver began grooming his face with a white paw. *Sorry, not sorry*, the cat seemed to be saying.

"I think I'll give Oliver a little more dinner right now," Holt said. He'd gotten that tip from Daphne. If he made the cat's dinnertime later, he'd likely sleep through the night. "Then he'll have a nice full belly and curl up to bed."

"'Kay, Daddy," Robby said with a yawn. He frowned, his face suddenly crumpling. "Daddy?"

Holt froze and then sat down on Robby's bed. "What's wrong, buddy?" He pushed his son's mop of brown bangs out of the way. Bentley jumped up and lay beside Robby to make sure his person was okay, and the boy put an arm around the sweet pooch.

"Do you think Gramps is still mad at me?" Robby asked.

Oh hell. A burst of anger radiated in Holt's gut. This was what Neal Dalton wanted? To worry a little kid so much that the first thing he thought of when he woke up in the middle of the night was that his grandfather was mad at him?

"Gramps loves you. I know that like I know my name. And yours. I promise you he does."

Robby shook his head. "But I'm loud and I break things."

"Gramps is just an impatient person. Something happens and he doesn't react well. Some people get mad if milk gets spilled or something breaks. Others, like Gram, take it a little easier. But Gramps loves you very much."

"Are you sure, Daddy?" his son asked, his expression less troubled.

"Yes. I'm sure." He *was* sure. His dad loved Robby like crazy; he had from the moment Robby was born. "Did I ever tell you what Gramps did right after coming to visit you in the hospital when you were just five minutes old?"

Robby giggled. "One million times, Daddy."

Okay, that was true. Holt pulled that one out of the hat so often because the story reminded him that his father *did* love the boy at the core, and it reminded Robby too in a way that seemed to settle inside his bones and cells, making him feel better.

"Well, I'm gonna tell you for the millionth and one time," Holt said, stretching out beside Robby and pulling his son against him. Bentley put his chin on Robby's belly with a sigh. "First your granddad stopped in the hospital gift shop, buying every single stuffed animal and like twenty 'It's A Boy!' balloons. Then he met you and held you for a long time, telling you how you were named after his favorite uncle who wasn't with us anymore. And when he bought Dalton's Grange, he planted an apple tree in the backyard that he named The Great Robby Dalton's Apple Tree."

Robby smiled. "I like my tree, Daddy. It gets bigger every year just like me."

"That's right. Your grandfather planted that in your honor, something superspecial that would last forever, right by the house."

"Gramps said he thought the tree would make apples in a few years," Robby said, letting out a giant yawn.

Holt nodded. "I'm already looking forward to the apple crumble you'll make me."

"I can't cook!" Robby said, laughing. But then he turned serious again. "Daddy, do you think my second grade teacher will like me?"

"Of course she will." The good news was that Robby had been assigned to Ms. Chang's classroom, and she had a reputation for being very patient and warm. "Warm and fuzzy" was good for Robby.

"Even though I'm in the worst reading group? I felt dumb when I was reading to Bentley and

Oliver. Do they think I'm dumb?" Tears filled his blue eyes again.

Oh no. "Robby," Holt said, drawing his son into his arms. "You are not dumb. You're very smart and you work very hard. Everyone learns to read at their own pace. Took me till the middle of second grade before I was considered a good reader. Just took me longer. Some things come easily and some things come harder. You can put together puzzles and Legos and figure out those crazy instructions. A lot of people can't."

"I am good at puzzles and Legos." His face brightened.

"Hey, did you know that Amanda works with kids at your school on reading and helping them improve? How would you like her to work with you the rest of the summer?"

In one day he'd gone from not having seen Amanda Jenkins for ten years to making an important decision—adopting Bentley and Oliver—in her presence and spending most of the evening with her. She'd met his parents—his entire family, actually. Then there was that amazing kiss. And now she'd be working with his son, probably a couple times a week for the rest of August. And August had barely begun.

Robby's face burst into a grin. "I'll be moved up from the worst reading group for sure!"

"I'll bet she can start working with you very soon." Holt liked the idea of having a very good reason to call Amanda in the morning. "You're a great kid. All you have to be is you, Robby. I love you just as you are. And so do Bentley and Oliver."

"Amanda likes me too," Robby said.

"She sure does."

Robby smiled, his entire countenance relaxing. "Good, Daddy."

"You feel better about everything?"

Robby nodded and yawned. "I'm so tired." He turned over and clutched his stuffed rodeo bull under his arm.

"I'm gonna go give Oliver that extra helping of food to calm him down. I think the thumps will stop and you'll be able to sleep."

"'Kay, Daddy. Love you."

Holt's heart was about to burst. "I love you too, Robby. Night."

"Night, Daddy," Robby said, his eyes closing.

Holt picked up Oliver, who wasn't having it and wiggled to be let down. "Fine, mister. You can follow me to the kitchen instead of having a perfectly good ride."

Which the cat did. As Holt put a little more dry food in the cat's bowl, Oliver padded over and began eating. *Ah, success*, he thought. *With a fully belly he'll settle down. No more thunks, for sure.*

As he put the bag of food away, he mentally added two items to his to-do list for the morning. One was to talk to his dad about how he was affecting Robby with his gruffness. The other was to ask Amanda to start working with Robby ASAP. Maybe even tomorrow.

Interesting that the thought of talking to Amanda made knowing he was going to have it out with his dad a lot easier.

Chapter Six

"I wish I had long nice hair like you."

Amanda glanced toward the voice. A little red-haired girl, three or four years old, with a chin-length bob, was staring at her from her seat at the big table in Tender Years Daycare, surrounded by kids practicing writing lower-case letters on wide-lined paper. Amanda was standing by the rows of cubbies, full of hoodies and lunchboxes, waiting for the daycare owner for their 10:00 a.m. marketing meeting.

"I love your hair," Amanda said.

The girl's face brightened. "Really? Mine was

long like yours but my little sister put gum in it and my mommy had to cut it."

Aww. "Really and truly. And sorry about the gum. That happened to me once. I'll bet by the holidays your hair will be much longer."

"Really?" the girl asked. "By Christmas?"

Amanda did the math in her head. It was now early August. The girl had a good five months to go, and at half an inch a month, her hair would be down to her shoulders by Christmas for sure. "Yup."

"Yay," the adorable redhead said, and finished coloring her picture of a cat.

Lucinda Banks, the owner of the daycare, gestured for Amanda to come back to her office. As she walked past the precious bunch of children working on their names, she took in their little faces, so full of concentration and wonder, their brightly colored sneakers and T-shirts, and her heart almost burst.

As she followed Lucinda to her office, she was grateful for the meeting this morning. Otherwise, she'd be working at home as usual and would be taking too many thinking-about-Holt breaks. She'd woken up with him on her mind. She'd had a quick breakfast in the kitchen with Brittany, who'd told her to keep an open mind about the sexy rancher. But she didn't want to. When you had your heart broken into pieces by someone, how you could trust them again? How could you let yourself be that vulnerable? Amanda had finished her coffee and made a firm decision to close her mind concerning Holt Dalton.

Inside Lucinda's office, one wall devoted to children's artwork, Amanda spent the next forty-five minutes sharing her PowerPoint presentation. Lucinda approved her campaign ideas for both radio and local newspaper advertising and social media outreach to target ideal customers. Amanda had one more meeting with Bronco Bank and Trust and then a few hours of work to do at home. Finally she'd drive over to Dalton's Grange for her first tutoring session with Robby.

When she got home, she'd spend some solid time going over materials she had from the school district and some online sites for approaches to help struggling readers. She already had a good background, but with some focused prep for Robby's particular needs—luckily she'd already gotten a sense of that when he'd read to Bentley and Oliver yesterday—she'd feel even more armored to get Robby Dalton out of that "worst group."

She was all too aware that she was looking forward to that part of her day the most. To help Robby—and to see Holt again. The man she not an hour ago had firmly decided to keep at double arm's length. Somehow, she would.

As she was heading out of Lucinda's office, she noticed the group of preschoolers were now in circle time around a big colorful rug in the center of the room. Amanda paused by the front door as the teacher addressed the group.

"Boys and girls, in a little while we'll be drawing pictures of something that makes us feel happy," the teacher said. "Let's go around the circle and say one thing that makes you feel happy. Everyone will have a turn."

Being with Holt and Robby, Amanda thought unbidden—and was unnerved by her immediate response.

The teacher held up a yellow happy face on a stick. "I'll go first. My students make me happy— all of *you*!" She smiled and passed the stick to a student with a long brown braid who said that chocolate chip cookies for dessert made her feel happy. The girl then passed the happy face to the boy next to her.

"Recess time!" the boy with curly blond hair said.

"When my aunt Maya visits cuz she always brings me a present and she's coming today!" the next girl said.

"Coloring."

"Chicken nuggets but no yucky sauce."

"When my mommy picks me up from here and we go home."

Aww. Amanda felt her heart grow bigger and bigger as each little kid squeezed inside it. Now it was the redhead's turn, the one whose little sister put gum in her hair.

The girl tilted her head and thought for a second. "My little sister makes me happy because she's my little sister."

Double triple awww. I want a child, she thought. *I want to be a mother*. Maybe she should look into adoption—an older child. But as she pictured a little hand in hers, there was a man beside her holding the child's other little hand.

This wasn't matching up with Amanda's plans to avoid love and romance. And now because of the call she'd gotten just five minutes ago from Holt as she'd pulled into the parking area of the daycare, she'd be seeing Holt and Robby later—and likely twice a week for the next three weeks while she worked with the little Dalton on reading. Holt's description of Robby's worried wake up in the middle of the night had had her agreeing to help ASAP, which meant starting today. She and Holt had discussed setting up a regular schedule then too.

A regular schedule of being in Holt's house. With him there.

Suddenly, the little hand she imagined in hers was Robby Dalton's. The man beside her holding the other little hand: Holt Dalton. Oh boy. She could clearly see their faces now. Robby with Bentley on a leash beside him, Oliver hitching a ride on Bentley's back, which made no sense, but neither did thinking of Robby as hers in the first place. And on the other side of the boy was Holt, tall, sexy, strong Holt.

She was falling for him all over again. And she was in even bigger trouble this time around because his seven-year-old son had managed to steal her heart in record time. Her roommate's words came back to her yet again, about having an open mind. Could she? Despite everything that had happened? Everything she knew would happen?

And she did know. Holt would break her heart—again. Never in a million years would she have thought that summer ten years ago that Holt would have left her, dumped her flat on her face, without a backward glance. How did a person go from acting like he was in love, showing that love, to just walking away and cutting all ties?

Tyler had done the same thing.

So how could Amanda think of giving Holt a second chance? *Come on. You can't be your own worst enemy in life, girl,* she told herself. *Be your own best friend. Be your own Brittany! Do not let that man past Go. Or even close to Go.*

Then again, Holt hadn't exactly said anything about a second chance. In fact, when she'd broken up that amazing kissing session on his deck, he'd said he shouldn't be getting involved with anyone either, that he had a lot on his plate.

He *told* you this time. Said straight out that he wasn't looking for a relationship. And what had been her grandpop's motto? *When someone tells you who they are, believe them.*

If she let herself fall head over heels in love with Holt Dalton again, she'd only have herself to blame, not Holt, who'd been honest.

So. Do. Not. Let. Him. Pass. Go.

With that firm in her head, Amanda pushed open the door to leave Tender Years just as someone pulled it open to enter. She almost crashed right into none other than Neal Dalton, Holt's dad. He wore a dark brown Stetson, a western shirt under a jacket and jeans.

What on earth could he be doing here?

"Mr. Dalton," she said. "How nice to see you again. It was so thoughtful of your wife to invite me to the house for dinner last night."

He tilted his head at her, as if trying to remember her name. "Ah yes, Amanda, Holt's friend—

from way back at that summer camp he had to attend."

Had to attend. Where had Neal Dalton been ten years ago when that one little word would have clued her in that Holt wasn't telling her everything? She couldn't help but think if he had told her everything, he wouldn't have felt the need to break up with her. He'd have known that she wouldn't have judged him—especially not after getting to know him and loving him. But of course, that wasn't what happened.

"Call me Neal," he said with nod. "Sorry you saw me get so upset during dessert at Holt's. But that's exactly why I'm here. Do you work at the daycare?"

Uh, *why* was he here?

"No, I do marketing outreach and social media for Tender Years. I just had a meeting with Lucinda, the owner. But, Neal," she dared to press, "what do you mean that's why you're here?" Perhaps he wanted to volunteer at the daycare to learn more about how kids operated, that they made mistakes, they made noise, and to watch the teachers for tips on how to handle issues that arise.

"I want to find out if there's an opening for Robby for the rest of the month so that Holt can concentrate on the ranch," Neal explained. "With the day camp not willing to take him anymore, Holt's out of options. He already went through about five sitters who all quit and said Robby was just too much."

Amanda frowned. Granted, she hadn't spent *a ton* of time with Robby, but certainly enough to know the boy was just very energetic and curious and easily distracted. Robby had a good heart and understood right and wrong. He just needed to be around adults who knew how to channel that energy and curiosity. Tender Years was an excellent daycare with warm and experienced teachers; Robby would fit in well here from what Amanda had seen over the past year. "I didn't realize Holt was looking for a slot here for Robby. I can introduce you to Lucinda—"

"Oh, I haven't talked to Holt yet," Neal said. "I figured I'd find out if there was an opening and offer to pay the monthly cost to sway Holt to enroll Robby."

Amanda was sure her face registered her surprise—and alarm. "You mean you're here because *you* want Robby in daycare?"

"That's right. Full time till school starts up at the end of the month. Robby's a great kid, but he needs more structured activity and direction. Right now, with camps no longer an option, Deborah is watching Robby while Holt works, and granted, his uncles also help out, but wouldn't the boy be happier with scheduled activities and kids his own age? I thought I'd just see if there's an opening and then talk to Holt about it."

Amanda doubted Holt would want to put his son in daycare. She knew how much he valued the boy being around family for the rest of the summer.

"Anyway," Neal continued. "As I said, I'm just seeing if there's an opening. No harm in that."

But there was. And would be.

"May I help you, sir?"

Amanda turned and there was Lucinda, extending her hand toward Neal.

"Ah, Mr. Dalton, right? I believe I met you and your wife at a fund-raising dinner for the ranchers' association a couple months ago. You own Dalton's Grange, right? What a grand and gorgeous property. And you have all those handsome sons."

Neal took off his Stetson and shook her hand. "That's right. And a very energetic grandson who could use a place here, if there's an opening."

"I have an opening for a full-time or two part-time attendees," Lucinda said. "Come to my office and we'll discuss."

Neal put his hat back on, then tipped it at Amanda. "Nice seeing you again."

Amanda managed a smile and swallowed.
This was not going to end well.

Holt spent most of the morning herding cattle—
one of his favorite jobs on the ranch—into a farther
pasture, then helped his brother Morgan go over
inventory, and now, fortified by two strong cups
of coffee, it was time to find his dad and have that
talk. He'd been looking for Neal Dalton all morning but hadn't seen him anywhere. He tried the
main barn again, and there his dad was with his
usual clipboard, flipping pages of his to-do list
in one hand, his travel mug of coffee in the other.

Holt took a deep breath and cleared his throat.
"Glad I found you, Dad. I've been looking for
you all morning."

Neal took a long sip of his coffee. "Well, you
found me." He looked up at Holt as if bracing
himself. His dad clearly knew Holt wouldn't let
go of what happened last night with Robby.

But before Holt could launch into the sort of
speech he'd prepared in his head but had already
gotten jumbled, his dad spoke.

"So is this Amanda your girlfriend?" Neal
asked.

I wish, Holt thought, the words coming quicker
than he could deny them to himself.

Luckily, Holt didn't have to respond because

his father quickly added, "I ran into her this morning. I was walking in, she was walking out. Small world."

He ran into Amanda? "Walking out of where?" he asked, figuring his dad was at the coffee shop.

"Tender Years Daycare," Neal said. "She does marketing work for the place."

Holt stared at his father, feeling his eyes narrow. "Why were *you* there?"

Neal took another swig of coffee. "Well, that's what I wanted to talk to you about. Turns out the daycare has a full-time slot open. Robby could start tomorrow and stay until school starts. The boy could use some structure the next few weeks."

Whoa. Overstepping much? "Between his grandmother and his uncles, he has plenty of structure. His relatives enjoy spending time with him." He emphasized the word *relatives*, feeling his eyes narrow on his father even more.

Neal Dalton lifted his chin. "I know they do. I do too. I love Robby, Holt. But he's a whirlwind. Just think about the idea of the daycare—that's all I'm asking."

"I won't think about it," Holt said. "I have a good arrangement the next few weeks with Mom and my brothers watching Robby when I can't. We all planned it that way together, so they'd get to spend some real time with him this summer. I can hire a sitter now and again."

"The last few refused to come back," Neal reminded him.

"So I'll find someone else. I'm going to do what feels right to me, Dad. End of story."

"You were always unnecessarily stubborn," Neal said. "Amazing that that lovely young woman still likes you from when you knew her ten years ago." He tried to add a smile to show he was kidding, but Holt knew his dad wasn't joking in the slightest.

Holt crossed his arms over his chest. "Why wouldn't she?"

"Come on, Holt. Getting into trouble. Arrested twice for stupid stuff you shouldn't have been doing."

"That was a long time ago," he said, turning away.

"Look, Holt, I don't want trouble between us. That's the last thing I want. It means the world to me that you're here at Dalton's Grange with Robby. You know that. I'm just saying that my grandson—and I love that boy like mad—is a lot like you were at his age. Rein in him now and save yourself problems down the road."

A hot flash of anger burned red in Holt's gut.

"Oh, so now Robby's a juvenile delinquent in the making?"

"He needs structure, Holt. Plain and simple. More than baking cookies with Gram or mucking out the calf stalls for twenty minutes with your uncles."

"I think I know what my son needs, Dad."

"Why don't you ask that nice Amanda her opinion," Neal said. "She knows you from back when you used to be a troublemaker headed down the wrong path. That's why she's so understanding about Robby. She clearly sees you in him." Neal Dalton nodded as if doubly agreeing with himself, flipped through his clipboard a couple times, then glanced at Holt. "She'll tell you structure is a good thing for a rowdy child. I was too lenient with you and I regret it. That's what this is all about."

Holt felt like a character from the animated TV show his son loved, about a bull with a temper who always had locomotive steam coming out of his ears.

"What Robby needs," Holt said through gritted teeth, "is love and guidance and supportive people around him. You are *way* too hard on him. He's seven years old. He's a good kid, but yes, he makes mistakes. Yes, he talks too much and too loud, he runs when he should walk, he's impulsive. But the way you bark at him doesn't change his behavior."

Neal frowned. "I don't mean to bark. But sometimes I can't help it."

"Well guess what? Neither can Robby. He needs to be around his family right now—that's what I believe. I like the arrangement as it is, with me, his mom and his uncles watching him the rest of the month. I'm *not* sending him to Tender Years, wonderful as the place may be. End of discussion."

Holt was more than done with this conversation.

"Hey, Neal," a deep voice said from outside. "Got a sec to talk about where you want the shipment of hay bales coming in at noon?"

Holt glanced out the barn doors. Brody Colter, one of the ranch hands, was standing there, looking at Neal expectantly.

"Sure thing," Neal said to the guy. "Stubborn," he tossed at Holt, shaking his head as he walked out with his clipboard and his thermos.

Like father, like son, he wanted to call after him.

Chapter Seven

At a few minutes before five o'clock, Amanda pulled up in the drive at Holt's beautiful cabin. She could see Robby throwing a ball in a large fenced pasture at the side of the house, Bentley racing to get it, his furry tail wagging in the breeze.

Holt threw another ball to Robby, who couldn't catch it, but the smiling boy didn't seem to mind one bit. He ran after the orange ball, Bentley trying to get it first, and Robby was laughing so hard he dropped to his knees.

"You're faster than me, Bentley!" Robby said, giving the dog a rubdown. "I love you so much!"

Bentley put a paw on Robby's leg, and the boy was up like a shot, throwing the ball, which the dog went chasing after.

"Wow," Amanda said as she approached the fence, her tote bag with her reading supplies on her shoulder. "I knew Bentley was going to a great home, but to see him running around with a happy little boy, chasing balls, well, it warms my heart."

Holt nodded. "And they'll both sleep very well tonight. Not sure about me, though." His face hardened and he shook his head. "Heard you ran into my dad at a daycare in town."

Phew, she thought. On the drive over here, she'd hoped his father had already talked to Holt about that. Because if Neal hadn't, being here and having all that in her head with Holt none the wiser would have made her feel awful.

"Yeah," she said, wincing. "I asked why he was there and he told me. I had a feeling the conversation between you two would not go well."

"It didn't."

"How many hours does your mom watch Robby?"

"Two. Three to five, Monday through Friday. Just for August. Maybe he's too much on her, even though she's never said anything. I can hire a sitter so that there's more back up. Someone with really good references in handling high-energy kids."

Amanda bit her lip, working over an idea in her mind. A good idea? Bad idea? You-are-crazy-Amanda idea? She looked at Robby, throwing the ball for Bentley, then trying to race the dog to get it, his laughter a beautiful sound.

"I'm your gal," she said with a nod, then felt her cheeks burn. "I mean, I'll take over that time slot if it turns out your mom does need a break. Robby and I can spend an hour on reading and then an hour on playing with Bentley and Oliver. I can give him some really good training tips."

Holt stared at her, his expression a combination of wonder and surprise. "You'd do that? I'd pay you an amazing rate."

"Nope," she said. "I won't take a penny for helping Robby with reading, and I won't take a penny for hanging out with him. It's just three weeks. And to be honest, Holt, I want the experience."

He raised an eyebrow. "You have plenty of that, though. I'd pay any rate you asked."

She shook her head. "I don't mean experience tutoring. That I've got." She looked away, suddenly not wanting to say it—the reason.

He tilted his head and looked at her. Waiting.

She sucked in a breath. "Well, I've come to a

realization. I want a child. Since that likely won't happen the traditional way, I've been starting to think about adopting as a single mother. I just know I want to be a mother more than anything. And spending some real time with Robby, not in a classroom setting like at school, a couple hours every day will really help me figure things out. Maybe I am meant to adopt an older child."

Holt was still staring at her, not saying anything, and she could see he had questions that he hadn't really formed yet. *Same here, guy.*

"What do you mean that it won't happen the traditional way?" he asked. "Why not?"

"I told you—I gave up on love and thinking my Mr. Right, the man I'm meant to spend my life with, will come along. I like the idea of adopting an older child who needs a family."

Still the dark brown eyes were on her intently. He was taking it all in, she realized. Processing.

"You gave up on love because of me," he finally said, grimacing, his head dropping. "I'm so damned sorry, Amanda. If I could—"

She shook her head. "I kept my more recent past to myself. Two years ago I was engaged to be married and my fiancé left me at the altar. Almost literally. We were in Las Vegas, minutes from our appointment at the wedding chapel."

He sucked in a breath. "I'm very sorry."

She shrugged. "Like I said, I'm done with love. Romantic love, I mean. But I do want a child. And you need a sitter and I'd like to do my own first-hand research of sorts by spending lots of time with a child."

He had that slightly confused look on his face again. The processing.

"Yay, Amanda's here!" Robby suddenly said, and she turned toward his voice. He was smiling and waving at her, then kneeled beside Bentley. "Bentley, guess what? Amanda's gonna teach me to read better."

Amanda managed a smile at Robby and waved. She wasn't sure she could bear to continue this conversation with Holt, so she was glad it had come to an end.

"Can we continue this conversation after the tutoring session?" he asked. "Or tonight, actually. I'd like to assure us some privacy away from big ears," he added, upping his chin at Robby.

"Okay," she said, answering before her brain had time to process the consequences. Privacy. The two of them, alone. At nighttime. Just what had she gotten herself into here?

He held her gaze and nodded, then turned toward his son. "Robby, collect the balls and drop them in the bucket by the gate," he called over to him. "Then we'll head in to wash up before you start reading time with Amanda."

"'Kay, Daddy!" Robby said. "Bentley, come help me. You get that ball and I'll get this one." He pointed to the orange ball, and what do you know, the dog picked it up with his mouth and looked at Robby for next steps. Robby gasped. "Daddy, he did what I told him!"

Holt flashed Robby a thumbs-up. "Like Bentley, like Robby?" he whispered to Amanda with a warm, hopeful smile.

Robby ran over to the bucket and dropped the ball and pointed to it, and the dog dropped the ball right inside. The boy covered Bentley with hugs and praise.

"I don't always make the right choices," Holt said to Amanda. "But this," he added, nodding his chin at his son coming out of the gate with Bentley. "I knocked it out of the park."

"You sure did," she agreed.

Did I make the right choice by suggesting this little arrangement? she wondered. One minute she was resolving to keep an emotional distance from Holt. Now she'd suggested learning about motherhood by spending a lot of quality time with his son.

Holt glanced over at the gate. "Robby, latch the gate—always, right?" he called.

"Oh, right, Daddy." The boy turned back and latched the gate, and they all headed into the cabin.

Holt told Robby to wash his hands, and the boy scampered off.

"He and Bentley really are so good together," Amanda said, needing to keep the subject light right now. "Talk about a bonded pair from the get-go."

Holt nodded, his dark eyes so focused on her that she had to look away. She was too aware of him. Tall and strong and masculine, Holt Dalton filled a room, and they were in the small front hall where his presence was overwhelming. In a good way. "So where do want to work with him?"

"Normally I'd suggest a kitchen table, but I think Robby and I should work in his room. I want him to be at ease, in his element when he reads. And have a dog and cat around for support."

Again the smile he sent her could warm the coldest heart. "Sounds good. I like how you really seem Robby-focused instead of just reading-focused. I have such a good feeling about this, Amanda. And if I haven't said how much I appreciate that you're here, working with him…"

"It's my pleasure. Really." And she meant it.

Robby returned from the bathroom. "I'm ready to get better at reading now." He held up his washed hands, which smelled faintly of green apples.

"Robby, while you and Amanda are reading together," Holt said, "I'm going to Grams and Gramp's house to talk to Gram for a bit. I'll be back very soon."

"'Kay, Daddy. Tell them Bentley and Oliver say hi."

"And what about you?" Holt asked with a smile.

"Of course me too, Daddy!" Robby said, rolling his eyes in an exaggerated way at Amanda.

She laughed. "Let's go read in your room. Bentley can come too."

"Later, guys," Holt said, and headed out the door.

Later, guys. Just like he was leaving for a while and coming back to the house they shared...as husband and wife.

I'm going bonkers, she thought, shaking the wayward thoughts out of her mind as Robby ran upstairs, Bentley on his heels. She'd told herself she could not be having these fantasies about Holt—similar to ones she'd had a long time ago when she really did believe they were headed for marriage and children and forever.

They hadn't been then, though. And she'd better remember that they weren't now either. Or she'd have her heart rehanded to her.

* * *

Holt walked the half mile to the main house, barely aware of the breeze he'd normally be grateful for on a warm August afternoon. Amanda had been left at the altar? Who the hell would walk away from—

He shook his head at himself. *You, idiot. That's who.* He'd been young and stupid ten years ago. *Two* years ago, if she'd been his, he would have picked her up in his arms and run carrying her to that chapel to say I do.

And now she was planning a life that didn't include a husband. Which meant he was out before he was entirely even sure he should be counted in.

He wanted something, though. A second chance. A shot. He'd loved Amanda fiercely ten years ago and she was that same beautiful person, inside and out—kind, compassionate, interesting, smart, funny. Except now, the girl who'd been so open was a guarded woman—for good reason.

He'd helped put up those walls and maybe he could try to take them down. If she let him anywhere near her heart again.

He did have the child she wanted and already seemed to adore, but Robby was a package deal with his dad. Holt frowned, kicking at a rock in his path. Usually Holt had to tell women that *he* was a package deal. Now, the woman he couldn't stop thinking about had no interest in getting involved with him.

Well, he certainly helped put that plan into motion for her ten years ago, and some jerk cemented it.

And that's it? he asked himself. *You're just gonna give up that easily? Show her who you are, that you've changed, that you wouldn't hurt her again, that you'd never walk away from her.*

He didn't know how to do that, though. It wasn't like she'd date him. She'd made that clear. He'd have to show her on the down-low, in the times they were together. Before and after the tutoring sessions. If Holt's mom *was* okay with her two hours a day of watching Robby on the weekdays, he could always suggest to Amanda that she simply come work with Robby every day on reading. That way, she'd still get a lot of time with him.

He reached the main house, struck as always by its grandeur. His father sure had hit the jackpot—literally. Holt wasn't a gambler, and poker and slot machines and the tables had ruined his father a time or two before, but he'd gotten very lucky and now he'd given his wife all this. His parents had gone from having barely anything to their name but a run-down small ranch to absolute wealth on anyone's terms. Holt tried to see the bright side of that, even if his mother would have been happy with a ranch a quarter of this size, this majestic. Deborah was about family, not money.

Which brought him back to why he'd come. He shook off his thoughts and entered the house, hearing the sound of talk radio coming from down the hall. He followed it to the "Mom-dom." That was his term for his mother's sanctuary, a large, sunlit room that was part home office, part library, part crafts room and *all* Deborah Dalton, down to the apricot-colored walls and watercolor paintings of the Montana wilderness. His mom sat at her desk and was on her computer, an invoice up on the screen, scrolling through an upcoming cattle auction.

"Hi there, Holt," Deborah said, smiling up at him, "Got my precious grandson with you?"

Now that was what he liked to hear. He certainly wasn't going to put his mother on the spot—or cause a problem between her and his father. He'd just feel things out and get a sense of how his mother felt. Deborah Dalton was a kind, loving person who tended to put others first. She'd never come out and say that Robby was too much for her, but Holt had always been able to read his mom well. He'd know.

"Actually, Robby's at the house with Amanda right now. She's tutoring him in reading starting today. She volunteers at the elementary school and has a lot of experience. And best of all, Robby really likes her."

"I can understand why. Amanda seems lovely. You really like her too?" his mother added with a sly smile.

"Actually yes," he admitted. "But I messed up ten years ago, and I doubt she'll give me another chance. She's already planning a future without me or even any husband in it."

His mother raised an eyebrow. "Really? What do you mean?"

He wasn't so sure he should be talking about Amanda's personal life this way, but he'd always been able to talk to his mom, and right now he needed some advice. "Between what I did ten years ago and getting left at the altar two year ago, she says she's done with love and romance. She wants a child, though, and is thinking about adopting an older kid. She even suggested working with Robby every day on his reading and then spending another hour just playing so she can get some 'mother experience.' In other words, in three weeks, when Robby goes back to school, I won't see her anymore."

"Well, I'll tell you, Holt. She may have given up on love—or think she has, anyway—but if you have feelings for her, then see what you can do about changing her mind. Minds can be changed. Trust me."

He glanced at his mom, wondering if she was referring to herself and the rough patches she'd had with his dad.

"I do, absolutely," he said.

She stood up and came around the desk and held out her arms. "You're never too old to hug your mama."

He smiled and let her wrap him in one of her big hugs, the kind Robby loved so much.

"Oh, you know, Holt, I wonder if Amanda's request to spend two hours a day with Robby might work out timewise. I signed up for an intensive knitting class that meets every weekday from three o'clock to five o'clock for the next two weeks. Usually I watch Robby at that time and figured I'd switch times with your brothers. But maybe Amanda can fill in?"

Could this have worked out any better? "She'd love to, so that's perfect. Listen, Mom, I want to ask you something and I want your complete honesty. Deal?" Now that she was off the hook, he felt comfortable coming right out with the question.

"Of course," she said, sitting back down.

"Is Robby too much?" he asked.

"For me? If you're asking if that's why I signed up for the knitting class, absolutely not. I adore my grandson and spending these two hours a day with him is a highlight, Holt. Yes, he's a whirlwind, but he's a sweetheart—and I'm not saying that because he's my grandson. Robby has a huge heart and means well. I love that boy to pieces, and there's no way I'm giving up my summertime with him. I'll split the difference with his uncles and get my Robby time that way."

He'd known before he walked in here that this was how his mother felt about his son, but hearing it filled him up.

"Dad thinks he's too much," he said quietly. He wanted his father to feel about Robby the way his mother did. Not want to get him out of his hair for the next three weeks.

"Your father thinks just about everything is too much," Deborah said, her blue eyes twinkling. "The price of feed. The news. The way Shep races his horse. The weather. I could go on." She shook her head with a smile.

"Thanks, Mom," he said, getting up, feeling like two heavy rocks had been lifted off his shoulders.

On the way home, it struck him that his mother's new knitting class sure seemed coincidental. Same time that she watched Robby? For the next two weeks? And it had come up just as he'd brought up Amanda being available? *Uh-huh. Sure, Mom.*

He had a feeling Deborah Dalton was playing matchmaker. And loved her even more for it.

Chapter Eight

When Holt came back to his house a half hour later, he could just make out Robby's voice upstairs. He heard laughter, a combination of his son's hearty laugh and Amanda's. Then he heard Robby say something and again more laughter. If the boy was having this much fun getting tutored in reading, Amanda deserved a million bucks and a gold medal. And his everlasting thanks.

And dinner, which he hoped she wouldn't find presumptuous. This morning, he'd promised Robby one of his favorites, chicken parm with spaghetti and garlic bread, and he did recall Amanda ordering a chicken parm sub from a pizza place on their trip into town on one of their days off from camp, so he knew she liked it. Maybe she'd say thanks but no thanks and leave. Or maybe she'd stay. He was hoping for *stay*. She'd been here for thirty minutes, which meant another thirty to go—exactly when dinner would be ready. No one could resist the smell of garlic bread, right?

By the time the cheese was melting and the garlic bread smelled so good that his stomach rumbled, he heard Robby running down the hall upstairs. "Daddy!" came his son's booming voice. "I smell something amazing! Amanda, doesn't that smell amazing?"

"Sure does," he heard her say.

Half a minute later, Robby was sniffing his way into the kitchen, Amanda right behind him.

"That really does smell intensely good," she said. "Garlic bread and what else?"

"Chicken parm!" Robby said, rubbing his hands together. "Daddy promised me he'd make it tonight."

"And I made enough for three," Holt said, catching Amanda's gaze. "Stay? We'd like to thank you for what definitely sounded like a good first day of reading practice."

"It was fun, Daddy," Robby said. "I read a

book—a chapter book!—to Amanda about a dog named Joey who has a cat for a best friend! Just like Bentley and Oliver. And Amanda said I can keep the book too. And yes, I said thank you."

Holt smiled. "Good. How about you go wash up for dinner and meet us in the dining room?"

Robby ran off, and Amanda moved closer into the kitchen, giving the air a sniff.

"I was just a little hungry before but now I'm starving," she said. "That just smells too good."

Thank you, universe, he sent heavenward. "Great."

She leaned against the counter, looking so sexy in her dark jeans and pale pink tank top, white stars embroidered on the V-neckline. Her hair was in a braid down one shoulder. She'd dressed casually, instead of more "teacher-like" to make Robby feel comfortable, he realized. "Talk go okay with your mom?"

He dragged his attention off how pretty she was and onto her question. "Better than okay. And you're on for the every weekday arrangement. Turns out my mom is taking an intensive knitting class that meets every day at that time for the next two weeks, so I'd need someone to fill in for her anyway. She wants to keep watching Robby, so she'll switch some morning hours with one of my brothers."

Her eyes widened as if she hadn't fully expected it to work out. "I'm glad. Wow, I'll really get to put my plan into motion—to get a sense of what it would be like to be a mom of a child Robby's age. I mean, not that spending two hours a day with him is anything close to what goes into raising a child, but I'll get a real sense, you know?"

"I think it's great that you want to be a mom and that you're thinking of an older child. That's beautiful, Amanda. There are a lot of kids out there who need loving homes." *There's also an open slot in my own small family for someone who loves kids and dogs and cats*, he thought.

Whoa—that notion slammed into him with startling force. He'd gone from thinking about the possibility of a second chance to marriage? Holt wasn't used to being led around by his heart, not that he'd used his brains much when he was younger either. But these days, he was six feet two inches of emotion. And given that Amanda had told him a second chance was off the table, he'd better be careful with himself.

But now Amanda was smiling so warmly at him that he wanted to gather her into his arms and just hold her and never let her go.

Luckily, Robby was back and dinner was ready, so he focused on plating everything. Robby carried the platter of garlic bread with two hands into the dining room, while Amanda brought in the salad and he carried the platter of chicken parm. They sat at the big table, big enough for his whole family and a guest or two, but because they were all at one end, it felt cozy. And right. Him. Robby. And Amanda.

Every time he looked at that chair, he'd be reminded of that open slot.

For his wife. For a mother for Robby.

Robby pronounced the chicken parm "too good for words," and Amanda seconded that. They ate and drank iced tea and talked about Robby's reading practice, and how patient Bentley was to sit through three books over the hour. They talked about their favorite seasons and foods and TV shows, and suddenly it was as if ten years hadn't gone by, and he and Amanda were those same two kids, lying on the grass by lake and holding hands, talking about everything. He could barely take his eyes off her during dinner. *I am you and you are me...*

With mere crumbs left on everyone's plate, Amanda insisted on helping him clear the table. In the kitchen, while he scooped out the ice cream for their dessert, he asked if she was okay staying a bit later after Robby went to bed so they could work up the schedule—and talk more about her idea to adopt. And why. Holt had said he wanted to continue that conversation, which had surprised her.

She hesitated for a moment, then said, "Sure. I can stay for a bit."

He smiled to himself, well aware that she was a little nervous about being alone with him, about their undeniable attraction, about whether despite what they'd agreed to, they'd end up kissing again.

Maybe they'd end up in bed, where Holt would love to spend some time with Amanda Jenkins.

He knew that was a pipe dream given all she'd said earlier, but he was still filled with anticipation about later. About possibilities. Maybe they *could* have a second chance. Maybe he *could* change her mind, let her see that he was someone she could trust.

Twenty minutes later, ice cream sundaes consumed, Amanda insisted on cleaning up since Holt had cooked, so Holt and Robby went into the yard with Bentley. Robby asked Amanda if she'd watch his favorite before-bed TV show with him, about the bull, so the three watched that together, Amanda on the big club chair perpendicular to the sofa, him and Robby on the couch. Through the show, Holt kept picturing the three of them sitting on the sofa—Robby between them—every night after dinner. Right now she was keeping a bit of a distance, which he totally understood.

After Robby's quick bath and a story and his good-night routine with Bentley and Oliver, which included having Robby say good-night to each from each, the boy was asleep in his bed, his arm wrapped around his stuffed rodeo bull. And he and Amanda finally were alone to talk.

He came downstairs to find her looking at the framed photographs on the fireplace mantel. There were a lot of pictures. Mostly of Robby, and a lot of the boy with his uncles and grandparents, plus a few from when Holt was a kid. He did have a photo of him and Amanda from ten years ago, which he kept in the drawer of his bedside table. Sometimes over the years he'd pull it out and wonder where she was, what she was doing.

Now she was right here.

"Robby did very well earlier," she said, turning around. "I think I can help him get moved up at least two levels by the time school starts."

"That's great, Amanda. Thank you. Really."

She sat back down in the club chair, avoiding being next to him on the sofa, unfortunately. "So the plan is that I'll come every day at three o'clock for reading time, then at four, we'll switch to playtime. I don't have to work with Robby on reading every day—maybe three times a week so that it doesn't feel like school. There are lots of ways to make reading feel joyful, but it's still hard work for him, so I need to be careful of not overdoing it."

"Sounds good. Scratch that—it sounds amazing. I don't know how I got so lucky, Amanda. The reading help from someone experienced and compassionate who really gets Robby. And the babysitting time. I know it helps you out too, but I really can't thank you enough."

"I'm really happy about the arrangement."

"I have no doubt you'll make an incredible mother, Amanda. You're loving and kind and Robby is nuts about you. He's a very good judge of character."

The big, happy smile on her beautiful face told him how much this plan of hers really meant to her. She might be at the starting gate with even thinking about motherhood, but being a mom was in her heart; he could clearly see that.

"I think about everything you're saying and how my son's own mother doesn't feel that way." He shook his head. "I hate that I had something to do with you giving up on love, though," he said with a grimace. "I know you got hurt again after our relationship, but I just wish I'd been different back then." He really needed to take a giant step back.

She looked at him for a moment, then said, "To the future, then. Everything is about what's ahead."

But here he was, focused on the past—and moving backward, not forward.

And now they were pretty much done with discussing the plan, but he wasn't ready for her to leave yet. Maybe there was more to say. "Coffee? We can clink to the new arrangement."

She smiled again. "Sure."

He got up to make it and brought it in the living room to find her once again looking through the photos on the mantel. As he set the tray of mugs and the sugar bowl and creamer on the coffee table, she sat down in front of it on the sofa. He sat beside her.

She added cream to her coffee. "I have a few pictures of you from that summer we were a couple. Sometimes I'd take one out and wonder where you were, what you were doing."

He turned and stared at her. "I did the same thing. And was just thinking about that when I came down and saw you looking at the family photos. When I got divorced I thought about looking you up, but—"

"But what?" she whispered.

It wasn't easy for him to think back to those days. "I guess I felt like I was in a bad place.

Newly divorced, a young son who didn't understand where his mother was."

She reached for his hand and gave it a gentle squeeze. He held on to her hand, looking into her eyes, leaning toward her a bit…leaning a bit more until their lips touched. She moved closer to him, his hands on either side of her face, then in her hair, across her back. He loved the feel of her, the lightly perfumed scent of her.

He couldn't get enough of Amanda, his hands now traveling up the back of her tank top, her soft bare skin driving him insane. He remembered the first time they made love, when they went camping on their day off, and he felt so much that he thought his heart might actually explode.

But now she was pulling away, fixing her tank top and smoothing her hair. "Holt, I can't. I said so. You said so. We can't do this."

"But if we both want to and clearly we do—"

She shook her head. "I'm attracted to you. No doubt. But like I said, I'm done with romance. And certainly with someone who broke my heart so bad I can still remember how hurt I was ten years later. I'm sorry, Holt. But I won't go there." She grabbed her bag and headed for the door. "I don't want to disappoint Robby, so I won't back out on him. But no more, Holt. We don't sit on the same sofa anymore. Got it?"

He managed something of a smile that he hardly felt. "Got it."

At least he knew for absolute sure that she was still attracted to him. The kiss last night could have been chalked up to nostalgia. But tonight had been pure chemistry and undeniable heat.

He just had to prove to her that he'd changed, that he was the guy she'd always thought he was. He had a solid two weeks to do that, while she was here every day.

And dammit, he'd do it.

"Good luck with that," Brittany said with a warm smile. She and Amanda sat at the kitchen table in their condo the next morning, Amanda on her second cup of coffee and a barely touched bagel after telling her roommate all that had happened yesterday. "Look, I get why you're wary of Holt. But like I said before, keep an open mind—even just a smidge open."

Amanda grimaced. "My mind *is* a smidge open—otherwise I wouldn't have kissed him back last night. My hands were all over his chest! That brought back some serious memories. For a second there, I was so lost in ten years ago that I forgot I'm supposed to sit far away from Holt whenever we're alone in a room together."

Brittany laughed, tucking an errant long ringlet behind her ear. "Yeah, good luck with that too. You like him too much. You have too much history. And you're too attracted to him for that. You know, Amanda, the read I'm getting based on everything you said happened yesterday and the day before is that Holt Dalton is still very much in love with you."

A little burst of sadness made its way from her stomach to her chest, stopping on the left side. She shook her head. "How in love could he have been, Brittany? He just walked away."

"Because he was going back to nothing, honey. Back to the guy he was before he met you."

Huh. Amanda hadn't thought of it that way. "Go on," she said. "I'm listening." Thank God for insightful roommates.

Brittany took a sip of her coffee. "He was headed down the wrong road in those days, right? Getting into trouble with the law for minor offenses. No plans for his life after dropping out of college. No job, no direction. And didn't you say he had some issues with his father? So he couldn't just go home. He had nowhere to go and that's where he thought he would take you, Amanda. So he broke up with you instead."

Amanda gasped. "You're right. You are one hundred percent right. That makes total sense to me." She sat back, kind of stunned. She'd never been able to understand how a guy who'd obviously loved her—and Holt had, she was sure of it—could have just dumped her that way, torn them apart and taken off as if the whole summer hadn't happened. Now she knew. He'd done it for *her*.

She stared at her sesame bagel, something poking at her heart. "But, Brittany, I could have helped turn his life around. He knew that too. I would have set him on the right path. He didn't trust in that. That says something too."

"Yeah, it says he didn't trust in love or people enough for that because of what he'd gone through in his own life. It's not about you, Amanda. I know it's hard not to take it personally. But his reasons and thought processes when he left you—it was about him."

"I hear you. I don't like it, but I hear you."

"I can be louder if you need it," Brittany said, grinning. "Any time you need some coaxing over to the love side, you just let me know."

"And what about you?" Amanda asked, raising an eyebrow.

"I date plenty. But I like my singlehood just the way it is."

Her roommate had met a lot of special someones. And she'd let them all go. When she was ready, she'd be ready. That was all there was to it.

Brittany had to get to work, so Amanda cleaned up, played with Poindexter for a few minutes and then sat down at her desk in her bedroom. She checked her email—for the millionth time—hoping there would be a response or two about her post on the chat group of people with adoption queries. She wanted to have good news for her friend and neighbor, Mel, about the whereabouts of Beatrix Abernathy—the long-lost baby that Mel's fiancé's great-grandfather had had to give up for adoption seventy-five years ago.

There *was* a response!

Dear Amanda, I hope you connect with the person you're looking for. I found a half sister I never knew existed through this group so don't give up hope if it takes a while to get a lead.

Amanda's heart sank that the response wasn't from someone who did have a lead on Beatrix, but at least some kind person out there was sending good wishes her way, particularly someone who had connected with the person she'd been looking for. Amanda did appreciate that. Especially because she had no idea how they'd ever find Beatrix otherwise with such little information to go on.

Someday I will find a way to bring her back to you...

Josiah Abernathy's words to his young love, Winona Cobbs, filled her mind, all the determination in that letter he'd tucked inside his journal, buried under the floorboards of his old ranch house for seventy-plus years.

Where are you, Beatrix Abernathy? she wondered. Right here in Bronco? For all Amanda knew, she'd walked past her in town countless times over the past two years. *I sure hope we find you.*

There were so many ways people, loved ones, got separated from one another.

You and Holt have a second chance. Stop resisting it, a little voice said.

Oh, you resist it, Amanda Jenkins, and hard! another, louder little voice said. *That man will crush your heart again. Mark my words. It was all about him then and it is now.*

Poindexter jumped up on her desk and sat right beside her laptop.

"What to do, Poin?" she asked the wise cat. "Give me a sign."

Poindexter began grooming his face with his paw, which told her nothing. Except that maybe she should start researching adoption instead of just thinking about it. She typed Wyoming Department of Family Services into the search engine and clicked on Foster Care and Adoption Requirements. She could foster a child or adopt as a single person—that was good. She read about how to become a foster parent, which seemed the way to begin the process since she wanted to adopt an older child. A half hour passed and she'd taken pages of notes, excited and a little scared at what a huge undertaking this would be.

She glanced at the time; she had to get into the shower and get cracking on her to-do list. She had a busy schedule of work at home and two meetings, and then she'd head back to Holt's house to work with Robby and spend time with her favorite seven-year-old.

She thought about Brittany's "good luck with that," which made her worry that this attraction thing with Holt was out of her hands, that she couldn't stop it or even try to. Amanda was pretty sure her roommate was right about that. Maybe all the reason to work harder at remembering how badly he'd hurt her, that it *had* been all about him so she wouldn't get her head all turned around.

She'd focus on Robby when she was at the Dalton home. Not his superhot dad.

Chapter Nine

"Guess what, Daddy?" Robby said when he and Amanda came in from the backyard. It was already five which meant Robby and Amanda's two hours together had come to an end. "I read a whole line today without having to stop. I didn't get messed up!"

Holt's heart moved in his chest and he smiled at his son. "I'm proud of you, Robby. You're working hard and it's already paying off."

Robby nodded. "Does that mean we can have pizza for dinner?"

Holt laughed. "I am dying for pizza, actually."

He turned to Amanda, once again hoping she'd say yes. "Join us? My treat."

"I'm getting pepperoni and mushroom, my favorite," Robby said. "What's your favorite pizza, Amanda?"

"My favorite is just plain cheese, actually. Just the crust, sauce and mozzarella cheese. Perfection. And now I can't stop thinking of having some pizza."

"Yay, Amanda's coming," Robby shouted, clapping his hands.

He smiled and glanced at Amanda. He had to give her an out to show her he had heard her last night and would respect how she felt about the two of them spending non-necessary time together. "Robby, Amanda might already have dinner plans."

She looked at him, then at Robby. "What? And miss pizza? No way. And besides, there's a great place not too far from my apartment building, so I'd be passing it anyway."

She'd definitely added that so he'd know this was strictly about convenience and a craving, but there was hope for a second chance here, he knew. And he was taking it.

Twenty minutes later they were inside Bronco Brick Oven Pizza, sitting at a round table and awaiting their orders. For the first time in a long time, Holt was sitting with his son and a woman inside a restaurant, and he liked it. Usually it was just him and Robby, all the time, everywhere they went. Yeah, his parents or brothers joined them sometimes, but there always seemed to be an absence. He knew that Robby wasn't aware of it most of the time; he knew his son very well—and he could always tell when Robby *was* aware of it. He certainly wasn't now. His adorable face was free of any kind of sadness. Robby had clearly had a good time with Amanda earlier, and was equally happy that she was with them now.

Just after the waiter set down their drinks, a cute kid about Robby's age with red hair and freckles came up to their table. A woman who looked a lot like him and a little girl were behind him.

"Hi, Robby!" the boy said.

Robby grinned. "Hi, Liam. The pizza here is soooo good, right?"

"I had like a million slices," Liam said with a big nod. "We just signed up for the fun run," he added, pointing to a poster and sign-up sheet on the far wall. "I want to win this year. Last year I was one of the last kids."

Holt smiled. "Well, it's a fun run so it's all about fun. Good for you for entering!" He smiled up at the mom, then turned to his son. "Robby, would you like to sign up?"

Robby nodded with a grin. "I love running and I'm good at it."

"The fun run really is fun," the woman said. "It's a mother-son event that the pizzeria is sponsoring."

Holt's stomach twisted at the words *mother-son*. He watched Robby's face fall as he stared down at his cup of soda.

"I can barely run half a mile," the woman continued, oblivious, "but I actually pulled it off last year. And it was great to do something like that with my son. Are you a runner?" She directed the question to Amanda. "You and Robby should enter!"

"I'm kind of a couch potato," Amanda said, glancing at Holt to interject—and fast.

"Well, think about it," the woman said before he could say a word. "Nice seeing you," she added before heading toward the door.

"I wish I could do the fun run but I can't because my mom isn't around," Robby said, tears filling his eyes and streaking down his face.

Holt stood up and knelt beside Robby. "Hey, there," he said, pulling his son into a hug. Robby cried harder, burying his face in Holt's shirt.

Holt looked at Amanda, sure his own his expression mirrored the heartbreak on hers.

Suddenly, she pointed at herself and mouthed, *I could run with him.*

He was so moved he could barely process it. Holt pressed his hand to his chest and mouthed back *thank you.*

"You know, Robby," Amanda said, "I might be a couch potato—meaning I'm usually on my couch instead of outside jogging—but I'd love to do the fun run with you. If you want."

Robby's face emerged and he wiped under his eyes. "But it's a mom and son run."

"I'll bet if I read the rules on the poster," Amanda said, "they'll say that you can run the race with me. I'll bet tutors are allowed."

Robby brightened. "Really? Can we check?" He ran over to the poster on the opposite side of the pizzeria.

Again, Holt was so touched by what she'd said that he couldn't find his voice. As she stood to follow Robby, he reached for her hand to stall her. "You're the absolute best, Amanda Jenkins."

She smiled, holding his gaze for a heartbeat, then glanced at where Robby was standing. "It would be my pleasure. Really."

This was about more than wanting experience at motherhood. *This*, right now, was about how she felt about Robby, one particular seven-year-old who happened to be his beloved child. She cared about Robby very much. Did she know how much that meant to him?

Robby was waving her over. As Holt and Amanda headed to the poster, he sent up a silent prayer that the rules didn't actually say mothers and sons only. That would be nuts, right? Not every child had a mother. "Can you help me read the rules, Amanda?"

Holt smiled to himself at that.

Amanda scanned the fine print, which was minimal. "Hmm, this event is open to boys ages five to eleven and an adult female relative, care-giver, teacher, or family friend." She turned to Robby. "That's me. Family friend. So let's do this!"

"Yay!" Robby said, jumping and clapping.

The people at the table closest smiled in that "he's kind of loud" way. Holt ignored them but ushered Robby and Amanda back to their seats just as their pizzas were served.

"I can't believe I get to do the fun run!" Robby said, picking up his slice of pizza.

Amanda lifted her plain slice too. "Hope you don't mind that I'm not very fast."

"I'm really glad because I'm not fast either," Robby said, giggling.

From tears to giggles just like that.

For the third or fourth time since Amanda Jenkins came back into his life, Holt felt his heart move inside his chest.

Holt had just left Robby's room after reading him a story and telling him a story—about the tortoise and the hare, which he loved—when the knocking on the front door began. He glanced at his phone for the time. Past nine.

That was weird. Since arriving in town a year ago, Holt had kept to himself, well, except for the dating he'd done when he'd first moved here, trying to find his Ms. Right and a mother for Robby and failing miserably on both counts. He hadn't made friends off the ranch; he simply had no time between work and raising his son. His brothers were his social life. And none of them would be banging on the door this late, knowing it was past Robby's bedtime.

Maybe it was Amanda. Maybe she'd changed her mind about doing the race with Robby. About their entire arrangement. Holt sure hoped that wasn't the case.

But no way would Amanda be knocking on the door right now. She wouldn't risk waking up Robby either; she would have texted to say she was outside.

Holt glanced out the window on the second-floor landing. A silver Range Rover was idling in the drive. Did he know anyone who drove a Range Rover? He didn't think so.

Bentley had come bounding out of Robby's room and stood at the top of the stairs, waiting for him. Luckily, the dog didn't bark and wake up Robby, who'd finally gotten to sleep after being so excited about participating in the fun run with Amanda. They headed down, Holt wondering who was on the other side of the front door.

With Bentley at his side, Holt opened the door to find a total stranger with a spitting mad expression. Whoa, dude. The man was in his late forties, maybe early fifties, with a receding hairline and a bit of a paunch. He wore expensive leather shoes—not the work boots or cowboy boots you saw on a cattle ranch.

"You Holt Dalton?" the man asked, anger radiating out of his narrowed blue eyes.

"I am," he said. Once upon a time, Holt would have deflected, given his troublemaking days. Now, he had nothing to hide. "What's this about?"

"I went to the main house and spoke to the owner of the ranch. A Neal Dalton. He said to talk to you."

Huh? His dad had told this man to come talk to Holt? "About?" he asked, wondering what the hell was going on. He stepped out onto the porch, letting Bentley out too, and keeping the front door just slightly ajar.

"One of your cowboys, ranch hands, whatever the hell they're called, is corrupting my daughter," the man said. "She's only eighteen and a college freshman. I want you to call him off."

Holt gaped at the man. "Call him off? What's the issue, exactly?"

"The issue is that he's a troublemaker who is not going to mess up my daughter's life. I want you to put an end to their relationship."

So this man had gone to the main house, spit out this request, and Holt's dad had sent the guy here? Why?

Because Holt had once been that cowboy? And Amanda had been that corruptible daughter who had to be protected from the likes of him at all costs? He'd never met Amanda's dad, but if the man had known about Holt's past he probably would have tried to talk her away from him too.

"Who's the hand?" Holt asked.

The man seemed to relax, as if he thought he was finally getting somewhere, that Holt would take care of it. Holt had no clue what he'd do. But he wanted to know who he was dealing with. Dalton's Grange employed a slew of cowboys, some part-time, particularly in the spring and summer.

"His name's Brody Colter. He's a real punk."

Brody. Holt knew who he was. It had been Holt who Neal had sent to bail the guy out of jail about three months ago. Brody had been charged with assault in a bar fight but the charges had been dropped. Holt didn't know the ranch hand well, but according to Neal, Brody was one of their best cowboys—never late, good at his job, respectful of others. He'd been working at the ranch part-time during high school and since he'd graduated in June had gone full-time. Getting into a bar brawl and ending up in jail—no one to bail him out but his boss—didn't fit with Holt's image of Brody Colter at all.

"In what way?" Holt asked.

"First of all, he's been in trouble with the law. Second, he practically lives at Wild Wesley's, that dive bar out in Bronco Valley, and I've heard stories about that place. And third, my daughter just graduated from high school two months ago. She's headed to college at the end of the month. Suddenly, she's saying she thinks she met the love of her life and that maybe she could take a year off. That punk is not the love of her life, and she's not losing her scholarship to Wyoming Western College. Over my dead body!"

"Mr..." Holt prompted.

"Thompson. Edward Thompson. I'm the senior

VP of new development for Thompson Paper—
a business that's been in my family and Bronco
Heights for almost a hundred years. My daughter's name is Piper. Short for Pauline. Do I have
your word you'll take care of this problem?"

"Mr. Thompson, you said your daughter is
eighteen. So is Brody. I'm not sure how anyone
can prevent them from dating."

Thompson crossed his arms over his chest.
"Apparently Brody likes this job. Threaten him
with it. Tell him he either stops seeing Piper or
he's fired. If the job means that much to him, he'll
move on to another pretty girl—this time from
Bronco *Valley.*"

This time from Bronco Valley. Until they'd
moved to Bronco Heights from Whitehorn, the
Daltons had always been from the wrong side of
town. So Holt knew exactly what the man meant,
and he didn't like it. Or Edward Thompson. What
a pompous—

"I said what I came to say," Thompson huffed.
"I'm a big donator to the ranchers' association,
and I think the powers that be over there would
want to keep me in their good graces."

Now he was threatening Holt and Dalton's
Grange? Thompson wouldn't make a donation
unless Holt intervened, and if Holt didn't, the loss

of big bucks to the association would be the Daltons' fault?

I don't think so, buster.

The man was down the porch steps before Holt could respond and that was probably for the best. He got in his silver Range Rover and drove off.

Holt sat down on the porch swing, shaking his head. "Believe that guy, Bentley?"

The dog rested his chin on Holt's knee, and he rubbed the sweet pooch's furry head.

Brody didn't live on Dalton's Grange. There were two bunkhouses a mile out back on the property that some full-time hands shared, but Holt recalled that Brody had his own tiny apartment, an efficiency, right above Wild Wesley's. Man, that had to be loud all night long, particularly Thursday to Saturday nights. He knew this detail about where Brody lived because he'd dropped the guy off there after bailing him out of jail, and Holt had said, "You just got busted for getting into a fight here, now you're going back for more? I don't like wasting my money, Brody."

And Brody had again insisted he didn't start the fight nor had he wanted to participate in it, then explained he lived above Wild Wesley's, thanked Holt again for bailing him out, then had gone in a narrow door wedged between the bar and a dark alleyway.

He'd talk to Brody tomorrow morning. Holt had no idea what he'd say yet. Maybe just relay the exchange between himself and Edward Thompson.

He pulled out his phone and called his dad. Neal Dalton answered on the third ring, his trademark.

"Thanks for the warning about the hothead, Dad." Seriously. Neal Dalton couldn't have given him a heads-up that some loose cannon was on his way?

"I'm sure you handled it fine, Holt."

"How, exactly, am I supposed to handle it? Brody's eighteen and so is Thompson's daughter. Oh and by the way—if I don't break up the relationship, he threatened to pull his big donation to the ranchers' association and make sure the powers that be know it's our fault."

"Classic," Neal said with almost respect in his voice. Whose side was his dad on?

"I'll talk to Brody in the morning when he turns up. Though I don't know why you sent Thompson to me when he was already at your house and you could have dealt with him."

"Because I figured you could talk him down, use your own experience but with hindsight, you know? I don't always have the answers even if I think I know everything."

Maybe his dad was coming around some. There didn't even seem to be a back-handed compliment in that. And good thing because Holt hated clapping back at his dad, hating being at odds with the man. Getting along meant the world to his mother, and Holt knew it.

"I'll see what I can do, Dad."

Which would clearly not include trying to explain to Edward Thompson that Holt couldn't stop his daughter from dating who she wanted. He'd tried that, and it was beside the point for Thompson. The *point* was separating the couple. Keeping Piper Thompson "uncorrupted." Making sure she left for college in three weeks, the Bronco Valley "punk" history.

Well, he couldn't blame his dad for thinking Holt knew something about that very topic.

"Kiss Robby good-night for me," his dad said and hung up.

Holt shook his head. His father made him want to throw something. He walked down the porch steps into the front yard and threw a stick as hard as he could. Bentley went flying after it, returning it and dropping it at his feet.

"Good dog," Holt said, giving Bentley's side a pat. Yup, that was what happened when you tried to avoid something, throw it away. It came right back, demanding to be dealt with.

Like Amanda maybe. She'd come back into his life for a reason. Now. Just when he was ready for her. That had to mean something.

He went back to the porch swing, Bentley trailing after him. Thompson had gotten under his skin and Holt knew why. Because in a parallel universe, the man could have easily been Amanda's father, furious about Holt and Amanda, and deep down Holt still felt like that twenty-two-year-old guy.

He'd changed his ways because of Robby, and seven years later, he led the most law-abiding, kid-focused life possible. His world was work and Robby and his family whereas ten years ago, before Amanda and in the few years after, his life had been about chasing a good time, pretty women and cold beer. His group of friends at the time were just like him. One had ended up in prison for a string of burglaries. Another had joined the army and had probably been straightened out. And another had tried to turn his life around when his older brother died of a drug overdose and had had to leave Whitehorn because no one would let him change, be a new person.

Sometimes Holt thought his dad didn't accept that he'd changed. Neal Dalton acted like Holt could revert at any time.

I coulda sworn you married that hard-edged gal because you knocked her up, his father had said at his and Sally Anne's wedding. *But she says she's not expecting.*

I married her because I love her, Holt had said.

He had loved Sally Anne. Yeah, she was rough around the edges—just like he was. They came from the same place, so to speak. They spoke the same language, understood each other. But Sally Anne had been even wilder than Holt, and she lived for attention.

What killed Holt now, and during the past four years since he'd been raising his son on his own, was that Holt's choices had put Robby in this position. To have a mother who'd walked out on him. To need his reading tutor to stand in at a mother-son fun run. To wonder why he wasn't special enough for his own mother to want to be in his life. Sometimes Holt thought about what his dad had said at the wedding and regretted not knowing better, not making sure that a woman who'd said she wasn't maternal, wasn't cut out for motherhood didn't get pregnant by accident. They'd been young and in love and tipsy most of the time—and careless.

Anyway, if Holt hadn't married Sally Anne, Robby wouldn't exist. And Holt wouldn't trade his life with his son for anything.

He got up and headed back inside with Bentley, giving Oliver his dinner reserve, which had the cat rushing over, then he shut the lights on the first floor. He, Bentley and Oliver went upstairs, Bentley going back into Robby's room and Oliver following Holt into his own bedroom. Usually the cat stuck with Bentley, but Holt was glad for the company tonight.

He sat down on the edge of his bed and opened the bottom drawer of his end table as Oliver jumped up on his bed and scratched at a spot and then curled up. Under a bunch of old keepsakes was one of the most precious of all: a photo of him and Amanda from ten years ago. They were sitting on the dock of the lake at Camp KidPower, Amanda's back against his chest, her legs straight out in front of him, his arms wrapped around her. They were both beaming. And so damned young.

He wondered what the story was with Brody and Piper, if they were in love like he and Amanda had been. Maybe Brody already planned to walk away from Piper, to let her head off to school and start her new life, which had no place for him. Or maybe the two had other ideas. In any case, they were adults, new ones but legally able to make their own decisions whether Thompson approved or not.

Holt would talk to Brody in the morning but he had to wonder: how could he advise Brody to walk away from Piper for her own good when doing exactly that with Amanda was the biggest mistake Holt had ever made?

Chapter Ten

The next morning, Amanda was happy to see her next-door neighbor Melanie Driscoll come out of her apartment as Amanda was leaving and locking up. Mel spent a lot of time at her fiancé's ranch, so Amanda didn't get to see her dear friend as often as she used to. As usual lately, Amanda's gaze went right to Mel's gorgeous diamond engagement ring.

What did *that* mean? Amanda used to be drawn to the ring kind of wistfully, as in, *That'll never happen for me because I've taken myself out of the game.* Now, the ring seemed to say something else to her. *I symbolize love and commitment and those things really do exist.*

Maybe Amanda *was* changing? Just a little? She hoped so. Being closed and guarded didn't feel great.

Amanda smiled at her friend, who looked beautiful as always. Mel's long blond hair was loose past her shoulders, and she wore the cutest outfit. Amanda glanced at her own outfit, which was professional meets superdull. She loved the way Mel and Brittany dressed with style and flair, but Amanda had always been a more fade-into-the-woodwork type. Maybe she'd ask Mel and Brittany to go shopping with her and let them suggest some upgrades to her ho-hum look.

The funny thing—and funny strange, not funny ha-ha—was that Holt seemed to find her sexy just as she was. He had ten years ago, too, which had shocked not only her but all the girls at camp. Amanda of the ponytail, no makeup, baggy T-shirts, and nose in a book had somehow stolen the attention of the cutest guy in camp. Once, when a girl asked Holt what he saw in her—Amanda had happened to be in eavesdropping distance but not visible—she'd heard Holt respond, *I see everything in Amanda—everything beautiful and everything that matters.* The girl had swooned. Amanda had burst into tears, unable to believe that someone, someone she'd fallen so hard for, had said something like that about her. She'd wanted to call her mom and tell her, but her mother wasn't the kind you shared stuff like that with. Amanda had held it close to her heart until he'd dumped her, when she'd stopped believing in anything Holt had said to her.

A few weeks into camp, Amanda had made a close girlfriend, another counselor who also had a boyfriend she was nuts about, and the two girls had told each everything. Daniella had been always been there for her over the years, and though she now lived in Alaska, Amanda would always feel close to her faraway friend. In fact, Daniella had paved the way for Amanda to open up to new girlfriends, and she'd easily become close to Brittany in college and then Mel when she moved next door. She trusted in girlfriends. Not so much boyfriends.

"Hi, Mel. I've been meaning to update you on my online search for Beatrix. So far, no leads on the one site I posted to—adoptees looking for information—but last night I posted on two other sites. I'm so hopeful."

"Me too," Mel said. "I want to find Beatrix so badly."

"You'll find her. I truly believe that."

Her own words shocked her. Maybe instead of

being so cynical, she was becoming more open to possibilities. She hoped so. She certainly wasn't looking to get hurt again, but her wise roommate's words kept coming back to her. *Keep an open mind—even just a smidge open.*

Did she dare do that when she was entering a race called the Mother-Son Fun Run with Holt's child? She already felt close to Robby Dalton. Being involved in something like this, given Robby's particular situation, pulled her in even more. She'd love to have a little boy just like Robby. But the thought of giving Holt another chance felt…scary. Truly scary. To allow herself to be that vulnerable, and then to be left heartbroken and alone… She couldn't do it. She wouldn't do it. She had a plan for a Robby of her own. She was researching, investigating, figuring out.

Amanda and Mel headed out into the perfect August Montana morning together, chatting about the search for Beatrix, then went their separate ways. Amanda couldn't stop thinking about Josiah Abernathy and Winona Cobbs during the short walk to the coffee shop, where she picked up an iced mocha latte to fortify herself for her presentation to a potential new client. Somewhere out there, a seventy-five-year-old woman may have been wondering about her birth parents all these years. That was if Beatrix even knew she'd been adopted at birth.

Amanda had so many questions. Had Josiah kept tabs on his baby girl from afar? He'd known where she was. Now, with Josiah suffering from Alzheimer's, he was unable to provide any answers about the past. It was up to Mel and the great search.

An hour later, after Amanda's meeting with the school district's superintendent about potentially taking on their social media needs, she stopped back in the coffee shop with her laptop to type up her notes and to work on a few other current campaigns. One thing she loved about her job was that she could do it anywhere. Such as while drinking a sweet iced tea and nibbling on a white chocolate and raspberry scone.

"CJ Donville is supercute," a voice whispered from the table beside her. "And omigosh, did you see that blond guy with the serious muscles at the health club last night? Hot!"

Amanda smiled to herself. She loved girl talk—even just listening. She'd noticed the two women, neither of whom she'd recognized, when she'd sat down. Both were in their midtwenties, one blond with great bangs, the other auburn-haired with killer eyebrows.

"I have my eye on a few Dalton brothers," the redhead said.

Amanda almost spit out her iced tea. Suddenly, she wasn't so sure she wanted to be hearing this.

The blonde nodded. "Five gorgeous brothers! Holt is so hot, but forget him. And Morgan—ooh la la. Ridiculously sexy. You should go for him."

Forget Holt? Why? Because he was involved with someone, namely Amanda? No one would know that, though. But they *had* been spending time together around town—Bronco's Brick Oven Pizza just last night. Maybe people thought they were a couple.

No, other women didn't look at Amanda and think the hottest guy in town would go for *her*.

The redhead shook her head and bit into her bagel. "Do you know Cheyenne, the junior Realtor at Bronco Properties? Tall, thin, huge chest, gorgeous? She has guys chasing her left and right. She asked Morgan out after running into him in the grocery store and he turned her down, made some excuse. So trust me, Morgan's no better."

No better? What did *that* mean?

"Yeah, neither of them seems to be interested in anyone right now," the blonde said, then sipped her drink. "I thought Holt stopped dating because no one could deal with his hyper kid."

Amanda narrowed her eyes. Hyper? How dare

she refer to Robby in an unkind manner! Kids were off-limits—worldwide rule.

"No, I heard he's seeing someone," the friend said.

Amanda had no doubt that someone *was* her. Might not be true, but she did like the idea of Holt being off the market. And clearly there was quite a market.

The blonde smirked. "Like that'll last. My cousin Lulu dated Holt last year when he first moved to town. He's gorgeous and a total gentleman, but he's a package deal and his kid's a nightmare. Never stops talking and has to be the center of attention. Holt told Lulu his son has to be his priority, not dating."

Amanda wanted to take her iced tea and dump it over the woman's head, then crumble the scone on top. What gossips! How dare they!

"Well, shouldn't his child have priority over his love life?" the redhead asked. "I think that's a good thing."

"I guess. He told Lulu he's looking for a mother for his son. She heard that and ran for the hills. Holt is seriously hot, but she knew she'd turn into the babysitter real quick and have the life sucked out of her. No thanks. No one needs a brat aging them ten years in a month! Who could afford that kind of Botox upkeep?"

The women laughed and clinked to that with a double amen.

Steam coming out of her ears, despite the air-conditioning in the coffee shop, Amanda packed up her laptop, stuffed her half-eaten scone into its little bag and into her tote and grabbed her tea. She stood up and turned to the women. "You're talking about a seven-year-old boy. And before you tell me to mind my own business, maybe consider that when you gossip about people in a coffee shop, you never know who's sitting next to you."

Both women's mouths dropped open. Amanda stalked out, fury climbing up her spine.

She was halfway down the block before it occurred to her that the old Amanda—Amanda of even a week ago—would never have spoken up like that. She would have been too shy and instead would have spent all night tossing and turning and thinking of comebacks she wished she could have been confident enough to hurl back at those hyenas in lip gloss.

You are *changing*, she realized, a smile forming on her lips.

Her phone pinged with a text. It was from Holt, and the way her heart leaped made her doubly sure she was changing, that she was letting him in. If just a smidge.

Robby woke up asking if it was all a dream, that he would get to be in the Mother-Son Fun Run with you. I assured him it was real. Thank you, thank you, thank you.

He'd added the emoji of a smiley face wearing a cowboy hat.

Amanda brought her hand to her heart, so touched she almost cried.

She was in deep trouble.

Holt had checked Brody Colter's schedule for the morning. The cowboy was on herding duty till eleven, then would be meeting the shipment of feed at eleven thirty. Holt planned to catch him right after the truck left. The two could stack the heavy bags—and talk.

Right on time, Holt saw the young hand loping his way to the barn, a metal water bottle in his hand. Neal Dalton had commented on Brody's good posture when he'd signed off on hiring him; his dad took that as a sign of something good. Holt watched the tall, lanky blonde swish his mop of bangs out of the way, then take a long drink and stuff the bottle in his backpack and grab a cereal bar, which he'd finished by the time the truck pulled in. Holt nodded at Brody and helped unload the truck, which seemed to surprise the cowboy. The Dalton guys didn't usually do the gruntiest of grunt labor.

"Brody, I'm gonna just come out with this," Holt said, grabbing a huge feed sack from the stack.

The guy whirled to him, alarm on his face. "I do something wrong?"

"I had a visit last night from Edward Thompson."

Brody's face fell and he let out a breath.

"He wants me to convince you to break up with his daughter for her own good," Holt said. "If not, he won't make his usual big donation to the ranchers' association and he'll blame Dalton's Grange for that."

Brody lifted his chin, squinting under the brim of his cowboy hat. "I'm not breaking up with Piper. She's stood up to her father ever since he found out about us. She was strong enough to do that, there's no way I'll let her down by walking away."

Good for you, kid, Holt thought. "You'd lose your job over Piper?" He headed into the barn and laid the bag of feed on the big pallet.

"You'd fire me?" Brody shot back, following him with another bag of feed.

The kid had conviction and Holt liked him. He also had a feeling Brody knew Holt wouldn't fire him. Dalton's Grange had a good reputation in town, despite the family only being in Bronco a year. The Daltons were known for being honest, even if some of the snobbier types in Bronco Heights referred to them as "new money." Holt had never understood why that was an insult; it meant someone came from nothing and made something of themselves. Granted, Neal Dalton had done that at the casino, but he was putting his blood, sweat and tears, and everything he was, into the ranch. Holt had learned long ago that it was what you did with your opportunities that counted.

Holt had thrown an opportunity named Amanda right out the window, hadn't he? He hadn't seen the situation with the same eyes he did now. If he had, he might have viewed his relationship with Amanda as a partnership, been honest with her, gotten her take on things. Instead, he'd basically lied about who he was and then made decisions for them. At least he could say he was young then. Now, he wouldn't squander an opportunity he knew was a good thing.

"Touché, Brody," he said as they headed back to the stack outside. "And no, I won't fire you. I don't like threats or ultimatums. You work for Dalton's Grange and that makes us Team Brody. We've got your back."

The cowboy's face broke into relief. "Really?"

Holt hefted another bag. "Yeah, really. Sounds like you really care about this young woman."

Brody nodded and grabbed a bag, balancing it over his shoulder. "I love her more than anything. She's the best thing that's ever happened to me. Piper makes me want to be better in every aspect of my life, you know?"

He did know. That was how he'd felt about Amanda ten years ago.

Brody was quiet for a minute as they finished getting the bags of feed into the barn.

"But her father thinks I'm a loser from the wrong side of the tracks," Brody continued, taking off his hat and using a bandanna from his pocket to wipe his forehead. "And I know that for a fact because I overheard him say so after I dropped her off at home one night. He kept asking Piper what she could possibly see in a ranch hand who smelled like cattle and was going nowhere in life."

Holt shook his head. "He's got you figured out at eighteen? Please."

Brody brightened some, clearly appreciating that Holt was on his side.

"A long time ago I once dated a girl from another world," Holt said. "I never felt like I had anything to offer her and that was wrong. I broke up with her because I thought she deserved better. I had no faith in myself at all. I'm glad you do, Brody."

"I don't know where it comes from. My mom died two years ago, and the day before my eighteenth birthday almost a year ago now, my father told me he was taking off with his girlfriend in her RV and they had no idea where they'd end up. It's why I live in that tiny one-room hovel above Wild Wesley's. I work there part-time, sweeping and mopping and loading the dishwashers."

So he didn't hang out in dive bars, like Edward Thompson had said. He worked there when he already had a full-time job on the ranch.

"That fight you got in—the one I bailed you out of jail for," Holt said. "You got caught in the middle of something?"

"I was bussing a table and some jerk said something really sexist to a waitress, so I told him that he was rude and he slugged me but missed, but then came after me. He was so drunk he kept missing, but I hit him once to get him off me and he called the cops."

Holt doubted Thompson would care about the details. "If you need more hours, Brody, I can take care of that. You can stay an extra hour every day or work a few on the weekends—whatever you want."

"Really?" Brody asked, brightening again.

"That'd be great. It would probably help with Piper's dad if I didn't work there anymore. She told him I had two jobs because I'm hardworking and want to build a nest egg to buy my own small ranch, and I heard him laugh and say a guy like me will never get past minimum wage and we were both kidding ourselves."

Edward Thompson was a real jerk.

Holt shook his head. "I have no doubt you'll achieve your dreams, Brody. That's what goals and hard work are about."

"Hope so," Brody said.

"Thompson said Piper's been saying she might not go to college after all. That seems to be what has him all riled up."

Brody looked off at the mountains for a second, then turned back to Holt. "She's afraid the distance will come between us, but I keep telling her we're too solid for anything to get in our way. I think she should go to college and that I should join the army—like my dad and uncle did after high school. My goal has always been to have my own ranch one day, but I like the idea of serving my country too. Piper can go to school for four years like she planned and I'll serve. Then we'll get married and start our lives together."

That also sounded solid to Holt. But Brody was biting his lip and looking away.

"Except?" Holt prompted.

"Except Piper doesn't want me going away for four years. She suggested I follow her to college and get a live-in job on a ranch nearby, but there aren't many ranches out there. She thinks we should buy a piece of land and start our own small homestead with like ten head of cattle and some sheep and chickens. She wants to make her own cheese and yogurt."

Holt smiled. "And what do you think of that idea?"

"I think it sounds like a fairy tale. Piper's the best, but she grew up in a fancy house in Bronco Heights and hasn't had to make milk or cheese to sell in order to have money for the power bill or groceries." His shoulders sagged. "Before I started working at the bar, I didn't have much left after paying my bills and ate those foam cups of noodle soup for a few days. Piper doesn't know what that's like and I don't want her to."

Holt nodded. "I think your idea of Piper going to school and you into the service is a great one, Brody. That'll let you both grow up some. You can remain committed as a couple. That's up to you two."

"That's what I think too. I just have to make her see it's the best plan for both of us. She seems to think I'm trying to end things. I just want her to have everything. And throwing away college and pissing off her dad isn't having everything."

"You're smart and focused, Brody. And it's admirable that you want her to stay on good terms with her dad. You two just need to get on the same page about where to go from here."

"What if we can't agree?"

Holt thought about that for a second. "Well, you know one thing for sure—you want to be together. Just keep that as the baseline. Whatever you do, make sure all roads lead to that."

"Mr. Thompson wants me out of Piper's life altogether. I hate coming between her and her father."

Holt really felt for Brody. He was in a tough situation and basically alone.

"Brody, help me for a sec," another ranch hand called.

"Coming," Brody said to him.

"Sorry to get mixed up in your business," Holt said. "Just know if you need to talk to someone, I'm here for you. And I mean it about the extra hours."

Brody smiled. "Thanks," he said, and walked toward the other cowboy, shoulders down, pressed by a weight that shouldn't be there.

Holt knew Edward Thompson was going to try to get his way here, and that things were going to get ugly. For *who*, exactly, in the end, Holt wasn't sure.

What was certain was that Brody was going to put Piper first. Holt had always thought that was what he was doing when he left Amanda a decade ago, but now he realized the opposite was true.

He hadn't been one-tenth the man Brody was now. Holt hadn't been putting Amanda first at all; he'd been afraid she'd discover who he really was out of that magical camp setting and everything would come falling down on his head. He'd believed who he really was wouldn't measure up and so he'd walked away. To save himself—not her.

He understood that now. And these few past days he thought he just needed to prove to Amanda that he'd changed. But *had* he changed?

The past ten years he hadn't been successful at anything. Yeah, he had a kid he loved. But Holt was a father who'd been told his son wasn't welcome back at camp because of his behavior. And Holt was a son who'd never figured out how to have a relationship with his father—and that relationship was now at an all-time low. And workwise? Here he was, working for someone else. His family, though, and he did like that more than he'd ever realized. Still, he'd never started his own ranch, which had once been his dream.

He hadn't made anything of himself in all these years. Not at home or at work or in love.

He was trying for a second chance with Amanda? Damn, maybe he should back the hell off. In fact, he'd do just that.

This time around he *was* going to put Amanda Jenkins first.

Chapter Eleven

The Mother-Son Fun Run started at eight o'clock and was located in a park close to Amanda's apartment building, so she let Holt know she'd meet him and Robby there. She could barely wait. She hadn't seen either Dalton yesterday. She'd planned on going over to tutor Robby as usual but Holt had canceled, saying "something came up." Amanda had always thought that was code for "making something up to get out of plans." If Holt had said Robby had a dentist appointment or he had a buddy coming over or a terribly tummy ache, she would have believed it.

Something came up. Humph. Something *was* up was more like it. But why would he want to stop her from coming over? She spent her time with Robby—not Holt. Maybe he'd explain this morning.

When she arrived at the park, the sight of all those mothers and boys in their matching race T-shirts almost took her breath. If Amanda was lucky, one day, she'd have two boys and two girls. But right now, she got to stand in as mom, and the idea gave her a little jolt of joy.

"Amanda!"

She turned to find Robby racing full speed ahead toward her. He slowed down a bit, thank heavens, before wrapping his arms around her. "Morning, partner!" she said, giving him a hug back.

He beamed up at her.

Holt was making his way over, weaving through the crowds, his expression neutral. What was going on with him?

"I'm so excited!" Robby said, taking her attention, for which she was glad. She'd spent way too many hard nights analyzing Holt Dalton, and she had to put a stop to it.

"Me too!" she said, giving Robby a high five. They'd both already picked up their registration packets from the town hall the other day and had their race shirts and bib numbers pinned on. The last three numbers were the same to show they were a pair.

As Holt joined them, Amanda could see he was definitely subdued. Maybe he'd had a run-in with his dad yesterday and that was why he'd canceled. Or a tough afternoon with Robby? Single parenting couldn't be easy; Amanda had no experience in that, but she wasn't kidding herself that it would be good times 24/7. In any case, she should stop speculating. Ten years ago, when he'd left her and hadn't looked back, she'd had no choice but to wonder about what had been going on in his head. Now, he was right here. All she had to do was ask if she wanted honesty about why he'd canceled. And why he seemed so…distant now. Subtle, but she could see it in his face and feel it in the air around them.

"That's the start line," Robby said, pointing at the huge banner across the grass. "And on the way back it becomes the finish line."

Amanda eyed the mile-long loop and hoped she didn't conk out halfway. She wasn't a runner and didn't belong to a gym. Her exercise came from walking around town—which, come to think of it, probably didn't count as exercise. Hey, at least it was something physical.

As Robby was talking about their matching

T-shirts and race bibs, a boy standing nearby turned and stared at him. He looked to be around Robby's age.

"Why are you here, Robby?" the boy asked, freckles dotting his cheeks.

"Same as you, Ethan!" Robby said, pointing to his blue sneakers. "I'm running."

Ethan tilted his head. "Yeah, but you don't have a mom. How can you run in the mother-son race if you don't have a mom?"

Amanda's stomach flip-flopped. Kids came out with whatever was on their minds. She glanced at Holt, who stood ramrod straight, his gaze on his son, whose expression had gone from happy and excited to sad and defeated.

"I have a mom," Robby said, frowning.

"No," Ethan insisted.

"Yes. She just lives far away."

The boy scrunched up his face. "That's weird."

"*You're* weird!" Robby said, and went to push the boy, but Holt clearly knew his son and scooped him up and away before he could.

"What is going on here?" asked a woman who looked a lot like Ethan.

"Robby said I was weird," the boy said, and stuck out his tongue.

"Mrs. Anderson said kids should mind their own business!" Robby shouted, tears in his eyes.

"Mrs. Anderson isn't our teacher anymore," Ethan said, his mother pulling him away.

Amanda shook her head. "Why don't we wait on the other side of the lineup?"

"Good idea," Holt said, and they moved a few feet away. Holt looked angry, Robby was about to cry, and Amanda's heart was breaking for the little guy.

"Is Ethan right?" Robby asked his father, tears falling down his face. "I can't run the race cuz I don't really have a mom?"

"Hey," Holt said, kneeling in front of him. "You saw the race rules—'mom' means anyone who feels like a mom. Someone special in your life who's kind and helps. Do you know someone like that?"

"Amanda's like that," Robby said, swiping under his eyes with his forearm.

Holt gently pushed Robby's bangs out of his eyes. "Right. So there's no problem with you running the race."

"There kind of is, Daddy," Robby said. The tears fell harder and Amanda bit her lip. "Why doesn't my mom want to live where I live?"

Holt glanced at Amanda, and she could plainly see the pain in his eyes. He looked at his son and put his hands on Robby's little shoulders. "I wish

I understood that myself, Robby. Because you're the best kid in the world."

That seemed to make Robby feel better. "But I always get in trouble. Is that why my mom doesn't come to see me?"

Oh Robby, Amanda thought.

"Robby Dalton, I promise you that you're a great kid, the very best I know. The reasons your mom lives far away don't have anything to do with you. That is the truest thing I know."

Amanda stared at Holt in wonder. She was so moved by his honesty and how he didn't try to change the subject. He was answering his son's questions the best way he knew how—questions that didn't have answers.

Robby was staring at the ground.

"I agree with your dad, Robby. You're a great kid."

Robby glanced up at Amanda and a smile broke out on his face.

"The race is gonna start soon," Holt said. "But if you don't feel like participating, that's okay."

"Do you still want to run with me, Amanda?" Robby asked.

She reached out her hand and he put his little one in hers. "You bet I do. I can't wait. This will be my very first race. Let's get to the start line!"

"I hope I'm faster than Ethan."

Amanda smiled and tapped his nose. "Ooh, I just thought of something. How about after this we go out for a special brunch? My treat."

Holt was staring at her. Uh-oh. She'd gotten so caught up with Robby that she wasn't thinking about the fact that Holt didn't want her in his orbit for some reason. But then his expression softened. "French toast sound good to me."

"Pancakes," Robby said. "Chocolate chip ones. And bacon."

"That's what I'm having too," Amanda said.

Robby was smiling and excited again.

"You know, Robby," Holt said, kneeling down in front of his son again, "I like the way you handled that conversation with Ethan. Except I got the feeling you were about to push him. You might have thought he deserved it because he wasn't being kind, but pushing someone is wrong. Same with hitting. Right?"

"Yeah. But I did want to push him *and* hit him. Teachers always say 'use your words,' but sometimes I don't know what to say."

"I completely understand," Holt said. "When you feel that way, just walk away. You can find me and we can talk it over, or if you're at school, you can tell your teacher."

"'Kay, Daddy."

"Family hug?" Holt said, holding out his arms.

Robby flung himself at his father, and Amanda realized just how much she wished she could be part of that family hug—and how attached she was to both Daltons.

A whistle blew and then a man's voice could be heard over a megaphone. "Time to line up, moms and sons!"

"That's us!" Amanda said, taking Robby's hand. "Ready?"

The smile on Robby's face almost made Amanda cry. "Ready!"

Amanda glanced at Holt, but again, he seemed…distant. Something was bothering him. Something that might have been exacerbated by what had just happened.

"See you two at the finish line," Holt said. "I'll be cheering you on."

The whistle blew again and the runners were off. Amanda felt like part of her heart was right beside her and the other part waiting at the finish line.

Holt had been prepared for his son to want to talk about his mother during brunch, but Robby hadn't brought up Sally Anne once, and now the three of them—Holt, Robby and Amanda—were just about finished with brunch. On one hand, Holt was relieved the subject hadn't come up; on the other, maybe he himself should have asked Robby outright if he had questions or wanted to talk about his mother. Waiting for cues from Robby had always been the way Holt had handled the topic, but maybe that was wrong. Maybe Holt should ask. He wished he had all the answers, all the right answers—to his own questions and to Robby's—but he didn't.

And maybe talking in front of Amanda wouldn't have been a good idea, anyway, though she seemed comfortable with the conversation in the park. She'd let him handle it, which he appreciated, and when she had joined in, it had been to back him up that Robby was a great kid, which he'd also appreciated.

During brunch, his son had been focused on talking about the run—that he'd finished without stopping, that he passed by that "mean Ethan Snowling" and that it was one of his favorite days of his entire life, maybe only after adopting Bentley and Oliver.

Because he'd had a "mom" for the morning? Because he'd simply had a fun time with his tutor, who he liked very much, his dad cheering them on?

Holt had thought he should distance himself from Amanda, that he should put any notion of a second chance out of his head, but maybe he had it wrong again. As he'd watched the mile-long race, Amanda and Robby running their hearts out, Robby smiling, focused, happy, Amanda so damned beautiful without a shred of makeup, her hair in a ponytail, wearing the bright blue race T-shirt, a thought had hit him. Hard. Their wants and needs were in perfect alignment.

Amanda wanted a child. He wanted a mother for Robby. Maybe the two of them finding what they needed in each other was the answer. Amanda had said she was done with love. And hell, maybe he was too. He didn't want to be, but after his marriage fiasco and trying to date to find Robby a good mom, he'd backed way off from trying to find a life partner.

They could both get they wanted. What they needed.

He'd just have to show her that she could trust him, that he was the guy she'd always thought he was.

The race had ended in a snap, so he'd had to put his thoughts out of his head so he could drive them all to the café without crashing into a pole. He'd done a good job of focusing on his breakfast companions, but now he was back to wondering. Was it possible—

"Earth to Holt, earth to Holt."

He started, realizing Amanda was talking to him.

Robby giggled and put down his little glass of orange juice. "Daddy, Amanda was saying your name but you were in another world like people say about me when I'm not paying attention to them. You were probably thinking of something really good, right?"

He smiled—and wanted to reach over and hug his son hard. "Yeah, I was thinking of something good." He turned to Amanda. "Sorry. What were you saying?"

"Hey, aren't those your brothers? See—by the painting of the dog with the cowboy hat on?"

Holt looked over and squinted. Huh. Dale and Shep were just getting up from their table. "Yup, you're right. Hey, Robby. I see your uncles over there. Wanna go say hi?"

Robby leaped up and raced over before Holt could remind him to walk. Luckily, a waitress with a tray of full plates wasn't anywhere in his path.

Holt tried to put cash on the table but Amanda reminded him this was her idea and her treat, and he relented. When the group met up at the door, Shep and Dale said they were headed to watch a rodeo competition a few towns over and invited Robby, who practically catapulted onto the ceiling in excitement—an opportunity to see Daring Drake. Holt took off Robby's race bib, and off the boy went with his uncles. Again, Holt was grateful that he'd moved to Bronco so that his son would have a big family who loved spending time with him.

Now he was also grateful he'd moved here because of Amanda.

"Take a walk?" he asked her. He bit his lip, wondering if he should come right out with his idea about them. It was a big deal, though, and something he should think over. He held open the door and out they went into the warm, bright sunshine.

"You're cutting me out, aren't you," she said, a statement, not a question. She stood stock-still, staring at him. "You canceled yesterday and you seemed conflicted this morning—before the conversation with Robby, I mean."

Since they were smack in the middle of town, he kept seeing people he knew and so did Amanda, so they decided to talk in his truck. Once they were both settled, he said, "I'm going to be honest with what's on my mind."

"Good," she said.

"You said you were done with love and romance, but I kept thinking maybe I could have a second chance here. But then I realized that I don't deserve it. I was selfish ten years ago—walking away from our relationship to protect myself. Not you, myself. I didn't want to get found out for the imposter I was."

She seemed to be taking that in. "Okay, I get that. But that was a decade ago. Now is another story. You're distancing yourself because…?"

He stared out the windshield, then turned to her. "I was thinking I should because nothing in my life is working out right now, Amanda. Relationships haven't worked out—from my marriage to the women I've dated the past year. I need to focus on Robby—get him more settled before school starts. I need to be more present for him, too, as evidenced by this morning and the conversation before the race about his mother. I need to focus on him. And I need to fix my problems with my dad—somehow."

"So, canceling a tutoring and babysitting session with me is helping Robby? I'm part of that 'get him settled' before school starts."

"Well, thinking I should back off from you was before I realized the opposite is true."

She narrowed her eyes. "What are you talking about exactly?"

Just come out with it, he told himself. *You don't risk, you don't get.* That was the damned truth. He looked at her, bracing himself. "I'm just saying let's give this a real shot, Amanda."

"Give what a shot—a relationship?"

He nodded. "You want a child. And you adore Robby. I need a wonderful, loving mother for him. Someone I trust. Neither of us is looking for…someone else to give us what we need. So… why not give us a chance?"

She was staring at him as though he'd grown an extra head. "You're serious, aren't you?"

"Very. I want to do what's right and best for Robby. That seems to perfectly align with what you want, Amanda."

Tears shimmered in her eyes. Oh hell. Did he mess this up?

"What are you thinking?" he asked gently.

"I'm thinking I don't know. That I just need to go think—alone."

"I understand." He didn't want her to get out of the truck. He just wanted her close.

"So, basically, Holt, you're asking me out. On a date. I mean, if we're gonna start something, it's gotta start with that first date."

A date. Yes. "We can see how it feels to be together on a date. And that date can be anything you want it to be, Amanda. We can take Bentley for a long walk and just talk and hang out. We can go out to dinner and share a bottle of wine. We can sit on the sofa and watch Marvel movies."

"You mean rom-coms," she said, sending him a half smile.

There was hope here. He could tell. "I'll watch any lovey-dovey movie you want."

She glanced out the window, then turned to him. "I'm not saying no. Or yes. I need to think about this, Holt." She took a deep breath. "I'll take the weekend to think about it. I'll be over Monday to tutor Robby and babysit. We can talk afterward, okay?"

How would he get through the weekend not knowing if she'd say yes?

"I'm just asking for a chance, Amanda. To show you who I am now."

She looked at him and he knew by her expression, by her eyes that she was halfway to yes already. She wanted a second chance just like he did, but after how he'd treated her, after getting left at the altar in her wedding dress, she was afraid to try again, afraid to even believe in love. She might say no, that dating—even one date— was out of the question.

"See you Monday," she said, getting out of the truck.

He wished she was still beside him.

Chapter Twelve

"Of course you're going on a date!" Brittany said. "And please, I'm not talking a dog walk in the woods in your unsexy hiking sandals. I'm talking Dinner. Candles. Wine. A good-night kiss…"

Amanda and her roommate were sitting on the balcony of their building, Amanda staring off at the mountains in the distance. She'd told Brittany every detail of the morning and conversation with Holt after brunch. When Amanda had gotten home, she'd tried to do some work but couldn't concentrate, and was grateful when her wise and insightful roommate had come in.

Amanda took a sip of her iced tea and stared out at the view, hoping the beautiful vistas would provide all the answers. No such luck. "I don't know how to just let go of everything I've been through, though. I don't trust anymore, Brittany. And I don't believe love even exists."

"I know it's not easy to put yourself out there. Especially with a guy who broke your heart. But love *definitely* exists. Case in point, our neighbor Mel, who's rarely home these days because she's with Gabe—and those two are big time in love. Ferociously so."

That was true. The early days of Mel's relationship with Gabriel Abernathy had been anything but "love at first sight" and happy-ever-after. They'd fought hard for how strongly they felt for each other, despite their issues. And love won.

Her roommate sipped her own drink, then pushed her long curls behind her shoulders. "Holt Dalton is asking you for a chance. And *one* date to see. A baby step. If you're at the restaurant and looking at him across the candlelit table with some soft music playing and you feel like throwing up, fine—then you're not meant to be dating him or anyone. But at least *see.*"

Amanda knew she wouldn't feel remotely nauseated or the slightest bit of dread if she were sitting across from Holt, both of them dressed up for a date. Butterflies, sure. But in a good way. Because Holt was so good-looking, so sexy, and he was part of her past and a big part of her present; she was already wrapped up in his life. So much so that she'd run a mother-son race with his son.

That was the problem, though. Being so invested in his life. The good butterflies. The real date. Everything that would be between them in that restaurant and hovering in the air. She'd have a taste of romance with Holt and be drawn right back in. Then down the line, whether two dates later or a few months, she'd be dumped again. *It's not you, it's me. This just isn't working out. I thought we could be what we each needed, but I was wrong...*

That was what she was afraid of. So why try at all? Why go on that one date when she'd end up with a broken heart, ugly-crying for days and eating Ben & Jerry's out of the container in bed with Poindexter?

She said exactly that to Brittany.

"And here I thought I was stubborn," her roommate said. "Honey, I don't get serious about the men I date because I'm not looking to be a wife and mama. You *are*. Everything you want, deep in your heart—which includes love and romance and happily-ever-after and a child—is possible with Holt Dalton. And I'll just come right out with this—the man you never stopped loving."

That was definitely true. "And if he hurts me again?" Amanda asked, biting her lip. She pictured herself waiting in a hotel room in Las Vegas, the veil she'd splurged on with the delicate beading that had reminded her of something Audrey Hepburn would have worn, her groom never appearing. *Holt*—never appearing.

She'd be knocked to her knees.

"Then, Amanda Jenkins," Brittany said, sitting up very straight and looking at her pointedly, "I'll be there to see you through the heartache, and in time, you'll open yourself up to going through it all over again because that's life. Love is everything."

"But not for you?" Amanda asked.

"Hey, I've got nothing against love. I just don't want marriage and kids. Right now. Maybe not ever. I don't know."

"Why is the subject of love so damned complicated?" Amanda asked with a sigh.

"Right?" Brittany said.

They clinked their iced tea glasses and sat in silence, looking out at the breathtaking view.

Amanda heard a sexy giggle, then a male voice say, "C'mere you." She turned to see that her next-door neighbor, Mel, and her fiancé had come out onto the adjacent balcony, locked in a very passionate kiss, eyes closed, arms wrapped around each other as they edged toward the railing.

"Um, don't fall over," Brittany called over, shooting Amanda a grin.

Mel opened an eye, her mouth forming an O at being caught in a hot PDA, before Gabe reclaimed her lips, taking off his cowboy hat and holding it to the side to shield the lovebirds from view.

Amanda and Brittany both laughed, but inside, Amanda was deep-sighing wistfully. That sure did bring back memories—of her two big romances and some littler ones. Love, desire, romance.

Dammit, she wanted in.

"I know what you need, Holt."

He glanced toward the voice—his dad's. Why did he doubt that Neal Dalton thought he knew what he needed?

Holt looked back down at the new-hire checklist on his iPad and clicked the first two boxes as the cowboy-trainee they'd hired mucked out the big pen at the far end of the barn. The guy was doing a great job so far. The worst duties on the ranch always fell to the new hire, and so far, the short, wiry cowboy was working hard, humming a country tune Holt recognized. Holt was trying

to pretend he was doing something else besides
assessing the guy, so it was a good thing his father had come along.

"And what's that?" Holt asked his dad.

"What you need," Neal said, pointing a finger at him, "is a *wife*. And not just any wife. One
who'll make a good mother for Robby. Someone
like the librarian with the curly red hair. Every
time your mother and I take Robby to the library
and anyone is noisy, she cuts them a look with
a serious shush and then there's blessed quiet."

Holt knew the shusher. There was a reason
she didn't often work the children's section. Holt
once overheard her nastily chastising a woman
for putting a book back in the wrong place, and
Holt walked up to the mean shusher and pointed
at the large framed sign on the wall that read
Choose Kindness. The shusher turned red, and the
chastised woman grinned. "Robby needs a loving mother above all. Someone who can be firm
when need be, yes. But loving is number one."

"Well, Charlotte—that's her name—seems
like a perfectly good candidate, and I took the
liberty of telling her that I have a son who has a
young child and maybe she'd like to join us for
dinner some time."

Oh God. "Dad, tell me you didn't try to set me
up on a date, especially with that woman."

"I sure as hell did. And guess what she said. She said, 'Oh, do you mean Holt? I know him and Robby. They come in every week. I'd love to get to know Holt better.' That means she can handle a boy like Robby."

A boy like Robby. And "direction" from someone like the redhead meant punishment not guidance.

Holt barely held his tongue. He wasn't interested in rehashing Robby's needs with his father. Besides, they'd had this conversation countless times over the past year. "Dad, there's one thing I agree with you on—I do need a good mother for Robby. But she'll be of my choosing. I don't need help in that department."

His father had perked up the moment Holt had said he did need a wife. "Well, your mother and I got hopeful about Amanda, but you two don't seem to be dating."

Maybe we will be. If things went his way. "I'm trying," Holt said. "We'll see."

His father tilted his head. "Ah, well in that case, I'll let you be and stop playing matchmaker. We like Amanda. And Robby clearly does too."

Holt smiled. "He certainly does. She's the whole package, as they say. Everything in one." She really was. Not only was Amanda Jenkins warm and compassionate and patient, but she was funny and charming and interesting and smart. Plus she was beautiful.

"Don't mess it up," Neal Dalton said.

Holt froze, then his skin got itchy, anger swirling in his gut. "Thanks for the vote of confidence."

"Just saying, Holt. Things didn't work out between you two once. Don't let her slip away again."

Out of the mouths of interfering fathers.

His phone pinged with a text. Amanda. How about we have that date tonight?

His heart soared. Perfect, he texted back. Robby is sleeping over in the main house tonight with Dale and Shep. They're having a camp-out in the backyard.

Pick me up at seven?

See you then.

Well. That she'd said they'd talk Monday and she hadn't been able to wait was a very good sign. *No, Dad, I'm not going to mess this up.*

Holt parked in the underground garage for Amanda's building, which sure was swanky. Lots of young men and women were around, coming and going to the pool. In the lobby he buzzed Amanda's apartment, and she told him to come on up.

When she opened the door, his knees almost gave out. He'd never seen her look like this. Ever. She wore a short sleeveless black dress and high-heeled sandals, her long hair loose past her shoulders. Her lips were a sexy red. And the hint of perfume around her was so scintillating it drew him closer.

He could not take his eyes off her and didn't want to. "You look stunning."

"My roommate's the expert on dressing up to go out. She helped me. Shook her head at all my choices for an outfit."

"Well, you'd look stunning in a burlap sack with tomato sauce on your head. But, wow, Amanda."

She laughed. "That may be one of the nicest—and strangest—things anyone's ever said to me."

He'd dressed up too. His brother Morgan had dragged him shopping after they'd moved to Bronco, shaking his own head at how Holt would wear a western shirt and jeans and his *good* cowboy boots to a nice restaurant on a date. Holt was all about cowboy clothes, but apparently, there was an unwritten dress code in fancy Bronco Heights. As he'd driven to Amanda's building, watching the guys walking around, particularly the ones carrying bouquets of flowers for their ladyloves on a Saturday night, he saw how right Morgan was. No one was wearing ranch gear in town tonight.

"You clean up real nice yourself," she said. "Well, let me grab my purse and say goodbye to Poindexter and we'll be off."

Holt glanced past Amanda to the cat sitting on the back of the sofa, grooming his face with a paw. He watched Amanda give the cat a little pat, and then she was back, smelling so delicious he wanted to just wrap himself around her.

He was so aware of her during the walk to the restaurant. Tonight held so many possibilities— for them, for their future and for Robby. Bronco had a couple of nice restaurants, and though he'd love nothing more than to sit down to a plate of DJ's Deluxe's finest ribs, he had something a lot more romantic in mind. There was a small Italian restaurant, low lit, with frescoes on the walls and candelabras. He'd made a reservation, leaving nothing to chance.

Amanda smiled as he led her inside. "I love this place. I've never been here before."

Perfect. A first for them both. They were seated at a round table by a window overlooking the side garden. As he looked at his date across the candlelight, he was taken back to ten years before, when they'd gone to a pizza place and he'd sat across from her so in love, unable to take his eyes off her then too, unable to believe she was his.

"I'm so glad you changed your mind about waiting to respond till Monday," he said. "I don't know how I would have made it through the weekend, not sure what you'd say."

She glanced up from the menu, surprise in her brown eyes. "I like how straightforward you are. You say what's on your mind."

"I've learned my lesson." He nodded.

Crud. Maybe that was the wrong thing to say. The wrong word to mention. She'd said many times that she'd learned her lesson about him, and he certainly didn't want to remind her.

She closed her menu and set it aside and so did he. A waiter took their drink and entrée orders.

"So tell me what brought you to Bronco," he asked. "I don't think we ever talked about that."

She took a sip of her water. "Well, after I got stood up by the man I was about to marry in Vegas, I found myself driving back home and realizing I needed a fresh start. I had a good friend from college who lived in Bronco and had heard such great things about living here, so off I went."

"I'm very sorry you got hurt by that dope in

Vegas, Amanda. But I'm not sorry that it made you available to be sitting right here with me."

"I always go back and forth about fate," she said. "Is this date, this reunion, meant to be? Or did circumstances just put us in the same place at the same time and so here we are?"

The waiter brought their wine and set a basket of Italian bread and a little dish of herb-infused olive oil between them.

"I think it's both," Holt said. "Half fate, half circumstances."

She laughed and lifted her glass. "I will toast to that."

They clinked glasses, the evening off to a great start. They weren't making awkward small talk. This date was about the past, the now and the future.

They talked so easily, Holt telling funny stories about his brothers, more serious ones about his mother's days of recuperation, and his favorite animals on the ranch. And Amanda told him about her clients, including a matchmaker whose success stories included two lonely seventy-somethings who'd recently gotten married and were honeymooning in Italy.

When their entrees came—chicken saltimbocca for him, spaghetti Bolognese for her—they shared bites, talking, laughing, eating, drinking. This evening could not be more perfect—

"Omigod! Holt?"

He glanced up at his name—at that voice—and he did a double take.

Sally Anne.

"Boy, did I surprise you!" Sally Anne said, looking a bit nervous. Then she slid her gaze to Amanda and held out her hand, her long red nails still her trademark, he saw. "I'm Sally Anne—the ex-wife. I'm sure you've heard all about me." She looked back to Holt. "I'm just in town real quick to help out an old friend or otherwise I'd have called."

"So," he said through gritted teeth. "You came to Bronco and didn't even call me to make arrangements to see Robby for even a half hour? You certainly had time to come here, Sally Anne. What the hell?"

"God, Holt. You haven't changed a damned bit. I just don't think I'll have time. My friend is in a bad way, okay? I'm here to pick up dinner for her and I'm leaving early tomorrow morning."

"Do you even care that you have a child?" he asked, red-hot anger pulsating in every part of him.

"I do, of course, I do, Holt. But sometimes

people are just who they damned are. I'm sorry. Just tell Robby I'm sorry."

She ran out of the restaurant.

Holt almost slammed his fist down on the table. "I hate knowing that she was here, right here in town and didn't even plan to see Robby. I hate it. And I hate that you had to witness all that, Amanda."

"Hey, it's okay."

He forced himself to calm down, to suck in a deep breath. It was a good thing they'd almost finished their meals because his appetite was gone, and from the way she pushed her plate away so was hers.

Of all the bad luck of running into her. If only his ex had picked somewhere else to order a meal to go, he never would have known she was in town. He never would have been reminded that she didn't give a rat's butt about her own child.

As Robby's sweet, precious face appeared in his mind, anguish mixed with the anger.

"Let's go, Holt. I'll drive."

He nodded, tossing cash on the table, enough to add a good tip. He needed to get out of here. And he could barely think straight, let alone drive to the ranch.

She didn't say a word on the ride over, didn't ask him questions or make small talk or try to lighten things up. She let him process and digest, which was what he needed.

When she pulled up to the drive at his house, he just sat there like a stone, and she left the engine idling. Maybe he should just send her home and deal with this Sally Anne debacle on his own, in his own way. Whatever the hell *that* meant.

But he needed to get out of the truck, he needed to gulp in some air. And he needed Amanda. He knew it with a certainty that made his chest tight.

What would happen when they went inside, he had no idea. Because he was in a bad place right now. And maybe being with Amanda in the middle of it was going to cost them both.

Chapter Thirteen

Sally Anne sure wasn't what Amanda had expected, not that she'd known what to expect. She really hadn't thought much about Holt's ex; Sally Anne had been just a concept, really, because she wasn't a part of his or Robby's life at all.

But there the woman had been at the tail end of her dinner with Holt. All Amanda wanted was a child and here was Holt's ex-wife, with absolutely no interest in the seven-year-old one she had. Amanda had no idea how that was possible.

The woman had driven away to a new life that didn't include her son. And it had been years.

Then she came to the very town where Holt and Robby lived and hadn't planned to spend any time with her son. That had floored Holt and it had stunned Amanda.

She glanced over at him, the idling engine making the only sound. "Listen Holt, if you need to just be alone right now, I can take the truck home and one of your brothers can bring you by to pick it up tomorrow morning. I'll totally understand if you just need some space."

He turned slightly to her, reaching for her hand and holding it. She liked the connection, that he wasn't shutting her out.

"I could use some coffee," he said. "How about you?"

She gave him a soft smile. "The entire pot, maybe."

She shut off the engine and they went inside, Bentley greeting them. Holt let out the dog, and they sat on the porch and watched Bentley sniff the grass and enjoy the beautiful summer evening weather, then they all headed back in.

She insisted on making the coffee, aware she was too comfortable in his kitchen, and then joined him on the couch, the mugs and a small plate of cookies on the coffee table.

He took a long slug of his coffee, then another,

and turned to her. "Do you get it? Because if you do, can you explain it to me?"

"Are you talking about how Robby's mother can have no interest in his life?" she asked.

He nodded slowly. "How? How is it possible? From the moment I knew he existed I loved him. And that feeling only intensified when the doctor placed him in my arms in the hospital. I love my son with everything I am. How can a parent not feel that way?"

She took a sip of her coffee. "I don't get it either, Holt. All I know is that some people are wired differently. You said Sally Anne left for good when Robby was three. How was she before that?"

"As expected. She didn't want to be a mother. She'd always said that."

"I'm so sorry for all you went through. And I'm so glad Robby had you. Sounds like you more than made up for what he was lacking in his other parent."

He leaned back, and she could almost see the heavy weight pressing on his shoulders. How she wanted to lift it. "A mom, a mom's love and devotion—I want him to have that too."

"I understand," she said, reaching for his hand.

He held it and turned to her again, touching her face. "I'm sorry she ruined our date."

"It's not ruined. In fact, she ended up bringing us closer. I mean, here we are, talking about
some very personal issues. You opened up to me,
and for that I'm glad."

"I just wish I could shake it," he said. "Just
blink that run-in away. But all I see is Robby's
face. I hear him asking why his mother isn't in
his life."

She wished she knew what to say, but there
really wasn't anything to say. She could just be
here and hopefully that would help.

He arched one shoulder and grimaced, and she
knew his muscles were likely very tight.

"Here, let me," she said, scooting closer and
putting her hands on his shoulders. "I remember you always appreciated my back massages at
camp after working in the kitchen all day."

She rubbed and kneaded, the soapy masculine
scent of him intoxicating. "You can take off your
shirt, if you'd like more pressure."

He didn't hesitate. The shirt came off, tossed
on the arm of the sofa.

Her hands moved on his bare, broad shoulders.
He let out little grunts and ahs, and she could feel
him relaxing under her touch.

He turned around, and for a moment, she was
dumbstruck by his naked chest. "I want to kiss
you," he whispered. "I *need* to kiss you."

There would be no turning back from this point. If they kissed, the kind of kiss she knew it would be—and very likely where it would lead— she'd be all in. Her heart would be his again.

Careful, a little voice said. He got the wind knocked out of him tonight, his faith in people, in the very concept of love was shaken hard; that she knew and understood. Maybe what he wanted and needed was less about her and more about *forgetting* the hard stuff, the hard truths. For tonight.

Then again, she thought, that was life. Stuff happened, and it could bring people closer or pull them apart. *Don't let this pull you and Holt apart when it has nothing to do with you or him—not really. This was about his ex's choices.*

Yes. That was very true.

So maybe she should just go with this. Both fate and circumstances had intervened tonight. So perhaps they should see this to where the evening had led it. Which was a proposed kiss. And, she knew, much more, in his bed. Maybe Holt did need to forget, if just for a little while, the pain deep in his chest, the truth in his head. She could understand that.

Timing is rarely right anyway so don't make it about that.

She leaned close and so did he and he kissed her, deeply. She remembered how she'd once felt about the way he kissed her—as if anything was possible.

"Maybe we shouldn't do this," he said, taking his hand off her back and moving a bit away from her on couch. "I know you wanted to move slowly, Amanda. And suddenly, instead of a candlelit table and a good-night kiss at your door, we're…in dangerous territory. Because I'm using everything I've got to tamp down how badly I want you right now."

There. This wasn't just about him needing to forget what happened earlier.

She stood up and took his hand. He looked at her, holding her gaze so intensely that her knees felt shaky, and she answered by leading the way down the hall and to his bedroom.

"You sure about this?" he asked, staring at her as they entered his bedroom.

She pushed the door closed. "Very." And this time, *she* kissed him, and he responded instantly, taking her face in both of his hands and kissing her so intensely that her knees really did almost buckle.

He turned her around and slowly unzipped the little black dress, then turned her back around and gave it a nudge on each side of her shoulders so that it would fall and slide past her hips onto the floor. She stepped out of it and kicked it aside.

She kissed his bare, muscled chest, which was even sexier than she'd remembered. He picked her up and carried her onto the bed, getting rid of his pants, and slowly taking off her lacy bra. His hands and mouth were all over her, exploring, enjoying, savoring. For the first time in a long time she didn't think; she just *felt*. And apparently, the same went for him.

Her eyes closed, she felt her lacy undies being pulled down and removed. She arched her back and kissed him, anticipating the feel of him on top of her. She opened her eyes, and he was reaching for his bedside table, opening a drawer. She watched him rip open the foil packet and then met his gaze as he leaned over her.

"To a fresh start," she whispered. "To the future."

"I will make love to that," he said.

And then every painful memory from the past and every new worry was replaced by pure sensation.

The faint sound of roosters crowing woke Holt at rancher's hours: before the crack of dawn. He glanced to the left, and there was Amanda, beautiful, sexy, loving Amanda, sleeping, her face turned away from him, her long dark hair down one shoulder.

To a fresh start...to the future.

Her words echoing in his head, Holt turned away, a chill creeping up his spine. Last night, those words had sounded so good. But suddenly…

Suddenly what? Why did he feel like bolting out of bed and making himself scarce?

Fight against it, he told himself. *You're just letting your old fears get to you. That this isn't going to work out. That you're not ever going to be enough for her.*

But something else was poking at him too. Something that said: *It's Robby who's going to get hurt when she leaves you. You'll disappoint her, Robby will be too much, more than she realized, and suddenly, your heart is handed back to you and your son is sobbing.*

Oh hell. That tightness in his chest was back, and he stared up at the ceiling. Last night was everything he remembered and so much more. He and Amanda had been perfect fits, in sync, in harmony, and he'd released what felt like years of pent-up frustration. All he'd kept thinking—when he'd been able to process thought—was that he had Amanda back, and everything in his world had felt right again.

But the weight of that world was now back, pressing down hard. He tried to keep it at bay, to just keep thinking about what he wanted for

Robby, but he couldn't stop all the echoes in his head. People, even those closest to you—*I'm talking about you, Dad*—couldn't be trusted. People walked out. *That's you, Sally Anne.* People disappointed. *That's me.*

Why had he thought he and Amanda could have a second chance, that they could find what they needed in each other? He'd believed he was thinking about his son's needs when he'd proposed they try again. But hadn't everything they'd been through hammered home that the fairy tale he sought for Robby didn't exist?

He wasn't letting anyone in to hurt Robby again, to turn Holt's life upside down. They had a good thing going here at Dalton's Grange. They had family, even with his issues with his dad. He had nothing to prove to his father anymore and hell if he'd make Robby prove anything to his grandfather. Right now, Robby was over at the main house, having a sleepover in the backyard with Shep and Dale. Between his grandmother and his uncles and Holt, Robby had all the love and support he needed. Holt wasn't going to let anyone come in and break his son's heart by leaving.

He could feel himself getting farther and farther away from thinking he and Amanda could have a shot, that their relationship would work out, that she would still find Robby so lovable after a few weeks.

Damn, you're cynical, he thought. Yeah, but how could he not be? There was Sally Anne's appearance and the sickening truth that she didn't care about Robby. And now there was Holt's disillusionment all over again when he'd just been building his faith in life and love back up.

What the hell was the point?

He felt Amanda stir beside him. And everything inside him went cold and hard, like stone. Now he was going to hurt her when she didn't deserve it. *He'd* brought up the second chance. *He'd* brought up the idea of them fulfilling each other's needs and hopes and dreams. She'd been saying all along that she didn't want to go back, that she couldn't.

And he'd brought her right in.

He wasn't too fond of himself at the moment.

Holt had thought he'd been taking his father's advice—his father's good advice—to not mess things up with Amanda. All Holt *had* done was mess up. Bad.

His phone rang, and Holt grabbed it off his bedside table. His dad. Calling at 5:52 a.m.?

He bolted upright. Had something happened to Robby?

Amanda sat up too, looking at him in with concern as she pulled the quilt up to cover herself.

"You'd better come get your son," Neal Dalton said—grumpily. "He woke up too early and is bouncing off the walls."

He shook his head. "Seriously, Dad."

"Oh, I'm being serious, all right," Neal said. "Robby took it upon himself to make his grandmother and me coffee and managed to break not only the carafe but a mug. It's just too much, Holt, and I want you to come get him right now."

"Look," Holt said. "I get that he broke something. But you can't just clean it up and ask him to be more careful? He thought he was doing something nice for you and Mom."

"Just come get him."

Holt hung up.

"Dammit," he said, reaching for his boxer briefs, which he quickly put on as surreptitiously as possible.

"What's going on?" Amanda asked.

He stalked to his dresser and pulled on jeans and a T-shirt. "I'm sorry, Amanda. But I've got to go get Robby. He woke up too early and is already breaking things by accident and driving my dad nuts. Why don't you take my truck home, and I'll have one of my brothers drive me over to get it later. You can leave the keys in the console."

She hesitated a second before saying, "Okay." Then another pause.

He didn't know how he'd expected this morning to go, but leaving her to drive herself home while he left wasn't it. The idea of that made him feel like hell, but having her here this early when he walked back in with Robby would be kind of awkward too.

He let out a breath and turned to look at her. "I'm sorry I'm being so abrupt. I woke up feeling kind of...unsettled, and then the phone rang and made it worse."

"Unsettled?" she asked, pulling on her clothes. Her movements were so fast and stiff, and he knew he'd made her feel off balance. All he wanted to do was take her in his arms and just hold her—not say anything because he had no idea what he wanted to say. But he had to go. And he needed the space to think anyway.

"Can we talk later, Amanda? I mean, really talk."

She stared at him for a second and then finally nodded.

He wasn't even sure what he planned to say.

Chapter Fourteen

Amanda very quietly entered her apartment, not wanting to wake up Brittany or be caught slinking in like this in last night's clothes. Brittany would want details, and Amanda would burst into tears. She'd been trying not to cry since she'd left Dalton's Grange—in Holt's truck.

Poindexter padded over for some attention, so she picked him up and nuzzled him, giving him a few good scratches along his back, then fed him breakfast. She could use coffee, but what she really needed was a hot, bracing shower.

It was under the water, washing away all traces

of last night, washing away Holt's scent, that she let herself give into how she was feeling—and she cried. Hard. Something had shifted deep within her. The way he'd let her inside, opened up to her, after such a tumultuous, emotional incident, had made her feel so close to him. And as she'd fallen asleep after they'd made love, she'd truly thought they were a united team, that they'd found their way to each other. Her heart had opened to him. Fully.

And this morning, she'd felt him close his own.

In her bathrobe, her hair damp down her back, she could swear she smelled coffee brewing, the chocolate-hazelnut roast she loved. Which meant that Brittany was awake. Thank God. Now that Amanda had gotten the crying out of her system, she could use some Brittany wisdom.

As she walked into the kitchen, her roommate, looking gorgeous as usual even though she'd just rolled out of bed, was studying her.

"So, I heard the door open and close a little while ago," Brittany said, her dark eyes shrewd. "Then I heard the shower start. That tells me a few things. But I hope I've got it wrong."

Amanda bit her lip. "You don't, I'm sure."

Brittany poured them each a mug of coffee and brought the creamer and sugar to the table. "That you didn't come home last night means the night started out great. That you didn't come home till 6:00 a.m. means the night *ended* great. But that you're home this early and taking a shower here means something went wrong this morning."

"Are you sure you're not clairvoyant?" Amanda asked, smiling for the first time since she woke up.

Brittany took a sip of her coffee. "Oh, just been there, experienced that. But I'm usually the one making something go wrong and leaving."

Maybe that was the way. Because then, you didn't get hurt. But Holt had seemed as conflicted as Amanda was. "Everything was going great and then disaster struck. More like a tornado. We were having an amazing time together at that little Italian place at the end of Main Street," Amanda said, thinking back to the restaurant, so romantic, the candlelit table, the delicious food, the good wine. "And toward the end of dinner, guess who suddenly appeared out of nowhere, picking up takeout. Holt's ex-wife."

Brittany raised an eyebrow. "The one who hasn't been around in a few years? Why was she here? To spend time with her son?"

"An old friend was having problems, apparently. She wasn't even planning on seeing Robby. I don't get it. Neither does Holt. They had words about that, and he was so upset about his ex's complete lack of regard for their child that I drove him home. Then we got to talking about it and one thing led to another and…we were in bed."

"Tell me that part was good," Brittany said with a gentle smile.

"Amazing. Beautiful. Everything I remember and everything I imagined being with him again would be like. I'm so damned in love with the guy, Brittany."

"I know," her roommate said, squeezing her hand. "So all the negative energy from the ex got pushed aside for something much better at his place last night, but then it all came back to him this morning?"

Amanda tilted her head. "You know, I didn't really think about it like that, but yeah, I guess it must have. He said he felt unsettled, and I'm sure that was why. And maybe both parts of his past coming at him." She sipped her coffee, wishing she understood better. "The ex-wife. The ex-girlfriend."

"So what caused you to come home?"

"His son had slept over at his grandparents and Holt got call to come get him. Robby was either too loud or broke something or both."

"Ah. The triple whammy. The ex-wife infuriating him. The hopeful second chance with the woman he never forgot. And his grumpy father, impatient with his son. All in one brief period of time. Enough to rattle the calmest of us."

That made her feel better for herself—and terrible for Holt. "You think so?"

"The ex-wife's appearance would be enough, Amanda. From everything you've said, Holt's a really devoted dad. His son is the world to him. And the boy's mother comes to town and doesn't even arrange to see her own kid?" She shook head. "Holt's probably just all tangled up. Wishing things could be different and knowing they can't be."

"Well, maybe he thinks *we* can't be either," Amanda said. "He just seemed so defeated this morning."

"Give him a little time. I have faith," Brittany said.

Amanda sighed. "Wish I did." Maybe she would if she hadn't been dumped by Holt once already.

"I know he picked you up last night, so you drove his car home this morning?"

Amanda nodded, then got up and headed for the fridge, needing some sourdough toast with butter and jam, pure comfort breakfast. "Want some?" she asked Brittany, holding up the sourdough bread.

"Sure do," Brittany said with a smile. "Well,

then he'll come by some time this morning to pick up the car. You'll talk then. And be smooching a big hot hello."

Amanda laughed, then her smile faded. "He told me to just leave the keys in the truck's console, so he doesn't even have to come up for them."

"Trust me, he'll come up."

Amanda hoped so. Or she'd go out of her mind wondering what was going on with them, what he was thinking. She didn't want to be shut out. Not when they'd both let each other *in*.

After breakfast, when Brittany left to take her own shower, Amanda headed over to her laptop on the coffee table and checked her email—and almost jumped.

There was a response to her last post on the group chat site about adoptees seeking information on their birth parents. Amanda hadn't had much information to share on the site, just the general birth year, possible birth place, which might not even be accurate, and the birth parents' names— she kept it surnames only for privacy—but she'd hoped that would be enough to connect with someone out there. And for Josiah Abernathy and Winona Cobbs to be reunited with the baby girl they'd had to give up—the baby girl Winona had been told had died.

Amanda clicked on the email.

Hi. My name is Bernadette Jefferson and I was born in Rust Creek Falls and placed for adoption with a loving family. When my parents passed on, I found a document in their keepsake trunk with the name Abernathy—it was with my birth certificate. Abernathy isn't a very common name so I think I might be who you're looking for. I know my birth parents would be very elderly if still alive. This is the first time I've had hope so thank you for that! Please be in touch at your earliest convenience.

With hope, Bernadette Jefferson

Amanda burst out of her chair, scooped up Poindexter and danced him around the living room. "Poin! I think we found the long-lost baby daughter of Winona Cobbs and Josiah Abernathy! After seventy-five years!"

Poindexter did not seem to care, but he liked being held so he went with the dance.

"Ooh, I have to text Mel right away!" She put down the cat and ran for her phone. It was six thirty, but she *had* to tell Mel this great news right away, even if it meant the notification would awaken her and possibly Gabe if she was at his ranch this morning. Amanda knew her friend would want to know about the response right away. Especially because it was so promising. Abernathy *wasn't* a common name. And the timing and birth place matched!

She copied and pasted the email into a text and sent it to Mel. Five seconds later, her phone pinged back.

Omigosh! Mel texted. You're amazing—thank you so much for helping us! This is our first real lead and it sounds so promising! I'll respond to her. Thanks again, Amanda!

The email and Mel's response had done wonders for Amanda's battered spirit.

The half-mile walk to the main house had done little to clear Holt's head. The way he'd treated Amanda... He'd reached for his phone three times to at least text her an *I'm sorry*, then put it back in his pocket. He had to break the urge to connect with her. The yearning for her. He had to let her go.

He'd taken Bentley with him, letting the dog walk along unleashed at his side. In the distance he could see Robby kicking a soccer ball, his grandmother sitting on the wraparound porch, cheering him on. Neal Dalton was nowhere to be found.

"Bentley!" Robby shouted, and came running, the border collie sprinting toward him. Robby dropped to his knees, hugging and kissing his beloved dog, the boy rolling on the grass and Bentley following suit.

This was what childhood was supposed to be, Holt thought. Exactly this. *And* making mistakes. And accepting the consequences for them. But those consequences right now included a grumpy, impatient grandfather. Holt had always thought Robby and Neal Dalton would have to meet each other halfway—Robby being more mindful, particularly when he was around his grandfather, and Neal being more patient and understanding that his grandson had a harder time controlling his impulses than some other kids.

If your father can't change, Holt's mother had said once, *I don't know why he expects a little boy to be able to change.*

Holt had appreciated that then, that his mother understood. But in the year Holt and Robby had been just a half mile away, the boy spending a lot of time with his grandparents, Neal Dalton hadn't become more accepting of his grandson.

As Holt got closer, Robby catapulted himself into his father's arms, and Holt lifted his boy up and held him tight. He loved this child with all his heart. *Everything* was right here.

His mother waved with a big smile and went inside, then came back out with a bowl of what looked like water, Holt's dad behind her. She set the bowl down by the door—for Bentley, he realized with a smile—then called Robby into the house for lemonade and a muffin. Thank God for his mother. She was the one who'd asked Holt to rethink his *no* about working for his father, living on Dalton's Grange, and he'd say yes all over again for his mother's sake. But it was time for him and his dad to come to terms about the way he responded to Robby. Given his father's expression right now, which was along the lines of I've-had-it-up-to-here and Holt's matching thought, he had no idea how this conversation would go.

Look, Robby's teacher had said when Holt had been honest about his dad's impatience with Robby at home. *That's part of the consequences of Robby's behavior. And part of your job is helping Robby manage that—from dealing with people's negative reactions to his behavior, from strangers to classmates and staff, to family. It's all valid, Holt.*

"Finally," Neal Dalton said as Holt got closer.

Holt glared at his dad. Sometimes, he'd see his father in front of the grand, majestic mansion and he'd try to reconcile the man he'd always known with this new rich Neal Dalton who owned this beautiful home and all this land. This success-ful ranch. His father had changed—because his wife's health scare and a big pile of money had given him a second chance.

It's what you do with what you have, Holt thought as his father came down the stairs.

So why the hell can't I apply that way of think-ing to me and Amanda? Why am I so sure it'll all fall apart?

Because it always does, he reminded himself, thinking of Sally Anne.

His mother came back out with a doggie bis-cuit, which she set on the cushy mat in front of Bentley, who was enjoying the shade. She gave the dog a pat.

"If you can't be more patient with Robby, then I don't think you should be around him, Dad. He needs people on his side. Yes, he needs guidance and correction—from me, his parent—not you. Do I make myself clear?"

His father seemed taken aback. "How dare you talk to me like that!"

"I dare because I have to."

Neal Dalton shook his head. "Trust me, Holt. You were the same way as Robby at his age and I said the same nonsense—oh, he'll grow out of it. And look what happened when you got older. Making trouble, getting arrested for nonsense.

Running wild. Marrying a woman who doesn't even care about her own child."

Holt winced, feeling like a left hook had just landed in his stomach. What the hell?

"You're done telling me who I am or who I was. I'm proud of the man I've become. And I'm damned proud of the father I am." He glanced behind his father to the house. "Robby!" he shouted. "Come on out, buddy. Time to go."

"'Kay, Daddy!" Robby shouted back, racing out the door and down the steps, half a muffin in his hand. It was clear from his tone that Robby hadn't heard any of what his grandfather had said. "Come on, Bentley. Race ya home!"

Robby and the dog went flying up the path.

"When Robby breaks his leg and lands face-first in that muffin in his hand," his father said, "don't cry to me."

Holt shook his head and turned to his mother. "Mom, if you'd like to see me or Robby, it'll have to be at my place. I love you but I'm done here." He hugged his mother, glared at his father and then turned and walked toward home, his heart heavier than it was when he'd left his house, and that was saying something.

On Monday afternoon Amanda arrived at Holt's house for the tutoring session with Robby, not sure he'd even open the door. But he did. He hadn't called or texted since yesterday morning when she'd left his bed. She'd thought for sure he wouldn't let the day pass without at least a text, just something, but not a word.

He stood in the doorway, looking both gorgeous and miserable.

"I'm here to tutor Robby," she said, lifting her chin. She wasn't going to let her issues with Holt stop her from keeping her commitment to help Robby with reading.

"I know I said we'd talk. And I want to, Amanda. Can you stay after?"

She nodded, and because she knew him better than she thought, she could tell he was relieved— that she was here, that she actually wanted to talk to him at all. Then again, *he* probably just wanted closure on this—to end their budding second chance.

She'd never felt so…up in the air. Before—with Holt, with Tyler and his hellish text right before their wedding—she'd had no doubt where she stood: a big fat nowhere. Things had been over, kaput. Now? This? She didn't know. And that was bad too. Hell yeah, they'd talk after.

Upstairs, she found Robby preparing for their tutoring session as he always did, taking his favorite books from his bookshelf and making a pile. Bentley was on his bed and Oliver was on his perch.

"Hey, Robby!" Amanda said.

He ran over for a hug, talking a mile a minute about his camp-out sleepover with his uncles at the main house, how they'd made s'mores and Shep had brought out his telescope and he saw the Big Dipper and a zillion stars and maybe even planets.

"But then I broke stuff in the kitchen and Gramps yelled at me," he said, tears welling in his big blue eyes. "He told me I never learn and he'd had it." He looked at Amanda, biting his lip. "Do you think that means he doesn't want to be my granddaddy anymore?"

Amanda felt her eyes sting with tears. She sat down on Robby's bed and patted the space beside her. He came and sat down, wiping under his eyes.

"Did you talk to your dad about this?" Amanda asked.

Robby nodded. "He said that my gramps will always be my gramps no matter what and that he loves me very much. And Daddy also said that Gramps needed more patience and that I needed to be more careful. But I tried to be, I really did. I just wanted to make my gram and gramps coffee."

Amanda put her arm around him. "I know,

sweetheart. And that was very thoughtful of you. I'm sorry it didn't work out the way you wanted. Maybe next time you want to do something like that, you could ask for a grown-up's help, like one of your uncles. That way, if anything breaks, *they'll* get in trouble and not you." She gave Robby an evil grin.

Robby laughed. "Hey, yeah, that's a really good idea. My dad is always saying I should think hard first before I decide to do something. And next time I'll think to ask someone for help." He nodded, brightening so much that Amanda's heart moved in her chest.

Oh, how she loved this boy.

"I picked out two books to read. Did you know that Rocco the Raccoon loves spinach? I tried it cuz of that and it wasn't as terrible as I thought it would be. Not like broccoli." He scrunched up his face. "I hate broccoli."

"I *looove* broccoli!" she said. "I can't wait to hear the Rocco story about spinach."

Robby grabbed the book and settled onto the floor on top of his round reading rug, white and blue with silver stars and lots of floor pillows. Bentley jumped down and curled up beside him. Oliver watched from his perch, then closed his eyes again.

As Robby sat beside her, tongue out in concentration, finger moving under the words, Amanda knew she wasn't giving up on this family. She loved both father and son with everything she was.

She'd give Holt his chance to say what he wanted to say. And then she'd make some decisions. Hard ones.

Chapter Fifteen

Turned out that the two youngest Dalton brothers, Shep and Dale, who lived in the main house, had filled in Morgan and Boone on what had happened with Robby that morning, so the four Daltons insisted on taking Robby to town for cheer-up burgers, fries and ice cream after his tutoring session. Another major plus in the working-for-his-dad column was that Holt and his brothers had gotten closer, and they all adored Robby. They also knew what a hothead their father could be.

Now, a few minutes after Robby had gone off with his uncles, Holt and Amanda sat across from each other at the kitchen table, a mug of coffee in front of each, neither saying a word. Amanda sipped her coffee. Holt stared out the window at the moment, trying to figure out where to start, what to say. How to do the least damage.

Amanda cleared her throat. "Before we started reading, Robby told me what happened at the main house this morning. He asked me if his grandfather didn't love him anymore."

Holt winced, but before he could respond, Amanda continued.

"I did my best to tell him that his grandfather *does* love him," she said. "As he told me you did. But it got me thinking, Holt. That's how I'm left feeling right now. Unsure of where I stand. Off balance. Last night, in your bed, in your arms, all I could think was how much I still love you. How I have you back. And then bam, all I feel is a cold draft."

How much I still love you...

He'd done a double take at those words, staring at her as if shocked she'd said such a thing. He kind of was, though. Shocked. That she felt that way. That she'd said it.

She met his gaze, but when he didn't say anything, she sighed and looked out the window.

He had no idea how he felt. Everything—all

the complex layers of what was going on in his life—was balled up so tight.

Dammit. This was not what he wanted. He'd made Amanda feel the way his father had made Robby feel. The way his father had made *him* feel. How had he screwed up to this degree?

Love was powerful and all-consuming and *everything*. And right now, he needed to reserve it all for Robby. "I thought I had things figured out," he said, staring at his coffee before looking up to face her. "I thought I could do this. But then I realized I can't. I'm not about to let Robby get hurt all over again."

Amanda gasped. "What? You think I'm going to hurt Robby?"

"You won't mean to. You won't want to. But you'll leave and he'll be devastated and think it's his fault. I went through all that with him once and the after-effects are horribly painful and long-lasting. We won't go through that again. I won't allow it."

Amanda stood up. "Are you kidding me? You're ending things between us—when we just got started—because you *expect* me to break both your hearts?"

He got up too, moving to the counter to lean against it. "Yes."

She glared at him, but then her expression softened into something more like sadness. "That's what you think of me? That's how little you trust me?"

"I don't trust anyone," he said. "Except Robby."

She was staring at him, sparks in her eyes. "Holt. This is no way to live. Expecting everyone to be like Sally Anne. Hell, *you* were Sally Anne in our last go around. Not me."

I did the same thing then that I'm doing now, he realized, his heart cracking. He was leaving Amanda before she could leave him. And this time—Robby.

He hated the wall he felt building around the weaker one she'd managed to get past. "I never wanted to hurt you, Amanda. You mean a lot to me. You know that. But I can't do this. I won't do this. I have to protect Robby."

She shook her head. "I know how much you love your son. I understand how you feel, Holt. I know what that run-in with Sally Anne did to you. But you're going to throw love away in case it doesn't work out? Does that really make sense to you?"

"I need to focus on my son, Amanda. There's no room in my life for anyone but him right now." There, he came out and said it, openly and honestly. No miscommunication. "I need to protect

Robby—heart, mind and soul," he added, hoping she understood.

Tears welled her in her eyes.

And I need to protect myself, he said silently.

Holt crossed his arms over his chest. "I'll take over working with him on reading. I'm not an expert, of course, but I did some research on how to help a struggling reader improve."

She barely nodded and headed for the door. "I guess this is goodbye, then." She whirled around. "For the record, though, Holt. I think you're wrong here. I love you and the two of us have something very special. And I love Robby, and he and I have a very special relationship too. Same goes for the three of us. We fit. We blend. We belong together, Holt. I'd lost my ability to believe in love, but my feelings for you and for Robby renewed it. I'm glad I believe—even if it means hurting this bad. And for a long time. Because at least I *feel*. At least I *try*."

She pulled open the door and left, and it took everything in him not to follow her, to keep her talking, keep her in sight. But he had to let her go. For everyone's sake. And that included her own.

"Goldilocks is gonna be okay, right, Daddy?" Robby asked, sitting beside Holt in the small barn where they were nursing one of their ill goats back to health. So far, so good.

For the goat, anyway. Holt was another story. Almost a week had passed since his awful conversation with Amanda. He hadn't called or texted and neither had she. Sometimes he missed her so much he felt sick. And there was no medicine. But spending the past few days with Robby and poor Goldilocks practically 24/7 had done wonders for the ill goat.

"I think she'll be fine," Holt assured his son. "She probably just needs a day or two more of round-the-clock care. Thanks to you, she's on the mend."

Robby beamed. "I did help, didn't I, Daddy?"

Holt nodded, slinging an arm around Robby's shoulders. "You did more than just help. You saved that goat's life. If you hadn't insisted on us sleeping right outside her pen, we might not have been there when she needed us at three in the morning two nights ago. You were right to argue for that." Goldilocks had needed constant fluids, but she'd worsened. Thanks to Robby's sweet insistence on camping outside her pen "just in case," they'd been ready with water when the goat had needed it.

He'd known, of course, that Robby cared about the animals on the ranch, from the cattle to the small number of farm animals like the goats and lambs, but the extent of his compassion and his interest in Goldie's illness had surprised him. Holt also knew that kids whose attention could generally be all over the place could focus intently on things that supremely held their interest. Robby had not only just wanted to sit outside Goldie's pen and monitor her, but he'd done his own research about her illness via a kid's farming website and had learned a lot about goats and illness in the process. A lot of text for a little boy who struggled with reading. But he'd worked hard. Granted, Robby was only seven, but for him to say he wanted to be a "doctor for farm animals" was a big deal.

And Robby looked so proud right now. Goldilocks was a favorite of Holt's mother, and she'd been out helping to care for the goat too. Holt had avoided his dad the past several days, easy to do on the vast ranch. The couple of times he'd seen his dad headed in his direction, Holt turned. And he'd kept Robby away from the main house too. That hadn't felt good at all. But the burn in his gut over his problems with his dad, especially where Robby was concerned, kept his mind off Amanda. Until late at night when he would try to sleep and all he could think about was her.

Their last night together.

How he missed her.

How he wished he could undo hurting her without undoing the part that kept him and Robby on the right track.

"I hear Goldie's better, thanks to you two," a familiar voice said.

Neal Dalton. He was in his work clothes, his jeans and a western shirt with a leather vest, and his black Stetson. He had his phone in his hand, as usual. His sons managed various aspects of the ranch and one of them was always contacting him. Holt had simply avoided checking in with his father about anything that had come up the past bunch of days. He'd just dealt with whatever needed dealing with.

"Gramps, guess what?" Robby said. "I helped mix Goldilocks's yogurt and honey. And she ate most of it!"

One of the pluses of Robby's impulsivity was that he didn't shy away from people who he knew were upset with him. That always helped smooth things over since Robby rarely cowered or ran off. But his grandfather was a tough customer.

Neal Dalton smiled and took off his hat. "I heard that you've taken real good care of her. You saved your gram's favorite goat. I'm proud of you, Robby."

"You are?" Robby asked, tilting his head.

"Sure am," Neal said.

Holt had never been able to read his father all that well, but the different emotions on the man's face clued him in that Neal Dalton was uncomfortable as heck right now. His father seemed about to say something, then clamped his mouth shut, glancing over at Goldie. Neal ran a hand under his right eye, then his left, and Holt peered more closely at him.

Was his father *crying*?

Robby got up, hay in his hair and all over his back. He walked over to his gramps and pulled out a baggie with carrot slices, which they'd packed just in case the goat got well enough to have the special teat. "I walked and didn't run this time. Do you want some carrots, Gramps? Goldilocks isn't feeling good enough to have them yet."

Neal Dalton slashed a quick hand under both eyes again, then wrapped Robby in a hug. "I'd love a carrot, Robby. And thank you for walking and not running."

Robby smiled. "Because sometimes it can make the animals feel scared. I wouldn't want Goldilocks to feel scared."

"I'll bet she really appreciates that you're taking such good care of her," Neal said, his eyes soft.

Robby grinned, glancing at the goat, then his face fell and he looked down at the floor.

"I'm sorry I'm not a good grandson." His eyes welled with tears. "I really am trying to be better, Gramps."

Holt closed his eyes for a second, his own eyes stinging. *Oh, Robby*, he thought, wanting to scoop up his boy and hold him close, save him, somehow, from this hurt.

And if his father blew his response, there'd be hell to pay.

He'd give Neal Dalton five seconds to make this right.

Neal Dalton's face almost crumpled. "You're a great grandson, Robby. Of course you are. I'm so glad you're my grandboy."

Holt almost gasped, his heart squeezing in his chest. Robby's face brightened, the tears abating.

"Now, it is true that sometimes you're a little too loud or fast or wild for me," Neal continued. "But I'm an impatient type. But you know what, Robby? I'm gonna try to be more patient because I love you and I want us to spend more time together. We'll both try."

Robby smiled and seemed about to jump up and down, then thought better of it. "Daddy always says that all we can do is try."

This time, Holt did gasp. As Amanda's words came back to him. *I'm glad I believe—even if it means hurting this bad. And for a long time. Because at least I* feel. *At least I try.*

He didn't want to think about this right now. Things were finally okay. Yeah, he missed the hell out of Amanda but this—him and Robby, on the ranch, his livelihood and future and Robby's legacy—was how it was supposed to be.

"I am very sorry for making you feel bad, Robby," Neal said. "I shouldn't have because I love you so much."

Robby smiled. "I love you, Gramps." The boy hugged his grandfather tight, Neal Dalton scooping Robby up and holding him close.

Well, *that* was all very unexpected. The relief that came over Holt undid muscles he hadn't even realized were bunch up and stiff. He was about to pull his dad aside and tell him how much all that meant to him when a gruff voice sounded from outside the barn.

"Holt Dalton!" a man called out. "I'm looking for Holt Dalton."

Holt frowned and eyed his dad and shrugged. "Robby, you wait with Goldie, okay?"

"Okay," Robby said, sitting on a stool just outside the pen with his Rocco the Raccoon book. "I'll read to her."

Holt nodded, and then he and his father walked

out. Standing in front of the barn, hands on hips, was Edward Thompson.

A vein was popping in the man's neck, his blue eyes shooting sparks. "My daughter informed me this morning that she and your ranch hand are engaged," Thompson said. "That is absolutely unacceptable, and I want to know how you're going to fix this mess."

Engaged. Holt wasn't surprised to hear that. That meant Brody and Piper had made their plan. "I did talk to Brody," Holt said. "He's a smart, levelheaded young man who loves your daughter very much. In fact, he has Piper's interests above his own. If he proposed, it's because he has a solid plan for their present and their future."

Thompson grimaced. "Oh please. All she is to him is a pretty girl with a rich daddy. Give me a break."

"That's how little respect you have for your daughter?" Neal Dalton asked, staring Edward Thompson down. "That she'd choose a man like that?"

"A *man*? The kid is eighteen," Thompson bellowed. He shook his head. "I guess I'll just have to take away the money I set aside for college. We'll see how fast she runs off with that boy when that part of her plan falls through. Love.

What the hell does either of them think they know about love?" He shook his head again.

"So you'd rather lose your daughter than try to see things through her eyes?" Holt asked. "To understand how she feels?"

"I'm coming down hard on her for her own good!" Thompson said, crossing his arms over his chest.

"No, Thompson," Neal said. "And it's too bad you can't love her for who she is instead of who you want her to be. I almost made that mistake myself with my grandson. And my son. But considering you don't give your daughter any credit…"

Huh. Would wonders never cease. His father was surprising him left and right this morning.

"Don't you tell me how I feel about my daughter!" the man boomed. "I love that girl with all my heart."

"If you did, you'd care how she'd felt," Neal said.

"I care how she feels," Thompson countered. "But she's throwing her life away!"

"Is she?" Neal asked. "Because she fell in love with a terrific young man who's making his own way? I heard you did too, that you started from nothing."

Edward Thompson lifted his chin. "I didn't

work so hard to own a very successful corporation so that my daughter could take up with a ranch hand."

"Interesting point of view," Neal said. "Because I heard a little bit about your family. Your wife, Marianne, eloped with you when you barely had a hundred dollars to your name. And you're happily married to this day."

Thompson seemed to think about that for a moment, but then he frowned. "Marianne was denied a lot for years. And worked hard right beside me. I don't want that for Piper."

"Well, Piper is her own person," Neal countered. "Give yourself some credit for how you raised her. And give her some credit too."

Holt could see the man was relenting. Slowly, but he was.

"Holt here was a ranch hand with nothing to his name at eighteen," Neal continued. "Now, I couldn't be prouder of the man he is." His father turned to him. "You tried to tell me and I wouldn't listen. I called *you* stubborn? No one is more stubborn than I am. Except for maybe Thompson here. I'm sorry, Holt. For everything. I hope you can forgive me."

Once again, Holt almost gasped. He certainly hadn't expected his father to say anything like that. And he could tell Neal Dalton had meant every word.

"You got it, Dad. We'll talk later?"

Neal nodded, then turned to their guest. "Look, Thompson, why don't you come up to the house for some coffee," Neal offered. "We've got a lot in common, more than either of us thought, most likely. Let's talk this through."

Thompson's shoulders slumped. "Guess I could use some caffeine."

And just like that, the two men nodded at Holt and then headed up the path toward the main house. Holt had a feeling his father and Thompson were going to be solid friends. And that Brody and Piper would end up with Edward Thompson's blessing. Maybe not today but very soon.

Holt went back into the barn and smiled at Robby. "How's Goldie doing?"

"She loves this book," Robby said. "I read the whole thing to her. And I only messed up a few times. I wish I could tell Amanda about that but she hasn't been around. How come, Daddy?"

Holt's stomach twisted and he sat back down beside his son, his knees drawn up to his chest. "Well, I decided I wanted to do your reading with you. That way I get to spend even more time with you before school starts. I can't believe the summer is coming to an end so soon."

"I miss Amanda, though, Daddy. She's so nice."

Holt's heart squeezed and he reached a hand over to brush back Robby's ever-present mop of bangs from his eyes. "Yeah, she is."

"Do you miss her too?"

"I do," Holt answered honestly.

"Then you should ask her to come over for lunch, Daddy. You make the best grilled cheese. And then the three of us can take Bentley for a walk in the woods."

"Not today," Holt said. "But I promise you that grilled cheese for lunch. And the walk in the woods."

Robby brightened. "I wish Oliver could come too. And Amanda."

Me, too, Holt thought.

"Daddy, if you and Amanda got into a fight, you just have to become friends again. Did I tell you that I saw Ethan at the burger place when my uncles took me, and Ethan came over and said he was sorry about being mean at the fun run and he asked if I wanted to help him build his new Lego set?"

Holt smiled. "Yup, you told me. And I'm really glad about it."

"Ethan said he didn't know he was being mean when he said those things about my mom."

Holt tilted his head. "What do you think about that?"

"I believe him. I think most kids have moms so they don't understand when someone's mom isn't around."

Holt nodded, again wishing he could protect Robby from this—from the truth. And that was crazy. He couldn't. Helping him deal with the truth, particularly when it reared its ugly head—that was what Holt could do for his son. "Yeah."

"But my mom isn't here and even though sometimes I get sad about it, I like to be happy."

Holt felt the backs of his eyes sting. "I'm so glad you do, Robby. That's a great attitude." It really was.

"You know what? I think people can choose to be grumpyheads like Gramps used to be. Or nice, like Gramps is now. Don't you think, Daddy?"

Holt smiled. "I suppose so. Though I guess sometimes people can't help how they feel."

"I don't know about that. Uncle Morgan said you can't make other people do what you want, but you can make yourself do what you want. I'm saying it wrong, but I think I knew what he meant."

So did Holt. That you couldn't control others, but you could control your reactions to them.

How did a seven-year-old get to be so wise?

Robby had this wonderful ability to take in the best parts, the positive parts, of chaos around him.

"Like Ethan," Robby continued. "He couldn't make me want to be friends with him after he was mean to me so he said sorry. And now we're friends."

On the very edges of Holt's consciousness, he knew there was a lesson in there for him, but the new wall he'd erected around himself was impenetrable. He'd made it that way.

"I'm gonna read Goldilocks another book about Rocco," Robby said. "You can listen too, Daddy."

"I will," he said, wanting to grab his son and hold him tight and never let him go. But also on the edges of that consciousness he knew he had to do just that. He had to have faith in his smart, caring, wonderful son to fight his own battles, work out his issues. Even at seven years old.

And Holt, at thirty-two, had to do the same. Damned if he knew how right now, though. Because when he thought about it, Holt had knocked *himself* out.

Chapter Sixteen

"Hi, Daring Drake!" a familiar little voice said as footsteps bounded. "I'm back to see you! How are you? How's life?"

Amanda's heart quickened as she rounded the "Adoptable Animals" barn at Happy Hearts Animal Sanctuary, expecting to see Robby Dalton any second since that was definitely his voice she'd heard. And yup, there he was, in an orange T-shirt and khaki shorts, standing pressed against the wooden fence where the dear old cows were grazing in their pasture.

Amanda braced herself to come face-to-face

with Holt, but she looked around and didn't see him anywhere. An entire week had gone by since she *had* seen him, the night he'd broken her heart all over again. Harder this time.

"Robby, wait up," a tall man with dark blond hair and a Stetson called. When he turned, Amanda saw it was Morgan Dalton, Holt's older brother—and the eldest of the five Daltons. Morgan noticed her coming his way and smiled. "Oh hey, Amanda. Nice to see you again."

At the sound of her name, Robby turned around, his mouth wide open. "Amanda!" He charged for her, wrapping his arms around her. The force of him almost knocked her over, but boy, it felt good to see him. She hugged him right back.

Amanda laughed. "Hi, Robby. And hello, Morgan. Nice to see you again too."

"Yay, Amanda's here!" Robby said.

"Robby, did you know that Daphne, who owns Happy Hearts Animal Sanctuary, officially named your very favorite cow in the pasture Daring Drake? It was as an extra thank you for adopting Bentley and Oliver and taking such great care of them."

"Really?" Robby said, beaming. "That's so awesome! If I ever meet the real Daring Drake, I'll tell him."

Daphne came out of the barn, and Morgan turned to Amanda. "Would you mind hanging with Robby for a couple minutes while I talk some business with Daphne?"

"Sure," Amanda said. *It'll break my heart to spend any time with Robby, but I sure am glad to. Wasn't that the way?* She and Daphne had had their meeting about a new outreach campaign Amanda had in mind for Happy Hearts, and Amanda had been about to leave. If the meeting had ended just a few minutes earlier, she might have missed seeing Robby at all. Fate and circumstances.

Robby walked back over to the fence and stared at Daring Drake. His whole expression had changed. From very happy to very sad. "I've been trying real hard to be better, but I guess I did something else wrong. I don't know what, though." He wiped under his eyes, and Amanda could see more tears welling.

"What do you mean, Robby?" Amanda asked, her heart going out to the boy.

"I musta done something to make you go away, Amanda," Robby said, looking up at her. "My mom left and now you left." Tears slipped down his cheeks. "Daddy said it wasn't my fault that my mom left and never visits. I believe that. But I know I musta done something to make you mad at me. I don't really even remember my mom but I remember you."

Oh, Robby, she thought, kneeling in front of him, her heart pinching in her chest. "Honey, you didn't do anything to make me mad at you. I promise, Robby. The reason I haven't been coming by is because your daddy and I had a dumb argument about me and him."

Robby brightened. "Really? Most fights *are* dumb. That's what my gram says."

"Your gram is right." Amanda gave a firm nod.

"So you don't like my dad anymore?" Robby asked. "If you two just talked and said sorry, you could be friends again like me and Ethan are."

Robby was so sweet and adorable and earnest that despite the ache in her heart, she smiled. "I do like your daddy. Very much."

"Then just tell him, Amanda. Just say sorry and he'll say sorry. And then you can come over for grilled cheese. Daddy makes the best grilled cheese." He pushed his brown bangs off his face and looked at her so expectantly.

"It's true, he does," Morgan said with a gentle smile. Amanda glanced up; she hadn't realized Holt's brother had returned. He held Amanda's gaze for a second, and by the compassion she saw in his eyes, she knew Morgan was letting her know he'd heard most of that conversation.

"And you know what, guys?" Morgan continued, "I agree that Amanda should come over and talk to your dad. Holt Dalton can be *very* stubborn."

Morgan was definitely trying to tell her something. But she'd said her piece to Holt. And he'd let her walk out of his house and life. All these days, not a word.

He was stubborn, sure. But she had her pride. Clearly Holt hadn't changed his mind or he would have come to see *her*.

"Oh yeah," Robby said, laughing. "Daddy sure is!"

Morgan grinned and ruffled his nephew's mop of hair. "Well, we'd better get going," he said, tipping his hat at Amanda.

"Bye, Amanda," Robby said, wrapping his arms around her again. "I love you."

Omigosh. He'd never said *that* before. Her heart was pure mush now. "I love you too, sweetheart." *Oh boy, do I*, she thought, watching them leave until the last bit of Robby's orange T-shirt was gone from view.

She sighed and turned to Daring Drake. "Should I go talk to Holt?" she asked the cow. "Even though the ball was left in his court?"

Daring Drake gave a little snort.

She smiled. "Was that a yes?"

I love you, Amanda... She heard Robby say it over and over in her mind. It was both very easy and very difficult to earn a child's love. It wasn't something she took lightly or for granted. She'd become special to Robby, and that meant something to him and to her.

And she loved him back. And his stubborn dad too.

Therefore, it had to be worth one more shot.

Maybe not today, though, she thought, unsure about this. She wanted Holt to come to her. He *should* come to her. That he hadn't meant he wasn't just being stubborn—he was sticking to his guns.

What to do, Daring Drake? What to do?

The day after Edward Thompson had walked off with Neal Dalton to have coffee at the main house at Dalton's Grange, ranch hand Brody Colter came grinning his way toward Holt in the big barn.

"You will never believe this," Brody said. "But Piper's dad gave us his blessing!"

Holt smiled. He wasn't the least bit surprised—now. "I'm very glad to hear that, Brody."

"He invited me over for dinner yesterday, and the four of us—me, Piper, and her parents—sat and talked. Even though we're both so young, her parents are okay that we got engaged. And like we talked about, I'm going to join the army and Piper will go to college, and once she graduates, we'll get married. Piper's mom said she was very excited to plan the wedding." Brody shook his head, a big smile on his face. "Can you believe this? I'll tell ya, man, just when you think people can't change, wham—they go ahead and change. And everyone's lives affected by them are better for it."

Holt stared at Brody, those words echoing in his head. *Just when you think people can't change*... How true was that? He thought of his father. But then he thought of himself. Holt the Unchanging.

"Mr. Thompson said he had some sense talked into him," Brody added. "If that was you, thank you. I owe you—big time."

Neal Dalton's face and trademark Stetson flashed into his mind, his father's words of wisdom turning Edward Thompson around. "Actually, you owe my dad. He did the heavy lifting."

"I'll thank him." Brody grinned. "Now I know just what people mean when say they can't wait to begin the rest of their lives. That's how I feel."

A delivery truck pulled up, and Brody put on his work gloves. Holt had to go check on Goldie, so he shook Brody's hand, wished him and Piper well and told him to call if he ever needed anything. Holt wouldn't be surprised to hear from Brody over the next bunch of years; life had a way of interfering even with the most well-thought-out plans and the fiercest of love, but he also had a very strong feeling that Brody Colter and Piper Thompson would be together forever.

As Holt entered the small barn and peered into Goldie's pen, the sweet black-and-white goat was standing up and munching on fresh hay. She was definitely out of the woods. He gave her a once-over, making a mental note to ask the vet to stop by for a final check, his thoughts drifting back to all Robby had said when the two of them had sat outside Goldilocks's pen two days straight, nursing the goat back to health.

I like to be happy.

Uncle Morgan said you can't make other people do what you want, but you can make yourself do what you want...

And then Amanda and her beautiful face came to mind.

I'd lost my ability to believe in love but my feelings for you and for Robby renewed it. I'm glad I believe—even if it means hurting this bad. Because at least I feel. At least I try.

That was what he needed to teach his son.

Or learn from his son. Robby was a lot wiser

than Holt in a lot of ways and seemed to know all about trying already. You *had* to try. Last night, during dinner, Robby had told Holt about him and his uncle Morgan running into Amanda at Happy Hearts.

Where it had all begun again.

He smiled as he recalled Robby's words as they'd eaten their grilled steaks and baked potatoes. *You say sorry and Amanda will say sorry and you'll be friends again.*

All around Holt, people were trying and believing, struggling and flailing, but putting themselves out there. From Amanda to Robby to Brody and Edward Thompson to Neal Dalton.

You couldn't stop trying. You couldn't give up on the most fundamental, most important thing in life: love.

Holt wasn't going to just instill that in Robby; he was going to *model* it.

He jogged the half mile back to his cabin, going to his bedroom and pulling something out from the bottom drawer of his dresser—something he'd kept hidden away for ten years.

He only hoped he wasn't too late.

When Holt arrived at Amanda's building in downtown Bronco Heights, a couple was leaving so he'd gone straight in without buzzing to let her know he was here. He didn't even know if she'd be home.

He was about to knock on her door when it opened and she took a step out, then froze, surprise lighting her beautiful face. She was dressed in exactly the outfit she'd been wearing when he ran into her at Happy Hearts. The yellow dress and short white blazer. Her dark hair was in a low ponytail.

"Holt? This is so crazy. I was just on my way to Dalton's Grange to see you."

"You were?" he asked.

She nodded. "I had something to say but since you're unexpectedly here, I'd rather you went first." She opened the door wide. "My roommate is at work, so this is good timing."

He came in, barely glancing around at the condo. He couldn't take his eyes off Amanda and wanted to tell her everything without taking a breath.

"You were wearing that outfit when we met at Happy Hearts after ten long years," he said.

She smiled and nodded. "I thought it meant the outfit is lucky."

He stared at her, hoping he understood her right. If she'd been on her way to see him and had put on her lucky outfit, the very one she wore when they ran into each other, then it wasn't too late. He could still make his comeback. *Their* comeback.

"I came over to show you something," he said. "And to ask you something." He reached into his pocket and pulled out a little pink box and opened it. "Toward the end of camp a decade ago, I bought this for you. With the money I earned that summer. I had to give half to the state to pay my fine, but the other half went toward this."

She gasped, staring at the tiny diamond, just a chip, really, on a thin gold band. She looked up at him, tears in her eyes. "I had no idea."

"I bought it back when I was still pretending to be something I wasn't. Or thought that's what I was doing. It took me until very recently to realize that *was* me that summer. The twenty-two-year-old who bought you this ring loved you, and that was all he needed to know. Then the doubts crept in and overtook him. I'm not letting that happen again."

She stared at him, waiting for him to continue.

"I'm so sorry I hurt you, Amanda. Then and now. But I love you so much. If you'll agree to give me that second chance again, I'd like to spend the rest of my life proving to you how much you mean to me, how much I want you to be my wife and Robby's mother."

Tears welled in Amanda's eyes. "You can definitely have that *second* second chance."

He put his arms around her and she wrapped hers around his neck. "Robby is going to be one happy little boy."

"We're going to be one happy little family," he said.

"Little? There's Bentley and Oliver and Poindexter, so that makes six, plus I figure we might have a kid or two in the future."

He held her tight. "I love you, Amanda Jenkins."

"I love you, Holt Dalton. And by the way, I love that ring. I love the pink box. I love that you bought it when you believed. It symbolizes a big piece of us, Holt."

She held out her left hand and he slipped the little ring with the barely visible diamond on her finger.

"One more thing," he said. "I made a stop before I got here. He reached into his other pocket and withdrew a black velvet box. When he opened it, Amanda gasped.

"Oh Holt, that is too gorgeous."

He got down on one knee, holding the box, the beautiful emerald-cut 1.5 carat diamond sparkling. "Amanda Jenkins, will you make me the happiest guy alive by marrying me and becoming my wife?"

"Yes," she whispered. "Yes!" she shouted.

He grinned and stood and slid the gold ring with the much bigger diamond right behind the little one.

She laughed and held up her hand. "Not many women can say they have two engagement rings from the same guy, bought ten years apart."

He looked at the rings on her finger, the two together symbolizing the past and present.

"Meow, me-owwww."

Holt glanced down to see Poindexter staring up at him. He picked up the big gray cat with the white paws. "Well, not many *men* can say they speak cat, but Poindexter was clearly saying he wanted to get in on the celebrating. I think you and Oliver and Bentley will make fast friends. What do you think, Poindexter?"

The cat stared at Holt with his amber eyes, but Holt didn't get another meow. He laughed and scratched the cat on his back by his tail and got a rub against his face for it. "That's a yes," he added.

"Definitely," Amanda said, her brown eyes misty. "Sorry, I'm just so overwhelmed with happiness right now I can barely form words."

"Then let's get to Dalton's Grange and tell

Robby his daddy's getting married and that he's about to get the mommy of his dreams. Robby is *never* at a loss for words." Poindexter wriggled out of his arms and jumped onto the back of the sofa, then meowed loudly as if in agreement.

"I promise you right now, Holt, I will be a great mother to Robby. I'll love him with all my heart—I do already. I'll be there for him, no matter what, in good times and bad."

"I know it," Holt said. "And thank you. For completing our lives."

"You might think this is nuts, Holt, but you know where I want to get married?"

He thought about that for a moment. "Wait. I think I do know. Is it somewhere that a cow named Daring Drake could wear a bowtie around her neck during the ceremony?"

Amanda grinned. "Exactly!"

"I think that's perfect. Happy Hearts it is."

With that settled, they headed out to Dalton's Grange to tell Robby—*their* son—that he was going to be the best man at a wedding this fall.

Happy hearts, indeed.

Epilogue

A week later, Holt was at the grill on the patio at his parents' house, keeping an eye on the burgers, chicken and ribs for many hungry Daltons, when he heard his son laughing.

He glanced over at Robby, wedged beside Amanda on one of the padded lounge chairs, a new chapter book that was two reading levels up in his hand. Bentley was on the grass beside the chair, chewing on a rawhide bone.

As Amanda ruffled Robby's hair, her engagement ring sparkled in the bright sun. They had a wedding to plan, and his son was going to be his best man, his brothers his groomsmen.

"Amanda, do you think you can find me a book about a kid who's really, really, really happy about his new mom?" Robby asked.

"I have a better idea. We can write that book together! You'll write a line, then I'll write a line. Before you know it, we'll have a whole chapter. Then another. Then another."

Robby leapt up. "Everybody, guess what? I'm getting a mom *and* I'm going to write a book!"

Neal Dalton, who was setting the huge rectangular patio table, put down the forks in his hand and walked over to his grandson for a high-five. Robby slapped him a hard one, and Neal grinned. "Are Bentley and Oliver going to be in the book?"

Robby laughed. "Yup. And you, too, Gramps. And Gram. And all my uncles. And Daring Drake. But it's mostly gonna be about how my dad and my great new mom met at Happy Hearts because I wanted a dog and Daddy said yes."

"And then Amanda said yes," Morgan quipped from his own lounge chair as he pushed his black sunglasses up on his head.

"Crazy woman," Boone added with a smirk.

Holt tossed one of Bentley's stuffed toys at Boone, which landed on his dad's shoe.

"Oh, good aim," Neal said, grinning.

Holt couldn't believe the changes in his dad in such a short time. He'd mellowed out considerably, stopping by the cabin at least once a day to see Robby, bringing a catnip toy for Oliver, throwing balls for Bentley in the yard, and letting his grandson take running leaps into his outstretched arms.

Morgan snatched the toy and chucked it, Bentley racing for it down the yard.

"Hey, Uncle Morgan," Robby said. "When are you getting married? You're older than Daddy."

That got a big laugh out of everyone.

"He's older but is he wiser?" Shep joked from his spot in a rocking chair.

Bentley brought the toy back to Morgan and dropped it at his feet. Robby ran over to his dog for a high-five, to praise how good Bentley was at playing fetch. He'd taught the dog how to high-five by giving him a ton of liver snaps for lifting up a paw to Robby's palm. The sight of that never failed to make Holt's heart skip a beat.

Morgan picked up the stuffed llama and threw it far again. "Well, Robby, if I ever meet a woman as super cool as your new mom-to-be, we'll see. But right now, the single life suits me just fine."

Holt eyed his older brother. Morgan dated—a lot. Women were always after him, handing him their cards or slips of paper with their cell phone numbers in the grocery store aisles and while in line at the coffee shop. But he never committed. Holt wondered if he ever would.

"Someday, all my sons are going to be married and giving me grandchildren," his mother said as she came out of the house with a huge bowl of homemade potato salad that she put in the center of the table.

"The more, the merrier," Neal called out, then sniffed the air. "Boy, does that smell good, Holt."

He grinned. "And everything's ready. Come and get it, folks!"

"Last one to the table is a rotten cheeseburger!" Robby shouted, taking a big head start.

"Hey, no fair," Neal said with a smile and raced him to the table.

His grandson beat him handily.

Holt laughed. He loved everyone in this yard so much. His parents, his brothers, his son, their dog.

And of course, his fiancée. He loved referring to Amanda that way but couldn't wait to replace that word with wife.

The crew headed for the table, stopping by the grill to admire Holt's skills with tongs and a spatula and knowing just when to flip. He made up two big platters of the food and set them on either end of the table.

Robby came charging at Holt and flung himself into his arms. Holt wouldn't change that about

Robby for anything. Amanda walked over, Bentley trailing, clearly hoping for his own burger.

"Can I get in on this family hug?" Amanda asked.

"Absolutely," Holt said, opening his arms wide.

Like his heart was.

* * * * *

COMING SOON!

We really hope you enjoyed reading this book.
If you're looking for more romance, be sure to
head to the shops when new books are
available on

Thursday 6th August

To see which titles are coming soon, please visit
millsandboon.co.uk/nextmonth

MILLS & BOON

MILLS & BOON

Coming next month

A WILL, A WISH, A WEDDING
Kate Hardy

'Miss Grey changed her will three months ago,' the solicitor confirmed, 'and she was of sound mind when she made her will.'

You could still be inveigled into doing something when you were of sound mind, Hugo thought. And Rosemary liked to make people happy. What kind of sob story had this woman spun to make his great-aunt give her the house?

'There are conditions to the bequest,' the solicitor continued. 'Dr Walters, you must undertake to finish the butterfly project, turn the house into an education centre — of which she would like you to assume the position of director, should you choose — and re-wild the garden.'

The garden re-wilding, Hugo could understand, because he knew how important his great-aunt's garden had been to her. And maybe the education centre; he'd always thought that Rosemary would've made a brilliant teacher. But, if Rosemary had left the house to his father, as her previous will had instructed, surely she knew that her family would've made absolutely sure her wishes were carried out? Why had his great-aunt left everything to a stranger instead? And he didn't understand the first condition. 'What project?'

'I'm editing the journals and co-writing the biography of Viola Ferrers,' Dr Walters said.

It was the first time he'd heard her speak. Her voice was quiet, and there was a bit of an accent that he couldn't quite place, except it was definitely Northern; and there was a lot of a challenge in her grey eyes.

Did she really think he didn't know who Viola Ferrers was?

'My great-great-great-grandmother,' he said crisply.

Her eyes widened, so he knew the barb had gone home. This was *his* family and *his* heritage. What right did this stranger have to muscle in on it?

'Miss Grey also specified that a butterfly house should be built,' the solicitor continued.

Rosemary had talked about that, three years ago; but Hugo had assumed that it was her way of distracting him, giving him something to think about other than the gaping hole Emma's death had left in his life. They'd never taken it further than an idea and a sketch or two.

'And said butterfly house,' the solicitor said, 'must be designed and built by you, Mr Grey.'

Continue reading
A WILL, A WISH, A WEDDING
Kate Hardy

Available next month
www.millsandboon.co.uk

LET'S TALK
Romance

For exclusive extracts, competitions
and special offers, find us online:

MILLS & BOON

THE HEART OF ROMANCE

A ROMANCE FOR EVERY KIND OF READER

MODERN
Prepare to be swept off your feet by sophisticated, sexy and seductive heroes, in some of the world's most glamourous and romantic locations, where power and passion collide.
8 stories per month.

HISTORICAL
Escape with historical heroes from time gone by. Whether your passion is for wicked Regency Rakes, muscled Vikings or rugged Highlanders, awaken the romance of the past.
6 stories per month.

MEDICAL
Set your pulse racing with dedicated, delectable doctors in the high-pressure world of medicine, where emotions run high and passion, comfort and love are the best medicine.
6 stories per month.

True Love
Celebrate true love with tender stories of heartfelt romance, from the rush of falling in love to the joy a new baby can bring, and a focus on the emotional heart of a relationship.
8 stories per month.

Desire
Indulge in secrets and scandal, intense drama and plenty of sizzling hot action with powerful and passionate heroes who have it all: wealth, status, good looks…everything but the right woman.
6 stories per month.

HEROES
Experience all the excitement of a gripping thriller, with an intense romance at its heart. Resourceful, true-to-life women and strong, fearless men face danger and desire - a killer combination!
8 stories per month.

DARE
Sensual love stories featuring smart, sassy heroines you'd want as a best friend, and compelling intense heroes who are worthy of them.
4 stories per month.

To see which titles are coming soon, please visit

millsandboon.co.uk/nextmonth

JOIN US ON SOCIAL MEDIA!

Stay up to date with our latest releases, author news and gossip, special offers and discounts, and all the behind-the-scenes action from Mills & Boon...

 millsandboon

 millsandboonuk

 millsandboon

It might just be true love...